Praise for internationally bestselling author Sherry Jo

FOUR SISTERS, ALL QUEENS

"A well-written novel set during fascinating times. The relationship among the sisters is believable and often heartbreaking."

—Library Journal

"A colorful portrait . . . and an insight into history."

—RT Book Reviews

"Jones captures the feel of the tension-filled thirteenth century. . . . Though you may already know the ending, Jones makes it feel like something you haven't heard of before. . . . *Four Sisters, All Queens* is not to be missed."

—Fresh Fiction

"Engrossing and vividly rendered. . . . A mesmerizing tableau of what it meant to be a queen."

—C. W. Gortner, author of The Confessions of Catherine de Medici

"Delightfully evokes the rich details and vivid personalities of a fascinating era. A feast for fans of historical fiction!"

—Gillian Bagwell, author of Venus in Winter

"Sherry Jones brings medieval Europe to life. . . . What a tale!"

—Catherine Delors, author of For the King

THE SWORD OF MEDINA

"Jones's fictionalized history comes alive with delicate, determined prose."

—Publishers Weekly (starred review)

ALSO BY SHERRY JONES

Four Sisters, All Queens

The Sword of Medina

The Jewel of Medina

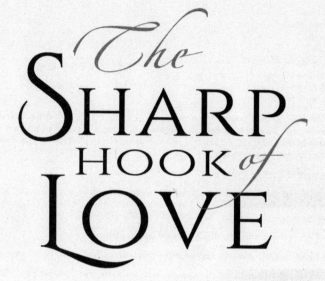

The SHARP HOOK of LOVE

SHERRY JONES

GALLERY BOOKS

NEW YORK   LONDON   TORONTO   SYDNEY   NEW DELHI

G

Gallery Books
A Division of Simon & Schuster, Inc.
1230 Avenue of the Americas
New York, NY 10020

First Gallery Books trade paperback edition October 2014

GALLERY BOOKS and colophon are registered trademarks of Simon & Schuster, Inc.

For information about special discounts for bulk purchases, please contact Simon & Schuster Special Sales at 1-866-506-1949 or business@simonandschuster.com.

The Simon & Schuster Speakers Bureau can bring authors to your live event. For more information or to book an event contact the Simon & Schuster Speakers Bureau at 1-866-248-3049 or visit our website at www.simonspeakers.com.

Interior design by Jaime Putorti
Cover art © SuperStock/ Getty Images
Design by Alan Dingman

Manufactured in the United States of America

10 9 8 7 6 5 4 3 2 1

Library of Congress Cataloging-in-Publication Data

Jones, Sherry
  The sharp hook of love / Sherry Jones.
    pages ; cm
1. Heloise, approximately 1095–1163 or 1164—Fiction. 2. Abelard, Peter, 1079–1142—Fiction. I. Title.
  PS3610.O6285S53 2014
  813'.6—dc23
                              2014020502

ISBN 978-1-4516-8479-7
ISBN 978-1-4516-8480-3 (ebook)

For Bobby:
amor, amicitia, dilectio, caritas.

For nothing is under less control than the heart—having no power to command it, we are forced to obey.

—HELOISE TO ABELARD

THE ROYAL ABBEY AT ARGENTEUIL
NORTH OF PARIS, FRANCE, DECEMBER 1114

I was born in silence, my wails quieted by the hand of the only friend my mother could trust. In silence I spent most of my youth, amid the nuns of Argenteuil floating through the dark abbey without sound, as though we lived under the sea. Only in my dreams did I dance, laughing with my mother in the sun, her voice like water, her kisses like dew falling on my cheek. I would awaken with tears instead, and an ache like hunger that never subsided.

Mother. Why did she leave me? Where had she gone? I begged God to return her to me. He answered me with a letter from her on my twelfth birthday, sent with a volume of Seneca's philosophy that I would cherish all my days.

I love you and long for you daily. Your uncle writes that you are an exceptional scholar, which brings me joy, for I, too, love to read the poets and philosophers as well as the Scriptures. I had planned to teach them all to you, but it was not to be, not in this life.

I shall never forget your tears on the day we parted; anguish fills my breast even now at the memory. I pray that you can forgive me, my beloved daughter. Forced to choose between loyalty to your father and life with you, I sent you away. I pray that, someday, you will understand.

In bed that night, I cried as never before. A fatal illness had not stricken my mother as it had the *maman* of my friend Merle, one of the other oblates. Mine had not brought me here to fulfill a promise to God, as Adela's mother had done. God had not called me to Argenteuil at all. My mother had abandoned me of her own free will: it was her choice. My soul's anguish gushed from my eyes, filling my mouth until I thought I would choke, in torrents that I thought would never cease. When at last I had depleted my store, I fell into a deep, dark sleep. The dreams of my mother ceased after that night, as did my tears.

Ten years after my arrival at the Royal Abbey, the Reverend Mother Basilia marched into the classroom and interrupted the lesson I was teaching on Paul's first letter to the Romans.

"Heloise, you have a visitor. Go and prepare yourself, then come to my office."

A visitor! When had anyone called for me? The familiar pucker of the Reverend Mother's mouth, as if she had eaten sour fruit, told me that I would be taken away. My mother had come at last! My feet seemed to sprout wings, and I flew out the door.

I would have run to the dormitory, shouting thanks to God, were such boisterous behavior permitted. Or perhaps I would not have done so, for in my fantasies I had always presented myself perfectly to Mother, poised and mature, a proper young lady on whom she would shine beams of pride and love. I washed my face, cleaned my teeth, and rebraided my hair, then dug into my trunk for the forbidden hand-mirror my friend Merle had given me. For the first time in my life—but not the last—I wished for beauty. My mother's hair had shone like spun gold, while mine dropped in a heavy, dark wave with a streak of pure white over my left eye. The hateful Adela used to tease me about it. *Is your father a badger?* I never replied, not knowing the answer myself. But I knew my mother, and now she awaited while I preened in the mirror. *Vanity of vanities; all is vanity.* I threw the mirror into the chest and hurried outdoors.

Mother had come! My pulse pounded all the way across the dry grass of the courtyard and on the stones paving the dank halls of the abbey. I must have passed—but do not remember doing so, in my excitement—the newly built refectory with its engraved face of the Virgin Mother looking placidly over the doorway. I did not even stop to cross myself before her, or to greet her with a whispered *Hail Mary, Mother of God.* Why should I, when my own mother waited for me in the flesh only a few steps away?

At the abbess's door I took a deep breath. Mothers love their children. Mine would love me no matter whether I was pretty or not, smart or not, poised or not. And I would love her, too, even if she had become as ugly and unpleasant as the Reverend Mother Basilia.

Yet my hand trembled so that I could hardly seize the latch and open the door.

The abbess stood before me, looking as if she might hit someone. Then, a rustle behind her; a movement. I prepared to greet my mother, my throat choked with unshed tears—but beheld, instead, a heavyset man with a ruddy complexion and thick, red lips.

"Your uncle, the canon Fulbert," the Reverend Mother said. Her voice sounded tired—she hated to lose her daughters—but not as tired as my uncle appeared to be.

His eyes reddened at the sight of me. "Dear God, how you resemble your mother," he breathed. "It is as if she had come to life again."

I cried out before he had even finished the sentence, knowing at once why he had come. A hole seemed to open inside me, filled only with darkness.

"Quiet yourself, Heloise," the abbess snapped. "You know that we do not allow such outbursts."

"I should think an exception might be made in this instance," my uncle said, knitting his thick eyebrows (and showing me whence I had inherited mine). "Her mother has died, after all."

His words in their awful finality hit me like a great stone thrown against my chest. I clutched a chair, dizzy and sick. *Mother.* I looked to my uncle for comfort and found it in the tears spilling down his face.

"I have come, Heloise, to take you home with me. It was your mother's final wish."

PART ONE

Amor

1

In you, I readily admit, there were two things especially
with which you could immediately win the heart of any
woman—the gift of composing, and the gift of singing.
—HELOISE TO ABELARD

THE NÔTRE-DAME CLOISTER
PARIS, MARCH 1115

*H*e sang to me of love from under curling eyelashes. In
the center of the market, amid the squawking hens,
the squealing children and the barking dogs, and the wine sellers
beating sticks against their bowls of *vin á broche*, he performed a
song of incomparable beauty without minstrel or lute, drawing
every eye—but singing only to me. His voice brought a warm
summer rain to mind. I felt a soaring within my breast, as if a
door had flung itself wide and my heart had flown through it.

When he had finished, he removed his hat with its peacock's
feather and bowed only to me in spite of the shouts of *Très beau!
Je t'adore!* from the women who had clustered around him, pretending to understand his Latin verse. As he bent over, dark curls
fell across his tonsure, which was no larger than a thumbprint on
his crown—the minimum required for a canon—a mark of the
irreverence that had, it was said, gained him not a few enemies.
He wore purple, a brocade of silk ribbon and gold thread, and

heavy boots. His lips pursed as he rose, as though he might burst into laughter or another song. His eyes gleamed triumph, as though he had won a contest with me as the prize.

My heart's beat faltered. His broad smile beckoned; his bold gaze dared me to refuse. Something shifted inside me, like the turning of a key in a lock. For a moment, I forgot everything I had ever known: the books I had read, the secrets I kept, my destiny that no one could alter. I would be no one's prize. Yet his smile shone like light across my face, pulling up the corners of my mouth, softening my eyes.

The cathedral bell tolled vespers. I started; his song had made me late. Uncle would want his flagon; Pauline, her capon. I bent to gather the sacks I had dropped at my feet.

A hand touched mine. I looked up and nearly fell into eyes of impossible blue. The sky at twilight could not compare. My breath caught in my throat.

"Heloise." His lips formed a kiss when he spoke my name. Pierre Abelard, the most famous—and infamous—scholar in Paris, offered my name to me like a gift. A sweet ache spread through my chest. "Allow me."

He took the packages from my arms: the capon in its flax-cloth sack, the flagon, and the second sack with the bread, vegetables, and strawberries, leaving me to carry the book of Ovid's writings I had borrowed that day, my sheepskin pouch with its wax tablet and stylus, and my wonderment.

The renowned teacher and poet now hastened to keep stride with *me*; he carried *my* packages, whistling a tune and beaming with pride as if I, not he, were the world's greatest philosopher. Envy slanted the eyes of the women we passed. They murmured his name—*Monsieur Abelard, darling Pierre, so handsome*—but he seemed not to notice.

As we walked, I slid glances at him. Slight of form as he

was—not much taller than I, and compactly built—he yet moved through the world as though he owned everything in it. His trampling steps left his mark in the damp-soft street, while I hopped from stone to stone to avoid the mud. At one point, lightning streaked the waxen clouds. The clap of thunder that followed nearly toppled me into a large puddle, but he stretched out a hand to steady me. His eyes' kindness made me want to lean into his arms. But why would a man of his status deign to help me, who had not even a father to give her a name?

"Take care, Heloise," he said. "Why don't you ride a horse? Surely your uncle would provide one for you."

"Master Petrus. How do you know me?"

A pair of canons lifted their brows at the sight of us together. We began to walk again. "Who," he said, "has not heard of the female scholar? A gift for letters is rare in a girl."

"Only because girls have no schools."

"You understood every word of my song." He studied me as if I had two heads.

In fact, I had mastered not only Latin but also Greek and now studied Hebrew with a rabbi on the rue des Juiveries. But how dare I boast to the master? I might speak every tongue in Babel, yet my accomplishments would pale in comparison to his.

"Do you truly think schools would make a difference? It is said that the female mind cannot comprehend complex ideas," he said.

"Complex ideas such as those in your song?" He failed to notice my wry tone. The song, so beautiful in its melody, had lacked complexity in its verse. I might have expected much more from the new headmaster of the Nôtre-Dame Cloister School.

"Ah, my poetry! What do you think of it? Women swoon over my songs. Baudri of Bourgueil, on the other hand, condemned them as too worldly." Abelard showed his teeth, looking every bit the hungry wolf. His eyes twinkled. "He says I ought to sing of heavenly angels, but I prefer the earthly ones."

I averted my gaze and widened the distance between us. A tonsured head, a vow of celibacy—these guaranteed nothing. To forbid the fruit only sweetens its flavor. Yet, he could not have achieved greatness at his age—not a strand of silver yet in his hair—had he whiled his hours with women. Time is the one loan that even a grateful recipient cannot repay.

Taught to respect my elders, I said nothing. The *magister*'s verses reminded me of a roasted peacock presented at the table with its brilliant feathers reattached: glorious to behold, but lacking in nourishment. He had sung of love as a flutter in the heart, as a burning in the loins, as a watering of the mouth. What could anyone learn from such nonsense? But I would not criticize the song he had sung especially for me.

"Everyone said, 'You must meet Heloise,'" he went on. "'She is a master of letters, and a trove of literary knowledge.' You are accused of inventing new words, and of writing poetry that rivals Ovid's." He glanced at the book in my hands. "Could such subtlety of thought truly belong to a woman?"

"I am fluent in Greek as well. And I am learning Hebrew." To prove myself, I quoted passages in both tongues, relishing the drop of his jaw.

"By God, how long have I waited to encounter a woman such as you? Indeed, I never imagined such a creature existed. Where have you hidden yourself all this time?"

"Not hiding from *you*, Master Petrus. I spend most hours at my books." I lowered my head to hide my pleasure. "One does not simply absorb knowledge, which Aristotle said is necessary to wisdom; nor is wisdom gained except by questioning."

Abelard stared at me. Cringing to hear myself crowing like a cock, I closed my mouth.

"She speaks in Greek and quotes from Aristotle!" We resumed our walk. "And I have lost my wager with Roger in the scriptorium. He told me about you, but I did not believe him."

I had to smile, thinking of men betting money on my knowledge. "I hope you will not forfeit a large sum."

"My purse may be empty, but my life is enriched, now that I have met you at last."

He tramped through a puddle, heedless of the mud splashing his hem, as he told of the effort he had expended to speak with me. "I stood for an hour in the *place* today, singing like the king's *bouffe*, waiting for you to appear."

"You waited for me?" Who had ever taken such measures for my sake? Not my mother, who had abandoned me; not my uncle, who would return me to cloistered life as soon as he pleased.

"I sang for you, yes. Or—no. I did it for myself, to alleviate the agony of watching you from afar."

He had admired me, he said, for several weeks, as I'd walked past his classroom on my daily errand to the place de Grève market. On the first warm day of spring, he moved his scholars onto the cathedral lawn, hoping to attract my attention. I had noticed him, his ringing voice, his waving arms, his excited laughter as he debated his students and always won. Feeling the eyes of his scholars upon me, I lowered my gaze as I hurried past, day upon day, increasing his frustration until, today, he ended the class and hurried after me. But I had disappeared into the scriptorium.

"I sang to lure you," he said. "I saw you stop yesterday to hear a minstrel perform a *chanson de geste* of inferior quality. I hoped my song might please you more." He winked. "Now I think it was my own pleasure that I desired to increase."

If so, he would be disappointed. If he sought pleasure from a woman, the sort that elicited winks, then he had already wasted his time with me. I would have told him so, but here came my uncle lumbering toward us, his great belly leading him like a horse pulling a cart, his face scowling at the sight of the victuals, still in sacks, that ought to be ready for his table by now. Noting my alarmed expression, Abelard turned, and Uncle's ill temper gave way to delight.

"Petrus Abaelardus!" He clapped the teacher on one shoulder as though they were old friends. "What a pleasant surprise— most pleasant! I hope my niece is not dulling your mind with frivolous woman's talk. By God, does she have you carrying her packages?" He took the sacks and the flagon from Abelard and thrust them at me with an admonishing frown.

Mirth leapt in Abelard's eyes, but seeing my brightening cheeks and hearing the murmur of my apology, he stepped forth and stretched out his hands. His fingers brushed mine. I nearly dropped everything into the mud.

"It is my honor to assist our cloister's esteemed subdeacon, Canon Fulbert," Abelard said. "Please allow me." And he gently took the packages from me again.

I assisted Pauline in the kitchen, simmering the fish she had pulled from the tank and gutted, preparing a salad of greens with strawberries, and ladling her capon brewet into a bowl. She worked as if the end of the world were near, slamming pots and pans on the countertops and stirring the sauce for the fish with one hand and the brewet with the other, sloshing both onto the coals. She'd pressed her mouth together in a grim line when I explained my delay: I had tarried in the scriptorium, undecided which book to borrow, I'd lied, blushing with guilt. Were I to mention Abelard's song, the smile budding on my lips would burst fully into bloom. One whiff of its fragrance, and everyone would know.

I had carried secrets all my life, each one as a great stone about my neck. This one, however, perched upon my shoulders, as light as a bird that seemed about, at any moment, to lift off and carry me away. When I carried the brewet into the great room, I beheld the slow unfolding of its wings in Abelard's eyes.

I set the bowl on the table and removed the lid. Steam rose, and aromas of thyme and rosemary from the savory broth Pauline had simmered. My mouth watered, anticipating the flavors as rich as liquid gold. I glanced at Abelard, proud to present Pauline's fare, which was, I knew, incomparable—but he was not looking at the brewet.

"Will you join us?" he said to me. The fingers of his left hand caressed the tablecloth.

I looked to my uncle, who sipped from the bowl with eyes closed in bliss—eyes that snapped open at Abelard's suggestion.

"We would only bore her with our talk, Petrus." Uncle's nostrils pinched themselves together.

"Then we must move to a new topic. Why speculate on who might become the next bishop of Amiens when neither king nor pope asks for our opinion? We might as well predict the weather. Sit, Heloise, I pray." My heart increased its beating at the sound of my name on Abelard's lips. He patted a spot on the bench beside him. "Come and tell me which writers you prefer. I noticed the Ovid you brought home."

I glanced at my uncle: Had he heard? He had forbidden me the *Ars amatoria*, calling it "lewd" and "inappropriate for a girl," and, in doing so, had made it irresistible. If he knew I had coaxed his assistant, Roger, into lending it to me, he would take it away. To my relief, he exhibited no interest in our discussion, but appeared lost in his unhappy thoughts, his lips moving in a silent curse. I knew why he fumed: One week ago, I had offended the bishop of Paris at this very table with my assertion that Eve ought not to be blamed for Adam's error. The bishop had colored several shades of red before abruptly taking his leave. Uncle feared I would embarrass him tonight, as well, no doubt.

"I enjoy Ovid's poetry, in particular his *Heroides*," Abelard said, oblivious of my uncle's scowl. "I used to prefer Boethius, but lately find his assertions flawed."

"Do you?" I ventured a step toward him, my appetite whetted no longer for food, but for discourse. "Which of Boethius's writings do you dispute?"

Uncle leapt to his feet in such haste that he nearly caused his precious wine to tip. "Niece, I beg for a word with you." He seized my arm and all but dragged me to the stairway. "Do you desire this man as your teacher? Then leave us," he muttered. The bird flapped its wings. My feet might have left the floor but for my uncle's grip. To study philosophy with Pierre Abelard would crown my achievements. I would be the most learned woman in the world, and ready to complete the task my mother had bequeathed to me.

I returned to the kitchen, but my thoughts remained upstairs with the men. Outdoors at the cook fire, my face glowed with heat. Would the great master assent and become my teacher? I pulled the pan of simmering fish from the coals and carried it inside. I handed it to Jean, Pauline's husband, for the table along with a green savory of parsley, thyme, dittany, sage, costus, and garlic, then assembled on a platter the carrots, onions, and garden greens Pauline had prepared. This I carried to the table myself with trembling hands, eager to gain the master's esteem, yes, but also curious to learn: With which of Boethius's precepts did he disagree? That ill fortune is of more use to men than good fortune? In my mind, I formed arguments in

Boethius's defense. Good fortune requires nothing more from us than enjoyment. When ill fortune strikes, however, we learn to endure, to accept, even to prevail. Clearly, we benefit more from our trials. Why, then, do we curse Fortune when she sends them, instead of thanking her?

But when I returned to the great room, the talk had moved beyond philosophy. Jean, attending the sideboard and the cup, refilled the *henap* with wine while my uncle pressed Abelard into service as my teacher.

"The idea intrigues me," the *magister* said, lifting his hand to refuse the drink Uncle offered. "To teach a girl! And yet, work already fills my days and nights."

"No girl surpasses my niece—*non*, and few men, either," Uncle said.

"She would need to possess an astonishing mind. Otherwise, why should I waste my time? I might as well teach a dog to talk as train a female in philosophy."

"You err, Petrus. My niece will become a great abbess—it is her destiny. At Fontevraud, no less—Fontevraud, heh-heh! Her mother was its prioress and would have become the abbess had she lived long enough. She wanted Heloise to follow in her path and finish the work she began. When Robert of Arbrissel meets my niece, he will beg her to join him there. Teach her the art of dialectic, and you will benefit the world—the world! Think of the letters she may write. Think of the arguments she may make, and the funds she may procure for the abbey, all for the glory of God!"

I closed my eyes and willed my uncle to rein in his tongue lest he make fools of us both. Of course Abelard would not desire to "waste time" with a girl. Teaching me would do nothing to enhance his reputation; my writings would never be published, and his detractors—who were many, I had heard—might scorn him for accepting a female student. As if to confirm my fears, he explained the demands on him. Since coming to the Nôtre-Dame Cloister a few months ago, he had expended much effort correcting the inferior teaching of the previous headmaster, William of Champeaux.

"You gasp, Canon Fulbert, but I do not lie," Abelard said, touching my uncle's arm as intimately as if the two were old friends. Watching them, I wanted, now, to take Uncle Fulbert aside for a warning. Had this man of intellect truly formed a bond so quickly with my slow-witted uncle?

"William taught my scholars that, in an argument, probable consequences are as true as necessary ones," Abelard said. Noting my uncle's bewildered frown, he added, "In other words, he taught that opinion is the same as fact. Let me illustrate. Provide me with an analogy."

Uncle merely blinked, as if the light of the other man's brilliance had blinded him.

" 'If Socrates is a man, then Socrates is an animal,' " I said. Uncle's frown told me to depart, but, for once, I defied him.

"That statement is a fact," my uncle said at last. "A man is, indeed, an animal."

"Only if Socrates is, indeed, a man," Abelard said. "But the analogy begins with a *possible* antecedent—*if*—which can only result in a *probable* consequence, not a necessary one."

"But one must infer that Socrates is an animal from the suggestion that he is a man." My uncle folded his arms across his chest as if he had just checkmated his opponent in a game of chess.

"Truth is based on necessity, not inference," Abelard said. "The consequence must be necessary to the antecedent."

My uncle appeared as a man wandering in the dark without a lantern, so I added, "Master Petrus means to say that the

antecedent of a true statement could not exist without the consequence."

"*Voilà,*" Abelard said, turning toward me now.

"I thought you were helping Pauline in the kitchen," Uncle
Fulbert growled.

"So if we say, 'Socrates is a man, therefore he is an animal,'
does the statement then become true?" I persisted.

"An astute question, Heloise." The beam of Abelard's approval
filled me with warmth. "The argument is necessary, and so would
appear to be true, but you have stated an incomplete argument."

"Incomplete because—" I struggled to discern what I had
omitted.

"Because it leaves open the possibility that Socrates does not
exist."

"But he did exist, by God," my uncle said.

"He *did* exist, yes. But, being dead, he exists no more," I said.

"Exactly!" Abelard leapt to his feet and grasped my hands. His
eyes shone.

"He exists either in heaven or hell," Uncle grumbled, but neither of us took notice. At the touch of Abelard's fingers, my pulse
had begun to thrum in my ears. I heard only my inner voices,
one praising God for sending this man as my teacher and one
urging me to run away, as far from him as I could go.

My uncle interrupted our moment. "She forgets she's a girl,
forgets her place—her place! She is her mother's daughter, imper-
tinent and proud. But I always say women are why God gave
men fists, heh-heh!"

I withdrew my hands to myself and closed my eyes, avoiding
my uncle's drunken sneer and, worse, the teacher's expression of
pity. I had hoped to elicit his admiration, but instead I felt like a
dog that had just been kicked.

"Heloise," Abelard said, but I could not meet his gaze now.

Heat flooded my skin. For the first time, I thanked God that I was unable to cry.

"Do you wish to study with me?"

The spoon in my hand clattered to the floor. "Why do you ask me—a mere girl?" I could not resist answering. "One might as well ask a hound whether it wishes to hunt, or a horse for its opinion regarding the bit in its mouth."

My uncle's gasp should have warned me, but Abelard's laughter drew my eyes to him until Uncle leapt up and struck me in the face.

"Impudent girl! Another remark such as that one, and you'll feel my riding crop on your *asne*." My cheek burned. My hands gripped the edge of the tabletop. "Pardon my niece's manners—very bad! All her years at Argenteuil—and at no small price—failed to teach her respect for her elders."

I reserve my respect for those who deserve it, I wanted to say—but my years at Argenteuil *had* taught me the futility of arguing with a tyrant.

"You will need to discipline her, Petrus," my uncle said. "I grant you full permission to do so."

But, Abelard pointed out, he had not agreed to teach me. First, he must have my consent. "An unwilling pupil learns nothing except how to vex his teacher."

A lump formed in my throat. No one had ever asked for my consent regarding anything.

"Sit with us, Heloise, I pray. Then we may become better acquainted and determine if we might work well together."

"I thank you, but I cannot do so this evening." My uncle's slap still burned on my cheek, as though he had struck me with a hot iron. I turned toward the stairs, my shoulders hunched, my arms folded across my chest.

"Niece! I command you to return—return! The master requires your presence," Uncle said, his speech slurring.

"Some other time, please, *magister.* My head aches, and I have lost my appetite for food." How could I sit at table with him now, reduced as I was even in my own eyes? I hastened to my room, a pulsing in my ears like laughter, away from the sound of my uncle's fist pounding the table and his voice shouting my name.

2

What king or philosopher could match your fame? When you appeared in public, who—I ask—did not hurry to catch a glimpse of you, or crane her neck and strain her eyes to follow your departure? Every wife, every young girl, desired you in your absence and was on fire in your presence.

—HELOISE TO ABELARD

My uncle's insulting words, his heavy hand—the memories clung to me like a bad smell. I placed a bowl of herbs and ointments in the window of my bedroom and let the scented breeze carry him away, then remembered the volume of Ovid that I had brought home. I might have been the only scholar in the world who had not read his *Ars amatoria*. The prioress had not taught it at Argenteuil, although we had studied the *Heroides* and his *Metamorphoses*. Roger, my uncle's assistant in the scriptorium, had praised the *Ars amatoria* as one of the great works of literature.

Now the first task for you who come as a raw recruit
Is to find out whom you might wish to love.
The next task is to make sure that she likes you:
The third, to see to it that the love will last.

What would Ovid recommend—that the man sing to his beloved as she walked by?

I dismissed the thought. Curiosity, not any hope of love, had sent the teacher to me: the novelty of a lettered female. Yet, if a man wished to attract a woman, what better way to draw her eye as well as her heart? Every woman in that crowd had envied me. My shame melted away at the memory, and a smile touched my lips.

Pierre Abelard had sung only for me. Who in the world had not heard of him, the poet whose verses rang out in every *place*, the philosopher whose brilliance blinded all who dared to peer into his light? As headmaster of the Nôtre-Dame School, he had reached the pinnacle of success. I had known him the moment I first saw him, months ago, surrounded by scholars shouting questions, challenging him, scowling as he drove home the final *riposte*, sharper than any sword. They always returned for more. Having spent only a few moments in his presence, I could easily discern why.

The memory of his eyes returned to me now, not only their dark blue beauty, like sapphires, but also the intensity of his gaze, as though he beheld my naked soul. When he took the parcels my uncle had so rudely thrust into my arms, his eyes had danced with amusement. For the first time, I'd seen Uncle not as a brute to be feared but as a sort of *bouffe*, graceless and awkward and as full of wind as a storm—and, as storms always pass, so did his temper. Why hadn't I thought to laugh at his clumsy antics, his fumbling words? Entering the cheerless convent at such a young age had stifled my joy—until today, when Abelard's eyes had prompted its return, and I had felt merriment bubbling in my mouth.

But why would a man of his eminence sing in the *place* for me? My star might rise, but would never shine as brightly as his. A woman, I was only a pale moon in a world of suns, reflecting the light of men but emitting none of my own. What use had the sun for the moon? What use had Pierre Abelard for me?

An answer whispered itself, and heat flooded my skin. *Non.* If he wished for that, he had only to snap his fingers. Girls and women far more beautiful than I filled the city, any of whom would open her arms—and legs—to the handsome poet willingly, even eagerly. Not I. Scandal would not an abbess make. I would teach girls in my own school—at the Fontevraud Abbey, if Uncle had his way.

A knocking at the door interrupted my thoughts. For a moment, I considered feigning sleep, fearing my uncle had come. Renouncing Gisele, his henna-haired mistress with a laugh like a raven's cry, had altered Uncle Fulbert in disturbing ways. At first a jolly and loving man who had earned my trust with his kindness, he now drank copiously every night until he either flew into a rage or fell into a stupor, or both. The hours between the commencement of drinking and the loss of consciousness had felt increasingly perilous for me since Gisele's abrupt departure the previous month.

He had not wanted to send her away. Like so many other men of the Church, Uncle had surrendered to the reformists' demands for the sake of his career. The bishop had tolerated my uncle's affair, for he indulged weaknesses of his own, as everyone knew. But the reformists had gained in strength. Thirty years had passed since Pope Gregory VII had revoked the authority of bishops who allowed priests to marry. My uncle, being not a priest but a canon, and not married but keeping a mistress, had enjoyed Gisele's companionship without penalty—until the fiery young monk Bernard of Clairvaux announced that he would come to Paris to speak. For him to point his finger at Bishop Galon would cause the old man's ruin. In his frenzy to rid himself of any taint, the bishop had commanded all his clergy, even canons, to practice not only celibacy—remaining unmarried—but strict continence, as well, abstaining from all sexual pleasure.

My uncle had to say good-bye to the woman he had loved since his youth. I shall never forget her tearstained face when she departed our home, all her possessions loaded on a cart and her eyes as empty as if she had run out of dreams. Uncle watched her go without a word, then rebuffed my sympathetic embrace. *It had to be done,* he growled. *I shall never advance to deacon by flouting the Church's rules.* Now the flagon was his mistress, and more dangerous to his advancement than any woman—and hazardous to me, as well.

The knock sounded again, hesitant, not at all like my uncle's fist, so I arose to open the door. Abelard stood on the other side, his hat in his hands, his eyes searching mine. I touched my fingers to my unbraided hair. Why had he come, alone, to my room?

"You did not say whether you want me for your teacher." His gaze brushed my cheek where my uncle had struck me, and it burned again. "Please let me in so we may discuss the matter."

"Does my uncle know that you are here?" I peered beyond him to the stairway. Uncle would punish me for any improprieties, no matter who was at fault.

"Your uncle sleeps."

"Did he fall asleep with his head on the table?" I closed my eyes against the image.

"He staggered into his room and did not return."

My eyes flew open. " 'Your uncle sleeps' is not a statement of truth, then, since sleeping is only a possible consequence of his entering his room." I took pleasure in Abelard's frown. "Although you stated it as a fact, 'he sleeps' is your opinion."

"I asked his servant to look in on him, and he reported that Fulbert was sleeping."

"Had my uncle instructed him to do so, Jean would have said, 'He sleeps.' Or he might have been dead, and Jean mistaken."

Abelard combed the fingers of one hand through his curls. "My God, how your mind leaps." His nostrils flared. "Like a caged animal."

I retreated into my room, and Abelard followed. "Caged? How so? I move about at will."

"But not for long, *non*? What else is an abbey if not a cage?"

"In the abbey, my mind will be free."

"Perhaps, then, you should liberate your body." He stepped toward me. "While yet you can."

"Is this why you have come, then? To discuss my body?" I crossed my arms over my chest and gave him a defiant look.

"I came for your answer. Do you desire me for your teacher, or not?"

"I do." I dropped my gaze to his feet, but resisted the urge to prostrate myself and beg him to accept me. He had already borne witness to my humiliation. "But why would you accept me, after seeing my uncle's ugly temper?"

"Forgive me, Heloise." I lifted my eyes in surprise; now, his was the head that hung in shame. "I should have defended you from Fulbert."

I shook my head. "Had you done so, he would have abused me more harshly once you had gone."

"But now? Do you fare well?"

"Of course. I have my book." I gestured toward the Ovid, which lay on my bed.

He stepped over to my bed and lifted the volume. "Ah, the *Ars amatoria*. 'The Art of Love.' Is love an art, or artifice?"

"I have only begun to read it."

"Would you learn about love from a book, Heloise?" His tone, gentle but chiding, made me want to seize the volume from his hands.

He lowered his eyelids as if sheltering a secret. Warmth flooded my skin. I should order him out of my room. But why should he respect me? My mother dead, my father unknown, I was as worthless as a foundling in Uncle's eyes—and now, perhaps, in the eyes of the *magister*, as well. I struggled to find the words to restore his high opinion. Otherwise, he would never deign to teach me anything.

"The Scriptures teach us all we need to know of love." I tossed my head, hoping I appeared more confident than I felt, and would have looked him directly in the eyes had they not followed the fall of my hair across my arms.

" 'How beautiful you are, my darling! Oh, how beautiful! Your eyes are doves,' " he murmured. I knew well his allusion, having read the Song of Songs many times. What would it be like to have a man whisper such words to me? I used to wonder. Suddenly thirsty, I took from my windowsill the gourd I used to collect rainwater and drank deeply from it.

" 'Love is patient; love is kind,' " I said when I had finished—returning Scripture for Scripture. " 'It does not envy; it does not boast; it is not proud. It does not dishonor others. It is not self-seeking; it is not easily angered; it keeps no record of wrongs.' "

He lowered his eyelids as I spoke, hiding his reaction. When I had finished, he peered out at me from beneath curling lashes. I heard, again, the song he had sung to me—could it be that very day? So much had changed since then. I pressed my hand to the wall behind me, steadying myself.

"There are several different kinds of love, Heloise," he said with a sly smile.

"Non, magister, you are wrong. There is only one."

3

❧

May the bestower of every art and the most bountiful giver of human talent fill the depths of my breast with the skill of the art of philosophy, in order that I might greet you in writing, most beloved, in accord with my will.
—HELOISE TO ABELARD

My uncle's horse nuzzled my shoulder and I clapped the tablet shut, as if the creature might read the words written upon it. As I stood on the mounting stone, Uncle's shrewd stare made me want to hide the tablet behind my back, but I did not. I had nothing to hide, or so I told myself.

"Another letter from Petrus?" he said as I climbed onto the mare he had brought with him. "By God, I wonder if he gives so much attention to all his scholars? If I didn't know the man to be continent, I might suspect him of seducing you, heh-heh."

I felt glad that he could not see the flush of heat that spread across my face.

To one who is sweeter from day to day, is loved now as much as possible and is always to be loved more than anything, he had written.

"Except for love, why else would a man write so many letters to a woman—why?" Uncle said.

We joined the tide of horses with their riders swelling toward the Saint-Etienne Cathedral for the great event—the long-anticipated

sermon by the renowned orator Bernard of Clairvaux. Even the mist-
ing rain that caused my teeth to chatter and stiffened my hands did
nothing, it seemed, to deter the Parisians from going to hear the man
who had denounced them, and their way of life, as degraded. Uncle
and I moved so slowly that I wished I had walked—but I would not
want to stain my tunic with mud, not when I had hopes of seeing
Abelard.

"He writes to you daily, *non*? Yesterday, I saw his messenger
thrice at our door. That sort of devotion usually means one thing."

I forced a laugh. "Why, Master Petrus is devoted to philosophy, and the teaching of it. You ought to appreciate his efforts on
my behalf."

"*Oui*, I ought, given the fortune I pay him—a fortune!" A dog
darted in front of us, startling our horse. Uncle's arms, on either
side of me, tightened. "Adelard of Bath commanded an equally
high fee, but he didn't show such a personal interest. It makes me
wonder what sort of lessons our Petrus intends for you."

"I do not know what you mean."

"Has he spoken of love to you? Has he touched you?"

I laughed again. "Master Petrus, in love with me? What philosopher ever squandered his time on women?"

"I have seen the way the girls crowd around him, young beauties, and wealthy widows, too, straining to touch the hem of his
garment as if he were the Christ—the Christ! No man could
resist such temptation."

"In his eyes, I am but a scholar, one of many under his care."

"I hope so, for his sake—and for yours. Be vigilant, my girl!
Guard your purity. Your future as an abbess depends upon it, as
does my career."

"I am well aware of that, dear uncle." I kept my tone light, reminding myself that, when he was sober, I had nothing to fear
from him.

"If he ever speaks of love or touches you in—in *that* way, I want to know. Do you understand?"

Before I could answer, my uncle's assistant, Roger, called his name and came toward us, waving his arms. "One of the deacons has fallen ill and cannot walk in the procession," he said, beaming. "The bishop of Paris wants you to take his place. Make haste, Canon Fulbert!"

As I followed my uncle into the Saint-Etienne Cathedral, I searched for Abelard in vain. Only by some miracle would I find him amid all these people. The entire city, it seemed, waited to hear the renowned monk, filling four of the great chapel's five naves and pressing against the marble columns: monks, clergy, and canons on either side of the center aisle; nobles along the far right side, their brilliant yellows, greens, and peacock blues competing with the colorful mosaics adorning the walls; merchants and townspeople on the far left; villeins and servants in the back, stretching their necks for a view of the proceedings. My uncle secured a place for me at the foot of the altar, with the nobles, then hastened to don his ceremonial robes and join the processional. As soon as he left, I slipped the wax tablet from the pouch on my belt and resumed reading Abelard's letter.

An unclouded night: would that it were with me!

The *magister* had suggested letter writing as our first exercise, to my surprise, for I had expected to learn the art of dialectic—of debate and discussion—for which he was famous.

"I have never lost a debate," he had said in our first lesson, his voice swaggering. "I humiliated William of Champeaux. I ground Anselm of Laon into the dust with the heel of my logic. I made Roscelin weep. The greatest teachers in the realm could not compete with me." He thumped his chest. "I may be the only true philosopher in the world."

"You have not debated me."

He laughed. "Debate a woman? That would be as unchival-rous as attacking you with my sword."

"Not so, master. You would best me with a sword." He laughed his lion's roar, delighted with my *riposte*.

Yet, after several weeks of lessons, I had learned little of philosophy or dialectic. Instead, we wrote letters—an art at which I must excel, Abelard said, to succeed as an abbess.

"Let us write as though we were lovers," he had said, slanting his eyes at me. "Then I shall discern how much you are learning from Ovid."

But all the books in the world could not begin to teach what I was already learning from this man.

To her heart's love, more sweetly scented than any spice, I wrote to him, *from she who is his in heart and body: the freshness of eternal happiness as the flowers fade of your youth.*

"Here," he said, tapping with his stylus the tablet on which I had written my first letter, "you have wished me 'the freshness of eternal happiness as the flowers fade of your youth.'" He smiled but his eyes held a dazed expression, as if staring into a too-bright sun.

"Do you approve of the greeting?" I thought it quite elegant and waited for his praise.

"As the flowers fade of my youth?" His smile slipped nearly off his face. "In your eyes, I am an old man."

I blinked, uncomprehending. What philosopher had ever concerned himself with such things? Who had heeded the wisdom of Socrates before that great thinker grew his beard? Christ himself had not taught until he was nearly Abelard's age.

"I had thought that, for a philosopher, youth would be a burden," I said.

"Not if youth is preferred by the woman he admires."

A song began to play inside me. I closed my eyes, which always revealed too much. My uncle had flown into rages because of my eyes. "*Chienne!* I know what you are thinking," he would snarl, lifting his hand against me. At Argenteuil, the abbess had read my sullen thoughts and wielded the cane herself, panting, her hand trembling as she'd lifted my skirt to deliver the blows.

"Heloise," Abelard had said. "Look at me."

When I lifted my gaze so shyly to his face, did he behold the girl dancing inside me? Could he hear the music playing so sweetly? At night, alone in the study of my uncle's house, reading the Porphyry assigned to me and writing my arguments, I would hear that tune begin quietly, as if played by a distant piper, then increase until it had filled me to overflowing and drowned out all thoughts but those of Abelard. How intently he gazed into my eyes as I spoke, pouring out my very soul to him in our long talks. Who had ever listened to anything that I said? Who had ever responded with smiles and compliments? With him, I became utterly myself as never before—and, to my astonishment, when I looked into his eyes like mirrors reflecting myself back to me, I admired the person I beheld there. Thinking of him, bathed in that sweet music, I would take up a new tablet and write verses to accompany that tune—words not of feigned love, as in our letters, but of the elation that had seized me on the day we met, and which aroused my spirit more with every moment I spent in his presence.

For him, I'd told myself, our letters made up an elaborate game of elocution, and no more. Every teacher played similarly with his scholars, writing letters as an exercise, an amusement. Love? What had a philosopher to do with love?

To one who is sweeter from day to day, is loved now as much as possible and is always to be loved more than anything. Standing in the cathedral, reading these words, I felt a fullness in my chest, as though my heart expanded. Who had ever loved me?

In the next instant, I berated myself. Abelard had written as a master to his scholar, from the mind and not from the heart.

Now I feared I would miss my chance to speak with him today at Bernard's sermon. Perhaps he stood in the processional outside the cathedral doors. I slipped the tablet into my pouch and turned my head to see—and heard his deep, rich laughter, already so dear. My pulse skipped a beat. There he stood, not far from me, also in the nobles' section, with a woman whose braids, shining from under a cloth of shimmering gold, rivaled the red in Abelard's tunic. Her slanting eyes gazed boldly into Abelard's; her pretty mouth curved upward as she told a tale that he seemed to find exceedingly amusing. I turned my attention to the choir. He could laugh with whomever he wished.

The choir halted its chant and the procession entered the cathedral, stepping slowly down the center aisle: the master of the boys, followed by four boys singing a verse and response; the cloister subdeacons, including my uncle, and deacons in green chasubles carrying oil, balsam, and candles; a boy holding the ceremonial cross; and the bishops and abbots in their vestments of white and gold. Galon, the bishop of Paris, stepped weakly on his aged legs, squinting to see with his rheumy eyes. Etienne of Garlande, the archdeacon of Paris and the king's chancellor, flashed his gold rings and looked over the crowd as though he were, as rumored, more powerful than the king. Then came Abelard's nemesis William of Champeaux, now bishop of Châlons-sur-Marne, flaring the nostrils of his long, sharp nose, followed by Bernard, in a hooded tunic of undyed wool. His head, tonsured nearly to baldness with only a small fringe of hair, glistened with perspiration; his face held a glum expression, as though he marched at his own funeral.

When they had ascended the stair to the altar, Galon stepped up to the pulpit. A hush fell over the room. In the voice he used for services—high, almost singing, pretentious—he introduced Bernard. The young monk had come on an important mission, Galon said: to denounce the spread of decadence in the Church.

"I have come to talk about decadence, yes," Bernard said when Galon had ceded the pulpit. In contrast to Galon's whine, his voice resonated like a struck bell.

"In particular, I wish to discuss the degradation occurring in our most sacred places. A foul influence corrupts what should be pure, namely, the hearts and souls of those of us chosen to serve the Almighty God." His stare fell upon Abelard's red-haired companion like an accusing finger, then shifted to me.

"Brothers," he said, "answer me this: If dogs defecated on the cathedral steps, would you not scrub them clean? Do you allow lepers to handle your saints' relics, or to urinate in your baptismal fountain?"

Murmurs spread in a low rumble, then swelled to a clamor. Abelard's friend waved an ivory fan before her face. Abelard wrapped a hand around her arm, as protective as a sibling—but his intimate glances were anything but brotherly.

"Then why," Bernard said when the din had settled, "do I see women in this cloister?"

His eyes flew open to stare at me with such loathing that I dropped my gaze all the way to the floor, my face as hot as if I had been caught in some unspeakable, indecent act.

"Women—daughters of Eve!" he cried. "Nay, you *are* Eve, the gateway of the devil. The one who unsealed the curse of the forbidden tree. The first to turn her back on the divine law. You are the one who persuaded him whom the devil was not capable of corrupting; you easily destroyed the image of God, that is, Adam."

I winced under the force of his words. For this occasion, why had Bernard resurrected a speech by Tertullian, the ancient

Roman whose disgust for women permeated his writings? 'Daughters of Eve'? Would the Church visit the iniquities of the mother upon the daughters? Didn't the Scriptures say, *Each one shall be put to death for his own sin*?

Bernard had become a monk only after the death of his mother, to whom he was said to be deeply attached. Now he praised the Virgin Mary as the supreme example of womanhood, apparently forgetting that, had his mother remained chaste, he would not have been born. Did only virgins merit God's love? Why, then, had the Lord given us wombs? And why did such men as Bernard blame women for the death of Man? Didn't God banish the first couple from the garden out of fear that they might eat from the Tree of Life and live forever? Weren't they, therefore, already destined to die?

As Bernard continued, his voice rising to a shout, his face reddening, a monk standing behind him—Suger, from the Saint-Denis monastery, I later discovered—narrowed his small, close-set eyes at me; his nostrils quivered as though I wafted a putrid odor. Flushing, I sought Abelard's eyes and found him whispering into *her* ear, his lips twitching with suppressed laughter. She smiled, showing teeth like matched pearls.

When the sermon had ended, my uncle joined me on the floor. I begged him to take me home. Never had I felt more unwelcome, and in the cathedral where I had so often prayed. He bade me to wait, however. We ought, at least, to speak with the *magister*, he said—but I knew he wanted to ingratiate himself with Bernard and also with Etienne of Garlande, who had descended to the floor and now talked with Abelard and his companion. Curious about the girl, I followed Uncle through the crowd of clerics and monks who now shrank back to avoid touching me.

"Remarkable," the girl was saying to Abelard and Etienne, the king's chief adviser. But my gaze did not remain on them for long: I could not help staring at the girl, whose *bliaut* fit her so tightly that I wondered how she could breathe, and whose neckline plunged to expose the curve and swell of her breasts—revealing attire, indeed, for the mass.

"What did you think of Bernard's sermon?" Abelard said to me.

My uncle, fearing I would embarrass him in front of the king's chancellor, squeezed my hand so hard I flinched from his grasp. But all waited for my reply. Pulling away from my uncle, I said, "Like your friend, I found it remarkable—for its irrelevance."

"*Voilà!* Your opinion is also mine," Abelard said. "I wonder if our reasoning is the same?"

"This is not the classroom, *magister*," the girl said, prodding him with an elbow. But he kept his eyes on me.

"The speech was written nine hundred years ago," I said.

"By Tertullianus!" Abelard cried in delight. "You have read him, also? Etienne. Agnes. Did I speak the truth about her, or not?"

"I knew the phrase 'daughters of Eve' sounded familiar," Etienne said.

"Blaming Eve for Adam's weakness is certainly convenient, isn't it?" Agnes said.

"Adam himself did so," I said.

"Now we know how far backward the reformists would take us all—to the days of Tertullianus, the second century. Soon they will call for the veiling of virgins," my uncle said, beaming at his own cleverness.

"Bernard has already done worse, in demanding that women be expelled from the cloister," Agnes said. "I wonder that you did not challenge him, Pierre."

Pierre? I lifted my eyebrows at him, but he was looking at her, not me.

"Challenge him? Why? I see no error in his remarks. We men *are* weak, and women are to blame for all our sins—especially lust." The grin Abelard exchanged with her sent a pang through my breast.

"Wickedness resides not in the bodies of women, but in the hearts of men," I said, more sharply than I had intended.

"*Non*—not in their hearts, but elsewhere," Agnes said, making Abelard laugh.

Etienne turned to me. "You bore Bernard's insults most gracefully."

"I did not consider them insults, since they did not pertain to me."

"Do you mean to say that you are neither a harlot nor a whore?" Agnes said. "How disappointing."

Abelard's gaze held mine—for only an instant, before returning to the red-haired girl. "Heloise is no harlot, but the most learned woman in Paris," he said.

"Of course." Etienne bowed. "Who has not heard of Heloise, our fair-sex scholar?" He introduced Agnes as his niece, who embraced me and declared me "the Minerva of Paris." The reference was flawed, for that goddess represents wisdom rather than knowledge—but I was wise enough, at least, not to contradict her.

"Now that we have all done our duty and gone to Sunday services, you must come to our house for dinner," she said, tucking her arm into mine. "Pierre will bring you—but only if you will divulge your secrets."

"Secrets?" I glanced at my uncle, whose fierce stare warned me to divulge nothing. *Your mother hid you away with good reason,* he had said this morning. *Her sins would have brought ruin and shame to our family. A single hint of scandal and I will never be promoted—never!*

"Your secrets—yes! I especially want to know how you provoked that sour-faced Bernard to glare only at you, when *I* stood at his feet." Agnes laughed, a sound as rich as butter. "I felt more than a pang of jealousy, I admit. I had anticipated the roll of his eye over me, daughter of Eve that I am. I even dressed for the occasion."

4

⚜

Love does not so easily forsake those whom it has once stung.

—HELOISE TO ABELARD

*I*n the hours between Bernard's sermon and Agnes's supper, she had transformed herself. Abelard and I entered Etienne's spacious house overlooking the Saint-Etienne Cathedral to find her even more breathtaking than before. She exuded the fragrance of roses. Her copper hair curled in ringlets against her flawless skin. Abelard stood more closely to her than necessary and breathed her in as though the roses embroidered on her gown were real. I looked on with a smile so broad it pained my face.

"You should have come sooner! You have missed the excitement," Agnes said as Abelard pretended to shield his eyes, dazzled, he said, by the sun. She had adorned herself in saffron from the boots whose toes curled up and around like ram's horns to the turban perched like a sunlit cloud atop her curls. Saffron! I caught my breath at the sheer extravagance. In my linen tunic of pale green—my favorite, until that moment—I felt like a common weed. As she lifted one perfumed cheek, then the other, to Abelard's smiling lips, I vowed to ask my uncle for new clothes.

"Which sultan did you charm into giving you his cap?" he teased as she led us across a Persian carpet of red and gold into the great room. There, Etienne stood with another man before large windows overlooking the city. Below, I saw the pale, bald Bishop Galon; Bernard, in his coarse, hooded tunic; and an elderly bishop with a stooped back all trotting away on horseback, talking and gesturing, oblivious of the crowds milling to and from the banks of the Seine.

"Do not tease! You know the count brought this turban from the Holy Land," Agnes said to Abelard.

"The count?" I asked.

"My grandfather Guy, the Count of Rochefort." She shrugged, as if everyone's grandfather were a count. "You should have come sooner, Pierre. The bishop of Paris has just departed in a rage with Yves, the bishop of Chartres. He and Bernard screamed at my uncle." Her voice rippled with pleasure.

"Did they come to discuss the bishopric in Amiens?" Godfrey, the current bishop, was said to be near death, Abelard told me, and Pope Paschal II wanted to name his successor—a privilege the king of France had always enjoyed. Bernard, Suger, and Yves, prominent reformists all, had come today on the pope's behalf, hoping Etienne might influence the king for Paschal.

"It was hardly a discussion," Agnes said. "Bernard foamed at the mouth, or nearly so. He spat every time he spoke the word *investiture*."

Seeing my frown, Abelard explained the situation further: The reformists, determined to enforce the former pope's decrees, insisted that the Church, not the king, must appoint bishops. King Louis did not agree. Bishops controlled vast domains, collected large sums in taxes, and commanded many foot soldiers and knights. The king would not relinquish his power to appoint bishops loyal to him.

"The pope cannot win this battle. He might as well try to move a mountain as to change King Louis's mind," Abelard said.

"So said Uncle Etienne. I thought Galon would excommunicate him and my father both."

"Galon did not expect an argument?"

"Yes, but he didn't expect my papa. Uncle tried to reason with them, but Papa was not so inclined. He said that, were it not for the king, Galon would not be bishop of Paris, but only the wiper of the pope's *asne*."

Abelard and Agnes laughed over this tale, while I cringed to imagine such abuse heaped upon a man of God—and a bishop, no less.

"Galon's insults were surprisingly imaginative for one so dull witted," Agnes said. "He could not compete with the bishop of Chartres, however. Yves called Uncle Etienne a gambler and a womanizer, and my father a drunkard."

As we reached the window, Etienne embraced us and introduced me to Agnes's father—his brother, Anseau, seneschal to King Louis. So alike were they that they might have been twins, except for their attire. Etienne had changed from his ceremonial robes to a fashionable *bliaut* of saffron silk with a blue, sleeveless cotte adorned with garnets about the neck and hem, while Anseau wore green silk embroidered with gold thread and trimmed in ermine.

"I hear that you have angered the bishops again," Abelard said to Etienne, taking the *henap* from him.

"Today, my brother is the devil's vassal," Anseau said. "His own bishop says it, so it must be truth."

"Galon is calling everyone 'the devil's vassal' except for me," Abelard said. His voice held a plaintive edge.

"Oh, but everyone knows that you are the devil himself," Anseau said.

Etienne took my hands with his soft, manicured ones and welcomed "Paris's famous woman scholar" to his home.

When I demurred, Anseau grunted and said he wished Agnes would apply herself to her studies with more diligence. "She thinks only of her wardrobe." He gave his daughter a pointed glance, but she heard only Abelard's whispers into her ear. "And, unceasingly, of marriage." Not marriage to "Pierre," surely, I wanted to say. The Church would never allow it.

A servant blew the dinner horn and we gathered around the table, Anseau and Etienne on one bench with Agnes between them, and Abelard beside me—directly across from Agnes, who gave him wanton looks as we washed our hands, her face bright with suppressed laughter. My stomach tightened. I had at first declined Agnes's invitation, stunned as I was by Bernard's hateful sermon, and wanting time alone to ponder the tide of sentiment rising against women in the Church. But Abelard had convinced me to join the gathering, saying a friendship with Etienne might help me gain the position I coveted at Fontevraud. Now, watching Abelard cast amorous glances at the beautiful Agnes, I wished I had remained at home.

"Bernard possesses very little learning and disdains books completely," Abelard said. "He actually boasts of his ignorance. 'Everything I need to know, I learned in the fields and the woods,' he says. As if God did not give men minds for a reason."

As the talk continued, I noticed that Abelard, who sat less than a hand's width away, had barely glanced at me. Yet, when he'd arrived at my uncle's house to fetch me, he hadn't been able to tear his gaze away.

"Heloise glows like a ruby in the sunlight, doesn't she, Jean?" he'd said to my uncle's servant.

Jean's eyes had narrowed in response. "A valuable jewel must be jealously guarded. She who makes herself a ewe will be eaten by the wolf."

"I will keep a special watch for wolves tonight." Abelard's

laughter had struck a false note through my uncle's great room—
as it did now at Etienne's table, after he declared that philosophers lacked time for women.

"Unless, of course, she is the most brilliant scholar in Paris."
He smiled at me.

"No time for women, Pierre? I have seen how they flock
around you, in love with your music and your blue eyes," Agnes
said. "Take care, Heloise—this man breaks hearts."

"Has he broken yours?" I could not help asking.

"Many times," Agnes said, giving Abelard a sly look—which
he returned. His hand dropped under the table to brush mine,
but I pushed it away. What had he written to me yesterday? *The
burning flame of love compels me.* Even knowing that the letter was
only an exercise, I had allowed myself to linger over the word
love. I wanted to leap up and run from the table.

"My lessons with Heloise are never dull," he told the Garlan-
des. "I would give my benefice to have her join my classes." His
knee brushed mine again. I moved my leg away.

"Why, then, don't you seek permission for me to attend the
school?" I asked.

He shrugged. "One might as well try to teach an ass to sing as
to convince Galon to mix the sexes in anything."

Servants glided into the hall with bowls of soup and plates of
bread. Abelard's hand dropped under the table to rest on his
knee, his fingertips barely touching my leg and yet commanding
all my thoughts.

"Galon is worse than Saint Augustine, frowning on carnal
pleasures as though Christ had never enjoyed even a back scratching," Agnes said.

"Or a woman's anointing his feet, then drying them with her
hair," I said.

"Or a cup of wine," Etienne said, lifting his *henap.*

"Or two," his brother said.

The servants replaced our soup with trenchers bearing salmon, lampreys, and bowls of buttered peas. As Abelard leaned forward to take some fish, his legs fell apart so that his left knee touched mine. My pulse quickened even as I moved away.

"Saint Augustine openly admitted his weakness for women," Etienne said. "But who in the Church dares to acknowledge Galon's vices?"

"Let Galon incur the bishop of Chartres's displeasure and we would hear accusations soon enough," I blurted, then blushed at my own irreverence.

As the others laughed, Abelard reached for bread at the same time as I, deliberately brushing my hand with his fingertips. Agnes lifted her eyebrows.

Abelard stretched his legs; Agnes giggled. I forbade myself even to glance down. Was he touching her foot with his? The bishop of Chartres had called the wrong man "womanizer," it seemed.

The meal went on, lamb and beef and lettuces, pastries and cherries and fine white bread, and conversation that flowed as co-piously as the wine: Guillaume of Poitiers's new, scandalous song, which Abelard performed to great merriment; the king's marriage to Adelaide of Maurienne, rumored to be quite ugly with a nose as large as a goose's beak; the declining health of the Amiens bishop Godfrey, with the men placing bets on the date of his death. I would have thrived on the *riposte* if not for Abelard. With him sitting beside me, his thigh pressing mine, his eyes on another woman, I had to force myself to listen. More than once, I reminded myself that others inhabited this room—this world— besides Abelard, Agnes of Garlande, and me.

O Abelard! The very name filled my body with yearning—to hear him whispering into my ear the words of love he had written to me, *always to be loved more than anything*, and to feel his breath hot on my cheek, the slide of his palms around my waist, and, yes, even the press of his body against mine. Every night prompted sweet imaginings and restless turmoil, and, now, the pain like a knife in my stomach as he glinted his eyes at another girl.

"Of course King Louis opposes the reforms." Etienne tore off a piece of bread. "The Church will do anything for wealth—even prevent clergymen from bequeathing their lands and titles to their sons."

"He opposes the reforms because they are unreasonable," Anseau said. "Forbidding bishops to marry was bad enough, a certain provocation to sin, for God bestowed urges upon men— but priests and canons, too? These so-called reforms tear families apart. They leave women without anyone to provide for them."

"And think of their children," Agnes said. "They will inherit nothing, not even their father's name. How will they marry? The poor things will have to join the abbey." She shuddered. "They might as well send them to the prison. Abbeys should not be permitted to accept oblates—children! Heloise, what do you think? You grew up in the Royal Abbey at Argenteuil, *non*?"

I frowned at Abelard. What had he whispered into Agnes's ear? She smiled, expecting to hear me speak ill of my childhood home, I knew. In truth, I had never felt so glad to leave any place. On the day my uncle had arrived for me, only his restraining hand stopped me from running out the door.

Under the table, Abelard's hand slid off his leg so that the backs of his fingers touched my thigh. I cleared my throat and shifted, causing the dishes to clatter on the table. He placed his hand back on the tabletop.

As the servants brought in eel pies—my favorite dish, and delectably seasoned—the conversation turned to Robert of

Arbrissel, the founder of the Fontevraud Abbey, where my mother had worked. He had agreed to preach a sermon in Paris, Abelard announced, pulling my attention away from my meal. Robert, coming here! Surely my uncle would take me to hear him speak. Perhaps Robert might tell me something of my mother—including what I most wished to know: my father's name.

"Robert declined to preach in the Saint-Etienne Cathedral, but will speak in the city, instead," Abelard said. "He said his message is meant not for the men of the cloister, but for all God's children, sinners as well as saints."

"Robert has a particular fondness for sinners, I hear," Anseau said. "Especially those of the fairer sex."

"He has ceased the practice, admittedly bizarre, of sleeping among the women." Abelard sent me a worried glance, noting my widened eyes. I had never heard of Robert's sleeping with the Fontevraud nuns. "His intentions were pure, at least. He did it to strengthen his resistance, he said."

"Who among us believes that tale?" Anseau said with a snort. "Being born a cat, he pursues mice. And the women love him—even more than they love you, Pierre. Prostitutes, widows, beautiful virgins—they stream to Fontevraud to touch the hem of his filthy tunic. They liken him to John the Baptist with his long hair and ragged clothes. They wait in line to wash his dirty feet, then give him their coins and their adoration. What man would not take advantage?"

Having reached the limits of my endurance with Anseau and his winking pronouncements—how odious, to take such pleasure in others' misfortunes—I could hold my tongue no longer. "Women join the abbey to escape from men, not to pursue them," I said, glaring.

"Our fair guest speaks the truth," Etienne said, "which makes Robert's betrayal of these women all the more reprehensible.

They come to him in trust, and he uses them for his own plea-sure—perhaps, yes, Pierre, only to tempt himself, although I agree with my brother that his tale is unlikely."

"Three thousand followers, and most of them women," Anseau said. "He must be a stallion in bed."

"Think about what you are saying!" I cried, looking around the table in horror. What monstrous creatures were these people, passing judgment on the cruel world from their cocoon of velvet and silk? "You malign one of our holiest men, as well as the women who seek refuge with him. Where is your Christian love? You sound like the very reformists whom you despise."

A long silence followed, during which everyone, including me, ate without so much as a murmur. Seeing all eyes cast down-ward, I realized that I had spoken too harshly, and without grati-tude for my host's hospitality.

"Please forgive my outburst," I said at last. "I should have con-trolled my temper."

"There is no denying that Robert of Arbrissel's soft spot for women has gotten him into some trouble," Etienne said.

"I thought his *hard* spot was the cause for concern," Agnes said, every bit her father's daughter.

Everyone laughed again, except for me. What did these men or the spoiled Agnes know of the desperation of women's lives? I had seen it for myself at Argenteuil: women born to the highest rank as well as the lowest, repudiated by their husbands, replaced with wives younger, richer, more beautiful, more fertile—or, simply, new.

"Many of the women at Fontevraud are the discarded wives of clergymen, for whom you expressed sympathy moments ago," I said. "Robert of Arbrissel provides them with shelter, food, and the solace of God's love. What have *you* done to help any of them?"

Abelard patted my arm, attempting to calm me, which infuriated me even more. He smiled, but with his lips closed, reminding me of my uncle's grimace when I had disgraced him before the bishop. My cheeks burned. I doubted that Abelard would ever bring me back to Etienne's house, or that, after this day, he would want to see me again at all.

"Heloise's mother was the first grand prioress of Fontevraud," Abelard explained.

"Who was your mother, child?" Etienne said. When I told him, he brightened. "Hersende of Champagne? Hear that, Agnes? She is a Montmorency! On your father's side," he said to me. I cringed inwardly, waiting for him to realize that I was far too young to be the daughter of Lord William of Montsoreau.

"My mother is a Montmorency," Agnes said with a smile of delight. "I knew we shared a special bond."

She stood and walked around the table, then held out her hands to me. "Cousin," she said. I gave her a thin smile as she sat between Abelard and me.

"*Oui*, I can see the family resemblance: those large, dark eyes; that generous mouth," she said. "You are a true Montmorency beauty." As the men around the table regarded me, I felt myself blush. Of what consequence was the color of my eyes? God sees not our bodies, but the soul within.

Agnes tugged at one of my braids. "You have the family's dark hair, as well. *I* am the outcast in that regard. But where"—she pointed above my left eye—"where did you acquire that streak of white? It must have come from your mother, *non*?"

My mother's hair had glistened like spun gold—but instead of responding, I lowered my eyes. *Please, let her change the course of her conversation,* I prayed. Soon, someone must realize that I was not her uncle's daughter.

"I wonder how Canon Fulbert could be related to such an *intelligent* girl," Anseau said.

"My uncle is not dull, *monsieur*," I lied, daring to send him an admonishing glance.

He cocked one eyebrow. "Then why haven't we heard before about his illustrious sister? Whenever I've encountered Fulbert, he talks unceasingly about himself. A man so anxious to advance his position would certainly make that connection known. Wouldn't you agree, Brother?"

"Given his ambition, it does seem strange that he hasn't mentioned her," Etienne said. "If Galon knew, Fulbert might be a bishop by now. What do you think, Pierre? You know Canon Fulbert the best."

Everyone looked at Abelard, who shrugged. "Fulbert talks much, *oui*, but he reveals little." Agnes burst into laughter, falling against Abelard's arm. Grinning, he amended, "He reveals little about himself, I intended to say."

Agnes rested her cheek on his shoulder and, with her eyes closed, sighed. Her cheeks flushed, rosy with wine. Her lips smiled, still, as though she expected a kiss, and Abelard gazed at her as fondly as if he might give her one. I turned my eyes, shuddering, and yet thanking God. He had shown me, today, the dangers of the path on which I had allowed my thoughts and desires to wander. A continent philosopher Abelard might be, but, like Robert of Arbrissel, he did not want for women. I thought of his kiss on my hand when last we had parted, how his lips had lingered, and his compliment: *Like the petals of a rose.* I felt like a toy played with once and then cast aside, forgotten.

5

To his brightest star, whose rays I have recently enjoyed: may she shine with such unfailing splendor that no cloud can obscure her.

—ABELARD TO HELOISE

He spoke of Aristotle's *Categories*, of Porphyry's Tree, of the classes of words that could be predicate to a subject. I gazed through the open window at the splendor of stars and tried not to think about the fragrance of roses rising from his clothes.

He had arrived late for our lesson, apologizing and giving me more parchment but not offering any explanation. But why should I need excuses? The roses spoke for themselves, and they shouted, not whispered, Agnes of Garlande's name.

He tapped my hand with his stylus. "Does Porphyry prove Aristotle's theory that all living things have souls, or does he disprove it?"

Had he embraced her and touched his lips to her cheek as he'd murmured her name?

"Heloise. What difference does Porphyry establish between 'accident' and 'essence'?" he prompted again.

He sat across from me, his eyes demanding, yet I could think only of roses. I walked to the window to stir the pot of herbs scenting the air. Four days had passed since the dinner at Etienne's home—four days since he had kissed my cheek at my uncle's door and breathed my name like a prayer. In four days, I had heard not a word from him, not even in response to my letters. Now that he had come, I could not even ask what had kept him away, for I dreaded his reply.

The tap of his stylus on the desktop; my blood's slow thrum; the cathedral bell's peal. I resumed my seat, but could not meet his demanding stare.

"I await your answer."

I admitted I had forgotten the question.

"Have you forgotten, too, that I am commanded to discipline you for idleness?"

I caught my breath, wondering what punishment he would inflict. Would he lift my skirt as the Reverend Mother Basilia had done and strike me with a cane?

"It is a wonder to me, then, that you have not pondered the *Isagoge*."

"I have read it, and pondered it, and written of it." I gestured toward the tablet. "As you have seen."

"I see words prettily arranged, nothing more. Where is the conviction behind your argument? Where is your passion?"

"I can hardly be expected to feel passion for the categorization of words. Does it matter whether the quality of being able to laugh is a *differentia* or a *propria*?" I would rather discuss whether plants and animals have souls, or which of the virtues is most desirable.

Abelard stood. "My topic fails to inspire you?" He took up his bag and walked to the door.

I cried out, asking where he was going, forgetting about roses for the time being.

"You have sat staring out the window since we began. I cannot compete with the beauty of the night. Let us go."

Quietly, so as not to awaken my uncle or Jean, we crept down the stairs and out the front door to confront the mysteries of the planets and wheeling stars, the moon hanging low like ripe fruit on a branch. He led me across the street and through the vine-yards to the river. I followed him to the bank's edge, tiptoeing over my misgivings. What did he intend for me out here, shielded by the vines from everyone's view? In the moon's orange glow I could see dark shapes all along the bank, couples lying in each other's arms or strolling beside the churning deep. Breezes soughed across the swift-moving waters, edging the night with chill. I rubbed my arms, wishing that I had brought a blanket or cotte.

When we reached the bank, he removed his cloak and laid it next to him, making a seat for me. He rummaged in his bag and extracted a bronze disk inscribed with symbols. I exclaimed: an astralabe! Mother had given one to me before taking me to Ar-genteuil. It was the only thing of hers I'd possessed, but the abbess had taken it away. *Everything here belongs to God.* As she'd snatched it into her hands, her eyes had snapped with greed.

"I have heard that the Saracens have found one thousand uses for an astralabe," he said, handing his to me. "Tonight, I am going to teach you one of them."

I cradled the instrument in my hands, admiring its cool weight, its ornate design, its surface inlaid with precious stones and carved with images of moons, stars, and planets. This work of beauty was made more precious by its power to unlock the se-crets of the universe. The scent of roses faded in the starry breeze.

He slid closer to me, his eyes on the astralabe, his hands touching the parts as he described them: the rete, on which the stars were inscribed; the tympanum, engraved with circles delin-eating altitude and latitude; the mater, or main body, with degree marks and numbers etched onto its rim. As he worked, his fingers touched mine, and his body's heat warmed my skin. No longer did I want for a cotte. I leaned into him and tipped my face toward the night, imbibing the silvered light shining from the moon and glossing his hair and brightening his face, which was now close to mine. He turned the astralabe over to show me the markings on its back and, along the edge, an inscription that, in the dim light, I could not read.

Where, I asked, did he acquire the remarkable instrument?

"From Agnes." The sound of her name on his lips set my teeth on edge. "She has befriended the king's astronomer and purchased it from him at my request."

I handed the astralabe back to him. "Far be it from me to tarnish its costly shine with my common hands."

He frowned as if he had not heard me clearly. "It was not so costly. She obtained it for a good price."

"Of that I have no doubt. I wonder what she gave besides her father's silver?" What besides money had Abelard given to her? The wind shifted, carrying the scent of roses again, filling my mouth with it, making me want to spit.

He cocked his head. "You do not care for Agnes? Then she has captured the hearts of all in the world but you."

"She certainly seems to hold yours in the palm of her hand."

"What do you find objectionable? Her nimble tongue? Her ready laugh? I had thought that, being of the same age, you might become friends."

How I cringed to hear him praise so readily this woman who, it was plain to me, excited his desire in ways that I could not.

"I do not befriend hypocrites," I said. "Agnes and her father profess concern for the wives and children of clergy, but do they help them?"

"I thought their repartee amusing."

"So I noticed."

"And did you notice also how I tried to compensate for your ill humor?"

"I call it 'discernment.'"

"I have yet to hear you laugh."

"And I hear you laughing all the time. I take life more seriously."

"Do you think me unserious because of my levity? Sometimes we must laugh in order not to cry."

"And what cause do you have for crying? You possess all you desire, it seems to me, including the admiration of every woman in the realm." I stood, blinking back tears, and walked away from him to the river's edge. Below, the water flowed deep and sullen.

"Only one woman's admiration matters to me, Heloise." Abelard's voice murmured against my ear, as close as a kiss. His hand pressed into the small of my back—rose-scented hands, wafting *her* fragrance. I cried out and struck at him, wishing I could fling him into the Seine—but I knocked the astralabe from his grip, instead—into the current, where it sank out of sight.

I fell to my knees and thrust my hands into the stream, rummaging as deeply as I could reach but grasping only water, numbingly cold. Where had it gone? Downstream? But it was surely too heavy to float away—wasn't it? *Dear God, please.* I wished that I, too, might hide in the water's dark, not only from Abelard but also from my foolish self. I bent over farther, stretching my fingers, seeking. Something brushed my fingertips and I lunged forward to seize it—then tumbled, headfirst, into the river.

Water filled my mouth, my nostrils, and all the pores of my skin. I heard a rushing in my ears and, as blackness enfolded me, the bubbling laughter of the river goddess Sequana. I grasped water in my flailing hands, thrashed it with my feet, strained my eyes against it, peering into the dark. My tunic twisted about my ankles as I kicked in a futile effort to find some toehold against which to push myself upward, toward the air. But I did not know which way was down, or which was up, seeing no light, not even the moon, but only darkness, as in a tomb. I struggled and turned, feeling the goddess tugging at me like possessive hands. The desire to breathe clawed at my lungs, but I knew in opening my mouth I would swallow death. *Abelard!* I cried out wordlessly as my foot touched a stone. Pushing against it, I sent myself upward, toward the water's surface, my heart now laboring for want of breath, my chest aching. Then I felt a hand grasp my wrist and pull me upward, and the water break around my head and pour from my eyes, my nose, and my mouth, and the grip of Abelard's arm around my waist.

"Heloise, thanks be to God. You are safe. Oof!" In my effort to shake off the goddess's grasp, I had struck him in the face. Abelard seized me more tightly and begged me to relax. "Still yourself. I am here and have you and will keep you safe."

My breath returning, I clung to him as he swam the short distance to the bank, letting the current carry us. Never had I felt so grateful to feel solid ground. I lay, panting, my eyes full of stars, marveling at the sight of them, at the breeze chilling my wet skin, at the fragrance of linden perfuming the night. I had not drowned.

Then I remembered why I had fallen into the Seine. A flush spread over me. Had I nearly died from jealousy of my teacher?

"You are shivering," Abelard said, pulling me to his bare chest—for he wore only his leggings and braies. My palms moved across his skin; my pulse sped up again, but not, this time, out of fear. His body, like mine, felt cold, but when I pressed the length of myself to him, we both warmed in the instant. I felt his heart's beat, his hand on my back, his fingers in my hair, his lips on my cheek.

"I feared I had lost you." His taking of my hand seemed, now, the most natural of acts.

"I cannot swim. Thanks be to God that you can."

"My father loves the sea. I learned to swim before I could walk. But—behold your stricken face! Heloise, are you crying?" I was not. He saw only water from the river glistening on my cheeks, for I had used all my tears sobbing for my mother, many years ago.

We sat still for a moment, swaying together in the breeze. "Did you think I loved Agnes?" Abelard finally said. "There is no one but you, Heloise. As God is my witness, I have never been with another, not even in my thoughts."

And then, O my beating heart! Under the spreading linden tree beside the Seine, in the air suffused with its sweetness, Abelard kissed me, his lips trembling with cold and his arms entwined around my waist. His mouth's tender press made me feel like moonlight itself, aglow and shimmering. A shiver ran through me. I tightened my hold, sliding my arms around his neck, and resisted my hands' urge to wander. Our lips parted and our tongues met, and I tasted his sweetness like that of a juicy apple. Warmth spread through me as though I were melting, and yet my skin tingled everywhere we touched. I wanted both to sigh and to sing.

"Heloise," he murmured, kissing my nose, my cheeks, my forehead. "Your softness; your delicious flavor; I would devour you, if I could." From under those curling eyelashes, his gaze dipped into mine and drew me in.

A shiver ran through him. I folded myself around him completely, holding him so close to me that I could feel his heart knocking at my chest, and willed myself to believe his words. *None other, even in my thoughts.*

"You are cold, and I am to blame. Forgive me, please, for my foolish behavior."

He kissed my cheek. The brush of his lips made me shudder. The linden's aroma enwrapped us like a sweet vine.

"I would hurl myself into the waters every night in order to feel your arms around me," Abelard said.

He would not need to do so, I nearly replied—but then I remembered what a dear price he had paid.

"Your beautiful astralabe. It is lost, because of me." I covered my face with my hands. "Seneca warned against jealousy. Why didn't I heed him?"

"Jealousy?" He kissed my hands, pulling them away from my face. "As if you had anything to envy in anyone—you, the swan among clucking hens, the glittering gem in the common stones."

"*Non*, not glittering, but dull with stupidity. And, now, deeply in your debt."

"A debt easily repaid." He kissed me again, more fervently than before, his breath in slow, deep pants warming my cheek while his hand caressed my waist. I longed to push him backward onto the bank, to spread myself over him like a blanket, to meld his body into mine.

But, alas, the moon shone full, exposing us to anyone who might pass, and the hour had grown late. We arose and made our way back to the place on the riverbank where we had begun, to retrieve Abelard's clothing. I sat upon a stone to wring out my hem as, whistling, he dried himself with his cloak. Let God be my witness: I averted my eyes. Yet the grace of his form—his smooth body; the glisten of him, taut curve and sinew, like a Roman sculpture—appears in my mind even now, as though he were a blinding star at which I had stared unblinking.

"Have you seen enough?" he said with a grin. "Or shall I tarry a few moments more?" I looked down at the water, where a glint of light caught my eye. I reached forth my hand and extracted, from the mud, the astralabe.

"Behold!" I cried, lifting it up. "My debt is paid." I offered it to Abelard, but he shook his head.

"There was never any debt, Heloise. That astralabe belongs to you."

"*Non.* You must not reward my foolishness with such a gift." Frowning, I held the instrument out to him.

He refused it with a laugh. "I bought it for your sake. I had it made for you."

"For me?" I lifted an eyebrow. "For what purpose?"

"Do you mean to ask what I wanted in return? I have already received far more than I expected." He winked.

My face burned. "Excuse me, please. I am not usually so . . . demonstrative. You saved my life."

"Therefore, you kissed me with mere gratitude? I do not think so. I felt much more." He lifted his eyebrows suggestively and laughed again. "But if that is how you express gratitude, then I will remind you daily how I rescued you from drowning in the Seine."

"I cannot accept this gift. Fashioned by the king's astronomer—this is too dear. You must keep it and bring it to our lessons for us to use together."

"There will be no more lessons for a while." We started up the bank together, toward my uncle's house. The breeze had stopped; the air was as still, now, as my wondering heart.

"No more lessons?" I longed, at that moment, to curl up on the sand, among the vineyards, and close my eyes. "I understand. After the way I have behaved tonight, I cannot blame you."

"It cannot be helped."

"You probably despise me, and with good reason."

"Despise you?" Abelard shook his head. "The opposite is closer to the truth."

"'*Anger is cruel and fury overwhelming, but who can stand before jealousy?*'" The proverb sprang to my lips. "With my jealousy, I have driven you away."

"Driven me away? Would that it were so, for then I might have the pleasure of changing my mind and remaining with you."

Duty called Abelard to his parents' home in Brittany, he said. His father had become ill, and his condition worsened every day. Abelard must hasten to him, as well as sign the papers giving his brother the lands and title Abelard had forfeited so long ago in embracing the philosopher's life.

"It is a mere formality," he said of relinquishing his birthright. "I chose knowledge and wisdom long ago over the life of a lord—the lap of Minerva over the court of Mars, as I like to say."

"Your father permitted you to choose?" The word coated my tongue like cream.

"My father served as a knight in the court of Anjou, where philosophy and song are revered as highly as God. He might have chosen the scholar's life for himself, had he not married my mother." Abelard halted his steps and turned to me, his eyes bright. "Were you truly jealous of Agnes?"

Heat flooded my face. "Does that amuse you?"

"It delights me. It tells me that you care."

My pulse throbbed sweetly. Questions filled Abelard's eyes once more, but I had no answers—only questions of my own.

"I hate leaving you now, when our feelings are only beginning to blossom." He reached out for my hand and held it as though it were a flower whose petals he feared crushing. "My greatest fear is that, when I return, you might be gone."

"Gone? But—where would I go?"

"To Fontevraud. Robert of Arbrissel will come to Paris in only a few weeks and might take you back with him."

"*Non.* I want to complete my studies with you."

"Your uncle may try to send you now. He told me so today. A widow named Petronille of Chemillé helped your mother build

Fontevraud, and she hopes Robert will appoint her as its abbess. If he does, it will ruin your uncle's plans."

Non, I wanted to say. Would Uncle Fulbert force me into the abbey again so soon, sacrificing my happiness on the altar of his ambition? Unlike Abelard, however, I would not be permitted to choose my fate.

I lowered my eyes. "I am dependent on my uncle and must do as he says." How could I meet Abelard's searching gaze, equal to equal, when another ruled me as completely as though I were his slave?

"I must convince Fulbert to keep you with him for a while longer, then. I did promise to help him gain a promotion. Perhaps as his friend I might influence him."

"He thinks you are friends now. He boasts of it even to the servants."

"And to every canon in the cloister. You should have seen Bishop Galon's puzzled frown on the day after Bernard's sermon. Your uncle told everyone at the dinner with Bernard and the rest that he and I are 'brothers in intellect.'"

"He thought to impress Bernard, I suppose." I sighed. Didn't my uncle know how Bernard hated knowledge and learning? While Abelard insisted that questioning could only strengthen one's faith, the reformists demanded blind obedience to the Church. "He wants so badly to advance. Poor Uncle."

Mirth filled Abelard's eyes, but neither of us laughed. At that time, at least, we respected my uncle.

At the door of Uncle Fulbert's house, Abelard tucked a strand of hair behind my ear, brushing my skin with his thumb and sending a shiver down my arms. He pulled the astralabe from his pouch and handed it to me in spite of my protests, telling me that he already possessed an astralabe and that he had bought this one especially for me.

Then he pointed upward to that bright and beautiful planet,

pink edged in gold on that night. "The loveliest body in the sky cannot compare to the one beside me now, but she will have to suffice. Venus is not difficult to find, except when clouds veil her." Using the astralabe, he showed me how to find her in position to the moon, and then in position to the place where we stood.

"I shall gaze at her bright face every night before bedtime and think of you," he said. "Will you do the same and think of me?"

"Shall I send you messages, too?" I teased. "Would you hear them over the singing of the spheres?"

"That music plays ever in my heart. It commenced on the day we first met and has not ceased."

Abelard pressed his lips to mine as softly as a sigh, making me forget, again, myself and all I had vowed I would never become. I yielded and submitted until my lips had parted to admit his tongue, whose flavor dissolved me in delicious bliss until we heard the shutters open over our heads. We looked up to see Jean in my window, searching out over the cloister for me. Abelard pressed a finger to my lips and then, after handing me the astralabe, slipped into the shadows and away.

"I am here, Jean, studying the stars," I called softly as I stood on the mounting stone with the astralabe in my hands.

"It is neither seemly nor safe for a maiden to be out alone at night. I beg you to come indoors, my lady." In a moment I heard the creak of the inner door, then the latch of the outer one, and there stood Jean with a lantern. As I stepped inside, my fingers felt the inscription on the mater, and I turned the astralabe over to read it in the light.

To his Venus, from her Adonis. The goddess of love and the god of beauty—and passionately in love. I smiled and might have burst into song but for Jean, who, watching me more closely than usual, narrowed his eyes. Then I remembered the rest of the lovers' tale, and my smile disappeared. As I passed him, I pressed my fingers and thumb against the engraved words, trying, in vain, to blot them out.

6

An equal to an equal, to a reddening rose under the spotless whiteness of lilies: whatever a lover gives to a lover . . . yet my breast blazes with the fervor of love.
—HELOISE TO ABELARD

obert of Arbrissel limped across the altar, his bare feet slapping the wood, his cane's tap punctuating each labored step. From behind me came a contemptuous snort. "Behold the mighty orator! He resembles a common beggar."

"He is ill, have you heard?" another replied. "This may be his final sermon."

"He is so thin and unkempt, how can anyone tell whether he is ill or well? His hair resembles a bird's nest, all tangled and dirty. And behold the scabs on his chin!"

"He shaves his beard without water, it is said."

"That tunic hangs on him like a sack, and full of holes. He ought to be ashamed, defiling God's holy house with such filth."

Having reached the front of the altar, the preacher lifted his cane and tossed it to the side, where it fell with a clatter onto the floor. His eyes, the same shade of gray as his wild hair, surveyed the crowded room: the canons in their white albs and rope cinctures; the priests in black; the tonsured monks in brown; the nuns, gathered like birds in their discrete flocks; and, in the front of the congregation, the colorful nobles, lords, and ladies and their families from Orléans, from Tours, from Paris itself. On a dais behind the altar, across from the choir, sat King Louis, who, although slightly younger than Abelard, appeared older by virtue of his protruding belly and the gray in his curling hair.

"Robert is overwhelmed," someone whispered. "He didn't expect the king to be here."

"Nonsense," came the reply. "Robert of Arbrissel has preached for the pope many times. He would not quaver before a king."

Then Robert's searching gaze fell upon me—and stopped. His lips moved. His right hand reached blindly; an altar boy handed him the cane he had dropped. He took it without moving his eyes from my face.

"He has seen you—seen you, my girl! I told you, *non*? You are so like your mother than he will beg you to take her place." Uncle, standing behind me, squeezed my shoulders, sharing an excitement I did not feel—until Robert spoke.

"Where are my people? I want my people," he cried, tapping the cane loudly on the stone floor. His voice rolled like thunder over the chapel. "I came to bring the good news of Christ's love to the wretched, not to hypocritical clerics, wealthy monks, and men with soft hands and silk braies."

Murmurs rustled through the room. "Why does he keep his eyes on me?" a woman said.

"*Non*. Not you, but me," another said.

In fact, he spoke to me, his clear eyes holding me rapt as he lifted his fist into the air and shook it, as he raged against vanity, against greed, against simony, against injustice—but not, as Bernard had done, against the wickedness of women. I moved through the crowd in a trance, pressing to the front, desiring only to be near him, and wondering where I had seen him before.

"Vanity of vanities; all is vanity," he was saying. "Whatever is under the sun is vanity and affliction of the spirit. Hypocrites, listen to me! The spirit of pride is bad, but the pretense of humility is worse." He raked his eyes over the nobles swathed in finery.

"The preacher ought to remove the beam from his own eye," the murmurer behind me said. "Dirty rags and bare legs are the worst sort of vanity if a man can afford better."

"The spirit of envy is bad, but the pretense of love is worse." Robert's voice rose.

I glanced at my uncle. His dark eyes peered shrewdly about the room; his fawning smile gave his mouth a greasy appearance. He would pretend to love the devil if doing so would gain him a promotion.

"The spirit of lust is bad"—Robert's voice broke, and he hung his head—"but the pretense of chastity is worse."

Silence fell over the room. I thought of Abelard, the headmaster, sworn to chastity yet touching my body with his eyes, his hands, his lips. My palms grew damp. Was this "the spirit of lust," or something more?

The sermon finished, a crowd of women swarmed about the great preacher.

Seeing that we could not get near him, my uncle led me, instead, to greet Etienne of Garlande, his new target in the quest for a deacon's post. Etienne took my hands in his and kissed my cheeks, and Agnes embraced me as though we were sisters. Engulfed by the scent of roses, I turned away from her.

"During all the time that man spoke, he never took his eyes off me," Agnes's father was saying with a nervous laugh. "One might think that it was I whom he called 'hypocrite.' But of course, he and I are not acquainted."

"He is known to be an excellent judge of character," Agnes teased, making me smile. Then, as the men discussed the sermon, she took my arm and pulled me close. "You and I must talk. My parents and I leave for Anjou tomorrow. May I come to you when we return?"

As I sought a polite way to say no—surely she wished to discuss Abelard, while I desired nothing less with her—my uncle tugged at one of my braids. "What are you girls plotting? Going to run away and join the famous nun-catcher? Nun-catcher! Heh-heh. Come, Heloise, let us introduce ourselves to Robert before the ladies devour him."

"Soon," Agnes said before Uncle led me away toward the altar clotted with women who strove to touch Robert as though he could cure them of their sex. His gaze captured mine and pulled me across the room to him. *Hersende,* he mouthed. Blushing at the intensity of his stare, I pulled my veil close and lowered my eyes.

When we had reached him, he kissed my hand. Power flowed through my fingers and into my arm, quickening my blood.

"Forgive me for my boldness," he said. "You remind me of someone I used to know. More than that—you are her very likeness."

"This is Heloise, the brightest star in Paris, and I am her uncle Fulbert, subdeacon in the Nôtre-Dame-of-Paris cloister."

Robert barely acknowledged him. "Perhaps you know of her," he said to me. "Her name was Hersende. She was the widow of the Lord of Montsoreau."

"I did know her," is all I said. I glanced at my uncle, not certain how much he wanted me to tell.

"Hersende was my sister—my sister!" my uncle said.

Robert turned to me, his eyes crinkling at the corners. His tanned skin stretched across high cheekbones as he smiled, revealing a chipped front tooth that only enhanced his handsome appearance. "You are related to Hersende, as well?"

"As Christ was to Mary," my uncle said.

"She was your mother?" Robert's lips parted. He stared at me. "How can that be? Hersende had only a son."

"And a daughter, too." My uncle cleared his throat. "As you can clearly see."

"Yes, the likeness is remarkable. I had not known of a daughter."

I began to perspire. At any moment he would ask about my father, and my uncle's hopes would shatter. Robert's scandalous acts had not harmed *him*—but he was a man. Would he appoint as his abbess a woman born in sin, without even a father's name to call her own?

"Behold your face. My God! You are her very likeness." Robert's hand faltered as he lifted it toward my cheek. I pulled my veil more tightly about my face, self-conscious, but in hiding my dark hair I must have increased my similarity to my mother.

"Hersende sent her to the Argenteuil convent for her schooling, the best in Paris for girls—the best," my uncle said. "She is proficient in Latin, Greek, Hebrew, astronomy, music, literature, all of it—the trivium and quadrivium. She's had an education fit for a queen—a queen! Or for an abbess, as my sister desired." He pulled out my mother's letter and handed it to Robert, who read it slowly, his eyes filling with tears.

"Your mother was the finest of women," he said to me.

"I barely knew her," I said, hoping he would tell me something of her. "I have only a few memories, but all of them are golden."

"Yes, that is how I remember her. As warm and golden as the sun. And her voice—ah! She sang like the angels. Do you sing, Heloise?"

"Her voice puts the angels to shame—to shame," Fulbert said. "Even the birds stop their song to hear my niece. She is her mother's daughter to the very core."

"And now you would follow in her path."

That phrase again. "Mother wished me to take my vows at Fontevraud, yes, and to be of service to you. It is my uncle's desire, also."

"My sister hoped that Heloise might become your abbess someday, or grand prioress," Fulbert said.

Robert drew his brows together. "I have not replaced Hersende, for to do so seems impossible. Petronille of Chemillé hopes to be chosen, and indeed I should have appointed her by now. Together, she and Hersende built Fontevraud."

"My sister always enjoyed being in command." My uncle, who often said this with bitterness, smiled as though he had lived to obey her.

"God gave her a talent for it, as well as beauty, grace, intelligence, and virtue. If I have not replaced her, it is because there is no replacement. No one on Earth compares to Hersende. Until now." The years fell away with his smile, transforming him. His eyes flashed. "We return to Fontevraud tomorrow. Come with us."

I caught my breath. Abelard had feared the preacher might take me with him, and I had dismissed his concern. My mother had left me behind; no one had wanted me since. Now I found myself torn between two men. My heart began to race—toward Abelard.

"Did you hear that, my dear girl?" my uncle said. "He wants you now. You can go, and I shall send your things along—"

"*Non*," I blurted.

Uncle scowled. "You don't—"

"I cannot, Uncle. Please! Not now. Not yet."

"If the abbot desires you to join him now, then now you shall go. No arguments. It is your time—your time!"

I would never see Abelard again. My only chance at love, gone. And although Robert of Arbrissel would surely tell me much about Mother, I still needed to know about my father—about myself, who I was, from where I came. I would never find the truth from within the walls of an abbey.

"*Non!* I cannot go with you now. I—I am sorry."

Uncle Fulbert's face colored and he eyed me with suspicion. *Abelard.* The name perched on my tongue but I knew better than to utter it.

"Must I leave you so soon, Uncle? I beg to remain in Paris a little while longer. I have only lived in my uncle's home for a short time," I said to Robert. "He is my only family, now that my mother is gone." Robert's gaze turned inward; he was remembering Mother, while I had forgotten even the sound of her voice.

"Uncle Fulbert and I have become very close, haven't we, Uncle?"

My uncle grunted. He licked his lips, thirsting, I knew, for his evening flagon.

"Please, Uncle, allow me a few more months with you. Can't I stay until—until next spring? That would give me time to finish my studies in dialectic."

"Dialectic is a fine course of study for an abbess," Robert said.

"And with none other than Petrus Abaelardus as her teacher," Uncle said.

I dropped my gaze, hiding my thrill at the very sound of his name.

"Pierre Abelard, the headmaster? That is most impressive."

"She is his finest scholar—his finest," my uncle said.

"By all means you must complete your schooling with him. Learn what you can of dialectic and debate, then bring your skills to me. I will introduce you to the richest, most parsimonious men in the realm, and you may convince them to fund the new oratory I want to build for the *meretrices* who have come to us.

But—when will you join us, Heloise?" Robert held my gaze, searching my soul, it seemed.

I leaned in to him, swaying as if blown by God's own breath. Yes, I wanted to go with this man, to bask in his light, which seemed to shine from within. *He can be very persuasive,* Abelard had said. I now understood what had drawn my mother to him so irresistibly, to this man who emanated love, who smelled of it, and the fragrance was that of every flower that had ever bloomed, including, yes, roses. I wanted to dive, headfirst, into that garden, to roll in those blossoms, to smother myself—and then, remembering how the silence at Argenteuil had smothered me with its unremitting hand, how the darkness and chill of the convent had stiffened my very bones, I shrank back from him, breaking the spell.

"I would like to remain in Paris for one more year," I said, my voice tearing like flesh on a nail.

"A year? That is too long—too long! The abbot needs an abbess, didn't you hear? I will send her to you in one month!" Uncle said. I caught my breath; when Abelard returned, I would be gone.

Robert's eyes turned fierce; his long hair flew about his head in the shifting breeze. He gripped my hands too hard; his fingers felt coarse and rough. "Taking the veil is not your desire. It is not your calling."

"Her mother willed it, by God—willed it!" my uncle said. "She has been training for it all her life."

"And what is Heloise's will?"

I searched my mind for the answer that, of late, had obscured itself even from me. "I wish to please God," I finally said.

"Good. Good." Robert pulled me close for an embrace that left me dizzy, as if I had taken too many breaths too quickly. "Until the spring. Come next June."

As we turned to leave, my uncle's faced flushed with pleasure as if he had quaffed from the flagon and it had filled itself again.

So my fate was decided. So would the remainder of my time with Abelard be parceled, one month at a time, a little more than one glorious year in which to dance and sing and perhaps to know true love. If Abelard loved me, the whole world and Paradise, too, would be mine, for a little while, at least. I wanted to dance in that moment, and I wanted to cry. *Hurry home, Abelard. Our time is short.*

7

❧❧❧

Your presence is my joy, your absence, my sorrow; in
either case, I love you.
— HELOISE TO ABELARD

J read Abelard's letter with a leaping joy. After two months
away, he was returning to Paris at last. In the study of my
uncle's home I took my own tablet from my pouch and composed a reply.

Glory of young men, companion of poets, how handsome you
are in appearance yet more distinguished in feeling. The words
flowed naturally, without artifice, as love should flow. Were
Abelard beside me now instead of this messenger with red ears,
I would breathe my ardor into his mouth until he overflowed
with it and returned it back to me.

He loved me. Of this I had little doubt, or no doubt at all
except in Agnes's presence. She was so beautiful and self-
assured—what man wouldn't love her? *Non*, it was *me* whom he
loved, me whom he had kissed, me to whom he had sent so many
messengers that Jean had asked *me* to answer the door. Had Abelard written passionate letters to Agnes, as well?

A pain stabbed my breast. No; he would not. *You are my sun,*
since you always illumine me with the most delightful brightness of
your face and make me shine, Abelard had written. *I have no light*

that does not come from you, and without you I am dull, dark, weak, and dead.

When I did not reply to him as promptly as he desired—feelings of inadequacy having palsied my hand and robbed my mind of confidence—he complained. *Envious time looms over our love, and yet you delay as if we were at leisure.*

Our love. A sweet tremor shook me. His words dispelled my fear, unlocking my hand, and I wrote to him not from my imperfect mind, but from my open heart.

I read my letter over, not satisfied, but the messenger awaited and I would not send him to Abelard again with empty hands. When the youth had gone, I crushed the herbs in the window pot, relishing thyme's woodslike scent, inhaling lavender's perfume, and remembering Abelard's fragrance, which, God willing, I would enjoy soon.

He loved me, yes. I'd seen love in his eyes when he'd kissed me under the linden tree, felt it in his embrace at my uncle's door. His every letter pulsed with love, and so did I, down to the marrow in my bones. It warmed me even on these chilly days, as though his arms perpetually encircled me. For the first time since my childhood, I felt not at all alone.

From outside my window I heard my name. I opened the shutters to see Agnes of Garlande below in a green silk *bliaut*, her copper curls springing about her face in spite of the braids she had tried to impose upon them. I felt, again in my plain, dark tunic, like a weed in a garden of roses. I sighed. Now that she had seen me, I must receive her.

She shimmered into the great room, all color and light. Her eyes sparkled as we embraced.

"Pierre is returning to Paris. Did you know?" she said.

"I received his letter today."

"He wrote to Uncle Etienne, also." Her bright smile did not

quite reach her eyes. "He has been away long enough, *non*? Paris seems dull without Pierre."

Jean entered and gave her the *henap*, whose stem she rubbed absently with her thumb and forefinger.

"I look forward to resuming my lessons with him," I said carefully. "I have much yet to learn."

"And in so short a time." She gave me a shrewd look. "I suppose you think the abbey to be your only recourse?"

"Is that why you have come?" My voice sounded colder than I felt, but I did not soften my tone. "You have heard of my plans to enter the abbey, and you wish to learn when I will go?"

"I have come to help you." She surveyed the room to make certain Jean had gone. "Heloise, I know about your father."

My body stiffened; my knees tensed, as though I might run. I heard my uncle's low growl: *No one must ever know.*

Controlling my voice with great effort, I asked her what she thought she knew. With whom had she spoken about me? Only her mother, she said, to exclaim over the cousin she had met.

"Mother insisted that I am mistaken. William of Montsoreau had no daughters, and he died seven or eight years before I was born. But—aren't you and I similar in age?"

"*Oui*, and we are not cousins, as you have discerned." I lifted my chin. "You bear no obligation to help me."

"But—are you truly returning to the cloistered life? How could you do so? When I mentioned Argenteuil at Uncle Etienne's dinner, you appeared stricken, as though someone had died."

I thought of my mother, her tear-streaked face, the letters she did not write. My body felt heavy, too great a weight for me to carry. I lowered myself into one of chairs Jean had set before the fire.

Agnes took the other chair and told me of her cousin whose husband had repudiated her for barrenness after six years of marriage. In shame she had taken refuge at Fontevraud. "I visited her there. The gardens are glorious; the cathedral is splendid—and the abbey is as dank as a tomb. Convents are where women go to die, not to live."

I closed my eyes against the dark and the cold of the abbey; the hunger and fatigue; the feeling that, if someone did not speak, I would lose my mind. And yet, was the nun's life worse than marriage?

"Better to die than live as a *meretrix* with a man I do not love," I said.

"*Pfft!* Love is for lovers, not for husbands and wives." She stood and took the *henap* from the mantel. "Women marry for money, and for children. Don't you want children?"

I felt a pang, thinking of the little girls at Argenteuil, their bony mischief, their shy smiles. How would it feel to hold my own baby to my breast, to kiss its fat cheeks, to sing for my child as my mother had done for me, lying together under the open window, stars spilling their light across the blanket? Sorrow pressed against my eyes.

"I do not want marriage," I said. "I have not imagined myself with children."

"But why? You come from a noble family. Who was your father?"

I denied myself the urge to confess, which was, in the face of her sympathy, nearly irresistible.

But my silence told her all she needed to know. "You do not know him." She sat beside me again and touched my arm, her eyes soft. "You poor dear. Do not fear, Heloise: I will not tell a soul—not even Pierre."

At the sound of Abelard's name on her lips I stood, brushing her hand away. "Is this why you have come today—to sink your teeth into a juicy tale that you can share with your friends in King Louis's court?"

"You are too young for the abbey, and too accomplished," she said, wrinkling her pretty brow. "On this, Pierre and I agree."

I narrowed my eyes. Had Agnes written to Abelard about me? *Poor Heloise. We must save her, Pierre!* Apparently, she had united herself with him in a common cause: me. What a brilliant strategist! I wondered if she played chess.

"Why concern yourself about my life?" I said. "When I am gone, you will have 'Pierre' to yourself."

"To myself?" She snorted. "To watch him preen and strut, and listen to him boast, or endure his unremitting teasing? And bear all that talk of 'genus' and 'species' and Plato and Porphyry—*merci, non!* Pierre amuses me most in the company of others, in *riposte*. His tongue is a veritable Damocles's sword."

This interested me. "How so? Do his words hang as a blade over his adversary's head?"

"Not over his adversary's head"—Agnes rolled her eyes—"but his own." She did not sound, to me, like a woman in love. "And he agrees that you are too young for the convent. Of course, he has reasons for wanting you to change your mind." She pressed a finger to her smiling lips. I looked at her askance. Was she laughing at me?

"And are you here today on your beloved Pierre's behalf?"

"My 'beloved Pierre'? Is that what you think?" She laughed again, but now the sound reminded me of a brook in springtime, frolicking over the rocks. "I am an heiress—a future countess. Would I squander my prospects on a *teacher*?" She grimaced as if the very word tasted sour.

"But you lay your head on his shoulder."

"Pierre used to bounce me on his knee. He put frogs in my boots." Agnes stuck out her tongue. "He is like a brother—a maddening, annoying, and very loving brother. *Mon Dieu*—behold your expression!" She laughed again. "It is exactly as I had hoped." Her eyes shone. "You love him."

8

﹥﹥◈◈﹤﹤

You are buried inside my breast for eternity, from which tomb you will never emerge as long as I live. There you lie; there you rest. You keep me company right until I fall asleep; while I sleep you never leave me, and after I wake, I see you, as soon as I open my eyes, even before the light of day itself.

—ABELARD TO HELOISE

*T*hat Abelard stood before me after so many weeks away seemed a miracle, or a dream.

No—were I dreaming, I would have thrown my arms about his neck and kissed his mouth as if it were a fountain from which I might refresh my soul, as I had done nightly in my dreams during his long absence. In the great room of my uncle's house, it was Uncle Fulbert who kissed Abelard in greeting while I murmured a shy welcome. His laughter rang out as familiar and dear as a long-forgotten song, drowning out, I hoped, the joyous, erratic thumping of my heart.

"Heloise." Even as my uncle embraced him, kissing his cheeks, slapping his back, Abelard's eyes never wavered from mine. "What a pleasure to see you"—he darted a glance at my uncle—"dear child. Have you behaved yourself while I was away?"

"Solitude prompts us to all kinds of evil," I teased. In fact, I had reread Abelard's *Dialectica*, preparing to debate him, and I had written him letters, taken cooking lessons from Pauline, and managed the household with alacrity, knowing that, so long as I pleased Uncle, he would leave me to myself so that I could retire to my room before bedtime. There, at my window, I gazed upon our Venus at the appointed hour and sent Abelard prayers and every sweetness of which I could think. I relived every moment we had spent together, feeling anew the thrill of his lips on my lips, smiling as his words returned to me—*The loveliest body in the sky cannot compare to the one beside me now*—and begging God to send him home. Now here he stood, thinner, yes, and as pale as if he had not ventured out of doors the entire fall, but with the same blue eyes beckoning, over my uncle's shoulder, like evening shadows.

"Welcome back, Petrus." Uncle Fulbert led him to the trestle table. "By God, if I had known you were coming, I would have had my niece buy a nice piece of salmon instead of these common eels." I held my tongue, thinking of the pinch of my uncle's fingers as he had parsed the coins for this meal.

"To health," Abelard said, lifting the *henap* of wine. "And to *home*, a word that, while bringing contentment to others, pricks me with melancholy." He handed the cup to my uncle. "In me, my friend, you see a man with no home."

"What—no home? No home, man, how can that be?"

"In Brittany, I forfeited my rights to my father's castle, and to the fertile lands that were my birthright." Abelard's voice broke, and he sighed deeply. "I am a wanderer, Fulbert, an itinerant scholar since my youth. Le Pallet is the only home I have ever known."

"I thought giving it up was your wish," I said, frowning. Had he wished to remain there?

"The Lord appreciates your sacrifice, Petrus," Uncle Fulbert said. " 'He who loses his life for my sake will save it,' et cetera. You suffer now, but your reward awaits in heaven."

"What you say is true, my friend. Yet I yearn for a home on Earth, a place of repose and rest."

"But didn't you take William of Champeaux's house here in the cloister? I have seen it, a fine place—fine! All the comforts, *non*?" My uncle handed the cup to Abelard, who gave it to me. The wine warmed my blood but, alas, did not calm my nerves.

"It is a fine house, yes—the perfect dwelling for an ascetic such as William, especially during the cold months. The winds blow inside nearly as freely as outdoors." Abelard shivered. "I dread another winter there, hunched at the fire in my blankets and cotte, my hands frozen and stiff."

"I wonder that you can do your work," I said, smirking. "How does one grip a stylus with frozen fingers or move it through cold-hardened wax?" He could well afford a warm house, I knew; the Nôtre-Dame canons earned the highest benefices of any in the realm.

Abelard winked at me. "And the expense, Fulbert! I cannot afford even a man to empty my chamber pot." Abelard sent a beseeching gaze to Jean, who had entered with the eels and a garden salad but, judging from his returning glance, no sympathy for the great scholar forced to contend with his own waste.

"Too great an expense! I am surprised to hear you say so— most surprised." Uncle drained the goblet again, shaking the last drops of wine into his mouth. "It seems to me that you might afford a castle given the price you command for teaching."

Uncle's insult made me grind my teeth. Seeing Abelard's eyes narrow, I braced myself—but rather than offer a scathing retort as he was perfectly capable of doing, he bared his teeth in a smile like that of the wolf poised to pounce on its prey.

"I had not heard you complain of my price, Fulbert. Is it too high? Perhaps you would rather hire one of my scholars to teach your niece?"

"Non!" I cried—then, seeing my uncle's frown, forced a laugh. "Robert of Arbrissel finds it most impressive that I am studying under the great Petrus Abaelardus," I said to Abelard. "It is the only reason he agreed to delay my going to Fontevraud until the spring."

"You are going . . . in the spring?" Suddenly, Abelard looked like a child who had lost his way.

"She leaves in June, yes, if I can afford to send her." My uncle called for more wine, although he had not taken more than a few bites of eel. "To attain a high position, my niece will need a substantial dowry. Her mother gave all *her* fortune to Robert. And now I am giving mine to you, in payment for Heloise's lessons."

"I would not hinder your niece's success, not for all the livres in France. And yet, I must have income. As you know, my position at the Nôtre-Dame School is precarious. Roscelin, Anseau, even William of Champeaux, burn with hatred for me."

"They burn with envy," I said. "The student outshines his masters."

"Would that I possessed their influence," Abelard said. "William of Champeaux, in particular, would love to cause my ruin—and he has the ear of the bishop of Paris. Etienne is my only protection, but only so long as King Louis loves him. Should the brothers from Garlande fall out of favor in the royal court, I would be forced to flee Paris."

"Where would you go, having signed away your inheritance?" I said.

Abelard shrugged. "I may claim it again at any time. That is my birthright, as my father's heir. To do so, however, would be far from my desire." Losing his position here would necessitate opening his own school, but how, when he had no money saved? The church demanded a high percentage of his students' fees.

"We must make a canon of you here, in Nôtre-Dame," Fulbert said. "You would receive a benefice with a substantial income, as well as prebends. When I become a deacon, I shall use my influence on your behalf."

"And as I have promised, I shall assist you in your bid for a promotion," Abelard said. "As archdeacon of Paris, Etienne will certainly aid in the cause."

"We will help each other." Uncle Fulbert's cheeks flushed with wine and excitement. "Help each other, as friends—friends!"

"*Oui*, but I want to help Heloise, too. Such a brilliant and capable girl deserves the best teaching." Abelard furrowed his brow, pondering—then brightened. "Fulbert—you possess a spare room, *non?*"

"The room on the top floor would accommodate one man. But it is a narrow, cramped space, far removed from any hearth."

"Believe me when I say that it cannot be colder than the warmest room in my house. How pleasant it would be to come home to you, my dear friend"—Uncle Fulbert wriggled with pleasure—"and Heloise, my brightest pupil. And your house is closer to the cathedral than my own." I looked down at my hands, scarcely able to believe what I heard.

"Not the attic, *non*," my uncle said. "The room is not worthy of you."

Jean returned to clear away the food.

"But your hearth is warm and your cook is exquisite. I would pay a king's ransom not to take another meal in the refectory." Abelard laughed. "I think the cook there procures his meat from the gallows at the place de Grève."

"A king's ransom, for my attic room?" My uncle shook his head. "I would not demand such a high rent. No, I would accept only the amount you charge to instruct my niece."

Listening to their negotiations, I pressed a hand to my skipping heart. Abelard, live here! The Lord had answered my prayers, and more: to spend every evening of our remaining months together was more than I had dared to ask.

I winced to hear my uncle's demands, however. Would he turn Abelard away for money's sake, rich as Uncle Fulbert was? He needed no rent; he had paid for his house long ago and earned as much as a count from his benefice. But even the greatest wealth cannot extinguish insatiable greed.

Abelard unleashed his lion's roar of a laugh and sent me another wink, dispelling my fears. "Fulbert, you fox! Are you suggesting I waive my teaching fee in exchange for a room in your attic?"

"Indeed not." My uncle glanced at Jean. "For that price I will give you Jean's room and move *him* into the attic."

Jean's eyes darted from side to side as he wiped the table. "You are giving my bedchambers to the headmaster? But who will guard Heloise? Didn't you place me next to her for that purpose?"

"That was your idea—yours. I never thought she needed guarding, and indeed she has not, chaste and devout girl that she is. They taught her well in the convent—very well! When I am away, however, your duty will be to watch the house—and, on all days, to empty Master Petrus's chamber pot." As my uncle laughed, Jean turned away with the dishes in hand—sending a dark look Abelard's way before stomping from the hall. When he had entered the kitchen, we heard a crash, then a string of expletives.

"I do not wish to cause difficulty," Abelard said, although his broad grin belied his protest. I had to look away or be consumed by the flame I saw leaping in his eyes. The corners of my mouth twitched with a smile of my own, which I suppressed, not wanting my elation to show. Living here, with me! Warmth spread through me as though the sun had taken residence in my chest.

"Jean has served me since I was young," Uncle Fulbert said with a wave of his hand. "Nearly thirty years! He will sleep anywhere I say, and happily. He's as faithful as a dog, eh, Heloise?"

Indeed. I could not understand why Jean endured my uncle's belligerent, wine-soaked rants and, when Uncle was especially drunk, his kicks and slaps. With a straight back and impassive eyes he bore Uncle's every insult, his every blow. Of course, I endured the same from Uncle Fulbert, but I had nowhere else to go.

"And so it is settled," my uncle said. "You will live with us. In exchange, you will instruct my niece—and we will both save money. Everyone is happy." He hoisted the *henap* in a toast, took a drink, and handed the cup to Abelard.

"Everyone is happy, yes, except poor Jean," I said, but Abelard's lips had curled in a slippery grin. I, however, did not like the twist of Jean's mouth upon his hearing that he must move upstairs. I had explored the attic room and found it dank and smelling of rats.

The meal finished, my uncle staggered to his chambers and I retired to the study, where I began work on a letter to Abelard.

In a few moments, as I had expected, he came in, rubbing his palms together. "Good fortune is mine once again."

"Good fortune? You have given up a substantial sum tonight."

"Yes, and gladly, in order to be near you." Abelard took my hand and pulled me close, then slid his arm about my waist. "My God, Heloise, you feel like heaven. I dreamt of this nightly while I was away."

"All this feels like a dream to me, too." I leaned against him, feeling as though I might melt. "To have you in Paris again is strange enough. It seems you might disappear at any moment, as though you were an apparition, or made of smoke. But to see you every night—I cannot believe it."

"I cannot believe how easily Fulbert fell into my trap." He laughed again. "And now he has consigned his little lamb to the wolf."

"You deceived him." I pulled away.

"Ah, but deception is not a sin." Abelard wagged his finger. "You have said so yourself."

"What I have said is that, in determining the sinfulness of an act, one ought to consider the doer's intentions."

"Behold the bold flush of your cheeks, the flash of your eyes!"

"My uncle trusts you, and yet you mock him as though he were a fool."

"I only did it to be with you, my lamb."

"Do not call me that."

"I only did it to be with you, light of my days. Think of it, Heloise—now we will see each other nightly. I will ride home with your uncle at vespers, and here you will be, your face shining with love—"

"Your presumption astonishes me." Yet I had to smile.

"Your face shining with pleasure at the prospect of another stimulating evening, first at supper and then, afterward, here, where we may talk into the night for as long as we desire. Your eyes bright with excitement, as they are now."

He pulled me closer than before, so that I felt his pulse thumping against my chest and another part of him pressing against my thigh. I gasped, sensing danger, as though an intruder lurked at my door. I shifted my hips and would have moved away, but his hands remained firm at my waist.

"Are you sorry I took such a liberty?" He pressed his cheek to mine.

"I worry that *you* will be sorry. You will regret this move, I fear."

"What shall I regret—giving up a salary I do not need? Yes, that's right, dear girl, I do not need your uncle's money. Do you hate me for pretending otherwise? Had I told him the truth, he would not have believed me. Such men cannot know what it means to despise worldly riches, as you and I do."

Truer words were never spoken. Abelard had given up a lord's château and all the privileges of landed wealth for the pursuit of knowledge. I, who had never owned anything, dreamed not of moneyed counts as Agnes did, but of heading the Fontevraud Abbey so that I might endow generations of girls with the gift of knowledge as my teacher, the prioress Beatrice, had done for me at Argenteuil. Never were two minds more alike than Abelard's and mine.

Our eyes met, and we joined ourselves in another kiss, becoming one in breath as in mind. Our mouths feasted hungrily, but, rather than sate my appetite, Abelard's kisses only made me yearn for more. I groaned.

"Shh! I feel the same way, but we do not want Fulbert to hear." Abelard laughed tentatively, as though tiptoeing across humor's prickly terrain.

"That is what I meant when I said you might regret this move. Are you certain you wish to take such a risk? What of the danger to you—to us both?"

His lips twitched. "'The wise man regards the reason for his actions, but not the results.'"

I had never agreed with Seneca on this. "I beg you to reconsider. If Uncle Fulbert discovers us, he will kill us."

"A man cannot kill you if he cannot see you." Abelard's gaze roamed across my throat, down to my breasts. "Or, if he sees two of you." He nuzzled my throat and stroked the small of my back, sending pleasure coursing up my spine. He smelled of woodsmoke and wine, and, underneath, of soap. "What should I reconsider—my agreement with your uncle or my feelings for you, which I could no sooner relinquish than my need for air?"

As he kissed my forehead, my cheeks, my nose, I relished the bristle of his unshaven cheek, his flavor like wine, his heat—Abelard, for whom I had ached these past months, Abelard at last. "I worry that the price will be too dear."

His voice broke and quivered. "For one night with you, my love, I would give my life, which, without you, would be no life at all."

His murmurs turned to whispers as he held me close, closer, kissing my ear, stroking my hair, *my love, my lovely Heloise,* words bubbling like a spring from his tongue. I, trembling against his chest, heard his heart's beat and, playing like a song, his words more beautiful than any poem: *my love my love my love.*

9

To her love most pure, worthy of inner fidelity; through
the state of true love, the secret of tender faith.
—HELOISE TO ABELARD

The sun shone more brightly, it seemed, after Abelard
came to live in our home. Warm breezes blew across
the city, delaying the autumn; the birds rivaled the morning
trumpet with their cheerful song. No more did I tarry in the
scriptorium and arrive home late for supper, but waited eagerly
for Abelard's arrival every day after the vespers bell. Home was
where we all wanted to be—all, that is, except Jean, who scowled
as the rest of us laughed at Abelard's witticisms, and as he compli-
mented Pauline on her cooking and begged her to divorce Jean
and marry him. Even I joined in the merriment, I who had not
truly laughed since my seventh year, when my mother and I had
danced in the sunlight singing nonsense songs and wearing
chains of daisies in our hair.

As much as I enjoyed our suppers, however, I cherished the
hours afterward even more, when Jean and Pauline's son, Jean-
Paul, had come to accompany his mother home and Jean and my
uncle had retired. Then Abelard would join me in the study, and
we would resume our lessons, in which I learned little of philosophy but much of love.

He spared no effort to please me, plumping the cushion for my chair; presenting me with a pen made from the quill of a peacock; taking his seat so near that I could scarcely breathe—and yet I would not have had him move away, not even were I gasping for air.

"Here you have wished me 'the secret of tender faith' through 'the state of true love,'" he said one evening, critiquing the letters I had sent to him in Brittany. "You have mistaken spiritual love, *caritas*"—he gestured toward the words I had written—"for carnal love, *amor*." His fingers brushed against my arm, standing the hair on its ends, as he spoke the word *carnal*.

"But love is love. It is all the same."

"Then why do we utter one word for God's love, another for the love of a friend, and another for erotic love?" His brusque tone made it clear that he did not expect an answer. "Of course a difference exists. Do you feel the same love for your uncle as you do for God?"

I did not feel love for my uncle, but only gratitude and, at times, fear—but I forbore straying from the topic at hand. "Are you saying that different types of love exist because of the words we use? Having read your *Dialectica*, I am surprised to hear you take this position."

"You have read *Dialectica*?" Pleasure shone on his face.

"I devoured every word."

"And what did you think of my arguments? The Count of Poitiers praised them as 'skillfully and subtly written.'"

"I cannot argue with that assessment, although I found the discourse rather *too* subtle at times. You dwell at length on the functions of words but little on the ideas which they express."

His expression changed. He slid his chair away from me. The chill night air blew into the space between us.

"The subject matter is too abstract for a woman's mind," he said.

"And yet I did appreciate your theories about universals and particulars."

"I cannot believe you have read my *Dialectica*." He gazed at me as fondly as if he were a proud papa, and I his child who had performed some difficult feat.

"And the classifications we give to things, you wrote, are mere words."

"My dear girl! Dialectic is not too abstract for your grasp at all." He reached for the stylus, pressing his knee against mine.

"But, master," I said, glancing away lest he detect the gleam of triumph in my eyes, "what of love?"

"As I said, a universal 'love' does not exist. Love comes in many forms."

"But are there truly different types of love, or do humans merely perceive them to differ?"

"They differ. It is a matter on which everyone can agree."

"Everyone, master? Are we all the same then, knowing the same things, feeling the same love, sharing the same 'world soul' as Plato described?"

He leapt to his feet and raked his fingers through his hair. "If you have read my work, then you know that the 'world soul' is a fallacy. Men do not share the same soul; we are not the same 'in essence.'"

"If each man and woman is unique, doesn't it follow that each of us loves uniquely?"

"Of course we experience love differently—in all its forms."

"And so isn't it possible that I could feel *caritas*, that beautiful, spiritual, unconditional love, not only for God but also for my beloved? Isn't that what Christ wanted from us—to enact *caritas* on Earth as he did, transforming God's love into love for our fellow men?"

Abelard's expression changed. He resumed his seat and reached over to touch my hand. My body's taut string plucked, I quivered and hummed.

"Heloise, you astonish me. Your mind—dear God! I can scarcely believe that you are—" He stopped, his face reddening.

"That I am a woman?" I rolled my eyes. "Given your propensity for insulting me, I can scarcely believe that *you* are a poet who makes women swoon."

"Shall I speak of your beauty instead of your mind?" He winked.

"It matters not to me whether you think me beautiful of face or form—"

"But I do think so." He slid his knees forward to press them against my thigh and touched my cheek with his fingertip.

"Do not flatter me." Suddenly short of breath, I could barely utter the words. I turned my head away from his touch, my eyes away from his gaze. "I consider only my soul of any importance, for that is what God sees."

"But he has given me eyes with which to behold your own eyes, as black and luminous as the water at night, and your lush, red mouth." His lowered lids, the softening of his mouth as it approached mine, made me leap from my seat and turn toward the open window, away from him. The stars, so near that it seemed I could touch them, shifted and wheeled in my dizzy sights. My heart beat so wildly that I cupped it with my hands, thinking it might fly away. I crossed my arms to cradle myself, trying to quell my blood's stirring, and heard the scrape of Abelard's chair on the floor. Then he stood behind me and stroked the backs of my arms.

I whirled around. "Master—"

"Call me Abelard," he murmured, moving his hands to my waist. "It is the name my scholars use—and many of my friends."

"Are we friends?" I said weakly, taking one step backward but no more, standing so close to the window's edge.

"We shall be the best of friends. How can it be otherwise? Who else, besides me, possesses a mind like yours? What other woman besides you approaches me in subtlety of thought and in sheer intellectual power?"

His modesty never failed to astound me, I wanted to retort—but I could hardly hear myself think over my pulse's throb. Heat rose from him like breath. When he grasped my waist and pulled me close to him, I thought I might burst into flame. A feral cry escaped my lips.

Abelard slipped his arms around me and murmured my name, a sound more delightful to my ear than angels' harps. I knew I should resist, but I had forgotten everything I had ever learned, forgotten even God and that he watched us, or, rather, I did not fear him. How could he be displeased, being the source of all love?

The rattle of the door latch caused us to fly apart. In the next moment Abelard sat in his chair, stylus in his hand, and I had turned to close the shutters of my window.

I had not yet smoothed my tunic or quelled the flush in my cheeks when the door swung open and my uncle walked into the room, a long switch of birch in his right hand. "I heard a cry."

I averted my gaze from the switch and from his glittering eyes, praying he would not notice my crimson face.

"I had to discipline your niece, as you predicted," Abelard lied. "We disagreed in our debate, and she called me a *bouffe*. Forgive me for losing my temper, friend."

"My niece must learn to control her tongue." Uncle glared at me. "I'm surprised you haven't needed to correct her before now." Turning to Abelard, he added, "My niece can be most obstinate—obstinate! She must learn to submit to authority, or she will never succeed at Fontevraud. You will need to punish her again, I am certain. But the cane you use on your scholars is too harsh for a woman's tender flesh." Uncle held the switch out to him.

"Thank you, Fulbert, my friend." Will I ever forget the gleam in Abelard's eyes as he took the weapon in hand? "Heloise, be forewarned. Do as I say—*everything* I say, or you will feel my sting."

He lifted the long, quivering branch and lashed it in my direction. I turned away; its tip grazed my backside, causing a brief, sharp flicker of pain. Heat flooded my face, and my bottom tingled where the switch had stung me. I looked down at my clasped hands, hiding my sudden elation. Never had I felt so vividly alive.

10

❦

I should be groaning over the sins I have committed, but I
can only sigh for what I have lost. Everything we did and
also the times and places where we did it are stamped on
my heart along with your image, so that I live through
them all again with you.

—HELOISE TO ABELARD

he months that followed recur to me, now, as a blur
of passion in which, as Abelard himself wrote, *more
words of love than of reading passed between us, and more kissing
than teaching*. I wonder if, in later years, he relived those nights as
I did, nights we spent warming each other in every new way we
could imagine. Did he blush to remember all the sweet and terrible things we did?

He opened my door without knocking as I worked one evening, then, undetected, moved across the floor to seize me from
behind. He covered my mouth with one hand while slipping the
other inside my chemise to cup my breast. It is a good thing that
he thought to silence me, for without his quieting hand my
moans might have alerted my slumbering uncle in the room beneath us, or Jean, who slept upstairs. My hips rocked as tension
gathered like a storm between my thighs, making me whimper
for release or for, at least, his touch in the moistly secret place
that he did not, at first, approach.

Another time, he unbound my hair and wrapped it around his fingers, then pulled me backward into his lap. There he explored me with his hands and eyes while I lay in complete and blissful surrender. Even when he lowered his head to kiss the places he had touched, I never thought to resist him but instead luxuriated in the joining of skin to skin, of Abelard to Heloise. When we were together in this way, I felt truly one with him, my shooting star, nay, my fixed one.

One evening, he sat beside me and I opened my notes, a dutiful student although a negligent scholar who whiled my hours dreaming of my teacher. When he saw how little I had done, he commanded me to lie across the desk, on my stomach. My breath became gasps, then pants of desire, when I felt him lift my long skirts, rustling the cloth, exposing my bottom to the chill autumn air. Then followed a slow tease, the light dance of the switch's tail over my skin, causing me to grip my hands and grind my teeth; then a light flick, a snap to revive the anticipation of a sting, and then, at last, the whoosh of the switch through the air before it lashed my backside. My cries could be heard, I know, throughout the house, for Uncle's face held a sternly satisfied expression the next morning. Abelard punished me, and I endured the blows, for Uncle's sake only, so that he might not suspect the true nature of our activities—or so we told each other. Yet, on the first night we spent alone—for my uncle had gone with the bishop of Paris to a synod in Rome, taking Jean with him—Abelard eschewed the stinging birch for the bruising cane, and I submitted.

When he had ceased his chastening and tears poured from my eyes, I felt Abelard's lips and tongue tracing the welts he had made, and his hands caressing and kneading pleasure into the places that throbbed with pain. In this way I learned that the boundary between ecstasy and agony can shift in a moment, or

even disappear. I began to associate love with a sweet ache, and
passion with the crack of my master's cane and the nip of his
teeth.

At what time did his fingers alter their course from caressing
the hurt places on my buttocks and legs to probing the area between them? So gradual was the shift that I barely perceived the
difference, although the tapping of his fingertips against the door
of my chastity did cause me to squirm from under his touch—at
first. When he lowered his head to kiss me there, I had to bite my
fist or scream in ecstasy. After all that pleasure, is it any wonder
that I would want to reciprocate? He guided my hand to his
verpa, whose terrible length and girth made me shudder with
desire and fear.

What were our studies, in those days? What use were my books
to me then, when love had offered herself to me in the form of
Abelard? I had only a few months in which to learn love's arts, and
from the most imaginative and skillful of teachers. Sitting beside
me at the desk, he would ask me to read aloud from one of my letters, which had become more explicit and love-filled as our daring
increased. As I read, he would untie my braids and loosen my
tresses, which hung, then, to my knees, then begin the touching
and teasing, which always led us to my bedroom. I remember the
curling hair on his chest between my gripping fingers, the outline
of every muscle in his back, his fragrance like linen, like ink, like
the aniseeds with which he sweetened his breath.

How closely we ventured, in those days, to fornication—or,
rather, to manifesting physically the full extent of our love for
each other. His *bliaut* lifted and the proof of his virility pressing
hard against my thighs, he begged me for permission to enter. I
sensed that to say no was a sin, as it was a wholly selfish act. Yet I
could not bring myself to take that final step, to plunge into that
fire from which neither of us could emerge unscathed.

11

What need is there for more words? Aflame with the fire of desire for you, I want to love you forever.

—HELOISE TO ABELARD

*I*t should have been Abelard whose breath quavered, he whose pulse fluttered, as we dismounted our horses and entered the royal palace. A minstrel would perform Abelard's songs that day before King Louis and Queen Adelaide and all their court; he, not I, would sup with them at the royal table. Yet, as the guards patted his clothes, searching for weapons, Abelard jested and laughed while I steadied myself with a hand at his elbow. My stomach felt unsettled, as though I had eaten something disagreeable, although I had not taken even one bite at dinner that day.

"I hear the king treats his guests very well, and his queen is said to be friendly," my uncle had said while Abelard drank Pauline's brewet with his usual appetite. "But the courtiers can be vicious, *non*? Like vipers, I hear—vipers!"

How would they regard me, a girl from the convent with almost no knowledge of their world? *Only two things matter to those people: blood and money,* my uncle had said. How would I fare under their scrutiny?

"Speak to no one—no one!" Uncle advised. "They will sink their fangs into your innocent heart." Abelard laughed: Uncle sounded as though Abelard were escorting me to a snake pit rather than a royal feast.

"I have found everyone in the king's court to be delightful—with the exception of the monk Suger. He's become especially disagreeable since Bernard's visit, I've heard. Of course," Abelard said, turning to me, "you will not even notice him in his monkish attire, not amid all the splendor. The courtiers will dazzle your eyes with their colors and gold, the ornaments about their necks, their rings on every finger. The Paris court is a garden of peacocks. And you, my girl, will be as a gazelle among them."

"A gazelle—yes," Uncle said. "Take care to remain as quiet as one, as well." His admonishing look told me what he meant: I must speak to no one about my family.

Now, walking through the enormous palace doorway, I clutched Abelard's arm so tightly that he laughed. "By God's head, will you faint? Perhaps you would like me to carry you into—Brother Suger! What a pleasant surprise."

Brother Suger's stiff, wiry hair; his downturned mouth; his tiny, black eyes, like those of a rat: he repulsed me now as much as he had the first time I'd seen him, at Bernard's sermon the previous spring. I lowered my gaze lest he see my eyes' expression. Here stood the king's former classmate at the Saint-Denis Priory, said to be beloved by him. Offending such an important man was far from my desire. Yet, when I had composed myself and raised my eyes to meet his, I saw contempt. My cheeks burned as though he had slapped them.

"Tell me, *magister*, how is it that a tonsured canon may disregard his vows in word and deed and suffer no punishment?" he said in the hearing of a dozen courtiers, men and women in velvet, silk, and fur who stood nearby.

"How, indeed?" Abelard said with an exaggerated gasp. "Tell me more of this shameful canon."

Suger narrowed his eyes. "He has written verses which extol the most venial of sins."

"Non!"

"Debauchery, drunkenness, fornication—"

"Please, Brother, I beg you to desist!" Abelard spoke more loudly than necessary, out of consideration for his audience, no doubt. With his free hand, he gestured broadly to me. "Have you failed to note the young lady on my arm?"

"*And* he frequents the company of young girls." The monk's eyes glittered at me.

Abelard shook his head. "This is most disturbing."

"I am pleased that you agree with me." Suger's accusatory glance made me want to cover my body with my arms.

"Brother Suger, will this man be at the feast today?" Abelard said, his tone somber.

"Indeed he will, master."

"I beg you to introduce me. Young girls!" Abelard clucked his tongue. Catching my eye for a moment, he sent me an almost imperceptible wink.

"And what would you say to this errant canon?" Suger's smirk said, *I have trapped him in my snare.*

"I would advise him to abandon this pursuit."

"I would do the same." Suger folded his hands beneath his stout belly.

"'Why waste your time with inexperienced girls?' I would say to him. 'Mature women know how to satisfy a man's needs and do not need to be coaxed.' As the poet wrote, 'They've more knowledge of the thing, and have that practice that alone makes the artist.' It is true, *non?*" Abelard nudged the monk with his elbow, grinning.

I do not know whose color deepened the most: Suger's in the face of such mockery, or mine as I wondered how much Abelard knew of mature women.

"My dear friends! How long has it been since you arrived?" Agnes greeted us with kisses, then took Abelard's free arm and led us away from the scowling monk into the great hall, where servants set up trestle tables with a clatter and tried to revive the fire smoldering in the enormous hearth.

"Forgive me for leaving you to that donkey Suger," Agnes said with a snort, apparently unconcerned that he might hear her. "He makes life in the court most tedious, with his dour face and somber presentments. The slightest hint of merriment makes him froth at the mouth."

"He will avoid today's festivities, then?" I said.

She laughed. "And miss the opportunity to chasten us? No, we'll see him at the king's table, as usual, darkening our enjoyment like a thundercloud."

She took us up the stone staircase to the women's chamber, a large room from whose ceiling cream-colored cloth billowed like sails and whose walls sparkled with tapestries depicting familiar scenes: Adam and Eve in a brilliant garden, contemplating a piece of fruit; Jason with his golden fleece, spurning the supplicant Medea. Rushes strewn with dried lavender fragranced the room as we stepped across the floor. Near the far wall a man wearing gloves without fingertips plucked the strings of a harp, while three handmaids laughed and danced in their taffeta gowns, all in the same style but each of a different color: pink, blue, and green. When they saw Abelard, they broke their circle and hastened to kiss and stroke him as if he were a child, or a pet.

"Pierre does look extraordinarily handsome today, *non*? I rarely see him in blue." Agnes took me aside to a cushioned bench, where we sat and watched Abelard laugh and tease the maids. Her knowing gaze made me blush. I could not deny that his *bliaut* of Frankish blue accentuated the color of his remarkable eyes, so much so that I could hardly keep my own eyes from turning to him constantly. Rather than admit to my friend my feelings, however, I changed the topic at hand.

"Is that your gown for the feast hanging on the pole? Agnes! I have never seen anything like it." Drenched in brilliant blue with sleeves of purple and green, it glittered with emeralds and embroidered peacocks with real feathers for tails. The mantle draping it was a deep, bright green with a bejeweled clasp of gold.

"I have a feathered turban, also," she said. "Now that we have dressed Queen Adelaide, I can help you get ready, and you can help me. Did you bring a change of clothes? You may have your servant bring them here. But—my dear! You had planned to wear this to the feast?" Frowning, she fingered my fine linen *bliaut* of midnight blue—a new garment made especially for this occasion, blue being the kingdom's official color —but then her expression brightened. In a moment she had led me to her chest of clothes and invited me to choose from its contents.

"You look lovely, of course, but that dark color will never do in this court. You must shine, Heloise, must sparkle and dazzle! You want to keep Pierre's attention on you, *non*? Every woman here is in love with him—except me, of course. Even the queen blushes when he kisses her hand."

As I hesitated—a moment earlier, I had felt beautiful in my new *bliaut*—Abelard came over to bid us farewell. He must meet with the minstrel performing his songs today and would not see us again until we gathered in the great hall.

"Pierre, tell her to listen to me," Agnes said. "She should not wear this gown. It is nearly black, not suitable for the court at all. Doesn't she look as though she had just arrived from the convent?"

"She appears perfect to me, as always. But do as you think best. I want my Heloise to shine, especially today."

I nearly protested—I was hardly "his" Heloise. I belonged to the convent—to God. Here in the king's court, I was Agnes's guest and would sit at one of the lower tables, below the salt. No one would notice me at all. Why should I wish to "shine"?

Soon, though, Agnes and the other maids had bedecked me in a blue linen chemise with a neckline that dipped to the swell of my breasts and an equally revealing *bliaut* of green *paile roé* silk— from Constantinople, Agnes said—woven with circles of blue. Under her direction, the maids laced my gown at the sides for a fit so tight I could barely breathe and laced my sleeves to the elbow, from where tippets trailed to the floor. They wound gold ribbon around my braids, cinched my waist with a blue silk girdle, and placed a gold band upon my head. Agnes herself adorned me with jewels: a sapphire necklace, gold earrings, rings on both my hands, and bracelets on my wrists. When she approached with a box of white powder and a brush, however, I demurred.

"Do you want to look your best for Pierre's sake, or not?" she said, planting a hand on her hip. "One would no sooner go to court with a bare face than with a bare *asne*. You are not a child, but you will resemble one compared to the women here today." I thought of Suger's calling me a young girl and relented. She applied the powder, using a cloth, all over my face, then rouged my cheeks and lips with vermilion.

Très belle! the other maids exclaimed. *Très sophistiqué!*

"Pierre will not recognize you," Agnes said, her grin sly. When she held the mirror up for me, I hardly recognized myself. I looked as pale as a ghost, nearly transparent, and my reddened cheeks and mouth appeared garish.

When I suggested the cosmetics detracted from my appearance rather than enhancing it, she laughed. "The men will buzz around you like bees to a flower." With a secretive smile she added, "All except for one, who has eyes only for me."

When we entered the great hall—where songbirds perched in its high rafters and a fire blazed in the tile hearth—courtiers filled the room, milling about with *henap*s of wine, their voices echoing off the stone walls as though they numbered in the thousands, not merely a few hundred. As Abelard had predicted, the brilliance of the courtiers' colors dazzled my eyes. In my modest gown, I would have been invisible—which I might have preferred to the linger of men's gazes upon my chest and the slanting eyes of women who whispered to one another as we passed. Why, I asked Agnes, did everyone stare at me?

"Because you are new to the court, and beautiful," she said. But how could they admire my beauty when they saw only a mask, not my face? Perhaps they thought me beautiful *because* my face was hidden.

A tall, thin man with a bejeweled wooden leg came forth to kiss Agnes's hand: the king's astronomer, she said, who had fashioned my astralabe. He dipped his head humbly as I exclaimed over his skill, but his eyes remained on her. Was this the man of whom she had spoken so slyly? But no, Agnes peered over his shoulder, seeking someone in the crowd.

We made our way about the hall, my eyes searching for Abelard, and Agnes seeking someone, also, her eyes as bright as stars. A handsome man with a small, pointed beard and light-colored hair falling in waves to his shoulders—the southern style—stepped into our path to kiss Agnes's hand and, to my surprise, mine.

"Were not the soft hands of ladies fashioned for the lips of men?" he said when I tried to withdraw.

I sent Agnes a wondering look, but she only smiled. "The Count of Poitiers is not accustomed to hearing no from women."

I caught my breath. "The poet?" In all the world, only his songs exceeded Abelard's in fame.

"By you, I prefer to be known as the lover." He continued to cradle my hand lightly in his own, no doubt so that he could feel my pulse increase as he told me with his eyes all the things he wanted to do to me. "See how she blushes, Agnes. Who is this innocent girl?"

"She is my cousin." Agnes lied to help avoid questions about my family.

"I am not so innocent," I said. "Nor is any woman who has heard your *Ab la dolchor del temps novel*: 'Let me live long enough, I pray, to bring my hand beneath her cloak.' That seems a dubious prayer to make to our Lord."

"I think that God, being male, would understand. He made woman for man's pleasure, *non*? And he had a taste of those pleasures himself when he impregnated that tender young virgin."

My gasp made him laugh. "You are not so innocent, you say? I must disagree." He lowered his lips to my hand again, but I snatched it away. "I think perhaps you are *too* innocent. Should you desire a remedy for this malady, come to see me."

"Poets," Agnes said as we walked away from him. "They think only of three things: love, love, and more love."

"Lust is what you mean. And, perhaps in his situation, blasphemy, as well. Has he no concern for his mortal soul?"

"He is a noble, and a man." She shrugged. "He does, and says, what he pleases."

Then, we heard a screech, and a woman's scream. The crowd before us parted to reveal a small, furry animal—a monkey—running across the floor, clutching a woman's beaded fillet. It leapt onto a trestle table, knocking the board to the floor, then leapt onto another before catching sight of the brilliant blue feathers rising like a fountain, or a bird's crest, from Agnes's turban.

"That monkey and I, we hate each other. Can you tell?" She shuddered. "I can't stand the way it looks. And when it comes close to me, I have to hold my breath. It smells like an old man who hasn't washed himself in years."

As if it had understood her, the creature bared its teeth, reminding me of Suger—except that instead of disgust, the monkey's eyes held a fanatical gleam.

"Pepin!" a man shouted, jumping up in attempt to see over the heads of the nobles. "Stop, Pepin! Come to me." He pushed his way through the intransigent crowd. "Please, allow me to pass. Pepin!"

But the creature had not heard or, if it had, paid no attention to its master. Staring at Agnes's hat, it ran to the end of the table and jumped, catapulting itself into the air, directly toward her. She stood perfectly still, her powdered face losing all its remaining color as it flew, shrieking like an infant, with arms outstretched and hands grasping. Around us, people scurried, removing themselves from the monkey's path, but not Agnes. I shouted her name and pulled at her arm, but she did not move. Terror had frozen her.

Everything happened so quickly, I do not know how I did anything while that monkey catapulted toward my friend. I looked to the nobles: Would none of them help her? But what could they do? The guards had taken everyone's weapons. I grabbed a goblet from someone's hands and threw it at the creature, but it struck the wall and clattered to the floor.

The cup missed its mark, but a man's hand did not—the hand of a man wearing costly scarlet cloth of the richest blue, who snatched the monkey from the space above Agnes's head.

The creature screamed again, struggling, but the man held it fast in his arms. "You are safe, Agnes."

"Amaury," she breathed.

The monkey's keeper arrived and took his pet, which writhed and struggled and screeched for Agnes's hat. "My poor little Pepin. His mother died two days ago, and he has not been himself since then."

"Then you should not have brought it here today." Agnes's voice frosted the already-chill air. I pulled my mantle over my arms.

"A trainer who cannot control his animals is worse than a nurse with no command of the children," Amaury said. The trainer flinched under his haughty tone. "Remove yourself from this palace, and your monkey, too. Go at once, before I seize you both and throw you into the prison."

When the tearful trainer had taken his pet out of sight, the man bowed and kissed Agnes's hand—lingering over her dainty fingers as if he might kiss each one in turn.

"Lord Amaury, what a bold display of courage and authority." Agnes's voice shook slightly—not from fright, I knew—as she withdrew her hand.

"I could not simply watch that dirty beast shred your beautiful dress." The roam of his gaze said he coveted that task for himself.

"I owe you a debt of gratitude," she said, never cringing under his eyes' assault, but, rather, seeming to enjoy it. *"Fortes fortuna juvat."* I lifted my brows to hear her speak Latin. *Fortune,* she had said, *favors the bold.*

"I warn you, my lady: I intend to collect on that debt. In full." His lips twitched. "Fortune willing."

She remembered me then and tucked her hand into the crook of my elbow. "Amaury, here is the one I've been telling you about. The daughter of your sister's friend, Hersende of Champagne."

"Lady Montsoreau was your mother?" He tore his eyes from Agnes to bend over my hand.

My pulse quickened to hear this stranger refer to her, and I sent Agnes a concerned glance—hadn't she promised me to tell no one about me? She, on the other hand, nodded as if she had done me a great favor.

"You knew her, my lord?"

"Your mother spent many hours in our home. But no one knew her better than my sister." He returned his gaze to Agnes's face, where it remained except when, from time to time, he allowed it to dip to her bosom. "Bertrade and Lady Montsoreau were the closest of friends."

Agnes squeezed my hand. "Heloise, have you heard of Queen Bertrade? Did your mother ever speak of her?"

"How could I fail to hear of her? She was the wife whom King Philip loved so much, he risked the fires of hell to keep her." But I had never heard my mother speak her name.

"Nothing could stop my sister from having anything that she wanted," Amaury said. "She wanted King Philip from the first time they met."

She'd knelt to kiss the king's ring, he said, and when she stood, he kissed her hand. *I shall not wash this hand until it belongs to you, along with the rest of me*, she told him. He carried her away from her husband's home that night, in secret, and brought her to Paris. He married her—although she was already married to Foulques, the Count of Anjou, and he was married to Queen Berthe, our King Louis's mother.

"After he'd possessed Bertrade, he bathed every inch of her," Amaury said, his eyes sending messages to Agnes. "That is as it should be, *non*? I would do the same."

The words spoken and unspoken stirred my blood, as did the heat pulsing like lightning between them. I looked upward, to the royal table, and saw Abelard standing too near a woman with hair like sunlight who leaned into him as the two shared a laugh. *Mon Dieu*, it was as Agnes had said: every woman in Paris wanted him. I ignored the stab in my breast and reminded myself that it was *I* whom he loved.

"Did you hear Amaury?" Agnes brought me back to the

conversation. "His sister lives in the Hautes-Bruyères Abbey, at Saint-Rémy-l'Honoré."

"It is not far from Paris," Amaury said.

"Heloise is my closest friend," Agnes said. "He who helps her, helps me."

"In that case, I shall take you to Bertrade myself," he said. "And Agnes can be our chaperone." He winked at her, and I wondered who would chaperone whom.

The trumpet sounded. We sank to our knees, bowing before the king and queen as they entered and settled themselves on the bench at the royal table, above the rest of the room. Then we stood and moved to the rear of the hall to sit with the queen's other handmaids.

"*Fortes fortuna juvat?*" I said as Agnes led me to our seats. "You told me you don't speak Latin."

"I've been studying it lately." She shrugged. "I heard Amaury speaking it with his wife in the court at Anjou. Apparently, they study it together. Of course, such a plain little mouse would have little else to do but conjugate verbs."

"He is married?"

"Of course he is married," she said, her voice terse. "He is lord of Montfort-l'Amaury and a future count and must have heirs. But his horse-faced wife has not even conceived." She slanted her eyes. "He will marry me next—as soon as the pope grants his petition for annulment. As it turns out, he and she are related."

"What a surprise." Every noble in the realm, it seemed, claimed kinship with his wife in order to put her aside.

Agnes did not notice my sarcasm. "I am relieved that you do not disapprove. I thought that, coming from the convent, you might have strict ideas about marriage."

"My only idea about marriage is to avoid it."

"Now you *really* sound like a nun." She poked me with a

finger. "But I've noticed the happiness on your face when Pierre is near. I think you would marry him if you could."

Reminded of him, I sought him out again. There he sat with the royals, next to that odious little monk Suger. To my satisfaction, Abelard appeared thoroughly bored.

"Wait until Pierre beholds you in your courtier's clothes," Agnes said. "The change in you will make him beg you for your hand—if only for one night."

Heat filled my body, and strange imaginings: Abelard's gaze rolling like a lover's tongue across my exposed bosom; his excitement to see me in this costume. Guillaume of Poitiers had all but eaten me alive with his eyes. Would my provocative dress inflame Abelard's desires, as well?

Suddenly shy, I asked Agnes to exchange seats with me so that I might sit behind the large column in front of our table, hidden from Abelard's sight. She happily did so, for the column had blocked her view of her precious seigneur.

"He did not bring his wife this time, hoping to spend some time alone with me," she said as the servants poured water over our hands. "Of course, I have refused him that privilege."

"But you love him, *non*? It shows in your eyes, Agnes."

"And that is why I must resist him. Once he has taken what he wants from me, he will lose interest and return to his wife. Men revel in the hunt, after all. If I want him to marry me, I must make him wait to claim his prize."

Positioning myself next to the wall proved a wise move, not only to hide myself from Abelard but also to avoid speaking to anyone who might question me about my family. As servants presented a stunning array of dishes—twenty different courses, at least, beginning with a broth of veal and ending with six different candied fruits—I found another reason to be glad for my hidden spot: I could, and did, eat as much as I desired, a fortuitous circumstance since the *henap* passed my way many times. Although we sat at one of the lower tables, the wine tasted more delicious than any other I had ever tried. I reminded myself to sip it slowly lest I embarrass myself—and Abelard.

The trumpet sounded again as the servants removed our trenchers, platters, and washing bowls. A man's voice rang through the hall, presenting Master Pierre Abelard, scholar and poet, and the greatest of both—Guillaume of Poitiers called out in protest, making everyone laugh—and announcing the minstrel Daurostre, who would perform the *magister*'s new songs. But first, the composer wished to speak a few words.

I leaned toward Agnes to watch as, standing, he addressed the hall. His cheeks glowed with the blush of wine, and his arms made sweeping gestures, as when he lectured to his scholars.

"Crude and humble though they be, I hope these songs will please you all, especially Your Grace and My Lady," Abelard said, bowing to the royal couple. "And, although I dedicate them to our king and queen, I ask that you share the dedication with another: with the most brilliant star in all of Paris—excepting myself of course."

Laughter filled the room as my face filled with heat.

"Ladies and gentlemen: Allow me to introduce my Muse, the inspiration for the songs you are about to hear, and my most accomplished scholar besides. Heloise of Argenteuil, would you stand? Where is she? Where is Heloise?"

"Stand," Agnes hissed. "You must bow before the king and queen. Hurry! And step out from behind that column. You must be seen."

Now I wished that I had not indulged my appetites, for my stomach turned at the necessity of presenting myself before all these people, especially in the too-tight gown I wore and with a mouth reddened by ocher and wine. The room fell silent as I dipped toward the floor, praying as I dropped that my breasts would not spill from my *bliaut*. When I rose, I met Abelard's gaze and beheld an expression that I could not decipher. Did it displease him to see me so attired and adorned—or did it excite him?

When I returned to my seat, Agnes had taken it and refused to move. "This is your day," she whispered. "You must be seen." When the minstrel began to sing, however, I wanted only to slide under the table. Abelard's new song declared his love for me to all who listened.

My reason for living: be kind to your faithful one.
Since all hope in my life resides in you.
I cannot say how much I love you.
Without you this life is night to me, and to live is death.

As Daurostre lifted his voice in my praise, repeating words I had read in Abelard's letters, *sweeter than honey and the honeycomb*, Agnes arched one of her painted eyebrows. From somewhere, her father's laugh rang out, evoking murmurs. At the table in front of us, a richly dressed woman with a heavily painted face turned and stared at me, then whispered into her husband's ear. *Meretrix*, I read on her lips. I pressed my hands to my chest, covering myself.

When the song ended, cheers filled the room. A beaming King Louis lifted his *henap*. "Encore," he commanded. "Sing us another of the poet's enchanting songs."

The minstrel cleared his throat, strummed his lute, and sang another, even more beautiful, song of despondency and love, one in which the poet begged *Heloise of my heart* to receive him and forgive his faults, adding, *May the day's risen light be the last that I see, if there lives a woman I could prefer over you*. I felt a blush spread over my face and bosom as everyone in the court, it seemed, stared at me. In naming me as his beloved, Abelard had either honored me or shamed me, or both.

"Exquisite," the king proclaimed, hushing the murmurs rolling like low thunder over the hall. "Delightful. Master Pierre, had not the bishop of Paris so wisely established you at the Nôtre-Dame School, we should bring you to court to write songs for us."

Abelard, who had stood to acknowledge the applause, fell to one knee to offer his thanks. "I fear the results would disappoint you, Your Grace. Parted from my Muse, my font of inspiration would run dry."

"I should like to dip *my* quill in her font." A young knight sniggered with his friends. Not having heard him, Abelard frowned in confusion at the shouts that followed.

I turned to face the knights. "Sir, I take exception to your remark. To do that, you would need a proper quill. Your pin-feather would not suffice."

Laughter flew like raucous crows through the hall. The nobles bared their teeth as if to devour me. "The *lupa* has captured her prey," I heard someone say.

I lowered my eyes in shame—for didn't *lupa* mean not only a wolf but also a prostitute?

"Is trading skins permitted in a canon's home?" The fleshy woman in front of me spoke more loudly this time. "In exchange for the master's parchment, Canon Fulbert's niece offers the teacher her hide."

"If Fulbert discovers the affair," said her husband, "he will skin them both alive."

12

❁

Day after day I burn more for your love, while you grow
cold.

—ABELARD TO HELOISE

When Daurostre had finished his performance and resumed his seat, and as the courtiers and nobles
laughed down their noses and called me a whore—the women
burning with jealousy, wanting the handsome poet for themselves, and the men livid with desire, wanting me—Abelard
stepped down from the dais and crossed the great hall with his
hand outstretched, beckoning, showing everyone whom he loved.
He bowed to me—he, the great composer and teacher, honoring
me—and then escorted me to the royal table.

"We have before us a living Muse, my lady!" King Louis said
to the queen. "Which one of the nine might she be?"

"She would be none other than Erato, Your Grace," Abelard
said. "The Muse of love poetry."

"Erato!" His Grace struck the arm of his throne, excited. "This
marks the second time in as many days that we have heard that
name." Another poet, he said, had invoked Erato the previous
evening while reciting a poem about Rhadine and Leontichus. I
knew the tale from my studies in Greek: Rhadine, forced to
marry, sailed away in sorrow to join her brutish husband in

Corinth, leaving behind the man she loved. But soon Leontichus rode to her, and they resumed the secret meetings they had enjoyed in their own city. When Rhadine's husband discovered their romance, he killed them both.

"Lovers make pilgrimages to their tomb," I said, sending Abelard a daring glance and thrilling to see his gaze fixed on my chest. "They think that touching it will bring good fortune in love."

"Ah, yes! Great fortune, indeed, to be murdered in one's bed," Abelard said. "Your Grace, I have changed my mind. Heloise is no Erato, after all, nor any other of the nine, but rather a tenth— a new Muse, inspiring poems about *happiness* in love."

"We did not care for last night's poem much," the king said. "We do not enjoy tragedy, especially in our songs of love." He patted the hand of his queen. "We are glad that the Muse Heloise does not inspire such unhappy tales."

"As am I," I said with a smile.

"What do you think?" Queen Adelaide said. "We have invited your poet to join our court, but he will not come without you. He needs his Muse." Her lips made a secretive smile when she said the word *Muse*.

Your poet. Light filled my body. Abelard had declared himself mine, in the hearing of all. No one mocked me now; I stood with him before the Queen of the Franks. Her slanting eyes said, *I know what you are doing with him*. Queen Adelaide's laugh rippled like a breeze.

I decided to give her a surprise. "If Master Pierre's claim is true, he will be of no use to you in any case. He will lose his ability to write poetry a little more than nine months from now, when I depart for the Fontevraud Abbey."

She did not gasp, as I had expected, but instead lowered her eyes. Her mouth drooped; she lost her queenly bearing. She reminded me of the paintings I had seen of the Virgin Mother, her face brimming with sorrow.

"To take the veil at such a young age—that ought to be a sin in itself," she said. "God gave us the world in which to live, and the convent in which to die."

I stared at her, remembering Agnes's words to the same effect. What did either of them know of abbey life? Not as much as I. Yet, when I wanted to argue with her, I could think of nothing to say without an argument's also springing to mind.

"But why despair over something that you cannot change?" The queen, having regained herself, lifted her *henap* in a toast. "Why not rejoice, instead, over what you possess? You have nine more months in which to love. That is more than many of us are given."

Abelard and I rode home slowly, woozy from too much wine, starlight falling like snow on our shoulders. The warm September breeze caressed my bosom like a lover's kiss; I yet wore Agnes's gown, she being too occupied with her seigneur to help me change. I hoped my uncle would be asleep. I did not wish to feel his eyes upon my bare skin or endure his rage at seeing me so scantily attired. Abelard's stare, however, roamed like fingers of heat over my cleavage; he could barely guide his horse.

"By God, are you the same girl?" he said when I tried, without success, to pull my mantle over my chest. "My plain little nun? My bookish scholar?" He slipped to one side, then shifted back into place, laughing and yanking the reins.

"If you thought me plain before, you have concealed it well."

"You are far from plain, as everyone in the court now knows. All of Paris would know it, as well, if you didn't conceal your virtues with high necklines and dark fabrics."

"I did not know that parts of the body constitute virtues. But I do know better than to argue with a drunken man."

"Drunken, me? I do not become drunken, my little cabbage. I can drink an infinite amount yet remain as sober as a horse."

"I imagine your horse would appreciate your being sober."

"Heloise," he said, slurring my name. "My beautiful Muse. 'My stars, if you should ask, are two. I know no others; I declare them to be those starry eyes of yours.'" He sang, his rich baritone as loud as if he needed to fill King Louis's great hall with it. "By God, I love you, Heloise." He sighed. "My beautiful Muse."

Now it was I who wanted to sing. Abelard had said it at last—he loved me! But then he slumped forward, his head drooping as though it were too heavy for his neck. He mumbled something unintelligible, and I felt my spirits plummet. He had spoken those precious words in drunkenness. Would he remember them tomorrow?

The horses stopped at my uncle's house. I paid the lantern boy while Jean helped Abelard to dismount, averting his face from his breath. I wondered if Jean smelled wine on me, as well. The *henap* had passed more times than I knew as Queen Adelaide and I had talked. Abbey life, especially, fascinated her. Her parents, the Count and Countess of Savoy, had sent her younger sister to study at an abbey, where the girl had recently taken the veil.

"I always wondered what sort of life she led there, if she was happy."

I thought of the girls I knew at Argenteuil, their haunted eyes. I must have appeared the same, abandonment stamped on my face like the mark of the beast. "One thing I learned in the abbey is this, my lady: happiness comes from within." Even a king may live in misery, I pointed out. If possessions or power could make one happy, those men should be the most content of all.

"And yet you left Argenteuil behind. Inner happiness did not suffice for you." Why, she asked, would I wish to return to that life? "God made the earth and all its treasures for our enjoyment. Can you hear the laughter of children in the convent, or an infant's cry?" I wanted to cover my ears. "Can minstrels come to play their merry music, and may you dance? And what of love?" I wanted to place my hands over her mouth, anything to stop these questions.

Her voice caught. She blinked rapidly and smiled as if she stared into the sun. "Forgive me, please. I know it is your choice. I—"

"But it is not my choice," I blurted. "To take the veil is my . . . destiny." I felt myself blush. The words sounded ridiculous even to my own ears.

Queen Adelaide tipped the final drops of wine into her mouth, then handed the beautiful *henap* to me—a gift, she said, for a new friend.

"What woman ever has a choice for how to live? We are like animals, *non*? Good for breeding, and nothing more. I wonder if this is what God intended when he fashioned Eve." Clearly, she spoke of herself. I would never bear a child.

Yet I could not deny anything that she said. Men belonged to themselves, while women belonged to men. The Church had owned me once and would again; in the meantime, my uncle could do with me as he willed. As I walked to the door of my uncle's house, the *henap* the queen had given me tucked into my belt, I pulled my mantle over my chest and clutched it tightly, holding it there, hoping again that Uncle had not stayed up past his usual hour to await us. As Jean opened the door, I lowered my head, not wanting to breathe in his direction lest he detect the scent of wine. Uncle Fulbert would ban me from the court if he thought it had corrupted me. Abelard, on the other hand, had drunk all he desired and now staggered up the steps, and no one would protest.

Jean lit a fire in my room, then offered to help Abelard undress. "I will sleep in my clothes," I heard him shout before I closed my door. In a few moments, I heard a knock.

"The master sleeps." Jean did not bother to whisper, knowing from experience the soundness of a wine-soaked slumber. "He is intoxicated and made a clamor, but I do not expect he will disturb you now." His gaze dropped to my exposed bust—I had removed the mantle—before I covered myself with a hand.

"You are mistaken about the master," I said, trying to draw him in with my smile, hoping to make him forget the tightness of my gown. "Wine does not intoxicate him. He remains sober no matter how much he drinks. He told me so tonight, on the ride home."

My jest had no effect. Jean remained as rigid as before. "Do you require anything more? If not, I will take your horses to the stable and then retire." He began to walk away, then stopped and turned toward me again. "It appears that my young mistress drank a bit of wine tonight, as well?"

"With the Queen of the Franks." I pulled from my belt the *henap* she had given to me and held it up for him to see. "This is her cup, my gift from her. Is it not remarkable? We became friends." Let him tell that to my uncle, and no harm would come to me. I thrust the cup toward him, offering it for a gift. I would have no use for it in the abbey, I said—but he refused. He said that my uncle paid him amply, but I knew the real reason he declined. If he became my ally, which was the reason I had offered the cup, he could not spy on me for Uncle Fulbert.

In my room, I undressed and lay on the bed to gaze at the fire and contemplate the night—the courtiers' glinting stares; Abelard's beautiful songs; the love for me that he had proclaimed; Queen Adelaide's knowing laugh and her disapproval of my plans to take the veil.

"Your poet loves you," she had said. "How can he permit you to do this?"

I longed to tell her about my past, and my parents—perhaps, then, she might understand that I had no choice—but I did not dare. Although I sensed that she would sympathize, I did not want to violate my uncle's trust. Or was that the reason I had held my tongue? I did not believe Queen Adelaide would betray any secret I confided to her. Tales, too, of my years at Argenteuil had formed on my lips, but I had swallowed them rather than reveal the unhappiness I had endured there. Admitting it to her meant admitting to myself the awful truth, one that would not serve me—and which might destroy me.

I did not want to go.

I sat up in bed, my pulse frantic.

At that moment, another knock sounded on my door, so quiet that I might have imagined it. I stared at the fire, gasping for breath. Something shifted inside me. I did not want to take the veil. I wanted—

The knocking sounded again, more loudly now, accompanied by Abelard's murmur. My heart leapt. I pulled on my pelisse, then opened the door and pulled him into my arms, sighing with wonder. He wrapped himself around me and kissed me, murmuring my name, *my precious love, more beautiful than any song*, filling me with his scents, clove and aniseed and wine, and with a certainty of life that I had never before known. I felt as though I might lift off the floor and glide to the heavens. Love in all its terrible beauty had presented itself to me, or, rather, God in his mercy had sent it to me so that I might know, at last, not only the true meaning of the word but also the purpose of life. How had Christ lived his own brief years on Earth? Had he begun a school or tonsured his head and retreated into an abbey or become a hermit in the woods? *Non.* He had drunk deeply of the flawed world, to the very dregs, healing the sick, helping the poor, touching the men and women around him every day with

the perfect love of God. Now, the Lord had sent Abelard to relieve my loneliness, and to fulfill the promise of God's love for
me. Would I forsake his gift?

"Ma chère," Abelard panted, kissing my throat. "My only
love." My blood quickened. My body seemed suddenly to ripen,
filling with moisture, swelling me until I felt I might burst open
like a juicy peach. He pulled open my pelisse and moved his
hands over my skin, cupping my breasts, which were heavy with
desire, and eliciting a moan from my throat.

"You were the most beautiful woman in that castle tonight,"
Abelard whispered. "A hundred men ravished you with their
eyes—but only I have the privilege of doing so with my body."

He picked me up and lowered me to the bed, where I opened
my arms and welcomed him. I wanted *this*; I wanted *him*. As we
kissed, my very essence seemed to overflow like a river flooding
its banks and pour from my mouth into his.

"Dear God, how I want you," he rasped, his breath hot on my
neck, my ear, my cheek. "Heloise, let me come in. I must feel you
encompassing me! I need to become one with you at last."

This was not the first time Abelard had asked for union
with me, but it was the first time his *mentula* had prodded my
inner thigh while he begged to enter. Never had we come so
close to the precipice. I wanted him, but I could not succumb—thinking of the pain, yes, but also of the danger that
we might be heard. I worried, also, about Abelard's intoxicated state. Tomorrow, when he had sobered, would he regret
breaking his vow of continence? Would he blame me for his
sin? I, who could find no iniquity in loving, dreaded his
pointing the finger of shame at me. So, consulting my heart
and finding it timid, I thought it best in spite of my body's
promptings to delay our joining until we both possessed ourselves fully and could unite in joy.

"I—I have drunk too much wine. I cannot, not tonight. But tomorrow, Abelard! Our minds, and hearts, will be clear then."

He sighed. The room fell into silence save for the cracks and pops of the fire. He rolled over and lay beside me, and I asked him to hold me for a while before returning to his bed. He slipped his arms around me and, kissing my hair and neck, murmured the sweetest words of love ever uttered. I pressed myself into him, molding myself to his form, wishing I might slip through his skin into his body and truly become one with Abelard.

Yet, to lie with him in this way, curled in his embrace, was enough. Here was where I belonged, in the arms of Abelard, my one and only love, and here would I remain—not in the abbey, not living according to the wishes of my mother, who had abandoned me, nor at my uncle's command, but only for Abelard. Here, I felt safe and protected as never before. Here, no one could harm me. Abelard's breath stroked the back of my neck like a calming hand until I slipped into a deep, dreamless sleep.

Or did I dream? For I felt, in my slumber, the graze of his lips on my breasts, the suckle of his mouth, the sweep of his hands, again, on my skin. I saw the dark shape of his head over mine, faintly limned by the moonlight slipping in through the shutters, and heard his quick, excited pants—

And awoke to a stabbing pain between my thighs. I would have cried out but his mouth was on mine, imbuing me with his breath, muffling my cries, which soon changed to delighted sighs. Pleasure filled me and grew with each slow stroke. I wanted this. I wrapped my legs around his waist and drew him in more deeply, reveling in the feeling of him atop me, around me, and inside me, as though we had indeed become one. It may be, as he had argued, that humans do not share the same essence, but in that moment Abelard and Heloise joined together in spirit as well as in body. Although the night covered his face, I could see him clearly, even the blue of his eyes, as his thrusting increased in force and speed. Then he stiffened, gasped, and sighed my name once more: *Heloise, my* singuläris, *you delight me more than I had even imagined.*

As he held me close, his pulse twitching against my ear, my teeth rattled with unquenched passion. I wanted more.

"Heloise, your body trembles. Have I hurt you, dearest?"

"No, my love." My voice quavered, as well.

"What? Are you crying? Dear Lord, what have I done?"

I lifted my eyes to his face, smiling, but he could not see me in the dark. "What have you done?" I said in my sweetest voice, about to tell him that he had made me the happiest woman in all the world, but before I could do so he uttered a curse.

"I have ruined the woman I love. God help me! Heloise, what did I do? I awoke with your soft, slender body in my arms and the fragrance rising from your hair, and I forgot everything. I forgot your desire to wait; I forgot my vows."

I drew back, dreading that he might rebuke me for our sin as Adam had blamed Eve. But how could Abelard point his finger at me? He had taken me while I slept; I had not assented. Or had I? I recalled his face above me in the dark, and the tug of his lips on my breasts. When had I awakened?

"Dear God, forgive me," he said. "But—why should he do so? Why should you?"

"There is nothing to forgive."

"How can you say that? I forced myself upon you, and most brutally—dear, dear Lord!" His voice broke, and when he kissed my cheek, he wet my face with his tears. "How can you ever forgive me? How will I ever forgive myself?"

"There is nothing to forgive, Abelard. I wanted it as much as you did."

He sat up and covered his face with his hands. "Please, avert your eyes. I cannot bear for you to look at me now, despicable creature that I am."

I sat up, too, and slipped my arms around him. Now he was the one whose body shook. Then we heard Jean's footsteps over our heads.

Abelard leapt from the bed. "Jean will find me here. I must leave you." He leaned down to kiss me, wetting my cheeks with his tears. "Heloise, I have wronged you most grievously and cast us both into sin. Do not despise me, I pray."

"I could never despise you." But I did not think he heard me. Snatching up his chemise and braies, he hurried across the room and out the door to his own bed before Jean might discover him here. If that happened, neither bribe nor cajoling would convince Jean to keep our secret. He had disliked Abelard from the first time they'd met, but having to move into the attic room had planted seeds of contempt in the servant's heart. His anger surely increased each time he emptied the *magister*'s chamber pot. Were he to learn our secret, he would tell it to my uncle—and who knew what Uncle Fulbert would do?

I smoothed the bedcovers where Abelard had lain, then turned onto my side and closed my eyes, feigning sleep and hoping that, when Jean came in to lay the fire, he would not hear the hammering of my anxious heart. Abelard and I had behaved carelessly, but we must not do so again. For myself I had little to fear except my uncle's heavy hand, and that my uncle might send me away sooner rather than later. But for Abelard, the consequences of betrayal would be disastrous. He'd laughed when I'd warned him of my uncle's temper, but I had felt Uncle's fist. What would he do to Abelard for betraying him under his own roof?

13

༄

So much pain sprouts and thrives in my heart that not even a whole year would suffice for its description. My body, too, is sad, my spirit transformed from its usual cheerfulness.

—HELOISE TO ABELARD

Pauline's eel pie, although delectable to the tongue, gave me no pleasure at dinner the following day. I choked down only a few bites, tasting nothing yet forcing myself to eat under my uncle's suspicious glare.

"You are corrupted—corrupted!" He smacked the table with his hand. "Jean told me how you came home in a whore's dress, stinking of wine. By God! I should not have allowed you to go to that pit of iniquity."

"I sat with the queen, at her invitation. She gave her *henap* to me and invited me to visit her again."

"That you shall never do. That court is the wickedest place in the realm—wicked! I have heard all about it from Suger. Gamblers, adulterers, fornicators: sin oozes from the very walls. By God, I should not have allowed you to go, but Petrus promised to protect you from harm."

"I am capable of protecting myself."

"Indeed. Behold your pale cheeks and trembling hands."

Uncle narrowed his eyes. "I know the ravages of excess as well as anyone."

I met his gaze. "Indeed."

"*Chienne!*" He bared his teeth and gripped my arm so tightly I cried out. "I ought to send you upstairs to put on that *meretrix*'s costume you wore last night. Then we can judge who is the greater hypocrite."

"Agnes has already sent her servant for the gown," I lied, pulling my arm from his grip. "But I assure you, it was no more revealing than any other costume I saw there, including the queen's own attire."

"And where was Petrus? I hold him responsible. You are degraded—degraded! He is to blame. Now I know why he did not come to dinner today."

My food stuck in my throat. I lowered my gaze lest my uncle note my distress. Why, indeed, had Abelard not come? Except for his months in Brittany, he had not missed a meal with us. *Men revel in the hunt,* Agnes had said during the feast in King Louis's court. Having finally claimed the prize he had pursued all these months, would he now forsake me?

I should not have opened my door to him. Or I should have sent him back to his bed rather than inviting him to lie with me. Now we shared the guilt in an act so unspeakable I could not even face him this morning. I had remained in bed all morning, feigning illness—not a falsehood, since I felt sick both in my head, which throbbed from too much wine, and in my heart, because of Abelard's remorse over what we had done and my part in it.

Agnes had suggested the revealing gown, but I had agreed to wear it, imagining, in truth, Abelard's arousal at seeing me so daringly attired. I had stirred his passions, then passed the cup with Queen Adelaide too many times, aware all the while of his gaze, which fixed itself again and again on my exposed bosom. My own desire stirred by his, I had welcomed him into my room when I should have turned him away. Had I heeded my own inner warnings against overindulging in wine, I should never have done so.

I had hoped to talk with him after dinner today, during *relevée*, while my uncle napped. Where had Abelard gone? To Etienne's house, to confess the act for which he felt only shame and self-loathing? I had rejoiced in our union, thinking only of myself even in the face of his torment.

After dinner I retired to my room, exhausted. I closed my shutters and lay down to wait until supper and the opportunity to face my love again. Did he despise me now, or did he yet love me after all? One look into those blue eyes, and I would know.

But at supper I sat again at the table with only my uncle. Abelard had not come. Neither had he sent a message excusing himself, a lapse that caused Uncle Fulbert to point the finger at me.

"Why isn't he here? Your face has guilt written in every pore. Tell me, girl—has something happened?" He narrowed his eyes. "By God's head, if you embarrassed him, or me, last night—"

"Nothing has happened, except that I have neglected to relay his message to you," I lied, a sin that paled next to the others I might confess. "King Louis invited him to court again this evening for a private lecture on philosophy."

"Good, good." Uncle nodded. "He may attempt again, if he forgot last night, to speak with Suger about supporting me for the deacon's post. Why do you frown?"

"I do not like Suger. He has the eyes of a vicious creature—the sort that lives underground and only emerges for the kill."

"He also has the ear of the bishop of Paris—the bishop!—and the heart of the king of the Franks." My uncle's eyes bulged. "By

God, did you tell him you are my niece? Did he see you in that whore's gown?"

I closed my eyes, remembering the monk Suger's accusing stare. *So begins the debasement of a great man,* he had murmured, unheard by anyone but me. *For his sins, God will banish Petrus from the garden of knowledge—and you, his temptress, will be crushed under your lover's heel.*

That night in my room, I tried to study while listening for the sound of my beloved's footsteps. Would he come for our lesson? My pulse quickened at the thought.

At last I heard his heavy tread. My heart beating wildly, I sprang across the room toward the door, ready to receive Abelard—but it opened to reveal Pauline.

"I am glad you are faring better, miss." From the sack in her hand she pulled the bedsheet, stained with the blood of my lost virginity, which she had removed from my bed and laundered. I sucked in my breath, but she only smiled.

"I know many remedies for female troubles. If you need it, I could provide you with something for your pain." I thanked her—but nothing could soothe me now.

The surge of energy Pauline's footsteps had produced now caused me to pace my floor from window to door and back again. If Abelard did not come to me when he arrived, I would approach him. I imagined the scene: his sorrowful eyes; my assurances that all was well; our joyous reunion. I tried to read, but not even Seneca could distract my thoughts. Minutes became hours; hours became lifetimes. The night deepened.

At last, I realized that Abelard would not return to my uncle's house that night. Perhaps he felt too ashamed to face me. Or perhaps Agnes had been right. What had she said of her future count? *Once he has taken what he wants from me, he will lose interest.*

I returned to my window, seeking Abelard's form on the street, but saw only shadows and stars. Even the dogs slept at this hour. What if I never saw him again? Of course he would return to me, whom he loved. But what if he did not? I knew where he taught; I knew where, in all probability, he spent this night. To-morrow, if he did not come to dinner, I would find him—and, God willing, I would soothe his anxious heart and bring him back to me.

I did not have to wait long for word from Abelard. The next morning, after my uncle had left for the cathedral, a message ar-rived. *Are you faring well?* I replied that I was, and that I wished to see him—but he did not respond. Was he faring well?

That afternoon, I ventured to Etienne's house in search of him. At the door, Ralph, Etienne's cold-eyed servant, turned me away with a face as impassive as stone. I stood in the gusting winds, hair stinging my eyes—for winter had swept in sud-denly—watching his lips form the word *non*. Abelard was not there, he told me. I did not believe him, but what could I do? I would not see him that day, wherever he might be. The wind shifted course as I walked, pushing me home.

I returned to Uncle's house to find Agnes there, her expression eager under her hat of snow-white ermine, her rosy cheeks re-flecting her *bliaut* of blood red.

"I have news for you," she said into my ear as we embraced. "Take me to your room?"

"No fire is lit, and Jean is out feeding the horses. It will be quite cold."

"Not cold to me, not under all this fur." She lifted her mantle. I marveled: ermine lined her cape in white, save for the black-tipped tails of the creatures, which lined the border. She also carried in her hands an ermine muff, similarly trimmed with tails.

"All that ermine must have cost your father a fortune."

"Not at all." She winked. "It was a gift from"—she slid her glance about the room—"someone else."

Not being so endowed with expensive fur, I led her with reluctance to my chilly room. I took up my pelisse, lined with lowly squirrel, and pulled it over my woolen gown.

No sooner had I closed the door than did she take my hands in hers. Her eyes shone. "Amaury and I talked all night after the feast."

"How unfortunate that he has a wife."

She lowered her voice. "He will not be married for much longer."

"But not even a year has passed since his wedding."

"How long does a man need to realize that he has erred? She not only lacks beauty, but also fire. She is more sister to him than wife, he told me."

I snorted. "He invents a convenient excuse for his own depravity. He wants you, and so he seeks reasons to repudiate her."

Did I truly expect to see Agnes cringe with shame? Instead, she dimpled and batted her eyelashes and smiled with pleasure.

"Amaury wants me? Do you truly think it is so?"

I lifted my brows. "So you talked all night. Did you come especially to bring me this news?"

She laughed. "*Non*, my dear. I have much more interesting—and important—information. Amaury's sister, our former queen, knows your father."

I withdrew my hands and placed them over my open mouth. "Queen Bertrade knows him? She is acquainted with him?" My thoughts raced. That would make him, in all likelihood, a nobleman, who might claim me as his own and save me from the confined life my uncle had ordained.

"She won't talk about him, or so she told Amaury. But she has invited you to visit her. Will you go? Amaury has promised to escort us. Behold your pale cheek, Heloise! Are you faint?"

She embraced me and I clung to her, steadying myself.

"Do not fear, *ma chère*: we shall persuade the queen to talk," Agnes said. "She will reveal everything to us. And then, at last, you will know the truth."

14

I am guilty, who compelled you to sin.
—ABELARD TO HELOISE

*O*f course my uncle entertained a guest that night: Roger, his assistant in the library, best known in the cloister for his wagging tongue. For a man who everyone knew could not keep a secret, he seemed privy to the most lurid details of people's lives—which he shared freely with us that evening. Canon Gaspard had fired his housekeeper after he'd dreamt of fornicating with her; some monks from Saint-Denis, visiting the Argenteuil Royal Abbey, had been discovered spying on the nuns in the bathhouse; Bishop Galon was said to be secretly married to a girl from la Marche; King Louis's most constant bed companion was not his queen, Adelaide, but his favored monk, Suger.

"That tale is ridiculous," I said. "I attended a feast in the court last week, and the king could hardly tear his gaze from the queen. Anyone who sees them together knows he loves her."

"You may be right, you may be right, indeed! And what of the queen, hmm? Does her head truly ache at night, or is she avoiding her conjugal duties? King Louis has already divorced one wife for failing to provide him with heirs."

"The monk is even less likely than Queen Adelaide to bear him a son," I retorted, causing my uncle to dismiss me.

I went to the study and opened Ovid's *Ars amatoria*. I read, *Make us believe (it's so easy) that we're loved.* For this, the poet recommended displays of emotion: tears, feigned jealousy, protests over the lover's long absence. I sighed. Tears might, indeed, help me coax Abelard back to me—if only I could summon them. But I had used up my supply years ago, crying for my mother.

The moon shone full and fertile. Jean set up my bed and built a fire, and still my uncle drank and gossiped with Roger. I took my book to bed and waited for him to sleep and imagined Abelard looking at me from under those curling eyelashes and calling me *singuläris* as he had done so often. *You are unlike any other woman,* he would say. *By God, Heloise, none can compare.* Now that he had conquered me, was I the same as every other woman? Perhaps that, and not guilt or shame, was why he had left me. I would find out soon enough.

When Roger had departed and Jean gone up to bed, I pulled on my cotte and slipped out the door, shaking my head to refuse the lantern boy, and slid through the shadows to Etienne's house. Ralph's eyes glinted as he again refused me entrance. I gritted my teeth and told him I would not depart, but would continue to knock each time he closed the door until he took me to Abelard. At last he relented, saying I would find the master in the guest quarters, in back of the main house. He took a lantern and led me to the gate.

"Does your uncle know where you have gone tonight?" he grumbled as he unlocked the gate. Without awaiting my answer he returned to the house, leaving me without any light but only a sliver of moon to guide me.

I could almost hear my heart knocking against my breast as I

stepped into the large courtyard with its trees reminiscent of skel-
etons and masses of shrubs resembling creatures poised for attack.
Etienne's large house loomed on my left; on my right stood a
confusing jumble of buildings whose functions I could scarcely
discern in the dark.

Walking through the doorway of the first building, I inhaled
the aromas of hay and manure and quickly discerned myself in a
stable; next door, a steeply pitched roof and narrow, rectangular
windows identified a chapel. As I stepped toward the third
building, I heard Abelard's voice shouting a curse so foul it
made me hesitate: Was he, again, intoxicated? Strong drink
might produce such outbursts in my uncle, I reminded myself,
but not in Abelard. He became jolly and effusive under the influence of too much wine, and his affections increased. My skin
turned hot at the memory. I pushed open the door—in time for
an object to fly past my head and hit the wall behind me with a
crack.

"Abelard! Do you now wish to kill me?"

"Heloise!" Abelard leapt from his seat and beheld me with
eyes as wide as if I had risen from a grave to haunt him. He wore
not his usual purple and gold but a short tunic of pale gray wool
and heavy stockings of a darker gray, with brown boots of calf-
skin, a brown leather girdle, and a green woolen cloak and
matching cap. The puffed skin under his eyes told me he had not
slept any more than I. But his eyes shone as brightly as if he had
just awakened from a beautiful dream.

He sprang across the room and pulled me into his arms. His
fervent lips on mine told me all I needed to know, and more.

"You have come."

"*Oui. I* could not keep myself from *you.*"

"Even after what I have done to you?"

I shook my head. "We committed the act together."

"Your virginity. I took it from you." His shoulders slumped and his hands dropped from my waist.

"I gave it willingly. Or—I would have done so, had you asked." I gave him a smile, which he did not return.

"But what about your vows?"

"I have not made them, as yet."

"And when you do?" He raked his hands through his hair. "Will you become the bride of Christ after having slept with a man?"

Many women did so, just as formerly married men became monks—but I held my tongue, not wanting to remind him of the vow *he* had broken. For a moment, I thought I would tell him of my decision not to go to Fontevraud, but I decided against that, as well. Too many uncertainties already lay before us.

"You possess my body," I said. "God wants only my soul."

Abelard gave me a crooked smile, one that, in combination with the cleft in his chin, gave him the appearance of a mischievous boy. "Are you certain? He has a reputation for jealousy, you know. But—Heloise, what of you? I have robbed you of your virtue."

"Losing my virginity means nothing to me. But if I have lost you, then I have lost everything."

"I am yours, Heloise," he murmured, and kissed me. Then he stepped over to the door and stooped to gather the broken tablet from the floor.

"I may be the one who loses everything," he said as he returned. He handed the pieces to me. *"Voilà."*

Sinking into his chair, he watched, his eyes wild and red-rimmed in the dim lamplight, as I examined the wax. I could not read anything written there, for each word had been scratched out at least once and, in some instances, several times.

"What is this?"

"I cannot write." He averted his face. "This has never happened before."

"Urania is capricious, Abelard. Has the Muse hidden herself from you?" I kept my voice light as I sat on the edge of his bed, across from him. "She shall return."

"Capricious, ha! The description is too kind. She beckons me with the shade of an idea and then, at the moment I reach for her, dances out of my grasp." His dark look made me shiver. "I think she is jealous of you."

"So *I* am to blame?" I could not help my wounded tone. Hadn't Abelard pursued me, singing to me in the *place*, bringing me gifts? Love had been the farthest thought from my mind on the day we had met.

Abelard groaned and sank to his knees before me. "Of course you are not to blame. I don't know what I am saying. I have—I have not been myself of late. I can think of nothing but you, Heloise, and everything we have said to each other, and all that we have done. I cannot fall asleep, and when I do, I dream of you. I lost control of my body with you—that has never happened before to me, either, I swear—and forced myself upon you. I disgust myself!" He covered his face with his hands, which I covered with my own. "What has happened to me?"

"Love," I whispered, afraid to utter the word he had given me lest he take it back.

"Yes! As God is my witness, I do love you." He removed his hands and lay his head in my lap, grasping my thighs. "Will you love me even when the world has forgotten me?"

"That shall never happen to you, the most renowned of men."

"My reputation hangs in the balance." He lifted his face to me again. "Bishop Galon came to me today, investigating an allegation that I had engaged in carnal relations with you."

"God help us." A lump formed in my throat. "What did he say?" How could the bishop know of our nights together when even my uncle did not suspect us?

"He said that if the charge proved true, he would dismiss me from the school."

"Dismiss you?" My heart began a slow, ponderous drumming like a roll of thunder. "For loving me? The bishop himself has done worse." Rumors said he lusted after young boys. "He ought to pull the log from his own eye before pointing to the speck in yours. When did the Church ever require continence of a minor canon?"

"When the canon is a teacher who seduces his scholar."

I opened my mouth to protest; he had not seduced me, but I had loved him willingly—from that first day, I now realized, when he had sung to me in the *place*. But when he hung his head I forgot my protest, wanting only to console him.

"Galon can offer no proof," I said with more conviction than I felt. "He cannot discipline you without evidence."

"He commanded me to sing 'Heloise of My Heart' for him."

"I feared this would happen." That song had been performed in every *place* in the city. Everyone in Paris knew it. "Why did you allow Daurostre to sing it in the king's court?"

"When did royal fetes or their amusements ever interest the Church?" Abelard narrowed his eyes. "Suger complained to Galon, I am certain."

The reformists despised Etienne for supporting King Philip's marriage to Queen Bertrade, Abelard told me. Bertrade having taken his mother's place, and her crown, King Louis had hated his father's new wife. Suger now used that hatred to his own advantage and whispered poisonous words to the king against the Garlande brothers.

"He wants to take Etienne's position in the court and gain power for himself and his reformist friends," Abelard said. "Tainting me with scandal would aid his cause."

A chill crawled down my spine. I had not liked the malevolent gleam in Suger's eyes as he had watched Abelard and me, both before and after the feast. He would harm Abelard, if he could. I stepped over to my beloved, reaching for his hands. How had Galon responded to his song?

Abelard grinned. "By the time I had finished it, he was scratching his head and wondering what had come over Suger, to see evil in such innocent verses. I shrugged and said that, as I recalled, the king's wine had flowed more freely than usual that night."

I widened my eyes. Galon had not thought the song a confession of guilt? "Did you sing 'May the day's risen light be the last that I see, if there lives a woman I could prefer over you'?"

"I did—and altered the words." He puffed out his chest. "'May the day's risen light be the last that I see,'" he sang, "'if there lives a girl endowed with greater virtue.'"

While yet the final note of his song hung in the air, he gleamed triumphant eyes and erupted in a great roar of laughter.

"He—he loved the song, Heloise, and—and he—he commended me for praising that which—which ought to be praised!" Abelard hiccuped, and tears streamed from his eyes.

A lightness rose through my body and, for the first time in ten years, laughter bubbled from my lips. I felt like a cup overflowing with joy.

"Hear your beautiful laugh!" Abelard cried. He embraced me and I knew again: I wanted *this*. We held each other until time stood still. I lifted my mouth to his. The only sound in the room was that of our mingling breaths, and, when the long kiss had ended, my sigh.

He turned and gathered his tablets and stylus and placed them in the pouch on his girdle. "Let us depart."

"Depart? But the hour is late."

"*Oui.*" He took my hand, smiling into my eyes. "It is time for us to go home."

15

Hour by hour I am bound closer to you, just like fire devouring wood; the more devouring, the more plentiful its fuel. . . . You glitter, with perpetual light and inextinguishable brightness immortally.

—ABELARD TO HELOISE

I slept past my usual hour the next morning, awakened by the sound of horses outside my window and Agnes calling my name. In the next moment, Jean had opened the door to her and she bounded into my room, exclaiming at the sight of me lying in bed, a smile on my lips as I recalled my time with Abelard the previous night. He had come back to me. *I am yours, Heloise.*

"Had you forgotten our plans for the day?" Agnes said, hands on her hips. In fact, I had forgotten—but now I arose in a hurry and pulled on my clothes. Today the seigneur Amaury would escort us to the Hautes-Bruyères Priory for an audience with the former queen Bertrade. On this day I might, at last, come to understand all that had happened to me, and why.

"Hurry!" Agnes said as she helped me braid my hair. Queen Bertrade expected our arrival midmorning, and we must not keep her waiting. We would take dinner in the abbey if the queen permitted it, Agnes said, as if I could even think of food.

"Where may I tell the canon that you have gone?" Jean said, frowning, as we stepped out the door. I gave him an explanation that I knew would please my uncle—that I hoped Queen Bertrade, having founded her priory and given it to the Fontevraud Abbey, might influence Robert of Arbrissel to make me his abbess.

We embarked on our journey not long after sunrise. Agnes eyed my dark-blue *bliaut*, which was, by now, familiar to her. She wore under her ermine cloak yet another gown that I had never seen: simple and flowing, of pale green silk embroidered with green leaves over a long-sleeved chemise of pale, fine linen, with a neckline that, for once, revealed not a hint of cleavage. When visiting an abbey, one must attire oneself modestly. Yet she had dabbed a hint of ocher on her lips, and on mine, as well. When meeting with one of the world's great beauties, one must appear at one's best.

My hands shook so that I could barely hold the reins. The queen had not only agreed to meet with me, but had said she anticipated with great pleasure a morning spent sharing memories of my mother. Perhaps she would reveal something about my father, as well.

"Heloise!" Agnes's insistent tone told me this was not her first call out to me. "Why don't you give your reins to Amaury"—his name rolled like butter over her tongue—"so that you do not stray off the road and into the vineyards? You are roaming so freely that I fear you will trample some poor villein, or, worse, injure your horse."

Coming to my senses, I saw that my palfrey had ventured close to the edge of the road, causing some workers to step back in alarm. I corrected its course and strove to keep my mind on the journey, but my imagination continued to spin dreams of Mother, and fanciful tales such as Bertrade might tell about her life. Surely Mother's closest friend would know why she had put me in the convent. But did I want to know?

"This invitation is special, indeed. My sister speaks of her friend Hersende to no one," Amaury said. "Baudri of Bourgueil interviewed Bertrade for his biography of Robert, but when he mentioned Lady Montsoreau, she sent him away."

"The queen will tell Heloise everything she wants to know," Agnes said. "I can be very persuasive."

"Of that, I have no doubt." Amaury's gaze flitted to her; he twitched his mustache.

I had to look away from them. Sly phrases, secret smiles, the sweet indulgences of blossoming love: these made up our own private language, Abelard's and mine. Watching Agnes and Amaury together made me blush—was this how we appeared to others? The sidelong glances, the surreptitious touches, the way the air around us seemed to shimmer—we thought our *riposte*, spiced with allusions to carnal pleasure, the cleverest in the history of lovers. Hearing them, I blushed. Abelard and I would need to be more careful in my uncle's presence.

The morning sun struggled upward in a tepid attempt to warm the day as we approached Hautes-Bruyères, with its elegant arched gates, stone walls, and tall trees whose red-and-gold leaves illuminated the pale sky. Amaury gestured toward the chapel with its slender spires. The priory, he told us, held two hundred women. Queen Bertrade had founded it, with Amaury's help, to atone for her sins with King Philip. He said this with pride, as though he weren't repeating his sister's sins with Agnes.

Soon we were inside the gate, accompanied by a fat nun who waddled through the large, light cloister to the prioress's study. The room impressed me: Bertrade of Montfort had furnished it in a manner befitting a queen. Colorful Persian carpets cushioned the stone floor; creamy silk tapestries lined the walls. A fire crackled in the exquisite fireplace of slender, rose-colored tiles laid in a herringbone pattern. Several lord's chairs with high, ornamented backs and arms lined the room's perimeter, and a large writing desk occupied a far corner. Sitting there was the prioress, who gathered herself and stood as befits a queen, her back and neck as straight as if she had been carved from ivory. She glided to us, or, rather, floated.

"Amaury, how handsome you appear! And this must be your Agnes." She kissed them both, then turned to me. She gasped when she saw me, and I might have done the same: even in her veil, and at her age—nearly fifty, a decade younger than my mother would have been—she was the most beautiful woman I had ever seen. Her skin gleamed like polished porcelain. Her sloe eyes lifted at the corners, their color so black as to be nearly purple. When she smiled at me, the room seemed to glow.

"My dear! You have your mother's face—her perfect little nose and her large, haunted eyes." Her own eyes shone, luminous with tears.

She invited us to sit, and two sisters entered to move chairs before the fire.

"*Alors*, Heloise," she said. "You have escaped from the convent, I see. *Bonne chance!* While I, the Dowager Queen of the Franks, have no other place to go."

Amaury cleared his throat. "I have tried to make these surroundings pleasant for you."

"They are pleasant enough, yes. But as you know, I would rather be riding a galloping steed than languishing inside these walls." She shot a glance at me. "That doesn't offend you? . . . Good. You are your mother's daughter, then. But you!" She leveled her gaze at Agnes, who had pressed a finger to her lips. "Something amuses you, *non*?"

"I beg your pardon, my lady. I had expected a different answer, given the life you have led."

Bertrade arched one eyebrow. "You thought I had repented for my sins? Indeed I have done so, but marrying King Philip is not one of them."

"But you built this priory to atone for it," I said.

"A mere display, to appease the Church. Those prudish popes would have excommunicated me straight to hell otherwise—but I intend to meet my husband in heaven. We married for love, as God intended." She turned to Agnes. "Was that what you thought I would say?"

"My lady, I thought you would say that, instead of living in this priory, you would rather be making love to the king."

"Indeed!" Bertrade brightened. "I would rather ride Philip's *verpa* than any horse." She broke into laughter, nearly drowning out the peals of the refectory bell. I turned wild eyes to Amaury. Had we traveled all morning for this?

"Heloise has come to ask you about her mother," Amaury said.

She arched a brow at me. "Your mother loved to laugh."

"Did you know of me?" I ventured to ask.

"Of course. I knew everything about Hersende."

"While I know almost nothing of her. She took me to the convent when I was seven, and I never saw her again."

"And Fulbert?" Bertrade narrowed her eyes. "What does *he* say about Hersende?"

I glanced at Agnes and Amaury, hesitant to repeat my uncle's slanders before them. The dinner bell pealed; Bertrade clapped her hands, and a young nun entered. At the queen's command, she escorted the pair to the refectory for dinner. When they had left, the queen resumed our talk.

"If the world has been silent regarding Hersende, it is because she insisted on silence," Bertrade said when she returned to me. "She gave birth to you in secret—I know because I was there, stifling her cries and yours. Most of her servants were gone, dismissed because she worried they'd talk about her growing belly. She felt terrified that her family would find out, all those brothers and that father of hers always talking honor, honor, honor. She hid her love affair even from me, for a time. She feared I might judge her." Bertrade wrinkled her brow. "As if I had never loved, nor suffered for it."

"Uncle said she was ashamed of what she did. That is why she went to Fontevraud."

"*Pfft*. The mirror he holds up to others, he should turn upon himself."

"Uncle Fulbert helped my mother."

She rolled her eyes. "Is that what he told you? He helped Hersende to avoid disgracing his precious family, yes. But what he forced your mother to do was far more shameful. And see how you have suffered, poor child!"

"What did he force her to do?"

"Ask that question of Fulbert. Ha! I would love to be there, to watch him cringe."

She narrowed her eyes. "Take care with him, my dear. For all his false piety, he is not a good man. Why do you stare at me so? If I held my peace, the very stones would cry out. But I have upset you, which was not my intent. I do not wish to discuss Fulbert with you, at any rate. It is dinnertime, and the very thought of that man has stolen my appetite. Is there anything more you would know about Hersende?"

"Was Mother ashamed of me, too?"

"Hersende adored you. After all, you were a part of herself— and of *him*, as well. She would have told the world about you, if she could. She was not ashamed of anything that she did, except, perhaps, placing you in Argenteuil at such a young age. Yet she did that, too, out of love. She didn't hide you away out of shame—this you must know. She was forced to take you there."

"Forced? By my father?"

Bertrade pressed her lips together and shook her head. Her eyes glittered like ice. "She did what was necessary to protect *him*. Had the world known about them—about *you*—it would have destroyed him."

"Is that why my father never acknowledged me?"

Compassion filled Bertrade's eyes. She squeezed my hand. "My dear, he never knew you existed."

PART TWO

Dilectio

1

Therefore my beloved, write something cheerful, sing something cheerful, live prosperously and happily. You who have almost forgotten me, my sweet, when shall I see you? Allow at least one happy hour for me.

—HELOISE TO ABELARD

PARIS

OCTOBER 1115

*A*t my door, Abelard enfolded me in his arms and kissed me with a fervor that bruised my lips.

"If only this night would never cease," he said, devouring my mouth, my throat, my bosom, "I would make love to you forever."

All on fire with desire, how could I turn him away from my bed? When he lifted me up and carried me into my room, his eyes reflecting the hearth's flames, I forgot our vow to forbear these indulgences in my uncle's house. The touch of his hands on my body obliterated every thought. He removed my clothing with excruciating slowness as if doing so would delay the dawn. I remember every detail: the scent of passion on his breath; the pluck of my body's strings by his nimble fingers; his tongue between my thighs; the press of his palm against my gasping mouth, stifling my ecstatic cries. These days and nights might be the last we spent in lovemaking for who knew how long? My uncle and Jean would return soon from Anjou, where they had gone with Galon to a synod of bishops. How, then, with even the birds throating songs about our love, would Abelard and I dare to take these risks under his very nose? So we rode slowly, savoring this night, prolonging it, wishing it never had to end.

Spent after our hours of delight, we lay entwined, my hair a river flooding his chest, his heartbeat murmuring, *Volupt, volupt, volupt.* How could I ever have doubted his love? In truth, it had outstripped my own, conferring upon me a debt that, too soon, I must repay.

A month had passed since our reunion at Etienne's, time spent in conversation rather than kisses, Abelard's fear of discovery having put its left foot against his desire, and my love for him compelling me to stifle my own. Possessing Abelard's love, I told myself, I needed nothing more. Why, then, did I feel adrift, as if set in a boat in the middle of the sea without an oar?

One day before my uncle's journey, I had lost my way walking to the market. Upon finding it at last, I tried to purchase some eels and realized I had left my money pouch at home. At supper, I wandered in my thoughts, causing my uncle to ask if I felt unwell. In my room, I vomited in my chamber pot.

Why? I knew well the answer. The sickness in my heart had made my body ill. I did not want to go to Fontevraud, but to remain with Abelard—which would be impossible to do. Even to voice my desires would be pointless. Who had ever asked for my thoughts concerning my life? I would depart in less than eight months' time. In the gown being sewn especially for the cere-mony—the fabric bloodred, the color of sacrifice—I would take my vows to God, then be shorn of all my hair and attired in a nun's habit and veil. I might never see Abelard again.

I did not want to go. I wanted to remain with my *speciälis*, not as his wife, for he could not marry, but as his mistress, as Gisele had been to my uncle, a position less honorable in the eyes of the Church but perfectly acceptable among Parisians. People in Paris pursed their lips in contempt over the reformists' insistence that clergymen remain chaste. Forcing men to deny their God-given desires was cruel and even unhealthy, many said.

Decades after Pope Gregory's reforms and his death, a new generation of zealots had begun to demand that priests and bishops live like monks, although, as everyone knew, monks themselves were not immune to temptations of the flesh. Unlike my ambitious uncle, however, many resisted these reforms. Abelard, who was neither priest nor deacon, might make a mistress of me without repercussions—were I not his scholar.

I lay on my bed that night, clenching my stomach. How would I tear myself from him? The wound would never heal. But I could not remain in Paris with him, either. Galon would know, then, that the rumors about us were true. He would eject Abelard from the school, covering him with disgrace. How would my dearest live? Could Etienne help him, given his own rivalry with Suger? To lift a finger on Abelard's behalf might prove too dangerous, friend or not.

My uncle would rage, too, of course. I shuddered: his hands were large; his fists, powerful. He had hurt me more than once for impudent remarks: *Just like your mother, thinking yourself above everyone else.* Who knew what he would do to Abelard for this betrayal?

Non, I could not remain here. My destiny sealed, I must go to Fontevraud in June. Cold, damp memories covered my skin in gooseflesh. Would I return to the life I had hated, and live in darkness and silence for the rest of my days? And yet, loving Abelard, did I have any choice? I would destroy my own life without hesitation rather than harm a single hair on his head.

Nausea rolled over me, then subsided.

In losing Abelard, I would lose a part of myself. Who else had ever listened to my deepest thoughts and encouraged me to dream? Who else among men considered anything that I had to say? Abelard engaged my ideas and challenged me to defend them. His arguments sharpened my mind and, at times, my tongue, and yet, as with everyone else who had ever tried, I had never defeated him. After each debate, though, he praised my intelligence and skill.

Who else had ever burst into song while walking through the *place* with me? Gesturing with open arms one rainy afternoon, he'd dropped my packages in the mud, spoiling our supper, but had returned to each vendor and purchased every item anew—as well as candied chestnuts for me. I, insisting now upon carrying the capons and bread, had encouraged him to resume his songs, but he'd only laughed and fed the sweets to me one by one as we walked. Who, now, would buy me candied chestnuts? Who would feed them to me and then lick the sugar from his own fingertips, declaring them sweeter for having touched my lips? Who, now, would make me laugh?

And who, when my uncle began to curse me, would lighten his mood with an amusing tale? Since moving into our home, Abelard had protected me from my uncle's anger. No longer did Uncle Fulbert raise his hand against me, not when Abelard's presence filled the room—*non*, it filled the entire house—blinding Uncle to my impertinences and dazzling us with bold, mirthful light.

If only we might continue in this manner forever. A prayer rose to my lips—but how could I speak it? Although I cherished the love, and life, we shared, I also hated deceiving my uncle. He trusted us, and we betrayed him whenever the opportunity arose: in his home, in the cloister stables, on the riverbank at night, and even—I cringed to think of it now, while my skin filled with heat—in the chapel behind Etienne's house. Our sins had increased in number until we had ceased counting them. We must end our deceptions soon or we would be discovered, torn apart, and cast into shame.

No, I must go to Fontevraud as planned, fulfill my destiny, and allow Abelard to fulfill his own—apart from me, but not completely. A part of me would remain with him for all time.

Love is not self-seeking. I remembered the Scripture I had recited to him to demonstrate my knowledge of love. Soon the time would come for me to practice what I had preached to Abelard that day. I would take my nun's vows to protect him, loving him as Christ had loved. And he, thinking I wanted to go, would never realize my sacrifice.

Knowing that the Scriptures admonish us not to boast of our good works, I resisted the temptation to confess the truth to Abelard. Instead, I demonstrated my feelings in other ways, offering love from my mouth as a fountain, or a spring, in the kisses we shared in my bed after my nausea had passed and the house was quiet.

And, oh! When he had carried me to heights never before known—into other worlds, it seemed—I clung to him, dizzy, as if the earth had turned itself over. When he peered into my eyes from under those sultry, half-lowered lids, I saw questions whose answers I had never thought to ponder. Now, alone with him in the house, entwined in my bed, the fire that he had just fed roaring in the hearth, I began to ask questions of my own. Why, I wondered, had he sung of our love to all the world, endangering us both?

"My love for you filled my body to overflowing." He smiled. "Had I tried to hold it in, I would have burst apart. You would not have wanted that to happen, *non?*"

"But what of my honor? Surely you heard the courtiers' murmurs that night in the palace. Surely you saw how they looked at me, as though I had fornicated with you on the floor before them all."

"They were only amusing themselves."

"And doing so at my expense!"

"They are nobles." He shrugged. "They amuse themselves at everyone's expense."

I sat up. "Noble birth ought to impose a higher standard of behavior, not excuse a lower one."

"And one might think that a girl so highly born would disregard the opinions of others. Indeed, such a girl might even laugh at her detractors."

"One might think that the man who loved that girl would defend her against defamatory remarks—*if* he were truly a man. And if he truly loved her."

"Were we on the field of battle, you might need my protection. For *riposte*, however, you are as well equipped as I."

"You said not a word to that disgusting old baron and his wife, who insulted me to my face."

"Would you rather that they did so when your back was turned?"

"Do not obscure my point with rhetorical questions."

"That old baron is a friend of Etienne's," Abelard said.

"What use could Etienne find in that decrepit old goat?"

"That 'goat' bathes himself in livres. He has the king's ear. And he supports Etienne against the reformists, who would have his head on a platter if they could."

"So he is Etienne's friend, and Etienne is your friend." I narrowed my eyes. "What, in the meantime, am I to you?"

"You are the love of my life, the brightest star in my constellation, my very soul and reason for being."

I kissed him, pleased with this response. "And you are my closest friend."

Confusion crossed his face. "I would have thought Agnes would hold that honor."

"Agnes?" I laughed. "You are the one to whom I reveal my soul. You alone understand my thirst for knowledge, for you share it with me. 'For he, indeed, who looks into the face of a friend beholds, as it were, a copy of himself.' How much more alike could any two people be?"

"But didn't Cicero say that friendship can exist only between men?"

"He lived more than one thousand years ago. Ours is a new era. More and more girls are becoming lettered. Soon we may see girls in the schools, studying alongside men. Why couldn't friendships form between them?"

Abelard laughed. "Didn't you hear Bernard's sermon? The reformists want to banish females from the cloisters and will never allow them in the schools. They might ask questions then, and who knows what would happen?"

"Well, *I* am a woman of letters, the likes of which Cicero never knew. Certainly he never knew a woman so like himself as I am to you. Our love, Abelard, has roots in the rich and ancient soil of friendship, of equal to equal."

"You call yourself my equal?" The quick flash of his teeth. The jerk of his chin.

"I call myself your friend."

His expression changed. He twisted my hair back with one hand and studied my naked face. "Perhaps you wish, then, to be a man." He turned me around and, pressing me into the mattress, took me from behind, as one man takes another. During that too-short week we had learned everything there was to know of each other's body, trying every new thing we could devise, limited only by our imaginations. We became artists in the bed, or, rather, musicians, or, rather, instruments of music. Struck by love, we resonated. We hummed and whispered, rustled the bed-coverings, sighed and moaned, hushed one another. Restraining my ecstatic song pushed my voice into a faint vibrato, chiming with passion, mingling with Abelard's gasps and groans, his murmur of my name in my hair, which, still coiled around his hand, he pressed to his mouth as he made me his in yet another new way. I submitted to him completely, and joyously, gasping with pain, quivering with pleasure, filling the room with our joyous noise—or, as we did not realize then, filling an entire house.

I heard a bang, and man's voice shouting, screaming, and then Abelard, who lay on top of me, was gone, the cold rushing to all the places where we had touched. I opened my eyes and saw him rising from the bed, and I saw my uncle Fulbert's face hot like a dragon's with eyes of bulging red.

"Rape!" he shouted. "Get off of her, you filthy beast." He lifted Abelard into the air and flung him down. I heard a crack as he hit the wall, and his grunt. My uncle's eyes ran over my naked body. *Fulbert will skin them both alive.* I yanked the covers to my chest and he turned away, to where Abelard was rising from the floor. Uncle gritted his teeth and balled his fists. Crying out a warning, I leapt up, but he swatted me to the bed with the back of his hand. I lay, dizzied, my ears ringing.

With a shake of my head I rose again, calling to Abelard once more, but Uncle had already seized him again and thrown him through the doorway, out of my room.

"You have stolen my innocent niece's virtue and my honor," Uncle growled. He pulled his knife from the sheath on his belt and pointed it at Abelard. "Now I'll make a eunuch of you, by God." Uncle breathed in deep pants, as though he had been running. His eyes rolled, out of focus.

"Uncle, no!" I screamed. "He didn't rape me! We love each other."

He turned to where I stood, still holding the bedcovers to my chest. I saw a glint in his eyes before he averted them, his face reddening. "What in God's name are you saying?"

"Abelard did not take my honor, or yours. I gave it willingly to him."

"Your mother's daughter," Uncle muttered. The anguish of betrayal twisted his features. From the corner of my eye I saw Abelard rising, his eyes watching the knife in my uncle's hand. Before he could attempt to wrest it from him, however, Jean ran into the room and seized Abelard from behind. Abelard hurled him over his back and onto the floor, where he lay like a bundle of twigs.

"What, now you've killed my servant, too? By God, your days on this earth are finished," my uncle snarled, lunging at Abelard.

Abelard leapt aside, narrowly missing the blade's point. As he cast about for an object with which to defend himself, Uncle thrust again, aiming for Abelard's private parts.

"Flee, Abelard!" I cried. "He will kill you. Run, my love; run far away!"

"And leave you? Never."

My uncle slashed the air in front of him, sending Abelard stumbling backward and tumbling down the stairs. I screamed and would have gone to him, but my uncle warded me off with the knife. "Have you no shame, *lupa* that you are? Go and hide your nakedness. There is nothing you can do to help your *magister* now."

"Uncle, please." Behind him, Abelard struggled to his feet again. "We have done nothing wrong."

"You have ruined my life, you ungrateful bitch—ruined it, ruined *me*!" Uncle yelled. "My honor, my reputation, my chance for a promotion, gone, all gone."

"Fulbert," Abelard said, standing now at the foot of the stairs, naked except for his hands, which he held in front of his most vulnerable place. "Heloise and I have spoken of our love to no one. Your honor is intact. And I will yet help you gain a promotion. I have already spoken to Etienne about it." How easily the untruths sprang to his lips!

"By God, I ought to kill you both—both!" My uncle leveled the knife at Abelard again. "Remove yourself from my house this instant, you Satan. As God is my witness, I'll make a woman of you." Uncle headed down the stairs, and I shrieked again at Abelard to run away.

"Should I step outdoors without even a fig leaf to cover me?" Abelard said, yet shielding his testes with his hands. "What would happen to your honor then, my friend?"

"Do not call me friend." Uncle narrowed his eyes, then shouted a command for me to retrieve Abelard's clothes. I ran upstairs, donned a *bliaut*, then took up the hose, boots, and other items he had been wearing and handed them to my uncle, who flung them at Abelard while ordering me, again, to my room. Out of his sight, I gathered all Abelard's belongings—his beautiful clothes, his lute, his books—and put them into a sack. When I heard the front door open, I ran to my window, flung open the shutters, and dropped his possessions down to him.

"I don't want to leave you alone with him," Abelard said.

"I have barred the door," I said, as my uncle began pounding on it and shouting my name. "But it will not hold for long, I am afraid, as angry as he is. Please, Abelard, hurry to Etienne's and tell him what has happened. Ask him to send a physician to look after Jean—and send him as quickly as possible, before my uncle injures me, too. Hurry!"

My uncle's fists beat against my door, and his shouts grew louder. Strength filled me, sent by God, I am certain, and I pulled my bed across the floor to block the door. I slid my heavy desk and chair against the bed, and my chests of clothes. Even so, I heard a loud thud, as though Uncle had thrown all his weight against the door, and the splintering of wood.

"Whore!" he screamed. "I should have known. My sweet niece, holy and pure. You're nothing but a liar and a slut—a filthy sinner—just like your mother."

Please dear God, send that physician now. My uncle would not lay a hand on me in his presence.

"Wait until I get my hands on you," he cried, slamming himself into the door, cracking it. "You want lessons? Uncle Fulbert has one for you, heh-heh, that you will never forget."

2

No one is unhappier than we who are simultaneously pulled in different directions by love and shame.
—ABELARD TO HELOISE

*L*ong after the physician had come and gone and Uncle's attempts to break down my door had ceased, I remained in my chambers, not daring to risk the blunt edge of my uncle's ire. After pulling the furnishings back into place, I lay on my bed, shutters closed against the night, remembering all that had occurred, shivering in the chill. Uncle's hurtful words echoed in my mind. *Filthy sinner—just like your mother.* Had I indeed become like her?

I pray that, someday, you will understand. How could I ever understand a mother's decision to abandon her child? Had she never realized that, by eating sour grapes, she might set her daughter's teeth on edge?

Why she had sent me away from her, I did not yet understand. But I had obtained a glimpse, at least, into the reasons why she had "spread her legs," as Uncle had put it, for my father. Loving Abelard had opened my eyes, my heart, and, yes, my legs, and joyously so. He and I might have sinned in the eyes of the Church, but in my eyes we had fulfilled the Lord's highest commandment. Although barred by the world from becoming husband and wife, we had nonetheless bound ourselves to each other by virtue of our great, and holy, love.

Yet, we had committed one grievous wrong in betraying my uncle's trust, and under his own roof. What terrible revenge would he wreak upon us? Would he follow the example of Mars, who, after finding Venus entangled with Adonis, caused Adonis to die? If I could prevent even a hair on Abelard's head from harm, I would willingly pay any price, even that of my pride. I would tell my uncle and the whole world that *I* had seduced *him*, and that, given the chance, I would do so again.

But now he was gone: My only friend, taken. My only love, lost. Never had I felt so utterly alone.

As I stared out the window, seeing nothing except the image of my uncle's murderous face, I heard a faint knocking.

"My lady?" Jean and Pauline's son, Jean-Paul, murmured from outside the door. "I bring you a message."

I pulled open the door. The boy, his dark eyes wide, handed me a tablet of green wax. *Write to me, sweetest, about how you fare, because I shall not be able to be healthy unless your well-being provides a reason for my health. Fare well and be happy, for as long as the wild boar loves the mountaintops.* The last sentence ran like a blade along my spine: A wild boar, sent by Diana as a favor to Mars, had killed Adonis. Abelard, too, worried what revenge my uncle might take.

"Tell the *magister* that I am well," I said to Jean-Paul, whose worried frown reminded me of his father's injury. How, I asked him, was Jean faring?

"My father lies senseless in the bed of the man who attacked him," Jean-Paul said. "Please, my lady, do not send me back to that murderer. I could not face him without committing a terrible sin that would break my mother's heart."

A correction sprang to my lips—Abelard had attacked no one but had been viciously assaulted and threatened—but I merely sighed. Was this household cursed? Did God now punish us all for the sins that Abelard and I had committed?

I stepped into Abelard's room. Jean lay on the bed, unconscious as his son had said, his feet and ankles jutting over the mattress's edge, his thin, gray hair spread on the pillow. I glanced about at the vestiges of Abelard: his desk of rich, dark wood, with its matching high-backed chair and footstool; the hanging tapestry dyed with saffron and embroidered with geometric designs of blue and green; and, on a small table, his astralabe. I picked it up and turned it over, imagining that I could feel the warmth from his hands. How long ago it seemed, that night when he had given mine to me, on the eve of his departure for Brittany.

How would I bear another separation from him, who had become a part of me? Too soon I would leave Abelard forever, never to see him again. We must find some way to be together in spite of my uncle—for I knew that he would use every method in his reach to keep us apart.

Tonight, perhaps, when Uncle Fulbert fell asleep, I might slip away to devise a plan with Abelard. I would return his astralabe, as well, so that we might send our love to each other by way of that bright planet. Venus's love had doomed Adonis to a bloody death. I shook off the thought. For all his threats, Uncle Fulbert was no murderer.

In the kitchen, Pauline pounded herbs with a pestle as if taking revenge upon them. She grunted when I asked how she fared, but offered nothing more. When I inquired about Jean, she dropped the pestle onto the floor. Cursing in French, she bent to retrieve it at the same time as I. Handing it to her, I saw her reddened eyes, and her glare that seemed to blame me for her troubles. I said nothing, having nothing to say. She resumed her pounding. At last, I asked her to bring some hot water to my room so that I might wash before supper.

My toilette complete, I ventured to the dining table. Although I had no appetite, I needed to speak with my uncle. I must discern his intentions toward my beloved, and I must dissuade him from seeking revenge. He could utterly destroy Abelard, and he needed no knife to do so but only words that I must convince him not to speak.

I found him not on the verge of drunkenness, as I had expected, but as sober as a stone, his mind—and tongue—sharpened only by anger.

"Ah, here is my little *meretrix*. Gave yourself willingly, eh? Willingly! Not even a thought for your uncle Fulbert, who trusted you."

"I had thought you trusted me to take care of your household and of myself. I have done both." I pulled a bench to the table and sat opposite him, wary of his pointed glare, his drumming fingers.

"A fine job you have done of caring for my household, conducting your sinful affair under my roof and risking my reputation."

"Why should your reputation suffer? It was I who sinned, not you."

"You have defiled yourself. I am your uncle and patron, and so am sullied, as well."

"I meant no harm to you."

"You were not thinking of me." He brought his fist down on the table, rattling the empty *henap*, the lighted candles. "You thought only of your own pleasure. It is no wonder that you saw me off so joyously—'Farewell, Uncle dear! Hurry home!' Deception—deception! You and your lover couldn't wait for my departure so that you could begin your rut."

Heat spread through my face and neck. "I will not allow you to debase our love."

"Love? Hmph. And listen to your haughty voice. Such pride—pride! Did they teach you that in the Royal Abbey? What of 'the meek shall inherit the Earth'?"

"What of 'judge you not, lest you be judged'?"

"I caught you in the act, stupid girl. I have no need for judging when the verdict is clear. Where is your contrition?"

"Contrition for loving Abelard? I might as well apologize for breathing."

"You ungrateful bitch!" He threw the *henap* against the wall and it clattered to the floor. Jean-Paul brought in our supper, his neck and ears reddening at my uncle's outburst as he set down the food, placed the cup on the table, then hurried away.

"After all I have done for you: paying for your schooling at Argenteuil, bringing you to Paris, preparing the way for your entry into a high position at Fontevraud—"

"All you have done benefits you. The more I prosper, the better your chance of success."

"And when everyone has discovered what you have done?"

Remain calm, Heloise. "How will everyone discover it? Are you going to tell them?"

"You're damned right I will!" He pounded the table again. "Bishop Galon deserves to know that his headmaster is a deceitful, lust-driven sinner."

"You would destroy the career of the world's most brilliant philosopher merely for falling in love? Can you not muster even a speck of compassion for Abelard—and for me?"

"Where is he now, eh? He hides, trembling in fear over the consequences of his foul deeds without a care for your welfare. Foul deeds!"

"What did he do that countless men have not done before him?"

"What? He seduced his own student, an innocent girl brought up in the convent, one already betrothed to Christ—to Christ!"

"I am twenty years of age, and capable of choosing for myself."

"I did think so, yes." His voice shook. He rang for some wine, and Jean-Paul rushed in with a flagon. "You were special, Heloise, a shining jewel of virtue." The drink Uncle took appeared to steady him. "Now Petrus Abaelardus has tarnished you. He has degraded you. And in doing so under my roof, he has degraded me and all our family."

"I do not feel degraded by his love, Uncle. I feel exalted."

"You poor, misguided child. I know you think yourself an adult, but you have little understanding of how the world works. Dear God, forgive me for my stupidity! I should have protected you." He sighed. "I am as much to blame as Petrus."

"No one is to blame." I placed my hand on his forearm, suddenly desiring to comfort him. "From the moment we met, Abelard and I knew we were destined to be together."

"And how could that be, with you headed to Fontevraud, and he rising like the sun in God's church? Some say he will become a bishop, as William of Champeaux did before him—a bishop, that serpent of deception! Petrus Abaelardus isn't fit to kiss the hem of my robe, I who have given up all for the Church and cannot even attain a deacon's post."

"And if you tell Galon what we have done? How would that help you, Uncle?"

"It would fill me with joy to see that traitor ruined, as he has ruined you." Uncle's smile flickered like a shadow. "Banished from teaching, exiled from Paris—Galon would make it so, and gladly. He appointed Petrus under pressure from the king, thanks to Etienne, but he despises his arrogance."

"And so—you will tell the bishop about us?" Tears did not form in my eyes, yet I sniffled and wiped my cheek and so deceived my uncle. "You would destroy my reputation, too?"

"Oh, no, I would never do that—not unless I were forced. Do you think I want the world to know that my niece is a whore like her mother?" He began to eat, then, and to drink, but moderately, pouring only a cup or two of wine for himself. Of all the nights to refrain, why would he do so on this one, when I wanted only for him to fall into his usual stupor so that I might go to Abelard?

The muscles around my stomach tightened, constricting my breath. I could not eat, but walked to the great windows overlooking the street. *Abelard, where are you?* Had he gone to Etienne's? Was he faring well? *God willing, I will see you soon, my love.* A dog skulked past, his teeth bared in warning to the hostile world.

"Seeking your lover?" My uncle came to where I stood and stared out the window beside me. "It is of no use. You will never see him again, not alone. I will make certain of it."

I wanted to laugh at his guilelessness. Did he think to keep us apart whose very spirits had mingled, whose love transcended all earthly concerns? When necessity had parted us, our souls had converged on a star. I was Abelard's, and he was mine, a fact that nothing could change.

Still, I trembled to think of the harm my uncle might do. Hoping to soften him toward me—toward *us*—I slipped my hand into his and asked again how his heart could be so hard. Had he never known love?

"I have had my share of female company." Seeing my eyes widen, he grinned. "Beautiful women—beautiful! Heiresses, servant girls, married women." He licked his lips.

"I do not speak of *that* sort of love."

"I know of what you speak." His voice was gruff. "I had it with Gisele."

I gaped at him. How, then, could he relinquish her? He looked as if he might cry. I placed my hand over his. "It sounds as if you loved her deeply."

"We loved each other." His voice rasped, gruff.

"As do Abelard and I."

He snatched his hand from mine. "Hmph. Petrus Abaelardus loves no one."

"No, Uncle, you are wrong—"

"Don't speak to me of that traitor—traitor!" He scowled. "Petrus arranged my journey to Anjou with the bishops, saying it would bind me more closely to Galon—but now I know his true reasoning. 'Take your manservant with you,' he said. 'Everyone else will have theirs along.' Hmph! Having coaxed me to do his bidding, he then cajoled his way into your bed. Love—hmph! That self-server knows nothing of love."

My uncle was mistaken about Abelard; of this I had no doubt. But I said nothing, not wanting to anger him.

Grumbling, Uncle Fulbert filled his *henap* and drained it at once, giving me hope that he might drink himself to sleep, after all. I forced a yawn and announced that I would retire to bed. Uncle sent me a suspicious glare as I stood. I slipped my arms around his neck and kissed his cheek, hoping to appease him.

"I am sorry for the pain I have caused you, Uncle. I swear that hurting you or your honor was the least of my intentions. Good night." I took a step toward the stairs.

"Would you depart from me so soon? I have tales to tell you from my journey—many tales! Ah, but if you are tired—let me come up and build a fire for you, since Jean cannot do it."

Only a girl harder of heart than I could watch without gratitude as my uncle carried wood from the stack outdoors up to my room. Only one with no heart at all could listen without softening to his grunts and mild curses as he struck flint to steel again and again, struggling to light the fire that would provide warmth to me as I slept. As he had said, he had given me everything, had shared with me all that he possessed. Perhaps he had loved me in the best way that he knew. In return, I had brought him only humiliation.

And yet—would I have done anything differently? Certainly not, for now I plotted to deceive him again.

"Good night, my dear child," he said, kissing my brow. "This day has gone hard for us both, but the worst is over now." If only his words had been true.

I walked to the hearth and held my hands up to the blaze, whose crackles and pops obscured the sound for which I listened—that of my uncle's steps descending the stairs. They did not, however, block the distinct sound of a turning key in my door.

I hastened to the door and rattled the latch, to no avail. "Uncle Fulbert!" I cried, banging on the wood. "What are you doing? Please, unlock my door."

"And have you run to your lover while I sleep tonight? I have been a fool—a fool!—but no more."

"But—how long shall I remain here? You cannot lock me up forever."

"Do not worry, you shall be free soon enough, heh-heh—when I have ensured that Petrus Abaelardus will never touch you again."

3

**My soul thirsts with incomparable love for the source of
your image, and it can never lead a happy life without
you.**

—HELOISE TO ABELARD

*I*mprisoned in my room, I hadn't the presence of mind to
think of escaping, or to worry about my uncle's threats. I
could think of nothing but Abelard. I went to the window and
gazed up at our planet, the "bright queen of the sky," shining as
brilliantly as my love for him. Had he lain in my arms only this
morning, holding me close, filling my senses with his fragrance
and his delicious heat? Now he had gone, I knew not where—although I could surmise—but this I believed: even as I looked up
at Venus, Abelard gazed at her, too, and yearned for me as I for
him.

Soon, exhausted by the day's travails, I slept and dreamed of
him—or, rather, of a man who said he was my father, although
he had Abelard's dark curls and eyes of laughing blue.

"Why do you worry?" he said. "I will take care of you."

I awoke and stared into the dark, thinking of the man for
whom my mother had given up her only daughter. How she
must have loved my father, to endure pregnancy, childbirth, and
motherhood alone and in utter secrecy, all for his sake.

Queen Bertrade knew him; of this, I felt certain. Kindness had filled her eyes when she'd spoken to me of him, and when I asked her to reveal his name, she'd bitten her lower lip in indecision. At last, she'd refused. Mother had wanted the secret kept, and Bertrade must honor her wishes.

"You will discover the truth for yourself, in time," she said. "You are closer now than you have been before." I departed from the Hautes-Bruyères Priory feeling as heavy as if all my hopes had turned into stones. To come so near to learning the truth pained me more than if I had not gone to Queen Bertrade at all.

"You should not have allowed her to send me off to dinner," Agnes said as we rode home. "I would have persuaded her to reveal all." Knowing my friend's fondness for scandal, I could not agree with her. Although she had helped me, I would not trust her with such a secret.

Yet, what a comfort it might have been to know my father. Even were I unable to contact him, I might have taken solace in some virtue of his, strength or courage or piety or lovingkindness, that I might claim as my own. I could say, "I am my father's daughter." Instead, I had never felt so alone. Even God seemed to have abandoned me; when I prayed, I heard the hollow wind in response and felt only its chill blowing in my window.

But I was not alone. Abelard was with me in spirit, at least. Knowing this provided me with some comfort, but I nonetheless ached for some word from him. My uncle's rage, like a sudden torrent sweeping him out of my reach, had brought a bitter end to the sweetest hours of my life.

During our week together, my heart had opened to Abelard, my precious light, as the tightly furled rosebud expands its petals to the sun. *My lily, my privet,* he'd murmured while filling me with his sweetness, increasing my delight with every touch.

In the morning I tried the latch again, to no avail. My

stomach churned with worry. Had Abelard suffered from his fall down the stairs? What further harm would my uncle wreak? Perhaps Uncle's night's sleep had dulled his anger's edge. I arose and dressed, shivering in the cold, perspiring and dizzy. My stomach felt as though it were falling; water filled my mouth. I lurched to the basin and retched and heaved, but nothing emerged except bile from my empty stomach. I pushed open the shutters and reached for my gourd filled with water from the light rain falling, slicking the street with mud. The lantern boy walked toward our house, waving something to beckon his drenched, mud-plastered dog. When he saw me, the two increased their pace, slapping the mud and dodging a donkey and cart of fish trundling to the market. I nearly cried out: his waving hand carried a wax tablet. Abelard had written to me.

The dog yelped; I lifted a finger to my lips and the boy slowed, murmuring to the animal. I regarded the street and, seeing no one, stripped the cover off my bed and lowered it, leaning over far so that the boy could grasp it. When he had tied the tablet into the cloth, I pulled it up again, then held up one finger. *One hour*, I mouthed: enough time to read the message and form a response.

My pulse ticced against my throat as I sat on my bed and broke the seal.

If that old bull Fulbert harms you, Uncle Etienne shall cut off his horns. Are you faring well, my dear friend? Please write and let me know when I may visit. Abelard had not written, after all, but Agnes. Yet, she knew something of what had occurred. She must have spoken with Abelard; she might be with him now.

I replied saying that I was well, but locked in my room. *Has Abelard taken refuge with Etienne? I must meet with him. Please tell him to write with a time and place.*

An hour passed. The lantern boy returned for my messages,

for I had written not only to Agnes but also to Abelard: *Caged like a bird, I would yet fly to you. Choose a suitable time for our meeting and let me know.* Another hour passed, then another, with no reply. I paced the floor of my room, imagining the worst.

Hunger gnawed at my stomach. Pauline came to the door with fruit, cheese, and bread, but shook her head when I asked her to free me.

"I cannot, or Canon Fulbert will dismiss me. He has already reprimanded me most severely for failing to report your . . . activity . . . with Master Pierre."

"But how could you have known? We took care to be quiet."

She blushed all the way down to her neckline. "You were not quiet."

I dropped my gaze, unable to meet her eyes. Consumed in passion's flame, Abelard and I had burned everyone we'd touched. Yet I could never repent of a single kiss. I could not have restrained myself any more than the wind can control its howling.

When Pauline had gone, I pondered my escape. The bedcover did not reach to the ground, not by any means, but I might climb as far down as I could go, then drop the rest of the way. Yet with the cloth above my reach, how would I climb back up? The truth is, I did not intend to do so.

The bells having tolled terce, the street roiled with horses and riders, dogs, canons stepping gingerly through the mud and around horse droppings, women carrying baskets of bread and meat home for the evening meal, and scholars laughing and jostling one another on their way home for the *relevée*. These were the busiest hours in the cloister library, when, during their long break between the morning and afternoon sessions, students kept my uncle occupied with their requests for books from the shelves. Now would be the perfect time for me to seek Abelard.

When at last the street had cleared, I let down the cloth. It dangled precariously far from the slippery ground; would I fall into the mud? I tied on a tunic from my clothing chests to lengthen the line, made certain the knots were fast, and began my descent.

My arms trembled from the effort as I lowered myself more slowly than I thought prudent, but as quickly as I could confidently go. I erred in looking down and saw the ground swaying below, dizzying me. *Help me, Father*, I prayed, and the Lord provided a surge of strength that enabled me to land softly on my feet.

I did not linger, but hastened to round the corner and step into the alley before anyone might see me. Hewing to the shadows, I slipped through the winding, stinking passage rife with rats and cats, covering my mouth against the steaming odors of garbage and feces. I must have resembled a lowly beggar, judging from the look in Ralph's eyes when he opened the door to me.

I dismissed his arched brow and haughty tone: Was that Abelard's laughter bursting forth from inside? Given my wretched state, it rang as an affront in my ears, or even an attack. He, at least, was faring well. And why should he not? He had not spent the night locked in a cold room or risked his neck escaping imprisonment. He had been deprived of nothing, it seemed, neither comfort nor good humor nor my assurance that I was unharmed. While I had gnashed my teeth imagining what vengeance my uncle might wreak, how had he occupied himself? With laughter as free as if the whole world existed only for him.

Whatever the jest, it certainly amused Ralph. The corners of his mouth twitched as he invited me indoors, then stepped away to fetch Abelard. I smoothed my hair, realizing that, in my haste, I had neglected to braid my hair or put on a fillet. How would I appear to Abelard?

Before I could finish the thought, he came around the corner looking as though someone had thrown cold water in his face. "Why have you come here? Did anyone see you?"

His accusing tone made me nearly forget my answer. Why, indeed, had I come? I hoped Abelard would save me from my uncle—indeed, I expected he would. He loved me, after all. But he stood motionless, his eyes darting about like that of a deer trapped by hounds. Thanks to God that Agnes came in at that moment and recognized what he did not.

"My poor dear! What has happened to you?" She embraced me—as Abelard had not done—and lifted her fingertips to the bruise blooming blue on my cheek. "Who did this? That awful uncle of yours?"

"He is deranged," Abelard said, opening the front door and peering out. "Possessed! Agnes, didn't I tell you so? He did not follow you here, Heloise, did he?"

I stared at him. Who was this thoughtless man with Abelard's perfect face, his eyes like a storm-tossed sea, his wary glance? My Abelard would have pulled me close by now, as Agnes was doing. He would have kissed my wounds, comforting me. He would have rejoiced to see me again so soon, or at all, given the perils we had faced.

"*Pffft*. Don't soil yourself, Pierre. Canon Fulbert cannot harm you here. Now close the door, lest you be seen. Come in, Heloise, and let me take care of you while Pierre regains his good sense," Agnes said.

When I had settled myself, Agnes asked again what had occurred to send me running from my uncle's house. But how could I tell anyone but Abelard? Even she, hearing how we had been discovered together, might judge me a wanton. I could only respond to her inquiries with a flushing face and averted eyes.

At last she left us alone. I stood to kiss her, then turned to

Abelard, expecting his rebuke. Instead, he slipped his arms around me and pulled me close to kiss the bruise on my cheek.

"What has happened? Has Fulbert further harmed you?"

"Not as much as you have done with your indifference."

His shoulders slumped and he released his hold on my waist. His eyes turned down at the corners. "Forgive me, Heloise. I have not known what to do." He paced, raking his fingers through his hair. "I sent you a message, but you did not reply." I told him of Jean-Paul's refusal to return to him. "I thought you blamed me for our being discovered or hated me for leaving you in that demon's care."

His eyes' expression told me that his heart felt as troubled as mine. Now I embraced him, but he soon pulled away.

"Did anyone see you come here?"

"I do not think so. What is wrong, my love?" I reached up to stroke his cheek, wanting only to comfort him—and thusly to be comforted—but he turned away.

"Heloise. You must return home, and quickly."

"What? Why, Abelard?" I tried to meet his gaze but he would not even look at me. "What has happened?"

His short laugh struck me like a slap. "Your uncle caught us in flagrante delicto, or had you forgotten?"

"Of course I had not forgotten." I pressed my hands to my burning face. "Nor had I forgotten the words of love you showered upon me in the moments before he appeared. However, it now seems as if *you* had forgotten them."

"Fulbert came here, uttering threats. I asked many times how you were faring, but he wanted only to exact my promise never to see you again."

"Which, of course, you did not provide."

His face reddened. "I had to do it, Heloise. It was the only way."

"You—you vowed not to see me?" I folded my arms across my stomach.

"His eyes gleamed when he spoke of punishing you, Heloise, and he called you the vilest names." Abelard shuddered. "I made the vow in exchange for his promise not to harm you."

"How could you promise not to see me?" I cried. "I will be gone very soon, locked away from you forever."

"Everything is changed, Heloise."

"We love each other. That will never change."

"But it must."

"Dear Lord, what has come over you?" Tears stung my eyes. "Having taken my virtue and my heart, will you now cast me aside at the first sign of turmoil?"

"Not turmoil, but disaster."

"Why disaster?" I stared at him, trying to comprehend. We had both known the consequences of being discovered together and had decided the rewards were well worth the risk. What of *our* vow to stand together no matter what might happen?

Abelard clasped my hands; his eyes shone with tears. "I shall never forget these months we have shared. I wish it could last forever, that we did not need to part, but—"

"Part!" I pulled my hands from his grasp and pressed them to my chest, trying to quell my heart's palpitations. "Why should we part?"

He frowned. "You know as well as I that we cannot continue as we have done."

"Not as we have done, no. But I can come to you here, as I did before."

"Non."

"But why? Is it because of my uncle's threats? He would not harm you—this you must know. To do so would destroy his career. Nor would he tell Galon about us, for fear of staining his own honor. Believe me, my love: I know my uncle well. We have nothing to fear from him."

"It is not Fulbert whom I fear." He grasped my shoulders and gave me a deep, dark look that sent tremors down my spine. "It is you, Heloise."

I forced a laugh. "I am not so evil, am I?"

"Not evil, but a beautiful distraction." His eyes' caress lifted my spirits, but his next words dashed them again. "I cannot write, Heloise. Not a word."

"Of course you cannot." In response to his anguished tone, I softened my own. "That is to be expected after all we have endured, *non*? Do not worry, my love, your gifts will return. Your Muse—"

"My Muse has abandoned me, and in the midst of my greatest work—a logical explanation of the Holy Trinity, a penetration of that great mystery so profound that it will shake the Church's very foundations. It will dispel every doubt that has ever plagued men." His face shone as though he beheld some faraway vision. "I aim to shine the light of knowledge on Father, Son, and Holy Spirit, illuminating them so that all may understand the threefold nature of God at last."

"Abelard! What a triumph." He turned his eyes to me, and they darkened again. "But why worry yourself? If God has inspired you, he will not forsake you."

"Not the Lord, but my own sin impedes me. I had nearly completed the work and had the final revelation in my grasp. As the clouds of obscurity had begun to part, revealing the light of knowledge—I met you."

He sighed and dropped into a chair, then covered his face with his hands. "I have not written a word since that day on the *place*."

"But your songs . . ." My voice trailed, smothered by inanity.

"I do not refer to those fatuous love songs." My blood ran cold: *fatuous* was the word Suger had used to describe Abelard's music. "The lofty thoughts which used to flood my mind and spill onto the wax will not come to me now. Instead, desire consumes me, and the pleasures of the flesh."

Silence hung between us, heavy with sorrow. Overcome, I seated myself next to him.

"All I had hoped to achieve, the light of understanding I had thought to bring to the world, all have been snuffed by the thick, hot breath of lust. Now I understand why the Church demands continence. Sex may sharpen the senses—never have I felt so alive!—but it dulls the mind. And now, because of my sin, God has taken from me the gifts he had bestowed. I am no longer the brilliant philosopher you thought me to be, but an utter failure."

"But our love is yet new," I said as brightly as I could. "Do you remember how the poet warned against the boredom that time brings to lovers? 'Quarreling's the marriage dowry.' Do you recall?" Ovid had also written that *sweet love must feed on gentle words*. I bit back the harsh ones that sprang, now, to my tongue. The *thick, hot breath of lust*? Was that all our love meant to him? "In time you shall tire of our pleasures, and your lofty thoughts will return."

"Tire of you? That shall never happen, as long as I live. My love for you is too strong—stronger than I by far. And it will destroy me." Abelard's expression closed like a heavy door between us. "Before I knew you, Urania was my Muse, and philosophy my only love. But the Muse is jealous: She gave herself to me freely as long as I devoted myself only to her. Now that I have found another, Urania has fled."

"That is ridiculous!" I leapt to my feet, balling my fists by my sides as if to strike this other "lover." "Urania is neither a woman nor a goddess but an invention, existing only in the imagination.

And *philosophy* is only a word invented to describe certain thoughts and ideas."

"I have taught you well," Abelard said with a smile too fleeting to arouse my hopes. "Call it what you may, philosophy has been my very life until now. I gave up my birthright for philosophy's sake; I have devoted my every hour to seeking, to knowing, and to illuminating the hidden nature of God for the perfection of men's faith. I cannot turn away from her—from it—now, when I have come so close to the prize."

"Let me help you," I said, swallowing my panic, willing myself to breathe.

"Yes. You can help me—yes." His eyes filled with tears afresh. "You can say good-bye to me forever, Heloise, and immediately accept the position at Fontevraud for which you are destined. Only when your sweet temptations are far removed will I be able to work again."

I stared at him, not believing my ears. He wished to part from me now, when so little time remained to us? Suddenly I could not remember my name, or why I had come. I turned and walked across the floor, over the carpets and under the lamps, out the front door, into the pouring rain, through the shit-stinking alley, and around the corner to my uncle's house—but where was my rope? I turned around, saw the gray dog trot by, washed clean by the rain and nearly white except for the red mud stringing from his paws. I looked up at the window again; the shutters were closed. Water ran in cold streams down my face. Shivering, I stepped to the door.

I pulled at the latch; it was locked. I knocked, but no one answered. I huddled against the house, under the eaves, waiting. I knocked again.

The door opened and there stood my uncle, his eyes red and glaring. "There is the last promise your Abelard will ever make to me."

I forbade myself to cringe as I approached. Uncle did not

move, but blocked my entry, leaving me standing in the down-pour.

"He has broken no promises to you today," I said, forbidding my teeth to chatter. I looked Uncle in the eyes. "I tried to see him, but he refused me."

A sickly grin spread across my uncle's face, and he stepped aside. I walked past him with my head high, my heart more knotted than if I had spoken the truth.

4

❦

*I am not a reed shaken by the wind; nor shall any severity
or weakness of any kind take me from you.*
—HELOISE TO ABELARD

In my youth, sorrow tasted of salt from the tears filling my
nose and mouth as I'd sobbed at night for my mother. But
having used all my tears in those days, now my sadness had a different flavor—that of the bile that rose in my throat every morning I awakened without Abelard in my life.

Every morning now, I held my aching stomach. Groaning
over my basin, I would purge myself of Abelard's soft hands, his
smile, his tender words—of everything that made up the sweetness of our love. Only sickness remained. I wished every day that
I had never been born.

Farewell, my sweetest, he wrote to me. *Farewell, more lovable
than anything that can be named.*

He wrote only to say good-bye. Is it any wonder that I did not
care to arise from bed, or that I did not reply? Yet, he continued
to write.

*Farewell, sweeter than everything known to be sweet. I earnestly
beg you to tell me how you are, because your good fortune is my greatest pleasure.* Why should I care about his pleasure? I copied his
letters, then sent them back unanswered. I had nothing to say to

him, who had abandoned me as my mother had done, whose promises of love meant as little as discussions of the weather.

"I have news to improve your spirits!" Uncle said one day when I entered the great room and gave him his morning kiss. He lifted a wax tablet from a table near the hearth and handed it to me.

"Your dowry—my brother has agreed to pay—to pay! Your letter convinced him. You are a master of rhetoric—a master. Petrus Abaelardus has given you that much, at least." He smacked his lips. "This comes at the most opportune time—most opportune. Now we can send you to Fontevraud. Should Robert name you as his abbess, your fame will spread throughout the realm. Galon must promote me then. He will have no choice—no choice!"

I wondered if he could hear my pounding pulse, like running footsteps. The kiss he gave before he departed for the library left a wet smear on my cheek, making my stomach turn over again. He noticed my expression, and his own hardened.

"Behold your face, like an open book!" he said, gripping my arm so tightly that I cried out. "I know what you are thinking, but it is no use, heh-heh. You will depart for Fontevraud as soon as the money arrives."

I turned away, suppressing a shudder, and nearly collided with Jean, now recovered, who watched me with a strange expression. Heat rushed to my face and I hastened down to the kitchen to consult with Pauline about today's dinner.

But Pauline had not arrived. She had fallen ill, meaning that I would need to shop this morning, and cook—and meaning, also, that Jean would accompany me to the market. Realizing that no lock could confine me, my uncle had ceased to imprison me in my bedchambers, but Jean now followed me like a shadow whenever I left the house. *Having marked its territory, the dog will return,* Uncle had said. The excitement in his eyes told me he hoped Abelard would do so and give my uncle an excuse to destroy him.

So I ventured forth for the first time in weeks, having been too proud to endure the humiliation of a guard. The cold weather had abated, although frost lined early-morning streets. Birds sang throaty welcomes to the warming day. I lifted my face to the sun. No matter what Fortune might hold in store for me, I had, at least, this glorious October morning. Yet not even my prayer of thanksgiving could quell my heart's skitter or dispel the dread clinging to me as persistently as my own shadow.

When confronted with the smells of the market, I felt unnaturally queasy and had to cover my nose. Capons roasting over the fire, pungent fish, and the sour odor of wet dogs and horse shit made a stew in my mouth that caused my stomach to lurch.

Was I well? Jean inquired. I nodded. Sorrow afflicted me, nothing more.

At the butcher's stall, I averted my gaze from the sausages and pigs' heads hanging overhead.

"*Bonjour*, pretty one. I have not seen you in such a long time. How does your uncle fare?" The butcher's wife greeted me with a smile that proudly displayed her rotting teeth. Her breath smelled of decay. I swallowed the water rushing to my mouth. She wagged her eyebrows and looked me up and down. "Or—do you live with a husband now?"

When I shook my head, she gave a tsk and pointed to my belly. "You poor girl! Who did this to you? I will send my husband for *his* head to hang in our display."

I murmured, as I purchased the sausages, that I had been ill. She clucked her tongue and shook her head, her lips suppressing a knowing smile. "After the love, the repentance, *non*?"

I did not know the meaning of her remark and said so.

She laughed with her mouth wide-open. "After the feast, the belly grows. You are with child? Of course you are."

Her coarse laugh mocked me as I hastened away, counting the weeks since my last menses. My heart began to pound as I recalled that I had missed my courses not only last month—which had scarcely bothered me, for I had missed a month before—but this month, as well. My uncle's attack and his threats, and Abelard's decision to relinquish our love, had occupied my thoughts, causing me to forget everything except my misery and twisting my stomach into knots, or so I had thought. Now I considered another cause for my illness and felt my sorrows melt away.

To bear his child! To have a part of him with me always, and to be bound to him for the rest of our days! God had heard my prayers, after all. My laughter, like the song of a bird freed from its cage, brought Jean trotting to my side.

"I am sorry I missed her jest," he said of the butcher's wife. "She must have been quite amusing."

"She was, indeed." I refrained from kissing his cheek, dancing in the *place*, falling to my knees in thanks. "I found her exceedingly delightful."

5

*M*y uncle's incessant talk barely drew my notice at dinner that day. Noting my distracted state, Uncle glowered, but why would I care? He would not touch me once he knew of my condition. Nor would Abelard allow me to come to harm. Given my precious cargo, he would certainly remove me at once from Uncle Fulbert's home and his reach.

I could hardly wait to share my news with Abelard. How his chest would puff at the proof of his virility! Even the humblest of men felt pride in their offspring—how much more so would Abelard boast, certain of the superiority of any child he might produce. Despair over his failures would disappear, replaced by joy at this blessing—for it *was* a blessing, a gift from God and a sign of his will for our lives. Without a doubt, the Lord desired that we should be together.

My spirits rose as I contemplated how Fortune's wheel had turned in my favor. I would not go, now, to Fontevraud or any abbey, but would bring up our child here, in Paris, in a home that Abelard would establish for us. I would spend my life not

in dreary, damp halls but in a sunny house; living not in silence but in laughter and play with our blue-eyed boy or girl;
suffering not the twin aches of longing and need as I lay at
night in my cold bed but enjoying Abelard's continued presence and, once Urania returned to inspire him, his joy. This
child would join us together forever. As for the rest, God
would provide.

Seeing my curving mouth and bright eyes, Uncle grinned.
"There's the girl I know, heh-heh." He squeezed my knee under
the table. "I thought I might never see your smile again. Ever
since Petrus came here to live, you have been much altered—
altered! You thought I didn't notice? A blind man would have
seen it. You couldn't take the time to talk with your old uncle
after supper anymore. You could hardly eat, eager for your
nightly lesson."

His expression darkened. He poured the cup's contents down
his throat, then slammed the *henap* onto the table.

"By God," he said, reddening. "You were with him all the
while, weren't you—all the while! As I sat here alone with only
the servants for company, the two of you rutted like beasts over
my head. Laughing at my ignorance, no doubt—at your stupid,
naïve uncle." He lowered his head, reminding me of a bull
before the charge. "I ought to beat you until you're black-and-
blue. I ought to hurt your body the way you've pained my
heart."

Does a stone feel pain? I wanted to retort. My uncle's pride,
not his heart, had suffered—but I held my tongue. He must
have read my thoughts in my eyes, for the hand with which he
had patted my knee now gripped my thigh cruelly, sinking his
fingernails into the skin. In another moment, he would strike
me. Thinking of the child's safety, I lowered my gaze and
begged his forgiveness. I had thought only of my own selfish

desires, and not of him at all, I said, an easy admission since it was true.

When I had placated him, I gave him a kiss on the cheek and, yawning, excused myself for a *relevée* nap. I would need to tell my uncle very soon that I carried a child—but first I must go to Abelard.

On my way to the staircase, I heard a knock at the front door and opened it to Agnes, who appeared as spring itself in a saffron *bliaut* embroidered with birds. I embraced her, wondering if she felt any rounding of my stomach. One question from her in my uncle's presence might arouse his suspicions—and cause him to lock me in my room again. I took her hands and led her into the garden, away from listening ears.

"Dear Lord, what has happened to you?" She perused my face and form with startled eyes. "You're as pale as a wraith. Have you been ill?"

I hesitated. Dared I tell her? But she knew of my love for Abelard and had encouraged it. Pressing a finger to my lips, I pointed to my womb.

She grasped my meaning in an instant; delight filled her eyes. "May it be so!" She took my hands in hers. "Then we might keep you with us. Yes, I am selfish. I don't wish to give you up to the convent." She pulled me close and held me, O splendid embrace, human touch elusive to me all my days and nights except those spent with Abelard. The warmth of her, her beating heart, the circle of her enfolding arms: Was that a tear of gratitude on my lashes? I lifted my finger to touch it, but it was gone.

"You must go to Pierre with your news, *non?*" She clapped her hands. "Then when you have seen him, tell us if he is faring poorly or well. He has barred himself in his quarters—to work, he says. I think he's nursing his broken heart. At any rate, he cannot turn *you* away, not now."

I frowned. That he might refuse my call had not occurred to me, for he had never done so before. Yet he had begged me to depart from him forever. Would my news change his mind, or would he resent me for interfering again in his work?

"I cannot bear the thought of his rejection," I said, pleading with my eyes. "What if he is displeased? Will he point the finger at me, as if I had conceived the child without his assistance?"

She laughed. "Such is the way of great men, *non*? They think themselves infallible, as they must."

I grasped her hands. "Agnes, will you tell him for me? Then you could send me a note informing me of his response. A note would not distress me nearly as much as seeing his eyes fill with bitterness."

She shook her head. "I would help you if I could, but he will not speak to me. When last I visited, he would not open his door—to me, and I have known him all my life. He sees no one. He eats very little, Ralph says; he doesn't sleep, but burns the lantern all night. He is working, but Uncle Etienne thinks he has lost all the pleasure his writing once provided him."

"For naught, then, has he abandoned me and rejected our love."

She widened her eyes. "Your bitter tone surprises me. How could Pierre do otherwise? Canon Fulbert threatened to cut off his *colei*." She grinned to see me flinch at the vulgar term. "But Abelard's love for you hasn't diminished. As much as he fears your uncle's blade, Uncle Etienne says, he worries even more that harm will come to you."

"If he fears for me, he has a strange way of showing it. Until today, I had not heard a word from him."

"And why do you think he wrote to you today? The lantern boy heard you crying out last night."

I stared at her. I had dreamed that my uncle was stabbing

Abelard with his knife and had awakened myself with my cries. The sound had brought Jean running to my room, but I had not realized I could be heard on the street.

"The lantern boy? He must have worked very late," I said.

"So he does every night. Pierre pays him to keep vigil at your uncle's house whenever Canon Fulbert is at home. At the first sign of trouble, Pierre would send someone to help you."

"But he would not come to me himself?"

"How could he do so? Did you know that Pierre's scholars have complained about him to Bishop Galon? He neglects his classes, they say. One word against Pierre from Canon Fulbert might cost him his position at the school. Would you want that to happen?" Agnes shook her head. "Selfish though I am, I would never wish the man I love to give up his life for me."

Soon I had bathed and dressed and slipped down the alleyways to Etienne's house to share my news with Abelard. A child of our own! Now reassured of his love for me, I hoped he would greet the news with as much joy as I felt. Abelard had watched over me. He had not withdrawn his love, but only his presence, and certainly not his protection from the danger my uncle posed. Now, by God's grace, I would bear his child, not as a consolation for losing him—for he had never left me—but as a gift to us both.

When I knocked on Etienne's door, not Ralph but Etienne himself opened it to me. "Welcome, Heloise. Agnes told me you would come. Please, come in and join me in the garden." He led me through the house into the courtyard. I seated myself on a bench in the shade and he sat beside me, his face expectant as though I had come to talk with *him*. Though I would not have insulted Etienne for anything in the world, I needed to speak with Abelard and told him so. But he shook his head. He had already knocked at Abelard's door and told him I would visit. *Send her home*, Abelard had said.

My face filled with heat, and I looked down at my clenched hands. What must Etienne think of my coming here after Abelard had commanded me to stay away? I must appear pitiful in his eyes, or careless of my beloved's desires. But when I looked up at Etienne, I saw only loving concern.

"I must speak with him," I said.

Etienne drew his brows together. Pierre admitted no one to his quarters, he said, not even Etienne himself. "When at first he hid himself away, I worried. But I had forgotten how he used to be. To make certain that he fared well, I opened a window and beheld him stooped over his desk, surrounded by trays of uneaten food, stumps of burned candles, and broken tablets, his beard grown like weeds over his face and his fingers clutching a stylus."

As Etienne watched, Abelard wrote, scratched out words, wrote some more, then scraped the wax clean to begin again, cursing and crying all the while.

Had a demon possessed him? Had he gone mad? I rose to my feet. "He needs me. You must take me to him, Etienne."

"He needs you least of all."

I stared at this man who had once professed friendship to me. Had he now become my foe?

"No one achieves what Pierre has done without complete dedication to his studies. God is my witness, Heloise: philosophy obsesses him, or it did before he met you. Pierre dined on ideas, drank deep drafts of discussion, dreamt about Plato and Porphyry. Every inhalation of breath provided a question, and every exhalation, an answer. I had never seen a man so possessed." Etienne paused. "Neither have I witnessed such a struggle as Pierre's these past months. His love for you has given him much pleasure, yes, but I have seen him falter in his work as though love were a rope binding him."

Abelard's love for me *had* caused paralysis—of his mind, Etienne said. "In earlier times, he lived for a higher purpose, but no more. Now, Heloise, he lives only for you, and for love."

Wherein lay the fault in living for love? I wanted to argue. If Abelard thought knowledge the way to God, he had erred. The only true path to goodness—to God—is love.

"We can see how this love has altered him," Etienne said. "He used to carry himself with pride, strutting like a cock. Now he stoops and walks like an old man. He is diminished."

I shook my head. If love had impaired Abelard in certain ways, I said, it had improved him in others. Having always taken what he wanted from life, he had learned to give. Now, he thought of another besides himself. Abelard had cared for me, consoled me, exalted me, and now, even in the midst of his crisis, watched over me to ensure my well-being. He had written beautiful songs for me, and not only for me but for all who knew love, which was why the minstrels still sang them in every *place*. Women adored Abelard because, with his songs, he'd taught men how to love them. I could find nothing to lament in the diminishment of his arrogance and pride.

Yet, his anguish over being unable to write had affected me deeply. Not for anything would I deprive him of his soul's sustenance—or so I had thought. Now I would do whatever I must for the sake of our child.

"Etienne, I love Abelard and do not wish to interfere with his work. But it cannot be helped. I have urgent news for him that he must hear." He shook his head, his eyes regretful. "Please, Etienne. As God is my witness, I will not ask again. If you are my friend—"

"Of course I am your friend."

"Then allow me to speak with Abelard once more. Only allow me to knock at his door, I pray. When he hears why I have come, he will admit me."

"Perhaps you would consider telling *me* your news. I would help you if I could."

My secret sprang to my lips—were I to tell Etienne of the child, he would lead me to Abelard in the instant, I knew. But I resisted the urge. Etienne had known Abelard for many years not only as a friend, but also as a benefactor. I would let my beloved decide whether to confide in him, and when.

How, then, to move Etienne to grant my request? If only I could cry! Tears would certainly influence him. Instead, I resorted to hyperbole.

"Etienne, I beg you," I tried once more, reaching for his hand. "I must speak with Abelard. It is a matter of life and death."

My words had the desired effect. He lifted his gaze sharply to mine before, at last, relenting. "How could I say no to such a heartfelt plea?" He rose to his feet, helping me to mine, and led me outdoors to the servants' quarters, where he rapped on the door. Hearing Abelard's reply, Etienne bowed to me before stepping across the courtyard and into his manor.

"For the love of God, why can't you all leave me be?" Abelard said through the door. "I am working and must have solitude."

"Please open the door. For the love of Heloise."

Silence was my answer. I pressed my ear to the door: Had he gone away?

I rapped on the wood with my knuckles, hoping he could hear me. "Abelard, I must speak with you. It is urgent." Still hearing no response, I added, "If you won't open your door for Heloise, then do it for our child."

I heard the bolt slide in the latch.

The door swung open and he stood before me, unkempt, nearly wild, his overgrown hair waving like a mane, his face unshaven and his eyes shot with blood, and the same plain tunic I had seen on my last visit hanging even more loosely on his thin frame.

"A child?" he said in a hoarse voice, then thrust out his chest and grinned. "The men of le Pallet are known for our fertile seed."

I laughed, dizzy with relief, and stepped into his arms, which he wrapped around me so tightly that I could hardly breathe. But who needs breath when one is attached, heart to heart, to the very source of life? My blood changed to wine, intoxicating me, as I inhaled his fragrances—apple, aniseed, and soap, for although unkempt he had, at least, bathed—and I forgot myself completely as he led me into the house to his bed.

"Show me," he said, lifting my *bliaut*.

I pulled the tunic over my head, revealing my belly, and his gaze wandered over it as though he could see the growing child within. He lowered his head and kissed me there, filling me with warmth. His hands stroked my waist, my back, and my thighs, making me gasp at the feeling, nearly forgotten, of flesh, his and mine, liquid with desire, running together like confluent streams.

"I must return to my uncle's soon," I protested as he began to remove the rest of my clothes, but he heeded me not and I did not resist. Soon I lay naked beneath his devouring mouth, ravished by kisses along the tender undersides of my arms, his lips suckling at my nipples and sending waves of pleasure coursing down to my *cunnus*, which became a well. The kisses he bestowed upon me there, the sight of his curly head between my parted thighs, the stroke of his fingers inside me, intensified my pleasure until I burst forth in a cry, or, rather, a song, a note struck deep within that reverberated through my being. On and on I sang as ecstasy rose to bliss, and bliss rose to oblivion. I forgot all else, for nothing else mattered but Abelard and me, together again until the end of our days.

"Heloise, my singular joy, my honey-dripping comb." Tears roughened his voice and shone on his face. "Life without you had lost all its sweetness." Kissing my lips, my hair, and my cheeks as though *I* were the one who cried, he begged forgiveness for abandoning me.

"It hurt me that you did so, but I understand your reasons." Deciding not to mention his jealous mistress, I added, "My uncle carries a sharp knife. Anyone would be afraid."

Abelard snorted. "I don't fear your uncle's knife. Let him try to touch me with it! *Non*, not his blade, but the sharp edge of his tongue frightened me. He could cut me off from everything that has ever mattered to me."

"And yet, knowing the dangers, you lie with me now."

"When the lantern boy reported your screams, I thought the worst had happened. If Fulbert had harmed you, I would have killed myself, I swear it." I suppressed a smile; Abelard loved himself too much to take his own life. "He can do to me what he likes, now. God is my witness, my jewel, my unique one: without you, I would not want to live. Because life is nothing to me without your love."

"I thought you lived for your mistress Urania," I could not resist saying now.

He waved his hands as if dispelling a fog. The Muses are mere inventions, he said, echoing the sentiments I had expressed. His difficulties with the stylus had nothing to do with the jealousy of imagined mistresses, he added—or with loving me.

"I could not write because I did not discipline myself. How shall I think great thoughts when I neglect to set aside the time?" He gestured toward his desk, upon which he had set many tablets one upon the other—all filled with words that he had *not* scratched out. "Philosophy requires diligence and commitment. I needed only devote myself to my studies now as in the past, and *voilà*. Urania returned to me. As you have done." He clutched me more tightly and kissed me all over my face. "If only we never had to part from each other again."

I laughed. "What could separate us now except death?"

He creased his brow. "But you will depart for Fontevraud soon."

"And take the veil while heavy with child? To do so may suffice for one of Robert's *meretrices*, but I have no intention of bringing up a boy or girl in the abbey, as I was raised." I shuddered. "And of course, *our* child will know its father."

He paled. "And what of the father himself? What will be his fate?"

"He shall continue on the path to glory, with a mistress and child always waiting to receive him."

"But you know that cannot be."

"Cannot be?" I frowned. "But why not? God has willed it."

"Does God will my ruin? I have taken a vow of continence, or had you forgotten?"

"And who demanded it of you? William of Champeaux, a mere schoolmaster. Surely no one expects you to emulate *him*, whom you have already surpassed—unless you wish to become a bishop, too, or a mad ascetic."

"I am supposed to set an example for my scholars—of virtue, not vice."

"To which vice do you refer? Love?"

"Lust. Fornication. Deception. Now the truth will be written on your body, for all to see. Dear God, how could we have let this happen?"

"How, indeed?" Emotion flooded me, sweeping me up from

the bed and onto my feet, where I pulled on my clothes with such force that I tore my tunic. "Suddenly I am asking myself that very question."

"My work, my reputation, my very life—I could lose all."

"Are you referring to the life which is nothing without my love?"

Abelard stood, too, and walked to the farthest end of the room. "Fulbert is to blame. You are in his care, and yet he gave you to me for the price of a few silver coins."

"He trusted you."

"'Would you trust timid doves to a hawk? Would you trust the full fold to a mountain wolf?'"

"I would not repeat those lines to him, were I you." My uncle had already blamed the *Ars amatoria* for my sins and returned the book to the scriptorium.

"Does it matter what I say? He will kill me, anyway."

"'There's no fairer law than that the murderous maker should perish by his art.'" I could quote from Ovid as readily as he.

"How can you speak so callously? Don't you care about my fate?"

"And what of mine?" My voice rose. "I hoped you would take me in—that you would bring me here to live with you."

"Are you possessed?" He stared at me as though I were strange to him.

"The child is growing, Abelard. Soon my condition will become visible. What will happen to me once my uncle notices?" *What he forced your mother to do was more shameful.* Queen Bertrade's words struck me with foreboding, like a fist to my chest. I sat on the bed's edge, trying to calm my careening pulse. Uncle would deprive me, too, of my child; indeed, he must do so in order to send me to Fontevraud.

"You, at least, do not have to fear for your life."

"If he takes our child from me, I shall kill myself."

"Take the child? Why would he do so?" Abelard frowned. "You are inventing difficulties before they arise."

I stood and crossed the room to him, holding out my hands, taking his in my own. "You will not allow it, will you, Abelard? You will protect us?"

"Protect you—from that demon? I could not defend you before." He withdrew his hands. "Indeed, the best protection for us both would be your return home, and an end to these meetings of ours."

I gasped. "Would you abandon me again? Would you cast aside the mother of your child? Would you leave me to the mercy of my uncle?"

"You speak of Fulbert as though he were a monster, or a demon. He will not harm you, Heloise, not when he learns about the child. The worst he would do is send you away, which might be better for us both."

"May God damn you!" I shouted. "You care only about yourself, and nothing for me. *Non.* Do not bother to protest. I see the expression on your face. A few moments ago, when my body was a source of pleasure to you, your eyes were as soft as a kitten's. But in the instant I mention responsibilities, you shut the door of your heart."

"At least I possess a heart."

"And I do not?"

"Our world is crumbling, I stand to lose my very life, and you have just cursed me. Where is *your* heart, Heloise? Where are your womanly tears?" His eyes flashed defiance; he thrust out his chin. "Do you realize that I have never seen you cry? It makes me wonder, yes, whether you possess a heart."

"And I wonder where are your *colei.*"

"I appreciate your concern for my testes, now that I stand an even greater chance of losing them."

I looked around for an object to hurl at him but, finding nothing, threw words, instead—words that would haunt me until the end of my days.

"If losing them would diminish your incredible arrogance, then I would cut them off myself."

6

Farewell, my bright star, golden constellation, jewel of virtues, sweet medicine for my body.
—HELOISE TO ABELARD

I was a brittle tree blown by the wind, on the verge of snapping. I was a pear left on that tree too long, bitter and rotting.

Abelard had cast me aside again, not only me but also his child, leaving us to the mercies of my uncle, who had awaited me in my room when I returned.

"You've been to see him, haven't you? Whore!" he screamed as he struck me to the floor. Panting, he seized my hair; I cried out as, with his other hand, he tore at my clothes and flesh, his eyes wild until, thanks be to God, Jean ran in, waving his arms, and shouted at him to stop. Uncle had no choice, then, but to release me, but not without a kick to my back, which I had turned to him, protecting my child—*our* child.

As I lay on the floor, cradling my belly and moaning, Jean made my bed, then lifted me onto it. Now I remained in my room, not locked in but refusing to leave, scorning my uncle's entreaties, fearing for my little one's very life. Perhaps Abelard had spoken the truth, and telling Uncle Fulbert about the child would stop him from striking me, but I dared not risk his wrath again. He might hurt the baby or, worse, take it from me, as he had taken me from my mother.

My uncle had forced her to abandon me—this I knew, as surely as I knew my own name. The memories now rushed in a great torrent: the lilt and ripple of my mother's voice, golden and warm; the powdery softness of her skin when she pressed her cheek to mine; and her fragrance, like the spring breeze. Mother! We must have had servants in our home, but perhaps, as Bertrade had said, she'd sent them away to avoid my being discovered, for in my mind there is only Mother, humming and laughing as she danced me, spinning, in her arms; Mother teaching me to read from a book of hours whose angels seemed nearly to leap from the page; Mother holding me close in her feather bed and singing me to sleep, her voice, that final night, choked with sobs.

I remembered our journey on her palfrey of gray, her arms about my waist as my uncle led us by the reins. The horse's rocking, as steady as the beating of my mother's heart, lulled me to sleep; when I awakened, with a pain in my neck that made me cry, she pointed to the stone buildings towering over us like rain clouds. Their gloomy appearance only increased my tears. When she bent down to kiss my cheek, her face was wet, also.

We stopped, and Uncle Fulbert came with raised arms to help me down. I clung to Mother, crying all the more, sensing that this strange man had nothing good in store for me. My mother's tears exceeded mine as she pulled my hands from around her neck and told me she was sorry, that she loved me, and that she would write to me often. Then my uncle carried me, squeezing the breath from me, through the great wooden doors of the Argenteuil Abbey. I flailed and kicked, screaming for my mother. He smacked my bottom so hard that, for days afterward, it hurt me to sit down.

"Keep still," he said. "My sister has spoiled you. He who spares the rod hates his child."

Inside the abbey's outer door, he set me down, his hand grasping my hair to stop me from fleeing.

"Dry your tears, now, and act like a lady. Our family is known here. Do you want to bring shame on us all?" When I wailed for my mother, he shook me so hard my teeth rattled. "They won't spare the rod here, do you hear me?"

Then, seeing that I did not comprehend, he snarled, "If you ever want to see your mother again, you will do as I say, and mind the abbess." No girl was ever so compliant, then, as I—until now.

Uncle would deprive me of my child, as well. How could I stop him? Being my guardian, he might do as he pleased. Even were I to murder him—I banished the thought as soon as it occurred—I would lose our baby, for the Church or the king would hang me by the neck for such a crime.

For days I heard nothing from Abelard, as I had expected. I knew well enough, by then, the vagaries of his temperament, how he shifted like the winds between desire and fear. My uncle's knife-waving threats had turned his dreams into nightmares—or, rather, night-stags. *Your uncle is not a good man.* I, too, feared Uncle Fulbert, and well understood Abelard's impulse to hide himself. If my uncle learned that Abelard had impregnated me, he certainly would hurt him.

But what of my sorrowing heart, and of my yearning for Abelard's words of comfort? Occupied with his own travails, he could not concern himself with me now—but I knew he would not stay away for long. My news had stricken him like a bolt of lightning; I had seen fear's glimmer in his eyes, and his hands' tremble. In time he would recover and tell me what we must do, and I would consent. In all the world, I never cared to please anyone else but Abelard.

I sat at my window, waiting for a message from him, or a sign. On the third day, I received his tablet—brought, to my great surprise, by Jean. Godfrey, the bishop of Amiens, had died. Bishop Galon and a delegation including my uncle would depart in the morning for his funeral. *Gather your belongings and come to me tomorrow at nightfall. Jean will help you. He has become our ally against Fulbert.*

The following night I packed my clothes, my astralabe, and our letters. Jean carried them as he followed me through the shadowed alleys to Etienne's courtyard, where Abelard waited with two saddled horses. He pulled me into his arms and kissed my mouth as Jean averted his gaze.

"Where are we going?"

Abelard jerked his chin toward Jean. "Not *we*, my love, but you and Jean." He could not abandon his classes and his students, especially in light of the complaints lodged against him. "Jean will care for you in my stead, won't you, Jean?"

"I shall give Heloise my full attention, *magister*."

"But where are we going?"

Abelard took me by the hand and led me indoors, to his chambers. "I am sending you away. Fulbert shall never find you."

"Away from you? But why can't I remain here?"

He pressed his lips together. "You know why." Soon my belly would grow, presenting proof of our sin to all and increasing my uncle's hatred.

"Jean told me what Fulbert did, how he hit you with his fist," Abelard said. "You cannot remain with him, and you cannot live here. Etienne has enemies and detractors of his own at court. We must not involve him in our troubles, especially if they involve a scandal."

In the face of these arguments I could only agree, but with the heaviest of hearts.

"But you will not part from me completely. I am sending you to Brittany, to my family's manor, to give birth to our child in the same room where I was born. Your wish, my love, will come true at last: you will greet my relatives. I only hope that, when all is finished, you will love me yet."

I fell upon him, then, with kisses and embraces and tears. "Nothing can alter my love for you."

His laughter rang like music. How I would long to hear that song during all the months that followed!

"You speak rashly, I fear," Abelard said. "You do not know my family."

Jean and I traveled through the night, I wearing a nun's habit that Etienne had provided. Agnes had assisted me with the cumbersome garment, so weighty and voluminous that I wondered how I would sit upright on the horse for long. To complete the disguise, she enfolded my head and neck in a wimple. My severe appearance reminded me of the Reverend Mother Basilia at Argenteuil.

"I hope that Jean will be guard enough for you on the highways," Agnes said as she adjusted the wimple. She arched her brows at Abelard, who stood ready to help me onto my horse.

"Jean grew up a villein, butchering his lord's cattle," Abelard said. "He knows well how to wield a knife."

"But will one man suffice to protect her against highwaymen? Journeying at night is especially dangerous."

"No one would attack a habit-wearing nun," Abelard said. "Even marauders fear for their mortal souls."

"Those who possess souls fear for them," Agnes said. "Didn't you hear of the two sisters traveling together last month? They were on pilgrimage to Saint-Jacques-de-Compostelle when robbers—knights, I heard—snatched them off their horses, raped them, and took their purses."

"But they did not contend with Jean," Abelard said, "or with the fearsome Sister Madeleine." He reached inside my habit and tied a knife in its sheath under my arm. The looks he gave me were meant to reassure, but I saw concern in his eyes. He handed me a purse filled with silver, which I tied to my girdle, also hidden under the folds of cloth. Jean would accompany me to Orléans, where a boatman would steer me down the Loire to Nantes, a journey of about seven days. From there, Abelard's brother Dagobert would escort me from Nantes to le Pallet, the family's manor.

A boat? I shuddered. Abelard knew well that I couldn't swim.

"It is the safest way for you, far from the reach of highway-men." He tossed his head, proud. "And so, you see, I have thought of everything and have arranged all to ensure your safe passage."

"But—seven days on a boat?" I remembered my fall into the Seine, how water had poured into my mouth and nose, how my tunic had dragged at my feet, pulling me down.

"Where is your strength, Heloise? You can do this. You must do it—for me, and for our child."

I mounted the horse—with difficulty, given the weight of my garments—and Abelard bowed to me. "Sister Madeleine, may God go with you."

Satisfied with the disguise he had given me—never mind the sin of wearing a nun's habit when I had not taken the veil—he smiled broadly, as though sending me on a voyage for pleasure. My own smile wavered. I did not want to leave Abelard; indeed, doing so was the furthest thing from my desires. Yet, in doing his bidding, I knew that I embodied the highest love. I had cast aside my own desires for his sake—he who mattered more to me than anyone else, including myself.

7

Nobody—except Death—will ever take you from me, because I would not hesitate to die for you.
—HELOISE TO ABELARD

*H*ad I worried about drowning in the Loire? That first night, as the rain poured down, weighting my woolen mantle, drenching my wimple, sending rivulets streaming into my eyes and dripping from my nose, I thought I might succumb to the water from the sky before even reaching the river. I thought I might dissolve into nothing with not even my soul left intact. We trotted our horses to Orléans as briskly as we dared with only the moon to light our way, for we must meet the boat at daybreak. My cold-stiffened hands barely grasped my palfrey's reins; the *ta ga da* of hooves on the wide stone road nearly, but not quite, kept pace with my frantic heart's beat. I worried that the ride might injure the infant I carried. I wondered why Abelard had not arranged a hiding place for me that was nearer to him. Had he sent me away so that he might put me out of his mind, as my mother had done? *Non*—sending me to Argenteuil had not been her will, but my uncle's. What would Abelard say when Uncle Fulbert returned to Paris and found me gone?

When first we stopped to rest, in the ruins of an old Roman building, I decided to ask Jean for his thoughts. First I wanted to know why he helped Abelard now when he disliked him so.

"Canon Fulbert went too far. I hate to see a man abusing a woman. It isn't right to use our God-given strength against creatures weaker than us, except our children when they need correcting."

"My uncle yet considers me a child, I suppose."

"Your slight figure and your quiet voice make you seem younger than your years. But Canon Fulbert should not drink so much wine as to forget himself like that."

Distraught by my uncle's behaviors, Jean had gone to warn Abelard of the dangers I faced.

"It broke my heart to see you lying on the floor. I wanted to quit my post, but Master Pierre urged me to remain—for your protection."

"And that of our child."

"Pardon?" One glance at Jean's expression and I knew that I had erred. But I could not take back my words. "Pardon? Did you say something about a child?"

Being an incompetent liar, I was forced to confess the truth.

Jean's eyes narrowed. "He has impregnated you? Very careless—very disgusting! Forgive me, but I do not know which of the two is more despicable, the canon or the master. Both have wronged you and caused you to suffer."

His face ticced with anger, which I felt compelled to relieve if I could. "No one has done anything to me, but rather I have done it to myself." Had I the opportunity, I would have done it all again—but this I did not say to Jean, not while he sneered in contempt over Abelard's "sin" and called him the "snake in the garden."

"I wonder on whose side you stand, Jean, my uncle's or that of Master Pierre?"

He jutted his jaw. "I stand with you."

I grasped his hand and squeezed it as I thanked him. Jean had always shown complete loyalty to me.

In spite of my misery I was almost sorry when the rain ceased, for Jean had said it kept the robbers in their caves. It did slow our progress, however, so that when the sun's light spilled over the horizon, we had to gallop our horses over the treacherous Roman road with its slippery stones. I fretted over the baby's safety, hating to jostle it, but I feared highwaymen even more. Then, when we had almost reached Orléans, the dreaded event occurred: two mounted men emerged from within the woods and, waving knives, demanded Jean's purse. Neither wasted more than a glance at the poor, bedraggled nun.

Jean's smile shimmered like a mirror. "If you want my purse, you will have to take it from me."

One of the men leapt from his horse, ran to me, and dragged me from my saddle. Almost without thinking I slipped my right hand into my left sleeve and grasped my knife.

"Now what do you say, old man?" the robber said, holding me fast against him. "Which do you value—your coins or her virtue?" He squeezed one of my breasts so hard that I cried out. His breath smelled of rotten eggs. As his hand moved down to pat my body—feeling for my purse, no doubt—I slashed his forearm. As he shrieked, Jean rushed forward with his own knife and stabbed him in the stomach. The robber doubled over, clutching his bleeding wound with both hands, and Jean turned to the other attacker—who turned tail to the wind and rode away. We left the injured man lying in the mud.

"We must help him," I said.

Jean shook his head. "No, he is paying the price for wickedness, as we all must do. He is in God's hands now, or the devil's, but you are in mine—and my task is to put you on the boat to Nantes."

So we rode away with the poor man's whimpers scratching at my soul.

We arrived at terce, several hours later than planned—but found the boat at the appointed place. "Monsieur Pierre promised me an additional livre if I waited for you," said the boatman, whose unshaven face made me want to scrub it with soap.

Jean frowned and said that no one had told him of the promise nor given him a sum that large. He paid the man two livres' worth of silver, causing him to scowl. "One livre pays the fare, and one is for your lodgings. You will receive two more when you have delivered the sister safely to Nantes—*if* you do so."

"*If* I do so? Of course I will." He cleared his throat and spat at Jean's feet. "That is what I think of your *if*, ha ha! Albert the Boatman always delivers his cargo unharmed, and in good time."

"Bretons," Jean muttered as he kissed me farewell. "As crude as swine, and not nearly as intelligent. I do not like leaving you in his care."

"I will be well. As you have seen, I can take care of myself."

Jean grinned. "Sister Madeleine, the Holy Terror. I hope that highwayman lives so that he may tell the tale."

The boat slipped slowly down the churning stream. Albert the Boatman never looked at me except to glare and rarely spoke. His manner suited me, as I had no desire to converse with him. I would rather he kept his eyes on the river. Merely to look at the murky water caused me to perspire; the boat's rocking motion made me grip the sides in a vain effort to steady myself. After several hours, exhausted from the nightlong ride, I curled up on the boat's bottom and fell asleep, awakening only at the lurch and scrape of our landing. I shivered and pulled my mantle close. Dusk had already begun to suck the light from the sky.

With a grunt the boatman lifted the lighter of my sacks, hoisting it over his shoulder, and left me to carry the heavier one up the bank to the tavern where we would sleep. With one look I could see that Albert the Boatman had no intention of spending Abelard's livre on lodgings. The timbered, two-story building, slumping on one side and leaning to the left, appeared as though it, too, had been built by the Romans. Inside, a crowd of men reeked of body odor and wine. The proprietor greeted the boatman with a grin and a flagon, which Albert took to a table with hardly a nod in my direction. The tavern keeper took both my sacks and led me up an unlit stairwell to a tiny room covered in grime and mouse droppings. Supper, he said, would be served downstairs.

In the dining hall, I forced down the thin, sour-tasting soup and dry, dark bread that passed for supper, thinking of the child in my womb, who needed nourishment. I kept my eyes before me, ignoring the stares directed my way. At the table beside mine, four men rolled dice and swore more loudly than necessary, and most foully—for my benefit, no doubt. When, finished with my supper, I passed them to return to my room, one of the men grabbed my habit and pulled me into his lap. I struggled to stand, my face burning. I reached inside my sleeve for my knife—but then rough hands pulled me up and tossed me aside, then flung the offender to the floor. Albert the Boatman had decided to take care of me, after all.

"I always deliver my cargo unharmed," he said, and commanded me to my room, where I went most willingly.

I spent the night with open eyes, every sound jarring me awake whenever I began to drift off to sleep: the scratching of a mouse in the corner; the thud of footsteps on the stair, and stumbles, and curses; and, once, the rattle of the latch on my door, which I had not been able to lock. I sat up in bed with a cry. The door opened and the boatman's face appeared.

"How do you fare, Sister?" he slurred. "Never fear. I am here to protect you." He closed the door; soon I heard the creak of hinges and, through the thin walls, his stumbling steps, as loud as if he were in my room. I heard his fall onto his bed, his mumbled curse, and, only a moment later, his snores, so jarring that I thought the groaning timbers of the hotel had given way at last. After a long while I slid back under the thin bedcovers to hunch against the cold, keep wide-eyed vigil against intruders and ro-dents, and ask, *Why?*

Why had Abelard sent me on this treacherous journey alone, placing me in the care of this loathsome stranger whose only con-cern was for his purse? Six days remained until we reached Nantes, and I knew already that every night would pass as this one had, in the most disreputable and unaccommodating hovels, as Albert the Boatman hoarded his coins. Abelard had thought little of my well-being, it seemed, in his haste to send me as far away as possible. A knot formed in my throat and my eyes burned. I pulled the covers over my head and closed my eyes and waited through the night for tears or sleep, neither of which ever came.

8

꧁꧂

I am the person I have been. Nothing has changed in me concerning my ardor for you, except that every day the flame of love for you rises even more.

—ABELARD TO HELOISE

As I had predicted, my ship's captain steered me from one pestilential port to another, each seemingly worse than before. One room lacked even a candle for light; morning revealed bloodstains on my mattress. I learned to sleep amid the cold, the filth, and the smells of rotting meat, urine, and excrement. Embarking on the river, which had terrified me at first, now came as a relief. There the air, although cold, blew fresh and moist on my face, and the banks offered an always-changing variety of sights. Villeins worked in the vineyards, collecting the remnants of the season's harvest, their voices rising in song. A herd of deer foraged at the river's edge. Trees waved their limbs in the soughing breeze, yellow leaves lighting the branches like candle flames at Christmas. A lump formed in my throat at the thought of the holiday just two months hence. I had looked forward to observing it with Uncle this year, with family for the first time since my childhood. Now I would celebrate our Lord's birth in a strange land, parted from the only one I love.

On the third night of our journey, as the tavern keeper showed me to yet another decrepit room, he asked if I were traveling to the Fontevraud Abbey. "I hear Robert of Arbrissel has returned from his preaching, and that he has taken ill." The man grinned. "Even as he lies at the door of death, the pretty women seek him out. By God's head, I should have been a preacher instead of a tavern keeper."

His remarks gave me an idea. I had planned to write to Robert once I had settled in with Abelard's family at le Pallet—but, with the abbey so near, why shouldn't I visit him, instead? Perhaps I might ask him about my mother and gain some clues to my father's identity. Indeed, hearing that he lay ill made me determined to do so, lest he die and carry my mother's secrets with him. But when I presented the plan to Albert, he refused.

"I was hired to take you directly to Nantes, and to arrive on Thursday afternoon," he said, thrusting out his jaw.

"But I must visit the abbey. Robert of Arbrissel is dying, and I must give him a message."

"If it's only a message, we could hire someone to deliver it, had we the coin."

I went into my room, loosened the money pouch on my girdle, and extracted two deniers.

"Would this suffice?" I offered him one of the coins.

His eyes bulged. "Such a large amount only to deliver a message? I would do it myself for less."

"Indeed, I meant the coin for you, should you do my bidding." Greed leapt in his eyes. "Will you take me, then, to Fontevraud?"

"I don't know. If we lose time, we may miss our man in Nantes—the man with the livres for your delivery." He winced as if decision-making hurt his head. I produced the second coin then, and the choice was made: we would stop at the river's confluence with the Vienne, and he would procure a horse and a guide for me. A short ride would take me to the abbey.

"You must return in a few hours," he said. "We have several days' journey to go, and Albert the Boatman always delivers his cargo in good time. I would not miss those livres."

As we made our way downstream, Albert paddling the boat so as to speed our progress, I thought of Robert, taken gravely ill. This hardly surprised me, as he had not appeared well when I had seen him last spring. Would he be able to answer my questions? I had hoped to hear all about my mother when I went to Fontevraud to take my vows. I'd anticipated long conversations in which he would tell me of her life, of her accomplishments, of her dreams and desires. I wanted to reminisce about her beautiful voice, her laugh like the lark's song, her fragrance like the morning breeze. I wanted to remember her, and to know her at last.

That I might learn something of my father, too, had occurred to me, but I had dismissed the notion. Robert had not known of me. I doubted my mother had told him of the man she had loved after her husband's death—for, surely, in doing so she would have mentioned the child she had relinquished. Yet, who knew what she had confessed during the long hours they'd spent together poring over building plans and discussing the administration of Fontevraud Abbey?

At the door of death, the man in the tavern had said of Robert. I clasped the crucifix around my neck and uttered a selfish prayer that his life might be prolonged until I could ask him about my mother.

We landed in a portage teeming with cargo-laden vessels, workers, mules and horses, and men and women in monks' and nuns' garments, all journeying to Fontevraud. Albert had no difficulty procuring a ride for me with a group of sisters departing down the rue de les Soeurs.

"Sister Madeleine?" a diminutive woman with a nose like the knot on a tree said, squinting her small eyes at me. "From

Argenteuil, you say? I visited that splendid abbey months ago, but I do not recall seeing you there."

"I lay in the infirmary, no doubt," I lied, "ill from dysentery. It plagued me for weeks."

"And yet, you do appear familiar." She eyed me more closely. "Perhaps I met you on one of my earlier visits? I have been learning the art of vineyard husbandry from the sisters there."

I told her that I had been committed to Argenteuil as an oblate.

"No, not as an oblate. I have seen you in your habit. Your face looks nearly as familiar to me as my own." No doubt she saw my mother's features, but I would not have said so. I would not spark whispers about Mother now when she could not explain herself.

Horses, riders, people, and carts filled the rue de les Soeurs, traveling both to and from the abbey. I kept my head down lest someone recognize me and allowed the talkative nun's stream of words to flow over me as if they were water—until she mentioned Robert.

"They say he will not last the year, God bless his soul."

"I have heard the same. What ails him?"

"Only the Lord knows for certain. But I think he is sick at heart." She sighed. "He has not been the same since our prioress died." She raised her eyes to my face then, and recognition flared—but, to my good fortune, the gates of Fontevraud rose before us, and the buildings behind them, gleaming white in the midmorning sun. I bade her farewell and urged my horse onward, leaving her staring after me.

I entered the abbey grounds through a high arch in a gate of white stone and found myself in another world, a dazzle of autumn flowers and manicured shrubs and a maze of white buildings with arched windows and doorways. The streets bustled with more activity than I had ever seen in the Nôtre-Dame de Paris Cloister: tonsured monks stooped beneath the building stones weighting their backs; mules pulling carts filled with shovels and picks and other tools; sisters walking in twos and threes. Above the scene rose the impressive cathedral with its high bell tower, rounded chapels spreading in a half circle from the main building, and roof tiled in a pattern resembling the scales of a fish. Mother had overseen the building of this edifice and had perhaps contributed to its design. I heard the ring of hammers striking chisels as workmen cut building blocks from the large quarried stones; saw monks mixing mortar in large vats, sweat pouring from their brows; and watched, fascinated, as a crane, by means of a wheel turned by men on the ground, lifted the chiseled blocks to workers on scaffolding high above. Emotion welled in me as I imagined my mother directing the laborers, arguing over the placement of a spire or a buttress, and jabbing her finger against a parchment that a broad-chested man held before her—as a woman did now, at the base of the nave being constructed.

This must be Petronille of Chemillé, my mother's assistant. I hastened to her in hopes that she might lead me to Robert. A petite woman with a face weathered by the sun, she lifted large, dark eyes to me and dropped her edge of the parchment.

"Hersende," she breathed.

"My name is Heloise. I have come to speak with Robert of Arbrissel."

She led me across the lawn to the abbey, a square building flanked on either side by long cloisters. Inside the main building, we passed through a refectory with low, wood-beamed ceilings, lined with wooden trestle tables and benches, and into a room with a writing desk and footstool, a chair, and shelves strewn with parchment and codices.

She closed the door and blinked up at me. "Please forgive me for staring. You bear a remarkable resemblance to . . . someone I once knew."

"You are Petronille?"

She lifted her eyebrows at the sound of her name.

"Hersende of Champagne was my mother."

She gasped. "I had not known that Hersende had a daughter. A son, yes, she spoke of him often. But a daughter?"

"You do not believe me."

"I may be dull at times, but I am hardly blind."

"Can you tell me anything about her?"

"Hersende was the best of women: lively, intelligent, strong— very strong. No man dared to argue with her, even when she was wrong." Petronille smiled to herself, remembering, then grew somber again. "But one felt sorry for her, too. An air of sadness surrounded her. One morning I entered this room and found her gazing out the open window, tears dropping from her cheeks. Outside, one of the girls was singing that lullaby: 'Sing, little nightingale, sing.'" Petronille's voice cracked as she rendered the tune, not at all musical as my mother's voice would have been, yet it evoked vivid memories of her.

"I never asked her why she cried, out of respect. Many come here to forget the past—I know that is why *I* came. Now, I think I know the reason for her sorrow."

"She left me when I was a child, to come here."

She eyed my habit. "And you have followed in her path, I see. So—why have you come today?"

"I must speak with Robert of Arbrissel."

"That is not possible." Her voice tightened. "Robert is very ill. The healers have bled him and used a green salve on his skin and the priests pray for him constantly, and yet he worsens daily." Her mouth quivered with love.

"But I must see him. It is urgent."

"In the morning, perhaps. He always seems improved in the mornings."

"*Non!* Sister, please."

The idea of sleeping here tonight, where my mother had lived and prayed and sung and commanded men, appealed to me, as did the thought of tormenting Albert the Boatman by failing to return to him that afternoon. Living by my word, however, I could not follow the promptings of my heart.

"He would want to speak with me, if he could. He has many questions, he said, about my mother, and my life. Please take me to him! Doesn't he deserve to decide for himself?"

"You have met Robert before? He did not speak of it to me." She sounded indignant.

"He came to Paris last spring and invited me to join you here."

"You are the woman scholar? From Paris?" She narrowed her eyes. "So you have come to us now, instead of in June. How convenient—when he is on the verge of naming an abbess for Fontevraud." She might have hissed. Pulling back her lips from her little teeth, she reminded me of a small, vicious animal.

"I have not come to vie for that position, or any other here—I assure you. I am here to tell him that I cannot join your abbey at all. My—my plans are altered."

"Altered?" She all but chirped the word. "Cannot join? Such a shame, my dear. Robert felt very excited to discover you. But, yes, you must tell him yourself." Suddenly in haste to bring me before her mentor, she linked arms with me and led me briskly to a small, square building—the infirmary.

The beds lining the barren room were filled with men, one with a cough so violent that I thought he might tear out his lungs; another whose face and body oozed with sores; a sweating, red-faced youth whose every breath wheezed with exertion. In their midst, a very old man with mottled skin and a mouth tight with annoyance waved away a priest burning incense and intoning the last rites. I gave Petronille a look of wonderment when I recognized the man as Robert of Arbrissel.

"He insists that he is not dying, but the healer says otherwise," Petronille whispered to me. "So often does he perch on the brink that the priest administers the unction to him three times a day." She glanced about to make certain we had no audience. "We cannot risk his death with any sin blotting his soul. We hope, when he has gone, to make a saint of him."

When the priest had taken his leave, Petronille ventured to Robert's bed and stroked his cheek with her fingertips. The intimate gesture made me wonder if he loved her, too—but then his eyes flew open to glare at her.

"You, again?" he snapped. "I tell you, I already have an abbess. A scholar, from the best of mothers. When she arrives, you shall see. The Lord will send her to me. You shall see."

"She is here," Petronille's voice rang with false cheer. "She has come to speak with you."

"Who?" He turned his head and looked at me—and something leapt in his eyes like glowing embers. He lifted his arms toward me, as if to draw me into them. "Hersende! Hersende! At last, you have arrived. My lovely angel—come to me! My darling. Let me hold you again, my dear, just once more."

"I am Heloise, from Paris." I moved to the foot of his bed, avoiding his grasping hands.

He widened his eyes. "Hersende."

"I am not Hersende. I am Heloise, her daughter. We met in Paris last May. I was to take the veil here in the spring."

"Your nun's habit confuses him," Petronille said. "Remove your wimple, *non*?"

I did so, and he gasped. His eyes bulged. "Your hair." He pointed. "That white streak. Dear Lord! I did not know. I did not know!"

The physician hastened to his side, glaring at me. "You have excited him. Please remove yourself, for his sake."

But how could I do so, staggering under the weight of all my questions? *Please, God, let me learn just one thing of my father today.*

Robert's gaze suddenly sharpened, and I knew he recognized me. "Heloise. Hersende's girl." Ecstasy shone on his face, and he opened his arms again. "Daughter! Come to me, my child."

I shrank back from him—was he mad, or merely delirious? I turned to Petronille, beheld her fear-stricken face, and knew the truth. God had heard my prayers and provided my answer.

Tears rolled like a tide over me, sweeping me into Robert's embrace. His arms enfolded me. I kissed his fevered brow. "Robert. Father, I have found you at last."

9

If I were there, I would wash away all cares from you, I would wipe sweetest tears from your starry eyes, I would surround your troubled breast with my embrace, I would restore your happiness completely.
—ABELARD TO HELOISE

LE PALLET, BRITTANY
AUGUST 1116

He had inherited Abelard's eyes. While it is true that all newborn eyes are innocent blue, our son's gaze resembled his father's not only in color but also in mirth. At birth in early June, he uttered a delighted squeal rather than the squall of outrage with which he ought to have greeted the world. I drew him to my breast with a fullness of emotion that I had never felt before, not even for Abelard. *Little prince, baby Pierre, O mon coeur,* my heart my heart my heart.

A sweet ache filled me as I watched him suckle. The midwife pulled the covers over my washed body, but for the first time since arriving at that chilly château I did not feel cold. Abelard's sister Denise entered the room, a cup of broth in her hands, her eyes covetous. She held out her arms, beseeching. I lowered my head; my hair fell over his greedy face. When I looked up again, Denise had gone. I felt a pang. Should I have offered him to her?

Surely she had seen that he was hungry. But not, it seemed, as hungry as she.

When I'd first met Denise, a woman with soft eyes and an ample body, her gaze had fallen to my belly and lingered there, with longing, I thought. I resisted the impulse to cover myself with my hands. Dagobert, Abelard's younger brother, introduced me in French as his brother's "friend," then spoke in a language I did not comprehend to the thin, pinch-faced woman beside him giving me sullen looks and wringing her hands.

"My wife, Elona, speaks Breton only. Pierre writes that you are talented with languages. Perhaps you can learn from her, and she from you?"

I kissed her stiff cheek in greeting and she pushed me away, then shouted something unintelligible.

"Silence!" Dagobert said, and she closed her small mouth, apparently knowing one word of French, at least.

I did not need words to comprehend. I could easily guess the questions that Abelard's sister-in-law might ask. What was I to Abelard? Contempt curled her lip. In her eyes, I was nothing more than a whore, and now I stood to interfere in her life, a stranger come to disrupt her home. Her glances at Denise spelled resentment, as well. If not for my exhaustion, I might have fled that dismal scene all the way back to Paris.

Why *had* Abelard sent me here, to live amid unhappiness? It could not bode well for our child. Why had I agreed to come, knowing nothing of the situation?

Such was my trust in my *speciälis* that I had done his bidding in spite of my concerns. Although I had already entertained fantasies of returning to Paris and begging Agnes or even my new friend Queen Adelaide for help, I knew that I would not do so. Abelard had decided the best course of action for us, and I would comply, desiring his happiness more than my own.

The autumn of my arrival had slipped quickly into winter, in which a succession of blizzards trapped us all in the house. Elona's scornful demeanor chilled me more than any snowstorm, however. At last I learned some Breton and could comprehend some of her outbursts. Elona not only resented me as another mouth to feed—repudiated by her husband, Denise had returned to the castle only one month before my arrival—but she feared losing her title as lady of le Pallet to me. Would Abelard come after me to reclaim his birthright, taking command of le Pallet and its income?

My only comfort came from Abelard's letters promising to join me upon the end of my lying-in period. For me, that day could not arrive quickly enough. Every moment without my love felt like an eternity. Here I could do nothing to protect him from my uncle's wrath.

"My brother will come to no harm as long as you are with us," Dagobert said when, before dinner one day, I mentioned my fears for Abelard's safety. "We Bretons avenge our own. If your uncle injures our brother, who knows what we might do to you?"

Is it any wonder that I wrestled daily with the demons of doubt? But then, when despair made me gnash my teeth, a letter from him would arrive.

Any single day I am forced to spend without you,
Sweet love, seems like three decades.
A day without your face rising like the sun over me,
Goes by without sun or the gift of its light.

Even as his words of love consoled me, however, they also increased my longing for him. Why must I endure the travails of pregnancy without him to comfort me? And what of the joys we could not share? Abelard never felt our baby kick against my womb. He never saw my body ripen, or my hair thicken and shine. When I awoke in the night hungering for arugula, I wanted his fingers to feed it to me.

Most of all, I needed his laughter. Until our child's birth, life at le Pallet held no joy for me. As my stomach grew, so did the resentment in Elona's eyes whenever she glanced my way. In the town with her, I noticed whispers and laughter following us, and the lewd stares of vendors. I came to learn that the word she spoke under her breath did, indeed, mean "whore." The whole world despised me, it seemed, for loving Abelard.

I thought nothing of others' opinions, but wanted only my beloved's presence even more keenly after the baby's birth. Our beautiful son, whom I named Pierre Astralabe, offered some new delight every day. Abelard did not witness the time when first, under my tickling fingers, our boy laughed, a sound more delightful than the music of angels. He could not note the alertness of his gaze at an age when, Denise said, most infants stare blankly, as though the world were made of shadows. He did not cheer, as did I, when our son first lifted his head and pushed his chest up from the bed, determined, it seemed, to crawl.

Declining a wet nurse—when Abelard came for us, I would need to feed our boy—I kept little Astralabe close under the cloying eye of Denise, who could not forbear offering advice on every aspect of his upbringing. I should not suckle him whenever he cried, but ought to let him learn to comfort himself. I ought to hand him over to her even when he protested, or he would always be diffident with strangers. I smiled and thanked her and clutched him to myself.

When my confinement had ended, Astralabe changed so completely in his temperament that I wondered if demons had stolen him in the night and replaced my happy child with an evil one. Where had his laughter gone? Now he screamed, clenching his little fists until they turned white, his face empurpled with rage. Denise tried to help by making funny faces and, at times, holding him in her arms, which increased his shrieks. For three days he cried, only stopping sporadically to nurse until, at nightfall, he would drink deeply from my breast, and exhausted, we would both fall asleep.

This is how Abelard found me after riding through the gates and crossing the drawbridge to the château of le Pallet that August afternoon: weeping, imploring, praying, walking with our babe in my arms, pleading for peace, for even one moment's worth of silence, rocking to and fro, patting his back, rubbing his head, thinking for one moment of dropping him into a well, of stuffing a washcloth into his mouth, of finding some way to silence the screams of this formerly delightful child. Having discovered the power crying gave him over me, he now refused to stop.

"Have I come at an inauspicious hour?" Abelard said as he entered my chambers. "Perhaps I should return—in a few years."

That I heard him at all was miraculous, for our son had redoubled his wails. I stopped pacing the floor and turned to Abelard, my heart lifting like a sail at the sight of his comical grimace, his starry eyes, his arms open wide to my leaping embrace. How long the months had been without my Abelard! He hardly seemed real. If not for the crying child in my arms, I might have thought myself in a dream.

"I am glad that *someone* is happy to see me," he said as I kissed him and Astralabe's screams intensified.

"I do not know what is causing him to cry." I held him out as if Abelard might know the answer. "I have consulted the healer, the midwife, and the priest, but no one knows how to placate him."

"Shh." Abelard bounced our infant so vigorously in his outstretched hands that I feared he might drop him. "Son, be quiet!"

Astralabe continued to shriek.

I took him and pulled him to my breast, where, mercifully, he nursed. Abelard's eyes bulged at the sight of my bosom and he reached for my free breast, but I pushed his hand away. Being suckled day and night, I did not desire to be touched there even by Abelard.

"I am jealous of an infant," he said with a grin.

I moved to the bed and lay with Astralabe close beside me, still feeding. Abelard lay down also and slid his arm around my waist. I closed my eyes, relishing his embrace. As he pulled himself more closely to me, his arousal prodded my thigh. I sighed and relaxed into him, my Abelard, beside me at last, his kisses moistening my neck and throat and his hands in my hair, his sonorant voice murmuring, "Beautiful mother, excellent wife." My blood stirred in spite of my fatigue. I settled our sleeping son in his cradle, then returned to Abelard's kisses and caresses. He stroked my belly, my thighs, my back, my buttocks. He lifted my skirt and pressed his skin against mine. Blood thrummed in my ears and throbbed between my legs. His breath smelled sweet, like aniseed, over the animal scent of him rising, enfolding, immersing me in heat like the sultriest of nights. My sighs mingled with his resonant moans—and then Astralabe awoke and erupted, again, in cries.

Abelard cursed. "What in God's name is wrong with him? I thought you said he was a cheerful child."

Indeed, I said, he had been so until the previous Monday.

Abelard laughed. "On that very day, I left Paris to journey here. The little rascal knew I was coming for his mother."

10

❦

You are not being fair to me, but have changed your ways,
and so trust is not secure anywhere.
—HELOISE TO ABELARD

*A*lthough Abelard's family had fed me well—if resent-
fully—my months in Brittany had whetted my
hunger for discussions such as my beloved and I had shared.
Dagobert had little to say to any woman, it seemed. Elona
gave me mostly hateful looks, even when I spoke Breton to
her. Denise, on the other hand, paid too much attention to
me, inquiring so often and so solicitously that I avoided her.
Then, after Astralabe's birth, she showed an interest in him
that I thought strange, even unnatural. One day I'd walked
into my bedchamber to find his cradle empty—and discovered
her napping with him on her own bed. When I'd reached out
for him, she had awakened and refused, at first, to hand him
to me.

Now that Abelard had come, everyone's behavior had
changed. Denise followed him about as a hen does its chicks.
Elona listened with alacrity, hanging on every word, as he and
Dagobert conversed. Dagobert spoke more words at dinner on
Abelard's second day than I had heard from him in a year's time,
telling of his villeins' laziness and their quarrels; describing each

of his crops and his successes or failures with them; and complaining of the unseasonably warm and dry spring.

"Father talked of digging a new well in the southern meadow," Abelard said.

"But he never did so, did he?" Dagobert pursed his lips.

"No, but I always thought he should. I would have done so—"

"If you had not given up your lands."

"Yes."

Dagobert said something to his wife in Breton; I recognized the words *brother* and *lord*. Denise spoke rapidly in her garbled tongue, her eyes snapping with demands. Abelard lifted his hands in a shrug and, smiling, began a reply, but she interrupted, raising her voice. Soon the two of them were shouting.

Dagobert leapt to his feet, waving his arms. "This is treachery!" he cried in French. "What other man would even consider taking back what he had freely given, and to his own brother?"

Abelard stood, as well. "What other man would deny his brother such a small favor, when that brother has relinquished everything to him?"

"A small favor? Ha! Let us petition the duke. He will decide who would inherit our father's lands, income, and title—one of his own sons or the illegitimate child you would have Elona bring up for you."

At these words, I felt a tightening around my heart. Elona, bring up Abelard's son?

"That 'illegitimate child' is your nephew," Abelard snarled. "And why shouldn't he inherit our father's estate? He could surely do as good a job as either of your sons. Had you heard? Three months of age and he already speaks!"

Denise, sitting beside Abelard, smiled and nodded. Although I did not believe her, she'd claimed to teach Astralabe to say *Maman*—to her, not to me.

"Listen to you, so proud of your seed!" Dagobert folded his arms across his chest. "But you always thought yourself superior to the rest of us." He pointed a finger at Abelard. "You are too good for le Pallet, too good for Brittany, your home—too good for your own family. You and your soft, scholarly hands, always with your face in a book, indulged by our father and pampered by our mother as if you were Christ himself."

"Papa and Maman loved all of us," Abelard said, frowning.

"It did not seem so to me. You never had to do a hard day's work, while I sweated in the fields with the villeins and had to practice swordsmanship until I thought my arm would fall off— and why? Because you wanted nothing to do with your birthright. You turned up your nose at all our father offered."

"Because I was born a philosopher."

"Because you were too lazy for real work and too cowardly to fight. You cannot bear the sight of blood, especially your own. Admit it!"

"I admit to nothing except having an *asne* for a brother."

"Stop!" I jumped to my feet, while Denise held my baby in her arms and kissed his cheeks as though he already belonged to her. "No one is going to bring up my baby except me," I said, glaring at Abelard.

I turned and snatched Astralabe to myself. Cradling him as if to shield him from a storm, I ran with my wailing infant into my bedchamber, where I fastened the latch against Abelard, against greedy Denise, against all the world, if need be.

"Shhh, poor baby, do not cry," I murmured. "Do not cry, and do not worry. No one will take you from me. Your mother would die before she would leave you."

An hour later, when both my son and I had drifted off to sleep in my chair, Abelard's pounding on my door awakened me. Forgetting my anger for the moment, I arose with sleep befuddling my brain and, after setting Astralabe into his cradle, opened the door.

"Ignore my brother's bad behavior." Abelard pushed his way into the room. "He once was a kind and gentle man, but he has changed. I blame that Breton woman he took to wife. Doesn't *Breton* stem from the same word as *brute*?"

At another time, I might have laughed at the clever jest. Abelard laughed enough for the two of us, however, and hooked his arm around my waist to pull me close—but I refused him.

"Are you annoyed with me? Why?" He lifted his eyebrows innocently.

"Because you want to take my son from me." I stepped over to the cradle and gazed down at his beautiful face.

"I want no such thing. I only asked for my brother's help should we need it. He said *non*, so we have nothing more to discuss. But I discovered why my sister has treated you as a leper. She fears Astralabe will take this estate from her own sons."

"But you signed your inheritance over to Dagobert."

Abelard shrugged. "My father wrote a provision into his will reserving inheritance rights for *my* son." He sighed. "Of course, I never expected to have a child. Papa must have known something that I did not."

My heart beat a little faster at the thought of living at le Pallet with Abelard and our child, far removed from rumors and scandal and far from my uncle. I imagined picnics on the grass, and singing and dancing together, the three of us, with chains of daisies in our hair as my mother used to string for me.

"To claim the estate, I must become a knight," Abelard said, having guessed my thoughts. "I would be required to fight battles for the Duke of Brittany."

I laughed at the notion of him with a sword—but his frown stopped me. "You are a scholar, not a fighter." I did not add that he would certainly be killed in his first battle—unless wits were the weapon. "Any man can flourish a blade, but your brilliant mind shall alter the world. Where can we go, instead? Paris is not safe for us."

"That has changed. I am at my ease in Paris now, and you will be, as well." His smile promised secrets.

"At ease? Have you told my uncle where I am living?"

"I have."

"And yet he no longer desires to harm you?"

"He will do me no harm." Abelard appeared so pleased with himself that I had to smile. "Sending you here was one of my more brilliant ideas. Fulbert did not dare lay a hand on me out of concern for you. He thinks that we Bretons are savages."

"Aren't you?"

"Haven't you guessed the answer by now?" Then he attacked me most savagely and most deliciously. I thrilled to the low growls issuing from his throat, his hands rough on my body, his mouth ravishing my skin—but we had matters to discuss.

"So we cannot remain here," I said, moving his hands from my overused breasts. "Your star did not rise in le Pallet, nor will it set here. But—where shall we go?"

"We return to Paris. My work awaits there, and my students."

"But if I am there, and not here, what will prevent my uncle from avenging himself against you?"

"I have befriended him, that is what. Ha! Disbelief writes itself across your face."

"My imagination has reached its limits, I admit. When last I saw the two of you together, my uncle brandished a knife."

"I have given him what he wants."

"What is that, pray tell?"

Abelard pulled me so close to him, I could feel the wings of his heart beating against my rib cage. "You and I are going to wed."

I laughed at his jest. "Thusly you demonstrate that intelligence is not the same as wisdom." Abelard frowned as if confused, so I added, "You ought to know better, by now, than to make false promises to my uncle."

"False promises?" He kissed me. "Let me remove those words from your lips for all time." He kissed me again. "I intend to marry you as soon as we return to Paris."

I extricated myself and walked to the window. In another life, I might swoon with pleasure to hear the man I loved begging for my hand, as I imagined the joys of children, shared meals, and my own household to command. Marriage would bring neither pleasure nor joy to Abelard and me, however, but the opposite: censure, scandal, and among his scholars, disillusionment.

"What are you doing there?" Abelard asked.

"I am searching for your good sense, since you seem to have lost it."

"To marry you makes perfect sense to me."

"And now, I think you must have misplaced your mind, as well." I turned to him. "Had it not occurred to you that I might wish to be consulted in this?"

"Is that the reason for your anger? Please, come to me." He held out his arms and I relented, letting him pull me back into the bed. "I am consulting you now, sweetness. Will you marry me?" His eyes gazed not with questions, however, but with answers—all of them in his favor.

"*Non.*"

He laughed and kissed my lips. "My darling contrarian. Have you forgotten that I read the Ovid before you? 'We can't stand sweetness: bitterness renews our taste.' But he was not speaking of me, I assure you."

"And I speak not from Ovid, but from the promptings of my own heart."

"Have you lost your love for me, then?"

"Did you read my letters?"

"Every word is imprinted in my memory."

"Then you know that I have pledged to love you eternally. I, for one, honor my promises."

"If you love me, then you must marry me."

"Because I love you, I cannot marry you. Abelard, you know that marriage would destroy you. A wife and children would diminish you in the world's eyes; you would never know glory."

"But you are wrong. Not to marry you, the mother of my child, would destroy me."

"If you do, the fruits of your labors will be lost—your reputation, your new book, perhaps even your position at the school. Not just your students, but all the world would be deprived of your brilliance."

"I must compliment you for originality. Never have I heard of a woman's refusing a suitor with such high praise."

"But I am not refusing you, my love."

"Are you not? To my ears, *non* sounds very much like a refusal."

"And have we not established that I will love you eternally? I am refusing marriage, not you."

"And when we return to Paris? Where would you live?"

"Why can't I live as your mistress? Many canons keep concubines. Given your fame and the scholars you attract to the cloister, the Church might even accept the arrangement. You might rent a house for Astralabe and me and visit us often."

He snorted. "Making you my mistress would placate Fulbert?"

"Not at first, no—but he would soon adjust."

"Having pleaded with your uncle for my life—for both our lives—I must disagree. And lest you say that we need not consider his opinions, let me remind you that he has already threatened to remove my testicles."

"Which he did not do, in spite of the knife in his hand."

"But he will kill me if I do not marry you." Abelard left the bed to pace the room and run worried fingers through his hair. "Everything is settled. Fulbert and I have reached an agreement. If I marry you, he will be appeased."

"You reached an agreement without consulting me?"

"I never thought you would object."

"In all the time you have known me, have you learned nothing of me? I prefer love to chains."

"I thought you might prefer to save my life."

"You overstate the danger. My uncle is not a murderer. And if we wed, you would lose your position at the school as soon as Galon heard the news."

"He will hear nothing. You and I shall marry in secret, with only your uncle, Etienne, and Agnes as our witnesses. Fulbert has agreed."

"A secret marriage? Now I know that you have lost your mind. Such an arrangement would never satisfy my uncle." Would a secret marriage end the talk about Abelard and me? Certainly not—in fact, the whispers would increase once everyone knew of my child with eyes the color of dusk and an indentation in his chin as a finger makes when pressed into clay.

"Fulbert and I have discussed the matter over many flagons of wine. He was reluctant, at first, to accept a marriage made in private. He talked endlessly about honor and his family, especially your mother and the scandal she caused. He blames her for his difficulties."

"Scandal? Mother kept me a secret all her days. Not even Robert of Arbrissel knew." I told Abelard about my visit to the Fontevraud Abbey and the state in which I found Robert. "Petronille of Chemillé worked beside my mother every day for years, and she did not know of my existence. Any scandal accompanying my birth exists only in Uncle's imagination."

I also told him of Petronille's revelation that, had my mother chosen to do so, she could have taken me with her to Fontevraud. Now that Robert had revealed the truth I understood why she had not. Everyone, including Robert, would have known who'd sired me: a streak of white had fallen over his left eye, too, before all his hair turned gray.

"When he extended his hands and called me 'daughter,' I could scarcely believe my ears. At first, I thought he must have mistaken me for one of his nuns. But the expression on Petronille's face told me all: Robert of Arbrissel is my father."

"Hermits and monks," Abelard said, smirking. "They are all the same."

I stiffened. His was the kind of remark my mother must have dreaded—and, surely, the reason she had relinquished me. "My mother loved Robert. She gave up everything, even her child, to protect him. She would not sacrifice his glory, not even for her own sake." *We hope to make a saint of him,* Petronille had said to me again, escorting me to my horse at the abbey gate. Were our secret known, the Church would not even consider sainthood for Robert.

"When he dies she will petition for sainthood, but no one thinks it will succeed," Abelard said.

I gasped. Did Robert yet live? He had appeared so close to the end when I had seen him last October.

"I thought you knew," Abelard said. "But of course, you would not have heard the news here." After my visit, Robert had recovered his health—a miracle, it was said, and I could not disagree—and appointed Petronille as his abbess "with much hesitation and eyes full of tears, causing many to say that he would never have chosen her were your mother alive." He had returned to preaching for several months but now lay deathly ill again in the infirmary at Orsan, Fontevraud's priory in Berry.

I lowered my eyes, thinking of Robert's kindness to me, and the smile, filled with warmth, that had encompassed his face when he had recognized me as his own.

"Even had you never been born, the Church would not canonize Robert," Abelard said.

"He has lived too much like Christ for the Church's liking."

"Yes, and, like Christ, he is beloved of women."

I remembered how Robert had called me to him, wanting to hold me in his arms. Had he lain with my mother in the convent? I had dared not ask Petronille, for fear she might say yes.

"Your uncle is convinced that scandal taints him, as well—and that your mother is to blame. He said that if our love becomes known, he will be ruined forever."

"If Uncle Fulbert wants the reason for his failure, he need look no farther than the flagon in his hand."

"But he will never admit to that."

"*Non.* Admitting the truth even to himself would be too difficult. He must blame someone else for his downfall. My mother is dead, so now he points his finger at us."

"Do you see now why we must wed? In Fulbert's eyes, marriage would sanctify us. Otherwise, we are sinners—and I have corrupted your soul. I swear, Heloise, he will kill me if I do not make you my wife."

"He will not. Nor would I marry you, or anyone, at the point of a sword. To do so would mean a life of misery for you, me, and for our child. I would rather be your mistress—or even your whore."

11

※

I looked for no marriage bond, no marriage portion, and
it was not my own pleasures and wishes I sought to grat-
ify, as you well know, but yours.

—HELOISE TO ABELARD

THE NÔTRE-DAME CLOISTER, PARIS
OCTOBER 1116

*O*urs was the most desolate of weddings, or would have
been except for the presence of our friends. Agnes stood
next to me, squeezing my elbow in sympathy. Etienne, conducting the sad ceremony, wore his ceremonial white robes, attempting to bestow dignity where grace was lacking—for what could
be more disgraceful than a forced union? Etienne's little chapel
felt cozy and quaint during the daylight hours when sunlight
streamed through its stained-glass windows, illuminating the
fleurs-de-lis, acanthus leaves, and lions on the capitals supporting
the ceiling's many arches. Now, however, in the hour before
dawn, the room felt gloomy and cold, the dimness of its lamplight only adding to my sense of doom.

This marriage was a mistake. My uncle's scowl as we entered the Saint-Aignan Chapel told me that, as I had argued,
he would not be satisfied by a wedding conducted in secret,
hidden from a world that honored hypocrisy more than love,

and blind obedience more than thought. Uncle Fulbert had educated me, but only so that his star might rise with mine. Now that I had fallen, like Eve, from my exalted status, his eyes held only contempt. I averted my gaze, hiding my own feelings. Uncle Fulbert, not my mother, had abandoned me at Argenteuil. Had he forced her to take her vows? I wanted to spit in his face.

"Ignore Fulbert," Abelard whispered, seeing my hands' tremor. "He cannot harm us now." If only I could believe Abelard, my trusting one! Or, rather, I wish that he had heeded *me* and realized the danger my uncle posed to us both. Seeing Uncle's hands clenched at his sides and rage compressing his features, I knew that Abelard had erred, and that I was in the right. This marriage would bring disaster upon our heads. My step faltered.

I turned beseeching eyes to Agnes, who mistook the reason for my distress. "The gown is perfection," she murmured, "and so are you." Before the wedding, I had cringed to behold the gown my uncle had provided: the bloodred *bliaut* sewn for me to wear as Christ's bride at Fontevraud. Yet, for this occasion, what could be more appropriate?

I said nothing in reply, for all eyes rested upon me now. This wedding bade ill for Abelard and me, as well as our son. We might have lived happily outside the cloister, perhaps in a house on the Grand-Pont; crowds of people passing by day and at night would have made splendid company. The new bishop, Guibert—Galon had died during my absence—would have frowned at the arrangement, but he might have allowed it. As for Uncle, yes, he would have hated to think of me as Abelard's mistress—at first. But the Parisian tongues would have ceased their wagging about us soon enough, as some other scandal erupted—a bishop found consorting with prostitutes, perhaps, or another priest forced to abandon his wife and children. Then, his ears no longing burning from the whispers about us, my uncle would have turned his thoughts elsewhere, as well.

Mine had been a perfectly sensible plan. Why had I consented to this one?

Why? Why? The question began to torment me as soon as we rode away from le Pallet, our child's cries pummeling my heart. Why had I agreed to leave my only son behind, doing the very thing I had sworn I would never do? Perhaps Abelard's constant entreaties had worn down my resistance, as soft water carves the hardest stone. He coaxed, wheedled, accused me of selfishness, uttered threats. He made promises that we both knew he could not keep. He ridiculed me, apologized, pretended to give up the fight, gave to me the most exquisite pleasures, and then, as I lay languid in his arms, tearfully begged me to do his bidding: "You possess the power to save me, or to destroy me."

When I pointed out that I had failed before to influence my uncle on his behalf, he said that, by bringing our child to Paris, I would oblige Uncle Fulbert to commit some public act against him. "We are friends again, Fulbert and I, thanks to my gifts of wine, my assurances that I can help him gain a higher position in the Church—I see your skepticism, but I have Etienne's friendship, remember—and my promise to marry you."

"My uncle, contrary to your opinion, is no fool. These deceptions, while soothing him now, will in the end bring disastrous results."

"Marrying you would be no deception," Abelard said as he lowered his head to touch his lips to mine.

I, keenly aware of his determination to prevail over me, turned my head away. "I cannot marry you. To do so would spell your ruin. Who has ever heard of a married philosopher?"

"Socrates wed Xanthippe."

"And he lived in misery."

"But I need suffer no harm should our marriage remain un-known."

"How long do you think my uncle will honor that agreement? Tongues will wag the instant we arrive in Paris with Astralabe. If Uncle blames my mother's indiscretion for his own failure, how much more vigilant would he be against any smear on *my* reputation?"

"You have just made the perfect argument in favor of leaving our son with my brother and Denise."

"I would rather die than do so."

"And I will die if you do not. Heloise, listen—Fulbert doesn't know about the child."

"You didn't tell him?" My voice rose, disturbing our sleeping son. Abelard arose to go to him, but I leapt between him and the cradle. "You will not take my son from me."

"No one is taking him away. It is only for a short time, until everyone has forgotten about you and me, and we may do as we please again."

"Meanwhile, my son will forget about me. Your sister will tell him that she is his mother. By the time we return for him, he will not want to leave her. Is that what you desire?"

"It will not be so long, my sweet, but only a few months. I promise you that."

So, having no more arguments to offer in the face of Abelard's logic, I conceded to his plan. If he had not told Uncle we had a child, then for me to ride into Paris with Astralabe in my arms would only enrage him further. Would he take our son, as he had wrested me from my mother? Without my husband's support, he might try. But, said Abelard, my uncle would be powerless to do so with Astralabe so far away, and in Dagobert's care.

I rode away from le Pallet that bitter morning with a tear-slicked face and my entire being already aching for our boy.

Denise, standing with Dagobert on the drawbridge, emanated joy even as she bounced Astralabe in her arms as if to shake him loose from his cries. I wanted to leap from my horse and snatch him from her.

Why, Abelard? Every hour of that long ride home I asked myself that question. Why had I left my child, born of my body and possessing a part of my soul, for even a few months? As Abelard and I rode, discussing a future with the three of us together, I noted that the shadows under his eyes had vanished, and his skin had regained its color. His leonine laugh, the self-assured toss of his curly head, the strut in his walk, all had returned, as well as his eyes' lively glint. At night, although we slept in separate rooms—in lodgings much more satisfactory than the boatman had provided. He came to me to imprint his love on my body with hidden pleasures and whispered bliss. By the time we arrived at the Saint-Aignan Chapel, I had found my answer at last. I had left our child behind out of love for Abelard, and a desire to protect him from harm. *Someday I hope that you will understand.* At last, my mother's wish had come true.

Yet, I did not think myself like Mother. While she had relinquished me to that strange, dark abbey for many years, I had left my son in the care of family members, and for only a short time. It seemed, however painful, a small sacrifice. Abelard's *Sic et Non*, when disseminated, might make him as famous as the saints. When that happened, he said, he might do anything he desired, even acknowledge me as his wife and Astralabe as our son. Until then, I would return to le Pallet from time to time so our babe would not forget me or, heaven forbid, think himself abandoned.

A child needs no vows to bind himself to his mother in love; nor did Abelard and I require them from each other. Yet as he promised himself to me before God and our witnesses, I felt my dread lift. He said that he would love and cherish me forever, and for a single, exalted moment, I believed in him, and in us. O Abelard! Light of my days! I pressed his hands with mine and told him with my eyes all that I felt. His shining face mirrored mine.

The strange, hushed ceremony finished, Agnes, Etienne, and my uncle embraced us and wished us well. I thought of the family that I could at last call my own and felt on my face a smile befitting a bride.

"I shall see you soon enough, my dear," Etienne said, holding my hands. "I have had Pierre's apartment cleaned and decorated for wedding-night nuptials. I hope you both will dine with me at terce today—and the Canon Fulbert, as well," he added hastily, seeing my uncle appear by my side.

Uncle's furrowed brow, his frowning mouth, the rigid set of his body, all told me that he wished to decline Etienne's invitation. He hated Abelard; I had no doubt. However, the notion still flourished in his mind that the powerful Garlande brothers might assist him somehow.

"We will come to dine, but my niece will return home with me after the meal," my uncle said as he clamped his hand around my arm. "Every eye in Paris will be upon her now, every tongue flicking with scandal—scandal!"

I sent Abelard a desperate look: Would he allow this? He frowned but said nothing as my uncle led me away.

"But, Uncle," I said as he pulled me toward the chapel door, "surely you do not object to our consummating the marriage that you demanded."

"Hush, you wanton," he hissed. "Consummate your marriage? Hmph! Everyone here knows that you have already ensnared your teacher in your web of deceit and womanly tricks. He came to you a continent man, holy and pure, but you tempted him with your forbidden fruit."

"Is that truly what people are saying?" Heat spread across my face. "Have you heard it whispered that I enticed Abelard into my bed?"

"I have heard much worse, you temptress. I did not believe it at first, but your detractor was very persuasive—very persuasive! He said, 'Heloise could not help herself, being a daughter of that seductress Eve.' "

"What man said this of me?" My cheeks burned. "Who would spread such slander?" Jean sprang to mind. Beneath his curtain of servility I had detected, more than once, a whiff of judgment. "As God is my witness, *he* is the one against whom you ought to seek revenge."

Uncle Fulbert's laugh slithered in my ear. He slid his fingers up the soft inner part of my arm, then gripped me again so brutally that he bruised my flesh.

"Revenge, yes, heh-heh! How I would have loved to hear your detractor beg for mercy—mercy! But, alas, he deprived me of that satisfaction today—by marrying you."

12

To the imperiled boat not having the anchor of faith,
[from] she who is not moved by the winds which fan your
faithlessness.

—HELOISE TO ABELARD

$\mathcal{I}$f I was a "daughter of Eve," as Tertullian had called all those of my sex, then Abelard was something worse: a true son of Adam, who, after freely partaking of the forbidden fruit, blamed Eve for his sin.

"I said only what he wanted to hear," he told me when, after an agonizing week apart, my uncle at last allowed me to go to him.

Be a good girl, and obey your uncle, Abelard had whispered during our wedding feast at Etienne's. *Hold your tongue; take care not to anger him. He will forget this wound to his pride when he has gained the promotion I have in mind for him.*

I cared nothing about my uncle's position or his pride, but I hid my true feelings for another reason. Abelard and I depended on my uncle's complicity now—on his silence regarding our marriage. So I submitted to him despite the bile that arose whenever I considered what he had done to my mother, and to me.

Stretched upon the bed where, after carrying me over the threshold, Abelard had laid me, I spoke not of the past but of the present. I told him what my uncle had said of him—that, accused of seducing me, Abelard had insisted I was to blame.

He lifted his brows in mischief. "Do you truly think that I would degrade your character to your uncle, who loves you, and so increase his wrath against me?"

I thought that Abelard would say, and do, anything to save himself, and I said as much.

"Have you no heart?" He kissed my shoulder, my collarbone. "Do you not comprehend the depth of my love for you?"

Was it love, I wondered, that had compelled him to take me in my sleep our first time? Had love inspired his songs that, sung far and wide, told the world of our sins? Yes, I'd enjoyed being known as mistress to the world's most brilliant man. Every woman had envied me, and every man had desired me. All was vanity! But in my uncle's eyes, Abelard had stolen my honor and Uncle's, as well. Like the first man, and all men who have followed, Abelard blamed a woman for his weakness.

"Fulbert misunderstood me," Abelard said. "I never blamed you for anything, but invoked Eve to deflect his ire."

"Deflecting it onto me."

"Not onto you, no, but your sex." He struck his breast with his fists. "'From the origins of the human race, beautiful women have ever brought the noblest of men to ruin.' Clever, *non*?" He caressed my cheek, then moved his fingers to the soft skin under my ear. Pleasure rippled my blood. "And you *are* beautiful, Heloise—more so than ever now that motherhood has softened you."

My features may have softened; not so my powers of insight. "You have regained my uncle's trust at my expense. He regards me as a *meretrix*."

"My *meretrix*." Something flared in Abelard's eyes. "And if you want to be paid, you wicked woman, you must lie still."

He touched his lips to the nape of my throat, sending shivers over my skin. He leaned into me, nudging me backward onto the pillows, cupping one of my breasts and rubbing his thumb across the nipple until I began to squirm. He unlaced my surcotte, slipped it off my shoulders and over my arms, then lifted my *bliaut* over my head. Melting under his attentions, I forgot about my uncle, about my yearning for our child, about my past, present, or future and all else save for the two of us, as alone together as though we were the first woman and the first man and no others existed. In all the world, only we remained: his serpent, and my fruit.

PART THREE

Caritas

1

**Now at last I understand, sweetest, that you are mine with
all your heart and all your soul.**
—ABELARD TO HELOISE

THE NÔTRE-DAME CLOISTER, PARIS
FEBRUARY 1117

*J*urged my palfrey over the pocked and rutted road to the
Hautes-Bruyères Priory. Nearing death, Queen Bertrade
had sent for me.

"She wants to see you at once." At my uncle's front door,
Agnes had shimmered with excitement for my sake or to see her
precious Amaury again, or both. The plain woolen *bliaut* she
wore under her surcotte told me that she had not even taken the
time to change her clothes. I sent Jean with a message to my
uncle, pulled on a cotte, hat, and riding boots, and departed with
her and her servant on the horse they had brought for me.

As we rode, my thoughts scattered like the stones under the
horses' hooves. What if the queen should die before I reached
her? *Please, God, do not take her yet.* No one else except my mother's dearest friend could answer the questions plaguing me yet
about my past.

Amaury greeted us, red eyed, at the door of the infirmary.

"You have arrived in good time. My sister is nearly gone," he said in a choking voice, and escorted us into Queen Bertrade's private chambers, where nuns and nobles stood around her bed, waiting like guests at death's dinner table.

"Thanks be to God," the queen said when she saw me. "Amaury, please take this morbid audience with you when you go. They are robbing me of air." Amaury ushered everyone out, including the healer, who sputtered and protested that he must remain near his lady until the priest could arrive.

"Fool. Does he think I would die before receiving the viaticum? I intend to join my husband in Paradise." She smiled at Agnes and me. "Behold your expressions of gloom! Do not mourn, please. I'll be in Philip's arms again before sunset. Now—give me another pillow so I can see you."

"But—you must not overextend yourself," I said.

"Lest I die?" She snorted. "I have saved my strength for your visit. After this final task, I will gladly go—depriving the leeches, I hope, of any more of my blood."

We propped her with a pillow; Agnes took up a comb from a table by her bed and ran it through her hair. I willed myself not to stare at her as the others in the room had done. Although her black eyes' fire had dimmed to a smolder, her beauty had not. Her long chestnut hair flowed like a river of silk over her shoulders and across her lap. Her skin stretched taut over her cheekbones and jaw, giving her the appearance of a sculpture. She was so pale and had lost so much weight that I thought she might fade away while I watched. Her intelligence had not diminished, however.

"I thought you would have taken charge of the Fontevraud Abbey by now," she said, a sly gleam in her eyes.

"I did not go there, my lady. Or—rather—I did, but only to tell Robert that I had changed my mind."

"You've changed your mind? Or did God change it for you?"

She grimaced. "Amaury told me about your 'secret' marriage. It won't remain a secret for long in Paris."

"We had only a few witnesses, and all of them vowed never to tell. But we will not need to seal our lips for long. Abelard's new book will propel him to glory, and then he may do as he pleases."

She arched an eyebrow. "Indeed? And what of the child?"

I caught my breath and glanced at Agnes, who blushed. "I did not tell her! I confided in Amaury, but no one else."

"My brother tells me *everything*," the queen said, giving Agnes a shrewd look.

I told the queen of leaving Astralabe in Brittany, and of Abelard's promise to take me to him soon. We planned to fetch him as soon as Abelard's songs about me had faded from the streets and rumors about us had ceased to wag tongues.

"Your Abelard craves attention too much to be forgotten." She closed her eyes. "You will never bring that child home."

"No, my lady, he has promised—"

"And so you follow your mother's path." She sighed. "One cannot escape destiny, after all."

I stared at her, speechless. Of course we would retrieve our son. If I had to do it myself, I would not hesitate. I had journeyed to Brittany before without Abelard and could do so again.

"And did you find your father?" Her eyes opened.

"I did." At last, we touched on the topic I had come to discuss with her. "He recognized me at Fontevraud."

Queen Bertrade's nostrils flared. "And did he tell you all?"

"He was delirious with fever, my lady. He could not tell me anything, and Petronille would not."

"Because she doesn't know anything. *Hmph.* I am the only one who knows."

Queen Bertrade first met Robert long before my mother did, she told me, while living with her husband, the womanizing

Count Foulques of Anjou. When Robert arrived in the court, she cast her eye on his *fier* form, tall and lean and dark, the streak of white emblazoned like the mark of God in his dark hair, and his gray eyes filled with light. Bertrade determined to have him for herself. When Robert, in her presence, chastised Count Foulques for repudiating his past wives and children to marry again and again—Bertrade was his fourth wife—she fell even more completely under Robert's spell. "No man had ever treated me with such respect," she said. In return, Bertrade gave him an apartment in which to live while he pursued his studies in divinity at the Angiers school.

But the handsome priest seemed immune to the charms not only of the beautiful Bertrade but of all the other women who adored him—as many did. They brought him food, cleaned his apartment—he had refused the servants Bertrade offered—and even emptied his chamber pot. In return, they basked in his love, which seemed limitless and pure. None suspected that, under his alb, Robert wore an iron tunic whose sharp blades pierced his skin whenever he moved. When he met my mother, however, he put the iron tunic away so that he would not harm her when he held her in his arms.

"Women were his weakness, and your mother his greatest temptation," Bertrade said. Mother's virtue and piety only made her more attractive to him; her intellect made her irresistible. She felt no compunction about loving him, whom God had sent to relieve her loneliness. She saw no reason why priests should not marry; had God desired men to live without women, why had he created Eve?

My mother and father's conversation began in the Angiers court at dinner with Foulques and Bertrade, and continued throughout the day and into the night while courtly life went on all around them: the servants' clearing the tables; the petitioners' filling the hall to await an audience with the count; the sweeping of the rushes and the replacing of them with fresh ones; the lighting of the candles and the replenishing of wood in the fireplace. Through it all my mother and Robert talked earnestly, discussing, debating, laughing, and developing a bond that would deepen throughout their lives.

No love is perfect, however. When their friendship turned to passion, guilt plagued Robert. He who had spent years in Brittany demanding that clergymen set aside their wives now lived in greater sin than those priests.

"He would have married Hersende but for the wife and children he had renounced," the queen said. His sins, adultery as well as fornication, made him weep many times in my mother's arms. Then, hearing whispers about Mother, he realized that he caused her to sin, as well, and put on his iron tunic again.

"That's when she knew he would leave her," Bertrade said.

Unable to bear the burden on his conscience, Robert fled Angiers in the dark of night without even saying good-bye. Mother wept for months and would have followed him, but no one knew where he had gone. He wandered, a hermit in bare, bleeding feet, in the forests at Craon, lost to her for years.

Near my seventh birthday Mother went to hear Robert preach, and he asked her to build his new abbey. She would not have agreed but for my uncle, who had come to rescue us from poverty with an offer of marriage from a count. When Mother refused, my uncle's anger rose. When I walked into the *salle*, she introduced us and he began to shout. From where had this child come? Who had fathered it? Now he understood why she refused to marry. What man of noble birth would want a whore as his wife?

Soon my uncle had arranged a place for me in the Royal Abbey at Argenteuil, to prevent my being known, he said, but also for my benefit. Argenteuil had housed many great ladies of France and boasted the finest teachers in the world. I would depart from the abbey with the best possible education, he told her.

"The girl cannot live here in secret for the rest of her life," he said. "She will be discovered, and the whole world will know— the world!" If my mother wished to keep me with her, she must produce my father, whom Fulbert and her other brothers would force to recognize me.

"Or you can marry the count and beg him to adopt her." Uncle leered. "Employ your womanly talents."

Deprived of me and forced into betrothal to a man she did not know, Mother fled to Robert's side. She worked closely with him for years, devising plans for his abbey and executing them, commanding men. But she never told Robert about me, fearing that guilt would pierce his heart and that he would flee from her again.

"What good would come of his knowing, anyway?" Bertrade said. "He could not claim you; nor, with that white streak in your hair, could Hersende take you along to Fontevraud. Everyone would know that Robert had sinned with her, and, worse, Robert would be reminded every time he beheld you." She snorted. "God knows what punishments he might have inflicted on himself."

"But did Robert love Mother?" I asked, remembering Abelard's sneering words about hermits and monks.

"Who can know what resides in the hearts of men? What we see in their loins is more reliable." The queen chuckled but, noting my drooping countenance, amended her comment. "Your mother, who did know Robert's heart, swore he loved her more than God."

Then Bertrade lifted her head off the pillow and gave me a fierce look, gripping my hand with a force that made her arm tremble. "Hersende would never have given you up unless she had been forced to do so. She loved Robert, but she loved you most of all."

I sank to my knees and bowed my head, still clasping her hand. "Thank you, my lady. You cannot imagine what your words mean to me."

"I didn't speak them for your sake." Queen Bertrade dropped my hand and closed her eyes. "I've done it, Hersende," she said with a sigh. "Your daughter knows the truth. Now, tell God to end my misery and bring me home."

2

〜〜〜

Having given up everything, I take refuge under your wings. I submit to your rule, resolutely following you in everything.

—HELOISE TO ABELARD

We began the night innocently, lying on Abelard's blanket and inventing constellations. He discerned a dragon, dubbed Drago; I, a wheel, which we named Fortuna. A chariot shape with two bright stars before it, as though being pulled by them, we named Atalanta and Hippomenes, not knowing how those ill-fated mythical lovers prefigured our destiny.

I reminded Abelard of their story: Consumed with lust, they copulated in the temple of the Mother of the Gods. An enraged Cybele changed them into lions and chained them to her chariot. Likewise, my mother and Robert pulled God's own chariot, the great Fontevraud Abbey, to which they gave their lives, sacrificing their love.

"Mother never agreed that, in loving each other, she and Robert had sinned," I said to Abelard that night. Monks such as Bernard of Clairvaux who had renounced the world now preached the most loudly against priests who continued to live in it. And what of the Paris synod that, forty years ago, had declared clerical celibacy to be a violation of human nature and reason? Were those bishops in the right, or did today's reformists reflect God's will?

As I told Abelard my parents' tale, warmth spread through my chest. I had not been conceived in sin, as Uncle had said, but in the purest love. Likewise, the hours I spent making love with Abelard were holier to me than any mass.

"And if you are formed in your mother's image, as they say, then I know how Robert must have felt about her." Abelard stroked my cheek, then slid his fingers along my jawbone and across my throat to the space between my reclining breasts. "You are exquisite, Heloise. I loved you from the moment I saw you."

I laughed, doubting whether he could have loved me without any knowledge of me. Did he behold in my eyes the promptings of my heart that day on the *place* as he sang to me? Did he discern the ethic of my soul by examining the capon in my hand? *Non.* Abelard most likely admired my buxom shape and large, dark eyes.

His own eyes crinkled when I said this to him. "Would I sing in the *place* for hours to meet a pair of breasts, or a set of doe's eyes? In looks you do not rank lowest, but in the extent of your learning you stand supreme. I wanted to match wits with the famed woman scholar."

"You hoped to humiliate me, *non*?"

He grinned. "A *magister* is only as eminent as his most recent victory."

"For what do you wait, then? When will you finally conquer me?"

"How do you know I have not already done so?"

"You have wrested nothing from me, but I have freely given all."

"By skillful persuasion I coax you to do my bidding, though you think your desires are your own. That is the surest form of conquest, *non*?"

"And so the yearning of my body for your hands is not my yearning, but the result of your 'skillful persuasion'?"

"*Voilà.*" He propped himself on one arm and caressed my breasts, sending tiny arrows of pleasure shooting downward. I moaned softly and closed my eyes. "Who is in control? I am. As your *magister*, I thought you would have learned this by now." I felt a prodding against my thigh. "But perhaps you need another lesson."

"A lesson in the pleasures of the body, or the mastery of the heart?"

"Between the two of us," he said between soft kisses, "there is no difference."

O Abelard! How exquisitely he made love to me that night, in Etienne's vineyard beside the Seine. Hidden by the clusters of ripening fruit and green leaves as broad as an outspread hand, sheltered by the ink-black sky resplendent with winking stars, under his mantle sheltering us against the cool March breeze, he unlaced my *bliaut* and lifted my chemise, exposing my breasts, and reached inside my skirt to remove my underpants. He touched my flower gently, taking care not to bruise the petals. I shuddered and strained against him, yearning for the press of his *verpa* between my thighs, but he delayed, teasing me, or, rather, torturing me. At last when he filled me with himself, I cried out, lost in the stars, at one with God.

"Quiet, my love," he whispered into my ear as he took his own pleasure. "We do not want to be discovered."

Now that he had tumbled me over that precipice, he hastened to it himself, increasing my excitement anew. Mindful of his warnings against being overheard, I bit down on my tongue to stop myself from screaming out, which was what I longed to do, but could not restrain the mewling, like that of a kitten, issuing from my constricted throat. My body, which should have been sated, demanded only more. I wriggled my hips to feel him all over—and he rasped in my ear, then shuddered against me with a great sigh. Deflated, he lay atop me for a long while, his pulse slamming against my chest.

"My perfect wife," he said at last, lifting himself up and kissing my face. "*You* have conquered *me*, my darling, I whom no woman could conquer. I would do anything for you. Anything." He lay down and wound his arms about me, one around my waist and one behind my neck, cradling me, his fingers in my hair, stroking my scalp. I wanted to purr. The constellations shifted. The planets clicked into alignment. I gazed into his blue eyes, dizzy, drunk. All, all was right in the world.

All except our son, who awaited us yet. "I wish Astralabe were with us now."

Abelard chuckled. "And I thank God that he is not."

"You do not yearn for him?"

"Of course I miss him. I also realize that, were he with us, our time tonight would not be nearly so exciting."

"I would gladly trade an hour of lovemaking every now and then to see the dimple in his chin, and to kiss his fat cheeks." I pressed a hand to my chest. "Oh, when will I see him again?"

A horse's nicker. The bells rang the compline hour. Leaves rustled in the slight breeze.

"Not yet," Abelard said. "Soon."

The lap of the waters; my liquid ache.

"So you have said for months now. Abelard, he is growing up! He will forget me."

"He will not forget you."

"He will think Denise is his mother." Her fawning eyes, her grasping hands.

"Denise has a new love, my brother says—a lord of some lands near Nantes. Soon she will no longer cling to our son as she does now."

"*I* want to cling to him!" A sob tore at my throat. I glared at Abelard, wondering what he had become. Was our child only an impediment to his carnal pleasures and his glory?

"*Shhh!* I heard a horse. If we are discovered here, Fulbert will tell the world that we are married." Abelard covered me again with his cloak. Diminished by our spent passions and by the universe above, we forgot ourselves and began the argument that would change the course of our lives.

"We have already discussed Astralabe and reached an agreement—or had you forgotten?" he murmured.

"Agreement? As I recall, you gave me no choice. Either I leave him in le Pallet or be responsible for your death."

"And so now you would rather have me dead?"

"Do you truly think that my uncle would do you harm?"

"Have you forgotten the flash of the blade in his hand?"

"But now that we are married, there is no dishonor in our having a child." How many times had I spoken these words to Abelard these past months?

His reply was ever the same. "Everyone will see him and will know that he was born before we wed. All of Paris will whisper against us—against you, most of all. Your uncle will blame me for the blot on your honor, and on his own."

"You told him that *I* was to blame, remember? He will punish me, not you. But I do not fear him as you do." I glared at Abelard. "I would gladly risk my life to be with our son. Whereas you think only of your own skin."

"I am thinking of my future—of *our* future. Did you not refuse to marry me at first out of the same concern? I will lose my position, my book, everything if the bishop discovers that"—he glanced around and lowered his voice—"that we are married."

"You should have thought of that before you forced me to become your wife."

"Who forced you to do anything? Did my hand drag you to the altar?"

I wished, then, not for the first time, that I could cry. Tears might have softened Abelard's heart, causing him to relent.

"I only want to see my son. You promised to obtain lodgings for me in Paris and bring him here to live with me. When will this happen, Abelard? Winter will soon be upon us, and I see no effort to abide by your promises."

"Shh," he said. "Lower your voice, I pray."

"Why? So you can continue to keep our love—and our child—a secret?" He worried more about being discovered than about my despair. "I am weary of secrets!" I cried.

Then we heard a rustle of leaves, and the sickening sound of snapping vines, like crunching bones.

"Who goes there? Is someone in distress?" A man wearing the canon's alb emerged from among the vines, his bald pate shining in the starlight, his little eyes like pinpricks of light focused on the sight of Abelard and me lying side by side, my bodice unlaced and skirt lifted, his braies removed and *mentula* exposed.

"Roger," I whispered, recognizing my uncle's assistant in the Nôtre-Dame library. I rolled over and hid my face.

Abelard cursed under his breath. "Leave this to me," he whispered. "Good evening, Roger." He stood, half-clothed, shielding me or attempting to do so.

"Master Abaelardus! And—is that Heloise?" He stretched his neck to peer at me. "*Mon Dieu!* Please forgive me—I heard a shout, and thought—"

"All is well. She and I have been stargazing." Roger's gaze dropped to our astralabes, lying where we had dropped them. "But the stars in the sky cannot compete with those in her eyes. Don't you agree?"

"So—it is true, what I have heard about the two of you." Roger chuckled with pleasure, already spinning his tale in his mind, no doubt, feeding as he did on others' misfortunes. "Canon Fulbert will be surprised to learn of it. He has defended you most vehemently against the rumors. The poor man. His shame!" Roger clucked his tongue, but continued to smile.

"My uncle knows about us," I said.

Roger lifted his eyebrows, and I saw that I had erred. "Fulbert condones his niece's affair with her *magister*?"

"We are in love and would marry," Abelard said. "But continence is required of me, as you know."

"Even the most devout of men may be allowed to rest in a woman's arms from time to time," Roger said, nodding.

Abelard cleared his throat and, stepping forward, took Roger aside. Sitting alone under the infinite stars, I lifted my face to the rolling, restless orb of the universe. Roger would tell all, to everyone who would listen.

I noted the grim set of Abelard's mouth as he bade farewell to Roger and returned to me.

"Roger loves nothing more than to talk."

"He enjoys talking, yes, especially about others." Abelard mustered a smile. "But he will not talk about us."

How could Abelard be so certain? I asked.

"Because as much as Roger loves slander and scandal, he loves money more. And I have promised to pay him handsomely for his silence."

But where would Abelard find the money? He had spent all his silver on our journeys to le Pallet. We needed more, and quickly, to seal Roger's lips.

I would talk to him myself, I decided, having caused our discovery. *Quarreling's the marriage dowry,* the poet wrote, but I should have subdued my protests. Now my indiscretion would bring our ruin unless I convinced Roger to hold his tongue for my sake. He had always dealt with me kindly and regarded me with fondness. I had no choice but to go to him and try the methods of argument Abelard had taught to coax the tale-teller to silence.

I hastened to the scriptorium the next morning, hoping my uncle would not be there. The Nôtre-Dame cantor, Alfred, had attained the deacon's post my uncle had wanted, but Uncle Fulbert had risen, as well. At the request of Bishop Guibert, who had taken note of his rich voice, Uncle had taken over Alfred's duties for the time being. Choral rehearsals now occupied most mornings.

I found Roger in the library alone, on a ladder, dusting the books on their shelves. When I entered, he climbed down and led me to the back of the room, behind a curtain and into a dim space containing parchment, inks in varying colors, and a large table used to repair damaged manuscripts.

"I need to speak with you about last night," I said in a low voice. "Master Petrus—"

"Has already spoken with me. Alas, he could not produce the sum he promised last night." Roger shook his head. "The *magister* is rich in promises, *non*?"

"How much did he offer?" I reached for my money pouch, which contained the few coins I had managed to set aside since returning to my uncle's house.

"Much more than you possess in that purse. But my loyalty cannot be purchased. I should have said as much to the master last night, had he not tempted me with his forty pieces of silver."

My hopes sank at these words. "Keeping our secret would be a betrayal? Should it become known, who would suffer more than I?"

"And through whose fault? None other than that of Master Petrus, a man with more years and experience than you—quite a few more years—who ought to know better than to take advantage of his scholar." Roger wagged his finger. "You, a girl of virtue as pure as snow. Master Petrus ought to be ashamed."

"You err, Roger. He did not 'take advantage.' Our love is mutual."

"*Non. You* err. A man such as Petrus Abaelardus does not love, not in the way you think. I wonder, I do, what promises he has made to *you*. Your uncle had every right to know about the teacher and his own niece, *non*? Compromising you in the vineyard, where anyone might find you! Be glad that I appeared, and not your uncle Fulbert."

"He—*had* a right to know?" I touched the wall to steady myself. "You have told my uncle about last night?"

"I did what I thought was proper. I spent long hours on my knees about it, yes, I did. The Lord showed me the right path. I marched straight to the cathedral, found Canon Fulbert, and unburdened myself. He paid me, too, the full amount that your *magister* had sworn to give. An honorable man, yes, Canon Fulbert. And now he knows that, of all the men in this cloister—including Bishop Guibert, who uses him like a servant—I alone am worthy of his trust. He knows that now, which is why he confided your secret to me." In the dark room I could see the gleam of his teeth.

"My secret?" My mind and tongue felt equally inept, leaving me to mimic him or speak inanities, like a parrot.

"Yes. You know—that you and Master Petrus are married."

"If only your words were true, how happy I should be!" I said, allowing my anguish, at least, to show.

"I do not understand."

"That is most apparent." I gave a little laugh. "Canon Roger, I am not married, although I would give my very soul to be Abelard's wife." As, indeed, I had done.

"But your uncle—"

"He is mistaken."

"He said there was a ceremony, in the Saint-Aignan Chapel. He said Etienne of Garlande officiated."

"God is my witness, Roger, that no such ceremony ever occurred." I shook my head. "And so it has come to this. Poor, poor Uncle."

" 'Poor Uncle'?" Roger's voice dropped to a near whisper. "Does Canon Fulbert suffer from a malady?"

"Visions," I murmured. Knowing he could not see my face clearly, I sniffed and wiped a feigned tear. "Or, rather, hallucinations. Delirium, Roger, brought on by his excessive love for wine. At first, he experienced terrors in the night, horrible dreams—but now they plague him during the day, as well. I've begged him to cease his drinking, but he will not. I fear for his sanity, and worse—his life."

"Dear, dear Lord in heaven." A fecund smell, like overripe fruit, wafted from his breath.

"I hope I may trust you to speak of this to no one, Roger—especially not my uncle, who would treat me harshly." I opened the closet door and stepped out with him into the library. "I assume Uncle Fulbert paid you for your silence, as well."

"Oh, no. Canon Fulbert urged me to scatter the news of your marriage like wheat grains at a wedding."

"Hmm. Well, do so at your own peril. When the truth becomes known that Master Petrus and I never married—and Guibert, hearing the rumor, would certainly ask Archdeacon Etienne—you, the spreader of the tale, might appear a greater *bouffe* than my uncle."

*   *   *

My next destination was the Royal Palace, where Agnes had invited me for dinner. I entered her *chambre* and found her sitting on her bed in her saffron tunic and white turban, surrounded by covered dishes and reading Guibert of Nogent's *Dei gesta per Francos*. Her seigneur had stimulated in her not only an interest in Latin, it seemed, but also a newfound love for reading.

"It's a fascinating account of the first campaign to Outremer, but I have yet to find a mention of my *grand-père*." She put it aside and stood to embrace me. "My dear, you look as if you want to cry! What has happened? Tell me all."

I did, and she burst into laughter. "Now Canon Roger will tell everyone that your uncle is a delirious drunk. This is perfection! But why do you frown?"

"Uncle is a proud man. I don't enjoy belittling him."

"*Pfft!* Canon Fulbert belittled himself by confiding your secret to the biggest mouth in Paris. And he urged Canon Roger to spread the news of your marriage, did he?" Her eyes glinted.

Hunching as though my uncle were already beating me with his whip, I slumped to her bed. "We would not have been discovered if not for my harping at Abelard."

"Harping? You have waited how long for your child? I would have ridden to Brittany and fetched the babe myself before now. Do not blame yourself for anything. Someone would have discovered the two of you eventually. No one keeps a secret in Paris."

"We had concealed ourselves well until last night."

"Heloise, I summoned you here for a reason. I, too, have heard talk about you and Pierre. Roger is not the first to have espied you together. Soon all of Paris will whisper about your illicit love, and Canon Fulbert will tell everyone that you are married."

"And I will continue to deny it. The rumors will surely cease, then."

"What teller of tales ever concerned himself with their veracity? You predicted this would occur, or have you forgotten? Your marriage will soon be known to all, including the bishop of Paris."

I hung my head. "I have abandoned my baby for naught."

"Not for naught, but for the love of his father."

"The same reason why my mother sent me to Argenteuil. Agnes! You should have heard little Astralabe's cries as we rode away. Dear God, what have I done? What can I do?"

"What would you have wished your mother to do?" She narrowed her eyes. "Your son needs you, and you him. You must convince Pierre to take you to le Pallet. Should he refuse, come and talk with me again. With my money and your wits, we shall find a way to reunite mother and child."

3

❧❧❧

There is nothing worse than a foolish man blessed by fortune.

—ABELARD TO HELOISE

I greeted Uncle as always, with his cup and a kiss. He knocked the *henap* from my hand, splashing wine like blood across my sleeve.

"The kiss of Judas," he spat. "Keep your traitorous lips far from me."

I stepped back, out of his reach. He reminded me of a rabid dog with his bared teeth and red eyes rolling. I took a calming breath and asked what was the matter.

"Deceitful woman. How dare you slander me?"

"If you are referring to Roger, I only adhered to the terms of our agreement." *As you did not,* I wanted to add.

"By spreading malicious tales? By God, he has told all who will listen that I imagined your wedding while drunk on wine! 'Your niece said your condition has worsened, and that you are prone to delirium,' he said. That is a fine story to reach the bishop's ears."

"Bishop Guibert surely knows, as does everyone, how Roger loves to talk, and with little regard for accuracy." Everyone also knew of my uncle's love for wine, a point that I did not think wise to make.

"And so what would you tell the bishop about your marriage to Petrus?"

"I would deny it, of course. We all agreed, did we not, to a secret wedding? Abelard cannot marry and yet continue to teach."

"And what of *my* position?" My uncle snatched up the empty goblet and filled it with more wine from the flagon on the table. "You speak freely against the one who has given you everything to enhance the one who has taken everything from you. You could not be more like your mother."

"My father gave my mother more than you know. Much more." I turned away from him, unable to bear the disgust that smeared his mouth when he spoke of my father.

"He gave her his *verpa*, of that I am certain. But did he provide even a single coin with which to feed you, or give you his name? Hersende was never one to complain; none of us is." How distorted was the mirror in which my uncle viewed himself! "But neither did she thank me for placing you in Argenteuil, and so discreetly. No one in the world knew of her sin—no one, not even Robert of Arbrissel, who made her his prioress. And yet for the rest of her days she refused my letters, blaming me, she said, for your loss—"

"She blamed you? Why?"

"She refused to see the truth of her situation. By God, I do not know what she thought—that she could stay with you in that manor forever, hiding you from the world? She was as blind to the consequences of her acts as you have been, and as ungrateful for my help."

"Help her? How? By forcing her to relinquish her child?" I snarled.

"Everything that you have become today is because of me." He jerked his thumb toward his chest. "As soon as she wrote to me, begging me for money, I knew what must be done—and I did it: found her a count to marry and arranged a place for you in a reputable abbey, all for my sister, who had cared for me when we were young, and whom I loved. But was she grateful? Are *you*?"

All was exactly as Queen Bertrade had said. I looked him in the eyes. "You forced Mother to abandon me."

He snorted. "I saved you, stupid girl. You had the best upbringing money could buy, the finest teachers, a pampered life in the Royal Abbey—the Royal Abbey! You wanted for nothing."

I had wanted for nothing except love.

"You, Uncle, are the reason she went to Fontevraud." Without me.

"She did so of her own volition, once you had gone. I did not require it. In fact, I offered her a dowry should she wish to remarry, but she refused. And—behold the edifice which she built! Fontevraud is hers, they say, and I do not doubt it. Had she lived, she would be its abbess today." Then, remembering his ambitions for me, he scowled again.

"And at what cost?" I cried, thinking of our little son, and my own empty arms. "You cannot imagine a mother's anguish at losing her child."

He shrugged and drew his bushy brows together. "Had Hersende revealed the father's name, she would have lost nothing. I would have given anything to learn it, for the sake of our family's honor. But she would say nothing of him." Of course she could not. The scandal would have destroyed Robert and undone all his good works.

"And besides—what do you know of a mother's anguish?" Uncle said. "The only product of all your reading, as far as I can see, is an overactive imagination."

"I know a mother's anguish," I said, barely hearing my own

words over the frantic pounding of my heart. "I know it all too well—for I have a child of my own."

"You"—he dropped his goblet onto the floor—"have a child?"

I sat on the bench. Employing my meekest voice, I told my uncle about Astralabe. I hoped, I suppose, that his sense of family would inspire him to bring my child to Paris. No sooner had I begun than did I realize my error. My uncle's complexion darkened, and he raised a fist.

"You left your son in that godforsaken place? My own flesh and blood, suckling at the teat of a Breton?"

"Abelard thought you would prefer it to scandal."

"When has that self-important cock cared about what I preferred—when? He has made a hostage of your child for his own protection, the same as he did to you. If you have left your baby with his family, it is for his sake, not mine."

His words resonated, having struck a chord my thoughts had played.

"A babe in your arms would still the tongues wagging about you now. Nothing makes a women more respectable than motherhood."

"Then—you will help me to bring him home?"

Uncle laughed. "That is between you and your husband— your husband! Soon all of Paris will know of your marriage, anyway. I see no harm the babe could do at that point. I, of course, will pretend to have known about it all along." He rubbed his palms together. "An illegitimate child will give me the perfect excuse for revenge against that traitor."

"Uncle," I said, standing. "Do not lay a hand on Abelard."

"By God's head, why not? What has he ever done for you—or for me?"

"He has spoken on your behalf to Bishop Guibert. You may become the next cantor. Isn't that what you want?"

"He swore to make me a deacon! His promises are as empty as his heart."

I averted my gaze from his challenging eyes.

"How quickly you have forgotten all Petrus's wrongdoings. What did he care about your reputation? What thought did he give to your future, to your plans to become abbess at Fontevraud?"

"I never wanted to be an abbess. The scheme was yours, not mine."

"Had you an idea of your own, I would have listened to it, although God knows what it might have been. Unable to marry, no inheritance—how did you expect to live? On whose income?"

"I would like to open my own school for girls. Now that the Church has forbidden oblates, where will girls learn to read and write?"

"And do you think Bishop Guibert and William of Champeaux and Abbot Suger would approve of this school? The very idea of thinking women makes them quake. Now, I am beginning to see why." He peered at me from under knitted brows. "And you have set a bad example for your scholars by fornicating with your teacher."

Seeing me flinch, he increased his attack.

"You hadn't considered that effect, had you? Heh-heh. The consequences of your actions go far beyond your own constricted world—far beyond it! And now your babe, too, is harmed. He forced you to leave the boy in Brittany, you say? What will he do next? He must be stopped." Uncle rubbed his hands together. "And I know exactly how it must be done."

"If you touch even one hair on his head, I will tell Guibert of your sins." My voice shook but I glared in defiance, thinking only to save Abelard from disgrace.

"*My* sins?" Uncle's face reddened.

"Yes. I will tell him how you drink to excess every night, a flagon or even two of wine that you steal from the Church . . ."

"Steal? First you call me a liar, and now a thief?" He leapt up, kicking aside the bench, and lunged across the table at me, then grasped both my arms and shook me with such violence that I feared my neck might snap. "I see the disdain in your eyes. You think yourself better than I—I, who could destroy you—destroy you!"

"As you did my mother?" With a mighty effort I wrested myself free from his grip—then had to restrain myself from attacking him. He was the reason for my misery all these years, the cause of my abandonment, perhaps the cause of my mother's death. Hadn't Petronille said she died of a broken heart?

"You cared nothing for Maman," I said. "You thought only of your reputation—which, should you lay even one hand on Abelard, I will quickly destroy."

"Impudent *chienne*!" My uncle's smiting hand swatted me to the floor. I lay still, my ears ringing from the blow, curling up to protect myself.

"This is how you repay me for all my kindnesses?" Grasping the collar of my tunic, he lifted me up like a rag doll and bared his teeth. "Not even your mother dared to utter threats against me. But she knew, yes, how the sight of blood only quickens my own." He drew out his blade.

"You would not kill your own flesh and blood."

"You are half kin to me, true, but what is in the other half of you? A piteous leper? A common highwayman? Or even Satan himself?" He turned the knife so that it reflected light into my eyes. "Perhaps I will cut out your tongue. You would tell no tales against me then."

I remained limp against his arm, not daring to struggle for fear of the blade. I must live, not for my own sake, but for that of my son, who needed his mother. *Dear Lord, help me to think.*

Then it came to me, how to defeat my uncle—using not my strength, which could never prevail against his, but my cunning. My words.

I looked him in the eyes. They flickered with uncertainty. I seized the moment God had given to me.

"Canon Fulbert!" I barely heard Jean's cry. "*Non, non!* I implore you to stop!"

I lifted my chin. "I am the daughter of Robert of Arbrissel."

His grin sent a shiver through my very bones.

"I know," he said.

4

Pity me, for I am truly constrained by love for you.
—HELOISE TO ABELARD

y horse wandered like a ship without moorings. In the saddle, I struggled to keep my eyes from closing. Sleep had eluded me these past two nights, or, rather, I had eluded sleep. To sleep was to dream of Argenteuil, and I would not enter that dreary place any sooner than necessary.

"We have not much farther to go," said Jean, riding up beside me and taking my horse's reins. "I see the chapel spire in the distance."

I closed my eyes. Argenteuil. "I have slowed our journey. You will not arrive home before my uncle tonight."

"I serve Canon Fulbert no longer."

"No longer?" I sat up, alert. "But you have been with him for so many years."

"His drinking has pushed him too far. He may shout at me and beat me all he wishes. I allow it for my own reasons—but for him to harm a delicate young woman? *Non.* This I cannot abide." His jaw ticced.

"Jean, you have served my uncle too well to abandon him now. He needs you." He needed Jean's influence in my favor, I wanted to say, especially now that he had turned me out of his house.

Yes, you are Robert's daughter—the product of an unholy alliance, Uncle had said. *An abbot and his abbess?* He spat on the floor. *Filthy—filthy! Even more so than a teacher and his student.* Sin, he said, was in my blood. *You defile my house. Let your husband care for you, as he ought to do.*

When, an hour later, I appeared on Abelard's doorstep with Jean and my bags, Abelard tried to send me back. "This could not have occurred at a worse time," he said, pacing from one side of his *chambre* to the other, and back again. "Guibert has heard the rumors of our marriage. I met with him today. 'She lives with her uncle, as always,' I said. But what will happen when he finds out that you have come here?"

"Uncle threatened to tell him about us, Abelard. If he does so, it will not matter where I am living."

His shoulders slumped. "If that happens, Guibert will remove me from my position. He said, 'A man cannot devote himself both to scholarship and the duties of the marital bed—as you should know, given your own students' complaints against you.' Ha! He has been waiting for months to make that insult."

When Abelard swore that he had not married me or anyone else, Guibert suggested Abelard end the rumors by taking a public vow of celibacy.

"A public vow, in the cathedral before all! By God, am I a respected scholar or a brainless monk?"

"Next he shall command you to become a eunuch and sing in the choir." Was I to pity him now?

"No, he shall forget me in a day or two, when some other, more pressing issue demands his attention. Unless, that is, he hears that we are living together." Abelard covered his face with his hands.

Perhaps the time had come to establish me in my own home, I suggested. Then I could bring Astralabe from le Pallet and begin the life that we had planned. But Abelard shook his head: The time was too soon. Because of Roger, the rumors about the two of us had not diminished, but had grown. Months must pass—five or six, he said—before Paris turned its watchful eye away from us again.

"Six months? No, Abelard, I cannot wait that long for our son."

"Then do as I say." He revealed his plan: I must enter the convent.

"Fontevraud? But it is far from Paris—so far from you. I do not want to be separated from you again."

"Not Fontevraud, *non*. I want you closer to me than that." He pulled me close and kissed me. "Didn't God say, 'It is not good that man should be alone'?"

"I will be alone no matter where I go, if I go without you."

"And I will hunger for you constantly. But you need only be there for a short while." I would live in the abbey as a secular canoness, not taking the veil, free to depart whenever I chose. "Your going to Argenteuil may convince Bishop Guibert that I spoke the truth and quell the malicious talk about the two of us."

"And my uncle? What will he think?"

Abelard put his arms around me. He pulled me close and kissed my cheek, then held me for a long time. "Fulbert cannot harm you there. Please go, heart of my heart, flesh of my flesh, soul of my soul."

"And you?" I pulled back to search his troubled eyes. "What will he do to you for sending me away?" Showing him the bruises my uncle had made in seizing my arm, I told of his threats.

Abelard cursed, and his eyes filled with tears. "This is all the more reason why you must do as I ask, sweetest." His voice trembled. "Do not worry yourself about me—*I* have Jean as my guard. But if you remain, and Fulbert touches you again, I won't need to call anyone. I shall kill your uncle myself."

So, agreeing that Argenteuil offered the most practical refuge for the time being, we arranged a place for me in that *donjon* to which I had vowed never to return. Now, as Jean and I approached its stone walls and high chapel tower, bells tolled like a dirge heralding death, or my arrival. My stomach churned.

The silent faces of the sisters, their lips sealed with suffering; the seep of water in the walls' crevices and its dripping, when it rained, from the ceiling; the chill emanating from the stones to permeate my skin; the faces, lined and exhausted, of the nuns who worked in the fields; my own constant fatigue from being awakened throughout the night for prayer: Was this how God intended his creatures to live—in deprivation and hunger, silence and cold?

I had argued until I'd depleted my store of words. But where else could I go? I knew no relatives, not even my own brother, with whom I could seek refuge, nor any friends except Agnes. Her father, along with Etienne, had fallen from the king's favor since the monk Suger had been appointed the royal chaplain. The brothers from Garlande could not involve themselves now in any dispute with the bishop of Paris or take any risk of scandal.

I have never believed in the climate as a sign of anything, yet the banging of the heavens by Jove's bolt seemed appropriate as we passed through Argenteuil's gates toward where Abelard awaited in the courtyard. The flash that accompanied the fearsome noise, causing my horse to jerk its reins from Jean's hand and turn about, might have portended a knife, or the fires of hell, or a rainstorm, or nothing. I laughed as my mare trotted away, but Jean urged his horse after us and, when I had dutifully pulled in the reins, led us around again toward my destiny and Abelard.

"Yours is a timely arrival." He grinned as he helped me to dismount. When I said nothing, his gaze turned sorrowful, and he kissed my mouth. "Do not fear, Heloise, the sisters will take care of you here. And I will come to see you tomorrow."

The chapel door opened. A smiling priest whom I did not recognize stood within, beckoning us to enter. Clinging to Abelard's outstretched hand, I stumbled toward the door, leaving Jean to tend to the horses and my belongings.

"God's head, Heloise, you are not marching to your doom," Abelard whispered. "They are helping us, or had you forgotten? You ought to strive, at least, for gratitude over sullenness."

Gratitude over sullenness; sweetness over anger; smiles over tears; Abelard over Heloise. But to be severely afflicted by one's own misfortunes is the token of self-love, not friendship. And so I did his bidding and summoned a smile for the father; then, in the guesthouse, I thanked the abbess—not Basilia, who had died the previous year, but Beatrice, the prioress who had comforted me when first I'd arrived at Argenteuil as a child.

"The Montmorency family has endowed our abbey so generously over the years," the Reverend Mother Beatrice said when, after pressing my lips to her hand, I said I hoped God would bless her for giving me shelter. "Providing aid to one of their daughters is the least we can do. The *magister* has told us of your troubles." I glanced at Abelard: What had he revealed to her? "But we are pleased that God has sent you back to us. When you left, you had met all the requirements for taking the veil. Perhaps you will consider doing so now?"

"I—" I glanced at Abelard again, but could not discern anything from his frown. "That would be impossible, Reverend Mother. I am married, and have a child."

She lifted her eyebrows. "You are married? This is most unusual." She turned to Abelard for an explanation.

"Yes, yes, she is my wife. We were married in secret—for obvious reasons."

"A secret marriage?" She pressed her hands together and brought them to her lips, pondering. "We must not violate God's law. We must not encourage sin."

"We were married before God, Reverend Mother, in God's own chapel," Abelard said. "And as I have told you, Heloise needs a place of safety from her uncle, who has developed a taste for strong drink." He gestured toward the blooming bruise on my cheek. "Is it a sin to help a woman escape from danger?"

"'Yea, though I walk through the valley of the shadow of death, I shall fear no evil.'" Beatrice took my hand. "Welcome back to Argenteuil, Heloise. You may abide here for as long as you wish."

"My stay will be brief," I said when Abelard did not. "My husband plans to find lodgings for me and my son near the Nôtre-Dame de Paris Cloister as soon as possible."

"*Oui, oui.*" He nodded. "As soon as possible, *oui.*"

5

At the beginning, you certainly aroused my hunger for
your letters, and you have not yet fully satisfied it.
—HELOISE TO ABELARD

xcept for the absence of the Reverend Mother Basilia,
life at Argenteuil had not altered since I had walked
out its front doors for the first time and, I thought then, the last.
Argenteuil had not changed, but I had, which made cloistered
life not only difficult for me but nearly unbearable.

The silence, always annoying, now threatened to drive me
mad. No one spoke except by using signs or in the night, when
whispers and muted giggles could be heard drifting through the
dormitory. I longed to join those gatherings and was invited to
do so, but dared not for fear of losing my residency. So I suffered
through each day without speaking a word, in spite of the inquis-
itive eyes asking why I had returned.

I had always hated rising from bed in the middle of the
night for prayers; now, doing so was a torment. Settling back to
sleep had never been easy, but now the turnings of my mind,
like a spinning wheel, prevented my doing so. Why hadn't Abelard written to me? When would he visit? What of our son—
was he faring well, was he still, as Dagobert had written, "hale
and robust"? Did his hair curl? Had his eyes remained blue?

Would he know me at all when, at last, I held him in my arms again?

Adding to my discomfort was the work that I had to do.

Abelard's one benefice, a parcel of wild ground near Champagne, yielded no income, unlike those my uncle had acquired during his years as canon. Because my husband could provide only a small amount to pay my expenses at Argenteuil, I knew I would have to perform extra work in the abbey. I had assumed that, given my education and background, I would work as a teacher or even a copyist or illuminator of manuscripts. Sister Adela, the nemesis of my youth and now a prioress, had other ideas.

"Given some notice, we might have arranged a position for you indoors." Her eyes glinted like needles. "We placed Sister Marguerite in the kitchen last week—but you were never an accomplished cook. The sewing room might be possible—but you are not a seamstress, *non*?"

"I speak Latin fluently," I said, although I knew she needed no reminding. She had been Mother Basilia's favorite among the oblates, but I had bested her in the classroom and gained the favor of Sister Beatrice, our teacher and, now, the abbess. Adela had spent most of our childhood in sullen resentment, trying without success to influence the other girls against me. Now she wielded power at last.

"Sister Helene helps me in the classroom." I forbore remarking that Adela must certainly need assistance, given her poor command of Latin. "We have no need for more teachers at present."

I suggested that I might become a scribe or illuminator, but her smile only widened. "The monks at Saint-Denis have taken those duties," she said brightly. "But we need workers in the vineyards. You always hated the darkness of the abbey, didn't you? Now you'll have sunshine and fresh air every day. Except, that is, when it snows." She laughed as if she had made a clever jest.

I might have complained to the Reverend Mother Beatrice about my assignment, but could not bring myself to do so. Was I superior to the other vineyard workers? Birth counted for nothing in the abbey unless one brought a dowry, which I had not. And besides, the life that I had led with Abelard made me less worthy than the nuns, most of whom had never sinned with a man.

So I bent and pulled and pruned in the vineyard with the sisters who, like me, had nothing to give to the abbey but painful toil, and the sweat of our brows. My body ached so acutely that first week that I could not move without wincing, as if I wore Robert's iron tunic. Blisters formed on my hands, and calluses, roughening my skin as though I were a villein or a man. At last I decided to petition the abbess for a change in my work assignment, but found that she had gone to Saint-Denis to visit the deathbed of the Argenteuil provost. I felt grateful that I could not cry for I would have shed many tears of self-pity, insulting the women who worked beside me.

My real sorrow, however, came not from Argenteuil's hardships but because of Abelard's neglect. Although he did come to me the day after my arrival—and made exquisite love to me in the guesthouse, where we had found privacy—his too-brief visit left me more bereft than before. Then he disappeared. One week passed, then two, without any word from him, in spite of the letters I sent at every opportunity and at great cost until my small supply of coins had trickled away. *The cold and your absence have turned my heart to ice, if not stone,* I wrote, and also, *If the vineyards do not break my back, your neglect of me will break my spirit.* Still he did not reply.

In those weeks, all my accumulated knowledge and the wisdom of the sages faded from my mind. I thought only of Abelard and my son, longed for them, prayed only for Abelard's imminent return so that I might share life with him at last, and with our apple-cheeked little boy.

Was it pity I saw in the eyes of my sisters as I sat by the courtyard, watching for messengers? The firm foundation of my trust in Abelard began to erode, leaving me as unsteady as a house built upon sand. Put out of his sight, I seemed to have vanished from his thoughts, as well. Shut off from Abelard, from our child, from love, from life itself, I felt alone as never before. I wandered the halls in silence, unable to cry, forbidden to speak, haunted by memories, taunted by doubt. Abelard, who had promised to love me forever, had abandoned me. And I, believing his promises, had abandoned our child as my *maman* had done to me.

Without Abelard's help, how would I claim my son again? I had no money that would enable me to travel to Brittany, and without Abelard's consent I doubted that Dagobert would allow me to take Astralabe anywhere. Even should I convince him, how would I care for a child? Bereft of Abelard, cut off from my uncle, I had no means of support. My arms ached for the weight of my little son; my breast yearned for his soft skin, the pats and squeezes of his tiny hands. *I pray that, someday, you will understand.* Yes, Mother, but not like this. Surely not.

Was this how she had felt while parted from me? She, at least, had the solace of Robert's love. Had she told him about me, everything might have been different. She might have taken me to Fontevraud with her, and my uncle would have been powerless to take me away. I would have posed no threat to the family's honor cloistered with her, the secret of my birth guarded like a precious heirloom. But she had not yet built an abbey when my uncle made his demands. Perhaps she did not yet realize her strength, or her capabilities.

I, on the other hand, had been abandoned as a child and given to the convent, but with God's help had survived. I had withstood my uncle's heavy hand and managed his household profitably. In my studies I had mastered all my masters—save one. I had loved not once, but twice—my son and his father—with all my heart. Pumping through that heart was the blood of Hersende of Champagne and Robert of Arbrissel, both of whom had dared to live their lives as each felt called to do, defying the strictures of men. Wasn't I as strong?

Giving up her child had been my mother's fate, but it would not be mine. No matter what Abelard desired, I would not leave my baby to be raised without me. On the seventeenth day with no word from Abelard, I decided to seek assistance elsewhere.

I had already written to Agnes, but she had returned to the court at Anjou and her beloved Amaury, who planned to repudiate his wife and marry her, she wrote. She sent several livres, enough to send me to Brittany and back, but the question remained of where, and how, Astralabe and I would live.

To ask Etienne for help was, of course, out of the question.

I thought of the brother I had never known. Where would I find him? I considered the distant uncle willing to help me with his funds but not, it seemed, with his love. So at last, holding the image of my son in my mind, I humbled myself with a beseeching letter to Uncle Fulbert requesting my dowry.

To gain his sympathy, I told him all that had occurred: Abelard's coaxing me to seek refuge at Argenteuil, then abandoning me there; our son's remaining in the care of the Bretons despite my wishes; and my own suffering. I told of my impoverishment and hard work, how I had to pull and prune vines with blistered hands and an aching back. I wrote with no other aim but that he might rescue me, again, from the hell in which I lived. I could not remain here. If I did, I would lose my sanity.

To my surprise, I received a summon only a few hours after sending the letter. A visitor had come, the sister signed. My pleas must have been effective, indeed, to bring Uncle Fulbert so quickly. I hurried from the vineyard to cleanse my hands and wipe the dust from my clothes, then went to the guesthouse. When I stepped inside, I greeted not my uncle but Abelard, standing in the center of the room with his arms open wide as if expecting me to run to him with joy.

"Abelard. I thought you had perished."

"Why the frown? Are you disappointed?" His booming laugh, nearly forgotten during these silent weeks, made me jump. "I am very much alive, my sweet bride, as you can see. You, on the other hand, appear barely so. What has happened to you?"

"Argenteuil has happened to me. I told you I would wither here."

"But I did not know you meant it literally. My God, how altered you are, in so short a time." He stared with horror at my brown hands, my chapped face.

"Seventeen days have passed."

"Have they?"

"Seventeen days with no word from you."

"I wanted to write, but I was afraid." His eyes darted from side to side. He lowered his voice nearly to a whisper. "I am being followed, Heloise."

"Followed? By whom?"

"Shh! By Fulbert, or Guibert, or someone else who would destroy me if he could. Perhaps Suger hopes for a scandal that could damage Etienne. I possess many enemies."

"And only one wife, whom you have neglected along with your son."

"Astralabe is doing well. He is truly talking Heloise and not even six months of age! Of course, his superior intelligence comes as no surprise." Abelard pulled a tablet from his pouch—from Dagobert, he said—and presented it to me. I read it hungrily, my heart leaping to imagine my son's sweet little voice sounding out words—and aching to think of him truly calling Denise "Maman" now.

"O Abelard! I cannot wait to see him, can you? Now that you have come for me, will we go to Brittany?"

"But I have not come for you, not yet. Forgive me, sweetest, but you must be patient a little while longer."

"You rode here to tell me this?"

"Not only for that." He stepped forward to slip his arms about my waist. "For this, as well." Sweet touch, sweeter kisses: how easily I succumbed to him, having been deprived of embraces. The heat of my beloved's breath; the spice of his scent; his hands on my back, my waist, my breasts; the taste of his mouth, the hum of my blood through my body like the tides, surging to the places he touched; the words of love he murmured as he lifted my *bliaut*—all carried me away from my sorrows of the past weeks to that place of bliss that I had visited so many times with him. Abelard had not abandoned me but had kept himself apart for fear of discovery, and a desire not to add further fuel to the fires of speculation.

He sat in a chair and pulled me into his lap. We joined our bodies, rocking, gazing into each other's eyes. Emotion filled me, spreading like the mist over the sea, encompassing all the world with love; my thoughts constricted to leave the world and center on only Abelard, my beloved, returned to me. When, spent, we clung to each other, I felt tears on my cheeks—but they were his, not mine.

"How I have yearned for this—for you. Heloise, I know you must think me weak and lacking in courage. Forgive me for neglecting you, my shining star. I swear, I never meant to cause you any pain."

"With great passion comes great pain." I pulled on my under-clothes and smoothed my garments. "But you must not keep yourself from me for so long."

"I will not need to do so, not anymore." He smiled as if pre-senting me with a gift. He had arranged to journey weekly to the Saint-Denis monastery, not far from Argenteuil, where the abbot wanted instruction in dialectic. Abelard would visit me after every lesson. "Once a week will not satisfy my hunger for you, but at least neither of us shall suffer long from being parted."

When, I asked, would he bring Astralabe and me to Paris as he had promised?

Soon, he said—always his answer. Seeing my displeasure, he added, "Fulbert is my greatest concern. I keep myself apart from him, but the cloister is small and, anyway, I cannot help seeing him at rehearsals and in services now that he is acting as cantor. You should behold his menacing stare! If he could accomplish with his eyes what he once threatened to do with his blade—" He shuddered.

"Abelard, you and I wed. Uncle gave me over into your care. He will not harm you. His sense of honor is too great, as is his ambition."

"He would not harm me now, thinking as he does that I have sent you to Brittany to collect our child."

"Did you tell him so? When?" I thought of my letter. *You spoke the truth about Abelard: he cares nothing for me. He deceived me into entering this convent and has left me here to die.*

"Would I speak to your uncle directly? *Non*, for I have no wish to die. One wrong word, and out would come his knife. I planted the tale in Jean's ear and had him tell it to Pauline at the market yesterday."

My admission about the letter perched on my lips—for his sake, Abelard ought to know the truth—but God is my witness that I could not bring myself to utter it. What good would come of increasing Abelard's fears? He already lived in terror for his life—needlessly so, in my opinion, for Uncle Fulbert would not do anything to endanger his own position. If my letter had increased Uncle's hatred, nothing Abelard could do or say would assuage him, anyway. Only I could do so—with another letter, which I would write as soon as Abelard had gone.

"But—will he believe such a tale? Does he truly think you would send me to Brittany alone?"

"I did it before, didn't I? Let us hope he believes it and ceases his spying. Perhaps he will put away his knife, as well." Abelard grimaced. "God forbid that he should discover the truth. Were he to learn that you live here, I hate to think what rage would prompt him to do."

6

Wholly guilty though I am, I am also, as you know, wholly innocent.

—HELOISE TO ABELARD

As soon as Abelard left for Saint-Denis—with a promise to return to me the following day—I wrote a second letter, telling Uncle Fulbert that Abelard had not abandoned me, after all. I sent it with the abbey's messenger the next morning.

Spies follow Abelard night and day, I wrote. *I pray that, if you are having him followed, you will desist. Only when he feels himself out of danger will he bring Astralabe and me home to Paris. The more others threaten him, the longer I must spend toiling in the vineyards here.*

I included the last sentence, I admit, in hope that my uncle would redress my situation, not liking the idea of his niece laboring in the fields. When Abelard returned to me the following afternoon, I felt an inner prompting to tell him what I had done. Again, I convinced myself not to do so—not for his sake, I realize now, but for my own, fearing he might abandon me again.

As we walked about, searching for a place to steal an hour's pleasure, I asked about our son. Had Abelard heard anything more of him?

"*Non*, I have no more news. Why don't we go to le Pallet and see him for ourselves?"

"Abelard—truly? Will you take me to your brother's house at last?"

"I wrote to Dagobert yesterday. Your grief moves me immensely, sweetest. I did listen to your complaints and have pondered them and found you in the right. And—Heloise! I have found us a perfect little house, with a windmill, on the ruga Saint-Germain." His entire face seemed alight. "It is time the three of us faced the world together, openly, and left all else to God."

I cried out, then, and clasped my hands in a prayer of thanks to heaven and Abelard.

"Shh," he said, smiling. "Or the sisters will send me away too soon." He winked.

The three of us together, in our own little house—with a windmill! I felt something turning in me, shifting, toward the light rather than the darkness I had imagined. Thoughts of telling Abelard about my letter to Uncle Fulbert flew from my mind. What would be the use in worrying him now? Soon we would ride to le Pallet, claim our child, and return to our home in Paris. My uncle would not dare to harm us; indeed, he would not desire to do so as long as Abelard took proper care of Astralabe and me. Our own, sweet house! And so I kept my error to myself, sowing the seeds for a lifetime of remorse.

"Of what are you thinking?" he asked, although his smile told me he already knew.

"I am thinking of kissing you."

"Once again, we share the same thoughts. Lead the way, my lady."

"But—there is nowhere."

"Surely there must be some private place. What about those shrubs?" He pointed to the cloister's eastern edge, near the refectory. As we looked around us but saw no one, he took my hand and led me into the bushes, where we kissed as though life depended on kisses and buried our hands in each other's clothes.

"My husband," I murmured. "Heart of my heart, you are everything to me, and I will love you forever," a vow that I have never broken nor regretted, not even for a moment.

Then, in the thick of passion, we heard voices, and a cough. Peering out, I spied Adela and a visiting priest walking toward us, engaged in deep conversation. My blood ran cold at the thought of them glimpsing us in the bushes, against the cold stone wall, groping and panting like wild creatures. Quickly we arranged our clothing and slipped inside the nearest door, over which hung a likeness of the Virgin Mother. Her expression, normally sorrowful, appeared stern to me now. *Mother of the Gods.* I shuddered, remembering the fate of Atalanta and Hippomenes, the lovers in Ovid's *Metamorphoses* who had dared to defile Cybele's temple.

This was the refectory, the large dining hall now empty save for the benches and dismantled trestle tables lining the perimeter. Light poured in through high, arched windows and bounced off the floor of smooth white clay, limning Abelard with gold. His hair shimmered, throwing off sparks. I felt giddy with light.

"Heloise. Behold your radiance. You look as if you might ascend into paradise."

"I feel as if I were already there," I breathed as he pulled me close. *Astralabe! We are coming for you.*

"No—not yet," he murmured. "But the kingdom of heaven is at hand, my love." He led me toward a bench and sat me down beside him and commenced the gentle rubbing and tender pinching and delicate nips of teeth that always made me forget myself. I shuddered as he moved his fingers more deeply, searching, probing, stroking—but the echo of my moans, bouncing from the ceiling to the stone walls and back to my own ears, awakened me as though from a delightful dream.

"*Non*, my love—wait! We cannot do this here." I pushed against him with my hands.

"Why can't we? The hall is empty. No one can see us, or hear us. And I want you, my beautiful dove."

"This hall is sacred." I gasped as he nuzzled my throat, sending chills down my spine and making my teeth gnash. "Dedicated to the Virgin Mother."

"Had you forgotten that we are married? There is no sin in this, Heloise." He slid his hand under my skirt, up my thigh.

"But we will defile her temple!" I thought, wildly, of Atalanta and Hippomenes, changed into lions as punishment.

Abelard knelt on the floor and pulled me down with him. "This is no temple, but a dining hall. But if you insist, I will pray. Thank you, Lord," he said, kissing my face, my neck, my breasts. "Thank you for my beautiful wife."

O Abelard! How could I resist his touch, his eyes of beseeching blue, his dimpled smile with its promise of bliss? Never once in our two years together did I say no to him, or, rather, although I begged him more than once to desist, I could not deny him anything he wanted from me. He pleasured me in that sacred hall until I quaked the building, not daring to loose the screams that had gathered like thunderclouds in my chest but lifting my voice, instead, in hushed, exultant song.

"Do you fare well?" he asked when, in the aftermath, I lay still as death beneath him, save for my heart's fist banging on my chest.

"My body fares well, yes. More than well. But my spirit feels torn and bruised." He raised himself to gaze into my eyes, but I averted them—half fearing, I think, that I would see a yellow mane covering his smooth neck, and his fingers bent into claws.

"Why be so worried, my only joy? No one has seen us except God, in whose eyes we are one." He arranged his clothing and I did the same, but with a burning face and shaking hands. We had defiled the sanctuary, just as Atalanta and Hippomenes had the temple of the Mother of the Gods. As punishment, Cybele had turned them into lions—creatures that could not mate with each other, so the Greeks had thought. What penalty would our Mother of God exact from Abelard and me?

7

⟨decorative ornament⟩

While I should be groaning over the sins I have committed, I can only sigh for what I have lost. . . .

—HELOISE TO ABELARD

I didn't have to worry for long about the penalty for defiling the Virgin's refectory. Mere days after our transgression, vengeance came in the tug of Sister Adela's hand on my sleeve. Someone awaited me in the guesthouse, she signaled. Adela's eyes glinted, as they had since Abelard's last visit—making me wonder if she had seen us enter the refectory together.

With a fluttering pulse and thoughts of our son I hastened across the courtyard, through the gardens, heedless of stares and the clapping of someone's hands meant to slow me down. I may have been the first person ever to run through those quiet halls and across those serene and sacred grounds. I pressed my hand to my chest, trying to quell my galloping pulse. Why had Abelard come again so soon? I could think of nothing except Astralabe. *Let him be safe, O Virgin, I pray.* But I thought my heart might stop altogether when I pushed open the guesthouse door and found Jean inside, his tall frame hunched over his hat, which he twisted in both hands, his eyes red and wild, his mouth a rictus of grief.

"A terrible accident," he said. My heart seemed, for a moment, to stop. Abelard! Had my uncle read my letter and avenged himself as he had so often threatened to do? But it was my uncle who lay in his bed, gravely injured, calling for me. I must depart for Paris without delay.

I turned to Sister Adela, who stood behind me with narrowed eyes, and asked her to inform the Reverend Mother Beatrice that I had gone, and why. As she protested that I could not simply leave the convent without settling my accounts, I turned and ran to the dormitory for my mantle and then out the abbey door to mount Jean's horse with him. I had taken no vow and did not wear the veil, and paid no heed, now, to the convent's rules or Adela's opinion of me.

I closed my eyes against the cold wind, clinging to Jean's waist as our horse sped down the wide road to Paris. Every bad thing I had done to my uncle replayed itself in my mind: my many deceptions with Abelard; the dislike I had tried, without success, to hide from him; the bitter words I had spoken; and, worse, the lies I had told against him to Roger, knowing they would be spread. Yet in spite of all, he called for me now. Perhaps he loved me, after all.

What had happened to him? Jean had not taken the time to say. A fall down the stairs after his nightly flagon seemed most likely, or a tumble from his horse. In my time with him I had come to expect that he would suffer some such tragedy, being consumed by wine, and reeling in vision, and stumbling in judgment. Why had I never admonished Uncle or expressed my concern for his well-being?

Now that his end was near, he had summoned me to his side. Would he repent of treating me so harshly? If so, I would readily forgive him. In fact, I should do more and beg *his* forgiveness. Yet I knew that I would not do so. For, in spite of the judgments of men, I never felt a speck of remorse for loving Abelard, the other half of my soul, with all my heart and, yes, body. Never did I feel closer to God than in the circle of my beloved's arms.

We arrived in Paris in less than an hour, perhaps even half an hour's time. As we slowed of necessity to a canter, then a walk, I gazed around at the city I loved. The noise of the children, the cries of the vendors, the rattle of cart wheels, the gurgle and splash of the Seine, the clopping of horses' hooves: all were as music to my ears after three weeks of uneasy silence broken only by the song of the abbey choir. The air, pungent with the smells of manure, dogs, rotting meat, baking bread, lavender, roses, smoke, ash, rain, even human feces and urine, exhilarated my senses in contrast to the dulling reek of incense at Argenteuil and, beneath it, the dank linger of mildew.

I took deep breaths, relishing the light snow on my face, the heat and prickle of the horse's flanks, the throb of my own heart in time to the pulse of life. I had come home to stay. I would never return to Argenteuil.

We entered the cloister gates and headed toward my uncle's house, not along the streets but, to my surprise, through the narrow, hidden alleys. Soon I heard a shout, followed by more voices, and looked to the right to see four men on horseback racing toward us, their faces grimly set. With a cry for me to hold tightly to him, Jean brought down his whip, sending the horse into a sudden run. Down the alley we sped, kicking loose piles of garbage; narrowly avoiding a flock of chickens pecking at scraps; scattering rocks, splattering mud. Then another horseman appeared in our path, and we halted so suddenly that I went tumbling over, off the horse and onto the icy street.

Dazed, I looked up at Jean, expecting to reassure him that I was unhurt, but his eyes had fixed on the men on horseback who now surrounded us.

"Apprehend him," someone said. Two men jumped to the ground and ran to Jean, then grabbed his kicking legs and pulled him off his horse. Someone clutched me from behind and lifted me to my feet, then, holding me by both arms, shoved me forward, toward the group that had pursued us.

"I have no money," I said. "Neither does he. Not even a single coin. Please, release us. My uncle—"

"Silence!" I stared at the red belts of the men who surrounded us—not thieves, after all, but the cloister's own gendarmes. My captor tied my hands behind my back and, taking me by an elbow, led me along with Jean toward the Saint-Denis-du-Pas Chapel.

"Jean, what is happening?" I said to him, but he would not reply or even look at me. "Please, there has been some mistake," I said to my captor. "You must let us go. My uncle—"

"Silence!" roared the man again, and tightened his grip, bruising my arm. Seeing my wince, Jean turned eyes to me that brimmed with tears.

"You must do as they say. For your own sake, I beseech you."

"Did you hear my friend call for silence?" snarled the man who held Jean. He lifted a booted foot and kicked Jean in the behind so forcefully that he fell to his knees. "I ought to push you all the way down and strangle you in the mud. But for what you have done to Monsieur Abelard that punishment would be too light."

"Abelard? What does he mean?" The gendarme holding me jerked my arm so abruptly that I cried out. "Please, monsieur. I have just arrived in the cloister and do not know anything. Has something happened to the headmaster?"

"We soon will find out what you know, and what you do not," the man said.

Inside the chapel, on cushioned chairs, sat Bishop Guibert and the monk Suger, whose roaming gaze seemed to penetrate my clothes. My skin crawled as though spiders scuttled over my body.

"We have captured the assailant," the provost said, pushing Jean forward so roughly that he stumbled. The word *assailant* clanged in my mind like dissonant bells, obscuring all else that he said.

"Jean," I cried, "what have you done?"

"No more and no less than he deserved," Jean said, but he would not meet my eyes.

The bishop sent him from the room, then turned to me. "What wrong has Master Petrus done to your uncle that he would command such a violent act?"

"Of what act do you speak? What has happened to Abelard? Is he alive?"

"He lives," Guibert said.

"At this moment, he may wish he were dead," Suger said with a grin.

"Canon Fulbert's temper is widely known, but you, Heloise?" Guibert's expression was grave. "What is your part in this terrible crime?"

"Terrible crime?" My voice rose. I looked from the bishop to the monk and back again. Neither answered, waiting, apparently, for me to confess something. "I do not know what you mean. Please tell me: What has happened to Abelard? Where is he?" My only love, injured at my uncle's behest? I would have turned and run from these men and their accusing eyes, their pointless questions, were it not for the ties binding my wrists and the gendarme who guarded the door.

"Petrus lies in his bed, groaning and mutilated, and will remain there for a long while," Suger said. "You will have ample opportunity to comfort him after you have told us all that you know."

"I took refuge in the convent at Argenteuil weeks ago. I know nothing of any attack."

"Why, then, were you riding with Jean, the doer of the deed?" Suger reminded me of a viper snapping its jaws.

"He came to fetch me. He said my uncle had been injured and was calling for me." Suger narrowed his eyes, skeptical, but confusion shadowed Guibert's face.

"The men who assisted Jean fled to your uncle's house. One of them returned to us and confessed, and the other we found hiding in Canon Fulbert's storeroom. We have not apprehended Canon Fulbert, but we will do so. Perhaps you know where we may find him?"

"As I have told you, I know nothing."

"Give her to the gendarmes," Suger said to the bishop. "She will confess to them soon enough."

"Please, Your Grace, I wish only to see Abelard. I beg you to take me to him, or to release me so that I may go to him."

"Do not be deceived by this woman, Your Grace," Suger said. "She feigns heartbreak, but where are her tears? Why did Jean bring her to Paris from Argenteuil?"

"Why not ask that question of Jean?" I said.

"I would like to know why you were living at Argenteuil, instead of with Canon Fulbert," Guibert said.

I paused, considering whether I ought to tell him the truth. Having sworn to keep our marriage a secret, however, I could only bring myself to reveal part of my tale. "Master Petrus took me there to escape my uncle's abuse. Uncle Fulbert had grown increasingly harsh with me. I lived with him in fear."

"And why did he deal with you so cruelly? Could it be that you deserved the treatment you received?" Suger asked.

"I did not," I said, returning his accusing glare with a level gaze.

At that moment, the door opened and two gendarmes hauled Jean back into the room. I gasped at the bruises on his face and stripes of the whip, oozing blood, on his bare back. But he would suffer much worse that day.

"He says Canon Fulbert ordered him to do it," one of the men said. "Fulbert held his wife hostage."

"Where is Canon Fulbert now?" the bishop asked.

"I do not know, Your Grace," Jean said in a slurring voice. His head drooped from his limp neck like a wilting flower. "My instructions were to meet him with the lady at his house."

Suger turned triumphant eyes to me.

"For what purpose?" Guibert said.

"I do not know, Your Grace. I fear that he planned to do her harm. He was—he was obsessed with Heloise."

My stomach turned.

"And what did the *lupa* think of that?" Suger licked his lips. "All of Paris knows of her wantonness. Have you heard Petrus's songs about her?"

"She is no *lupa*, but a married woman." Jean's voice rose and his skin reddened. "A virtuous woman, as well, even if she has that scoundrel for a husband."

"Married?" Guibert arched his brows. "To Petrus?"

"Has a teacher—nay, the headmaster of our school—taken to bed his own scholar?" Suger said. "How disgusting." He leered at me. "Who seduced whom?"

"He moved into our house and made himself her teacher, then forced himself upon her," Jean said.

I stared at him, barely able to comprehend what he said.

"But Petrus has taken a vow of continence." Guibert's frown caused me to lower my gaze.

"And so, you attacked Master Petrus at the uncle's command—and with his wife's permission?" Suger said, his voice now gentle, as if to coax from Jean the answer he wanted.

"She knew nothing of it. If she had, she would have run to his side. I never saw a woman more in love—or a man less deserving." A sob escaped Jean's lips. "Please forgive me, my lady. I had no choice in what I did, but I did it with pleasure. He is not good enough to kiss your feet."

When the gendarme had taken the quivering, crying Jean out the door again, the bishop ordered my hands untied. As I rubbed my wrists, he apologized for my treatment. "This heinous act has thrown us all into confusion." He gave me permission to go. I dipped low to kiss his ring and thanked him for his kindness— and then, as he was about to turn away, I asked again what calamity had befallen my husband. Instead of answering, the bishop cleared his throat. A flush spread like fire across his face and neck.

Suger, however, seemed eager to answer. "Who would have surmised that the drunkard Fulbert would prove to be such a . . . *man*? He has outstripped us all with his magnificent feat." Suger's eyes, gazing at some far-off delight, held me transfixed as I waited for him to finish. " 'An eye for an eye, and a tooth for a tooth.' With his servant's blade, Fulbert has cut off the instrument of your husband's dishonor."

By now, Suger could barely restrain himself from laughing. "Petrus Abaelardus is gelded. He will not sin again."

8

❦

Is it the general lot of women to bring total ruin on great men?

—HELOISE TO ABELARD

How would I reach Abelard when all of Paris blocked my way? Canons, clergy, students, servants, merchants, husbands, wives, and children pressed against Etienne's gate, shouting and exclaiming, impervious to my efforts to push through, ignoring my pleas for passage.

"Please, he is calling for me," I said, but the group of scholars in front of me only laughed.

"He might have done so before, but not anymore," one of them said, prompting laughter all around.

"Who is she?" someone asked.

"Heloise," I heard another say. "His whore."

"Master Petrus can't do anything for you now, sweetheart," the first youth said. "But I can."

Someone groped at my tunic; I felt a hand on my bottom. I cried out in protest, but who could hear me over the chants and calls of the crowd?

"There he is!" I shouted. "Master Petrus—I see him coming."

As the youths stretched their necks to see, I took advantage of their distraction to plunge more deeply into the crowd. Yet the gate seemed no closer than before. I could barely glimpse its brown stones, or the windows of the large house behind it—which, as I watched, opened to reveal Etienne in his alb and bejeweled stole of red.

"I beg you to leave us," he called over the din. "The *magister* has been grievously injured, perhaps gravely so. He needs rest. Please depart and allow him some peace."

Gravely injured? I raised my voice, adding it to the noise, wishing for wings so I could fly up and over the obstinate crowd, through Etienne's window. My mind's eye pictured Abelard pale and bleeding, seeping life, in need of my comfort. I strained, again, for the gate as the few who heeded Etienne's words began to trickle away.

But then one of the unruly scholars grasped my tunic and yanked me backward, into his arms. "Where are you going, Heloise? Do not leave us, my beauty. Your lover has nothing for you." He clamped an arm around my waist and, with his free hand, pressed between my legs.

I struggled, my heart throwing itself against my rib cage, my elbows flailing, trying without avail to strike my captor. Laughing, he nuzzled my neck. I waved my arms, hoping to draw Etienne's eyes—but, shaking his head at our refusal to disperse, he reached out to close the window.

"Etienne!" I screamed at the top of my lungs. "Etienne, it is I, Heloise! Etienne! Let me in, please!" He heard not a word over the shouts coming from the crowd, but continued to pull the window shut.

"Heloise!" a man shouted. "It is Heloise, his lover!"

"Heloise of his heart," another cried, referring to Abelard's song. "Let her pass!"

"Abelard's seductress," called a man's gruff voice. "Canon Fulbert's niece."

"Her uncle's man did the deed. Heloise is to blame for this crime!" Angry faces turned my way. Someone—my assailant, perhaps—snatched at my chemise, tearing the sleeve. I screamed again, shouting Etienne's name with all my might.

Alerted by the commotion, Etienne paused, looked over the crowd, and spied me at last. "Release her!" his voice boomed over the melee, drawing everyone's attention. He glared at the youth who, laughing, yet clasped me to him. In an instant, all hands fell away and I was free—but surrounded, now, by dark and murderous faces, the scowls of people who, loving Abelard, blamed me for his injury.

"Heloise, come to the gate," Etienne called. "All of you—clear a path! Allow her to pass unmolested. I am watching and can see everything from here. If any of you lays even a finger on her person, I will have you arrested on the spot. Come, Heloise! Pierre needs you now."

Slowly the crowd parted and I made my way to the gate, keeping my head down, not wanting to see the angry looks that I knew would assail me. Reputation is the first of all things to abandon the unfortunate.

"Daughter of Eve," a man snarled as I passed. I kept my eyes upon my feet lest anyone see my blush. Just as the first woman had brought about the downfall of the first man, so had I caused Abelard's ruin. These people blamed me for what had happened to Abelard, and they were not entirely wrong to do so. My face burned as I remembered the letter I had written complaining that Abelard had abandoned me and begging Uncle for rescue.

"*Meretrix,*" I heard someone mutter as I passed. How, in that moment, could I disagree? Now I must pay the price for my error, no matter how high. If the rumors about Abelard's injury proved true, nothing I might do would atone for what I had already done.

Yet, amid the anger and insults, I also found compassion in the crowd.

"The poor girl," I heard a woman say, "behold her trembling. She loves him."

And, also: "Why would her uncle do such a thing? Did he want her for himself?"

My hand reached for the gate latch, but it opened before me. I lifted my eyes to see, not Ralph, but a gray-haired servant whose kind expression made me lower my gaze again, unable to bear his mercy.

"My lady." The familiar voice drew my attention as I was about to step through the gate, and I looked around to see Pauline, her large eyes luminous and moist. She gripped my hand, causing me to wince in pain.

"Pauline! Why have you come?"

"I am looking for Jean." A tear slipped down her face. "Have you seen him? No one can tell me where he is."

The servant rattled the gate. "Young lady, will you enter?"

"I must go," I said to her. I placed my hand on her arm. "Pauline, Jean has been arrested and is with the bishop in the Saint-Denis-du-Pas Chapel."

"With the bishop!" She squeezed my hand more tightly. "What will they do to him? Please, you must help us."

"After what he has done?" I shook my head.

"For our son." I stared at her, uncomprehending, and she added, "Jean-Paul is missing. I cannot find him anywhere."

"Please, miss," the servant said. "Make haste, or the mob will try to come in."

I tugged at Pauline's hand, pulling her through the gate with me. I would talk with her after I had seen Abelard.

The servant led us into the house, where Etienne greeted me with a kiss. "I did not realize that you had come," he said. "I sent a servant to Argenteuil for you."

"Jean brought me home. Where is Abelard?"

"Jean?" Etienne scowled. "So that is why my men did not capture him. Where is he now?"

"He is in the bishop's custody. Where is Abelard?"

"Fortunate fellow, that Jean—he will get a trial." Some of Abelard's scholars, Etienne said, had captured the men who had assisted Jean—Etienne's own servants, including the sneering Ralph—and blinded and gelded them in the street.

"They would have done worse to that traitor Jean. God damn him!" Etienne said, surprising me with his vehemence. He made a fist. "Had those boys captured him, I would have wielded the knife myself, and with pleasure."

I could not help staring. Was this truly Etienne, my kind friend? Hearing him, Pauline uttered a cry, drawing his attention. I introduced her, then asked again where I might find Abelard. He rested in Etienne's own bedchambers, he said, next to the hearth. "The physician said we must keep him warm. He shivered for hours after the attack."

I hastened into the room, trembling all over myself, wanting only to comfort Abelard. *Dear God, forgive me for betraying him.* As soon as I entered the room, however, he turned his back to me, and his face to the wall.

"Abelard," I said, sitting next to him, "I came as quickly as I could."

He curled around himself, drawing his knees up as if to protect himself from further harm.

"Light of my life, how do you fare?" I touched his shoulder, longing to see his face, to pour my love into his eyes and perhaps assuage his pain, which, unbeknownst to him, I had caused. "Abelard!" My voice rose. "Can you hear me? Dear God, have you lost your hearing, as well?"

"As well as what?" he snapped. His bitter tone made me recoil. Did he suspect my treachery? I wanted to throw myself at his feet and beg his forgiveness, but was loath to tell him anything that he did not already know.

"Are you in pain, sweetest?"

"In body or in spirit?"

"Either, my love. But—why speak so harshly to me? I have come to comfort you."

"Can the cause of my misery bring me ease?"

"My uncle, Abelard. Not I." My mouth felt so dry that I could barely speak the words.

" 'The woman whom you gave to be with me, she gave me of the tree, and I did eat.' "

"I gave you my love, Abelard. I give it to you still."

"My position at the school. My reputation, my vitality, my manhood—gone! My life is ended." He pressed his hands to himself and curled even more tightly as he succumbed to sobs.

"Your life is not over, my soul, but only just beginning. Soon we shall bring Astralabe home. As soon as you are healed, we may collect him at le Pallet as we planned and live all together in our house."

"Live together?" He gave a harsh laugh that tore at the edges of my soul. "You, our son, and his eunuch father?"

"Abelard, I do not care about that. I love you for yourself."

"I am not myself. I am not even a man."

"Do not say that." How I longed to lie down beside him and wrap my arms around him, to offer him comfort and consolation. When I touched him, however, he pushed my hand away. "You are one of the world's great men. No one can take that away from you."

Then, with a sudden movement, he flung the bedcovers from his body and turned to me at last. "Behold your husband," he said. "Mutilated. Unmanned."

I forced myself to gaze upon the wound, which, save for a small line of stitches where his testes had been, appeared less a wound than a lack. Jean had performed his task so cleanly that Abelard did not even need a bandage. Yet, the sight of him so diminished, and the contortion of rage and shame on his face, would haunt my nights and days for a long time. He was as altered as I had heard, and I was to blame.

"Behold your uncle's handiwork." I looked only into his eyes now and smoothed the hair from his sweating brow. "In stealing my manhood, Fulbert has robbed us of a life together. We are finished."

"Finished, my love?" I smiled. "How can that be? We love each other. And we have a child, or had you forgotten?"

"My brother and sister have our child, and thank God for that."

"A child who needs his parents."

"Parents mocked and scorned by all the world? Dagobert, at least, will protect our son from this shame."

"Who would mock you, the most brilliant man in all the world?" Even as I said the words, I thought of the scholars outside Etienne's house who had sniggered over Abelard's loss. *Your lover has nothing for you now.* Even Suger had seemed amused, his mouth lingering over the word *gelded* as though it were a piece of sweet fruit. Yet I could not agree that our son should live in Brittany, far from me, deprived of my love and his father's because of a scandal that would surely diminish with time.

"From this day forward, none shall remember my writings, or the arguments I won." He turned his back to me again. "I shall be known as Abelard the eunuch, the *castrato*. And nothing I write, not my *Sic et Non*, not even my brilliant work on the Holy Trinity, will ever be disseminated or read by anyone."

With great effort, I willed my tongue to still itself. Could Abelard think only of himself, of his loss, of his pain? I had not lost a part of my body, but now, in refusing me my son, he threatened me with a greater harm than he had suffered.

"Sweet Abelard," I said, summoning all my compassion. I laid my hand on his arm but he withdrew it. "How can you think clearly now, after such a horrible night? I cannot even imagine the pain you have endured."

"Jean drugged my wine. I remember nothing. I awoke this morning with a burning between my legs, yes, and emptiness where my manhood used to be. But my thoughts, I assure you, are as clear as ice. I have never before felt such clarity, in fact."

"Try not to think. You need to rest."

"Rest, when Fulbert remains free? Who knows what he will do to me when next I close my eyes?"

"All of Paris searches for him. He cannot escape capture for long. Try not to think of anything except regaining your strength."

"Yes, I will need my strength to stand tall and look the bishop of Paris in the eyes as he humiliates me." Abelard's own eyes glittered. "He will remove me from my post, as you know. All I have worked for, all is lost to me now."

And what of me? I wanted to ask. My uncle had meant to wreak revenge upon Abelard alone, but he might as well have plunged that knife into my chest.

9

It is not the deed but the intention of the doer which makes the crime, and justice should weigh not what was done but the spirit in which it was done.
—HELOISE TO ABELARD

At last, having coaxed Abelard to drink a glass of wine in which I had slipped a tincture of valerian root, I left him sleeping by a freshly stoked fire. In the great room, Etienne sat in a chair beside the weeping Pauline. One of the canons had brought news of Jean, saying that he had collapsed after hours of whippings and beatings.

"He refuses to confess out of concern for me," Pauline said. "He does not know that I have escaped."

Sipping from a cup of wine Etienne had given to calm her, she told us what had happened the night before. As she'd prepared to leave my uncle's house for the night, he had grabbed hold of her, stuffed a rag into her mouth, and tied her to a column.

"I was so frightened, Your Grace, even though Canon Fulbert promised that he would not harm me. He even sent a message to Jean-Paul saying that I was needed overnight and that I would come home the next day. But then, oh! He made me stand on my feet all night, after working in the house all day long. You could not imagine how my legs ached, the sharp pains. See how swollen my feet are even now! I tried to untie the ropes, but they were too tight." She held out her wrists to show the red marks the ropes had caused.

"My God! To treat a woman so cruelly. Is he mad or possessed?" Etienne said, leaping to his feet. I sat next to Pauline and took her wrists in my hands, massaging them gently, trying to ease everyone's pain that day, it seemed, except my own. Alas, no remedy could abate the cracking of my heart, or the shattering of my dreams. *Abelard. Astralabe.* I had never felt so alone, but, for me, it was only the beginning.

"I wondered the same, Your Grace, but of course I could not ask, my mouth being filled with rags. And Canon Fulbert had been drinking even more wine than usual. He gives me such a fright when he drinks! I usually go home before he has too much, especially since Jean left him to work for Master Abelard and cannot protect me."

"He had become increasingly violent," I said to Etienne. "Abelard feared for my safety, or he would not have taken me to Argenteuil."

"The day your letter arrived, Canon Fulbert came home early from work." My heart seemed to jump about in my chest, and I had to cup both hands around the *henap* to stop their shaking. "He had already begun drinking, even before vespers. When he read your message, he threw the tablet against the wall and broke it in two. That evening, Jean came. I did not know why, and he never told me. Canon Fulbert sent me home so they could talk alone. Now I know they were plotting revenge against Master Abelard."

Etienne turned to me. "What did your letter contain?"

I stared at him, openmouthed, uncertain what to say. If I confessed my error, would he tell Abelard what I had done? Abelard might blame me, then, for my uncle's cruel deed, and I would lose him forever. But what choice did I have? Were I the most accomplished liar in the world, I could not deceive Etienne, not after all the times he had helped Abelard and me.

And so I told him everything. I told how Abelard had installed me at Argenteuil and then failed to answer my letters, leaving me to believe that he had abandoned me. I told him how Sister Adela had forced me to toil in the vineyards. And I told him of our son, of his secret birth and Abelard's promise to take me to Brittany on a date that he continually delayed. Although I dared not ask for Etienne's help, a part of me hoped that he might do what Abelard would not and bring Astralabe home to me.

Instead, he cursed and leapt to his feet, striding toward the chambers where Abelard slept, then turning around and walking back to us, running his hands through his hair.

"A child, born out of wedlock!" With a great sigh, he slumped back into his chair. "This is disturbing news. Who else knows?"

"No one except the two of you—and Agnes, and Jean, who took me to the boat." We both looked at Pauline, who raised her hands toward heaven and swore before God that, although she knew about the child, she had never told a soul and would not.

"I hope you are telling the truth," Etienne said to her. To me, he added: "Breaking the vow of continence is punishable in itself, but impregnating his own scholar would cost Pierre everything. The Church would show little mercy for such a sin."

"Abelard and I sinned, but our hearts remained pure. We loved each other. We could not marry because of his vow of continence, but our souls joined as one from the moment we first kissed. By the time we consummated our love, we had married in our hearts." At that moment, my soul wanted only for me to join my *speciälïs* in his bed and hold his wounded and cringing body, crippled by a scandal from which neither of us would recover.

"Married in your hearts? I appreciate the sentiment, but the bishop will not."

Etienne spoke the truth, I knew. Love, in the eyes of the Church, did not excuse the flaunting of its rules. King Louis's father, King Philip, had married Bertrade of Montfort for love—setting aside the wife he had taken out of duty. In return, the pope excommunicated him several times, punishing not only the king but his subjects. The realm's cathedrals closed, depriving even the dying of the final blessings that would allow their souls to enter heaven. Lamentations rent the skies; rioters converged on the royal palace, throwing stones and shouting demands that the king repudiate his whore. No one, least of all the Church fathers, cared whether he loved her. How could we, not royals but mere mortals, expect their sympathy? That we loved each other counted for nothing except in our own hearts, and in the eyes of God—or so I pray.

Now I, too, had been called *whore* by the students who loved Abelard, and *daughter of Eve* by others who had forgotten, it seemed, that God is love. In daring to live life on our own terms, he and I now stood to lose all. Indeed, judging from Abelard's behavior, I might have lost him already. And Etienne, I realized, would not help me to regain my son. He could ill afford to be seen as endorsing our love while the rest of the world, including the king's favored chaplain, condemned it.

"Has Jean spoken to anyone of the child?" Etienne demanded of Pauline.

"I do not know, Your Grace," she said, drawing back from him. "We have not discussed it much. After my husband left to work for Master Pierre, we saw each other only on Sundays, our day off from work. We did not spend our precious hours discussing our employers, as I am sure you can imagine." Her skin colored.

"I must know." Etienne stood and rang for his manservant, then commanded him to bring three horses to the mounting block. Turning to Pauline, Etienne said, "I shall arrange for you to see your husband."

Pauline's eyes lit up. "God bless you, Your Grace! How can I ever repay your kindness?"

"You can find out whether Jean has told anyone of Master Pierre's child, and whom. And, for God's sake, ask him where Canon Fulbert is hiding."

How had I never noticed their love?

The tears in her eyes, the way she lifted her hands to his battered face as though her touch might heal his bruises; his steady gaze, the understanding that passed between them without need of words—how could anyone see Pauline and Jean together and not notice? But my uncle knew and had used their love to his advantage. Holding Pauline as his hostage, he had coerced Jean into committing his crime for him. But my uncle had gone to such lengths needlessly, Jean told me.

"Had Canon Fulbert asked, I would gladly have done the deed before that devil could even think of dishonoring you," Jean said in the cold stone room set aside for visitors to the prison. He spoke with difficulty through a mouth swollen and bleeding, struck many times during his interrogation by a gendarme's heavily ringed hand.

"I saw right away what Master Pierre wanted. So did Pauline." She nodded and squeezed Jean's hand. "We know too many women whose employers have taken advantage of their innocence, then cast them aside like dogs after the hunt. Pauline was in this situation when I met her. Her employer cast her out when at last she refused his demands. She was fortunate, indeed, that

Canon Fulbert hired her when he did, for she had spent nearly all the money that devil had paid her for her silence—and she had a babe to feed." Jean spat on the floor as if telling the tale had embittered his mouth.

Suspecting Abelard's motives, Jean had tried to dissuade my uncle from renting a room to him—but Uncle would not listen.

"He fancied himself Master Petrus's friend, which vaunted his pride to no end." But pride goes before destruction, and haughtiness before a fall, and my uncle before long found himself utterly humiliated by Abelard's—by our—deception.

"Drink gets the best of him at times, but Canon Fulbert is a good man," Jean added staunchly. "He always had the best of intentions for you, my lady. But he didn't protect you, and he feels bad for it. His only fault is that he trusted that womanizer."

I frowned. I'd been twenty years of age when Abelard and I first met, hardly in need of protection. What had Jean said of Abelard, or what might he say under the gendarme's blows?

I hastened to correct Jean: Abelard, I said, had not seduced me. We loved each other. "To change Abelard's feelings for me, you would have to cut out his heart."

Jean shook his head, his eyes fathomless pools of sorrow. "I hope you are right. But I fear, for your sake, that you are badly mistaken. No man who loves a woman treats her as he has treated you."

"It does not matter what we think, my lady," Pauline said. "You will see for yourself very soon whether his love comes from his heart, or from another part of his body."

10

❧

I beg you, then, as you set about tending the wounds that others have dealt, heal the wounds you have yourself inflicted.

—HELOISE TO ABELARD

*H*aving gained Jean's assurance that he had told no one, not even my uncle, of our child—"I would not cause harm to you for anything in this world, my lady," he said, apparently not realizing that, in assaulting Abelard, he had destroyed me—Pauline and I left him at the prison, where he would remain until my uncle's arrest. Jean swore that he did not know where Uncle Fulbert had gone, but having been deceived so thoroughly by him before, I did not know whether to believe him.

"Jean," Pauline said before we departed, wringing his hand, "I have a message for you from Canon Fulbert. He told it to me before he fled. *Non!*" She stood and pressed both palms against her cheeks. "Jean-Paul! Dear Lord—I have just remembered. I must find him."

"What is it, Pauline?" I said. "What did my uncle say?"

She turned back toward her husband. "He said that if you were captured, Jean, you must not speak a word against Canon Fulbert. He said, 'Tell Jean he must confess to the crime completely. If they ask of my involvement, say I knew nothing about it.'" She began to tremble. "Jean, he had tied me to the post. He slid the dull edge of his blade across my neck. He said he would hurt our son."

"Jean-Paul." Jean's strength returned to him. He stood and grasped his wife by her shoulders. "Where is he?"

"I—I don't know." She stared into his eyes. "I can't find him."

"Go and seek him at home. He must be there! Pauline, you must find him now. I have told the bishop all about Canon Fulbert. I . . . could not endure the torture." Jean held out his hands to show the bleeding, torn skin where his fingernails had been.

In moments we were riding through the cloister gates, accompanied by Etienne's manservant, into the city. Rather than turn toward the south, we rode over the Petit Pont and the Grand-Pont to an area in the shadow of the northern wall. This was a part of Paris that I had never before visited. My stomach turned at the squalor we encountered. Garbage littered the streets and alleys, attracting dogs, pigs, and flies, and sending up a stench that mingled with the reek of feces and urine flung from chamber pots and left to rot. Dirty children ran barefoot through the muck, squealing with laughter and smearing their hands and clothes with filth. The houses, made of rotting wood, crowded together, blocking nearly all the day's light from the narrow street. A woman with arms as muscled as a man's hung clothes on a line stretched across her window, a child swelling her belly and another in a sling around her neck. Pauline waved and called her by name; when the woman smiled, I saw that she had just one tooth.

"How do these poor people live?" I asked Pauline.

"With hope, always with hope of better times in this life or the next."

At the end of the street, the neighborhood brightened. The houses turned to stone and masonry; shops, rather than butchers' stalls, occupied the ground level, selling soap and candles and linen fabric and cooking pots. A lone rooster crossed ahead of us.

"That place back there is sickening, *non*? I used to live there," Pauline said, "before I married Jean." Jean-Paul's father, her former employer, had put her there, she said, and, except for the few coins he sent from time to time, utterly neglected her and his son.

"He was terrified that his father, a count, would find out what he had done to me and force him into the priesthood. And so he hid me there with the lepers, the prostitutes, and the rats." Her eyes drooped at the corners. She pressed her mouth shut, but her chin trembled. "It was the worst year of my life. You cannot imagine."

I stared at her. No, I could not imagine living in such misery.

Why didn't she appeal to the man's father for aid? I asked. Surely he would not wish to have his grandson brought up in such a place.

"And have Jean-Paul taken from me to be raised in his castle? My son would never have known me. You may think me selfish, but I loved him too much to let him go. He was all I had in the world." When, at his birth, he slipped into the world like a breath, as thin as a reed and too weak even to cry, she worried that she had made the wrong choice. She wrote to the boy's father, threatening to tell the count about Jean-Paul unless he gave her more help. In a few days she had a job cooking for my uncle, where she met Jean, who married her and claimed Jean-Paul as his own name.

"Now it seems my job is finished. Jean-Paul has just begun work as a servant to the new bishop. What will happen to him now that his father is disgraced? What will happen to us all?" Her eyes shone—not with light, but darkness.

I tried to think of some way I could ease her distress. "Pauline, you are the best cook in Paris. You will find work." I would help her if I could. Agnes loved Pauline's brewet and would need a cook when she married her seigneur. "But first, let us find that son of yours."

She stopped her horse before a fabric shop, in whose window a rosy-faced man laid out rolls of linen and cotton before a woman in a brown-and-pink gown.

"*Bonjour*, Pauline!" the merchant called as we passed, lifting his brows at the sight of my clothes—a saffron chemise and blue *bliaut* embroidered with golden crosses, my attempt to add cheer to the gray-and-black world of Argenteuil. "Did Jean-Paul find you? He left a little while ago for your canon's house."

"He went to Canon Fulbert's?" Pauline's voice rose. She turned to me with panic in her eyes. "What will he do to my son?" she cried.

We turned our horses and rode as quickly as we dared through the crowded, ice-slicked streets to my uncle's house, where we found Jean-Paul sitting on the mounting stone and wondering what had become of his parents.

"Thanks be to God, thanks be to God," Pauline said softly as the boy stood.

"Where have you been, Maman? I looked for you indoors but no one is at home. Where is Papa?" He offered a hand to help her dismount.

"*Non*, we must go from here, and as soon as possible," she said to him. "Save your questions. I need you at home with me now."

As he untied his horse from the post, she turned to me. "You have done enough for me, considering all you have suffered. I hope you can forgive Jean someday. He only gave Master Pierre what he deserved. Believe me, I know."

I did not respond. All the world, it seemed, wished to pass judgment upon us. Who, looking upon a building's facade, can discern the size or number of rooms within, or the quality of their furnishings? In like manner, none could comprehend the nature and extent of our love. Every marriage, every relationship—indeed, every man and woman—remains a mystery to those outside it, as distant as the stars, as unfathomable as the Holy Trinity. Others might frown and whisper and shake their heads and say that Abelard had used me—but I knew the truth. He had loved me. I prayed that he loved me still. Twenty years after his death—and as my own approaches—none of that has changed.

When they had gone, I dismissed Etienne's servant, wanting some time to myself. I sat for a while outside my uncle's house, its shutters latched against the light of desire, its doors barred against the sweet warmth of love. In the same manner, Uncle Fulbert had closed his heart the previous year, when he had given up Gisele. Those empty chambers, dark and cold, made a fit dwelling for Satan, who eagerly takes up residence wherever *caritas* is banished—the true abomination of desolation.

Where was my uncle hiding? Every man in the cloister sought him even now. Did he cower in the scriptorium amid the rolls of parchment and stacks of books waiting to be repaired or copied? Had he fled to someone's home? I could not imagine who would harbor him except Roger. But my uncle would never trust that tale-teller.

To hide in the cloister, small and close as it was, would require extraordinary abilities—cunning, a large group of loyal friends, immense wealth—none of which my uncle possessed. Yet, he could not have gone far. Entering the city's gates with Jean, I had seen sentries posted in double their usual numbers, stopping all who attempted to pass out of Paris. He must be somewhere inside the walls. But where?

One idea, then another, entered my mind, only to be rejected. Finding him seemed impossible, and yet none of us—neither

Abelard nor I, nor Jean and Pauline and Jean-Paul, nor Etienne—would rest while Uncle Fulbert remained free. Why had
he sent Jean to fetch me from Argenteuil—so he could make me
his hostage and ensure his escape? If so, he had not needed me,
after all, or so it seemed.

The gendarmes had searched his house to no avail, but now I
wondered if I might find a clue to his whereabouts. I rose and
went to the door. I pushed it open and stepped inside quietly, as
if entering a chapel or—I shuddered—a tomb.

I caught my breath at what I saw. The house had been ran-
sacked: chairs toppled, fireplace ashes scattered as someone had
stepped into the hearth, then trailed footprints across the floor.
On a shelf lay a familiar knife with a trace of blood smearing its
blade. I picked it up and turned it over in my hands, studying the
ornate ivory handle with its grimacing demon on one side, a
garnet glinting where its eye should be, and, on the other side, a
crucified Christ, drooping on an ornate cross. This was my uncle's knife, with which he had threatened Abelard on the day he'd
caught us together—the knife that had haunted Abelard's dreams
ever since. Had Jean committed his crime with it? I could not
understand how the gendarmes had failed to see it when searching the house this morning.

Unless . . .

"He felt no pain," my uncle said.

I gasped and nearly dropped the knife—before my fingers
curled around it to grip the ivory, smooth and warm as a man's
flesh. My uncle ascended the final step from the first floor, where
he had either come in from the outdoors or, as I guessed, from
some hiding place downstairs—perhaps in the cellar. As he
walked toward me, I pointed the blade at him, but he only
smirked.

"Jean drugged your lover's wine at dinnertime—drugged him,

heh-heh. Not even the most excruciating torture could have awakened him." Uncle licked his lips, staring at the knife as though he yearned for its kiss, then turned his strange stare to me. His eyes blazed as red as the demon's on the knife handle. I wondered, watching him sway, how long it had been since he had slept.

"But this is your knife," I said dumbly.

"None other would do—none other!" He rubbed his hands together as if anticipating a meal. "My blade to avenge my niece."

"Jean said that *he* cut Abelard."

"True, true. I could not very well do the deed myself, could I? Jean gelded many a bawling calf when he was young." Uncle looked around the great room. "Did he bring you here? Where is he?"

"The gendarmes arrested him."

Uncle sucked in his breath. "The cloister gendarmes? Or the king's?"

"Suger questioned him this afternoon." I closed my eyes, remembering Jean's swollen mouth, lips split by a man's ring; his bloody fingertips.

"Holy Mary, Mother of God," Uncle whispered, clutching the rosary on his belt. "But—Jean would not talk. He swore never to say a word."

"He swore it to whom—you? Or the devil?"

"To the devil with *you*, holding a knife against your own uncle." He lunged toward me to seize the blade from my trembling hand, but I jerked away and, in doing so, cut a long gash in his palm.

"Ungrateful *chienne*," he snarled, pressing the wound to stop the bleeding. "God damn you—damn you! You're like your mother in every way."

"Thank you, Uncle. I consider that the highest praise." Although my heart pummeled my chest like two frantic fists, my voice resonated with power. The instant I'd felt the blade strike my uncle's hand, clarity had descended upon me. I smelled my own fear, rising like perspiration from my skin. I heard each labored breath my uncle took as he tore a strip from his alb and wrapped it around his bleeding hand.

"Or maybe it's your father in you I see. Simple and pious to the eye; corrupt to the bone. I warned Hersende, but she was as blind to his ways as you have been to Petrus's."

"If you knew Robert was my father, why didn't you send me with Mother to Fontevraud?" I held the knife high to repel him. "He accepted many women with their children. Surely he would have welcomed his own."

"Your mother would not hear of it. He would know you were his child, she said. As well he ought, was my opinion, but she pleaded with me not to tell him, or anyone. You should have heard her weep, clinging to my hem like a beggar. 'It would ruin him.' And indeed it would have—indeed! All his followers, then, would know him as a sinner."

" 'All have sinned, and fall short of the glory of God.' " I gave him a pointed look. "You possess weaknesses, as well."

"Weaknesses, yes." His mouth quivered. "I trusted you, for instance. And I believed your teacher when he said he was my friend."

Confronted with the sorrow in his eyes, I averted my own, thinking of all the nights Abelard and I had sinned under his roof. We had thought ourselves in the right, justified by love. Were we to blame for the impediments to happiness that the world had placed between us? Yet, we had laughed together more than once, like naughty schoolchildren, at my uncle's oblivion to that which all of Paris knew.

"I am no dullard. I had my suspicions, yes. But he called me *amicus*, and I thought you loved me. Perhaps I *am* a dullard—or I was one. No longer! Now my eyes are opened, and I know what you truly love, heh-heh." His eyes narrowed, and then, again, he lunged—and again, I eluded him.

"I shall have you, eventually." He took up a fireplace poker and waved it in the air. "I stand between you and the door, you know. That makes you my captive." He grinned as if engaged in a game.

"What do you want with me, Uncle?"

He licked his lips. "To beat some good sense into your head, for one thing."

"*I* am not the one being hunted by the gendarmes. I am not the one in hiding."

"Fleeing to the convent is not hiding?"

"I did so to escape from you."

"You went because your husband commanded it!" he shouted, his face now a furious red. "*He* hid you, not from me but from himself—and from all the world." He told me how Abelard had laughed with the Countess of Anjou after mass, while I waited in Argenteuil to hear from him. He'd caressed her face with his blue eyes as though he and she were lovers, Uncle said.

"I knew what he was doing. I'd seen him do the same with you. That woman gazed at him as if he were the second coming of Christ."

"Women are drawn to Abelard, but he would never betray me."

"He betrayed you the instant he left you at Argenteuil. He betrayed you before that day, when he took your maidenhead."

"He took nothing that I did not willingly give to him."

"That is what your mother said when I asked her about Robert. Two beans in the same pod, you and Hersende. I only regret that I ever trusted Petrus—that I ever trusted you. I should have known that you'd share your mother's whorish nature."

"I love Abelard, and he loves me."

"That's what Hersende said about Robert of Arbrissel. But he used her, didn't he? Used her for his own pleasure, then cast her aside. Men like him—like your precious Abelard—are all the same: so charming, so confident, so arrogant. And hungry for ad-oration—he's desperate for it! Men like that love no one except themselves. I tried to warn Hersende, but she wouldn't listen to me."

"You were wrong. Robert would have loved me. He did love me."

"I should have done more to protect my sister." His mouth's cruel twist crumpled to a babyish pout. "I failed Hersende. But, by God's head, I have not failed you."

"You destroyed Abelard's life—*my* life."

"I did it for you. Petrus tried to destroy you: hiding you in an abbey, telling you any lies that sprang to his lips to keep you there. He never meant to bring you home."

"He did. He had found a house on the ruga Saint-Germain. A beautiful little house with a windmill."

Uncle's scowl disappeared. His eyes' expression softened. "He never went there, or to any other house," he said gently. "I had a man follow him."

"*Non!*" I cried. "You are wrong. Abelard would not lie to me." Yet, I could not look at his face, could not bear to see him pitying me, poor Heloise, brought up in the convent and now seduced, deceived, discarded. Poor, stupid girl. I lowered my head.

And felt the knife slip from my fingers and my uncle's hand clamp around my arm.

"I told you I would have you, heh-heh. You thought you

could outfox the fox, eh?" He prodded my chin with the tip of the blade. "How readily you believed my tale—as naïve as a child—a child! Who is the dullard now?"

In my relief to hear that Abelard had *not* deceived me, clarity of thought returned. "What is your plan?" I said, glaring at my uncle. "You could do no worse to me than you have already done."

"You will help me escape. Seeing you at the point of my knife, no one will stop me from riding through the cloister gates."

"And what of your honor? Everyone will think you fled in shame over your crime. The whole world will pity Abelard and condemn you."

His face reddened. "He will use the situation to his advantage, I have no doubt."

"Who would not do so, in his position? He was mutilated at your behest. Now, instead of telling the world why you attacked him, you flee like dog with its tail between its legs."

With a sigh, he released his hold on me. "I feel no shame for avenging you. He deserved worse than he got."

I stepped backward, just out of his reach. I stole a glance toward the stairs, calculating their distance. If I could only distract his attention away from me, I might run past him and out the door. "If you think so, then what do you fear?"

"Fear? Who said I was afraid?" He stepped toward me again, forcing me against the wall. I looked him in the eyes, denying all my own feelings so that he would see only peace, and calm.

He lifted his chin and took my arm again, but more gently this time. "Let us depart." He began pulling me toward the stairs.

"Where are you taking me?" I tried to wrest free, but he tightened his grip. What would he do to me now? Inside, I felt as though I were falling. I wished only to go to Abelard, my love.

"Calm yourself, silly girl. I'm taking you to the chapel." He dragged me to the front door and threw it open. "It is time the bishop knew, and all the world besides, what that deceiver Petrus Abaelardus did to you, and to me."

11

If everyone kept silent, the facts themselves would cry out.
—HELOISE TO ABELARD

My life had ended. This I had known the instant Abelard revealed his wound, his eyes glittering, defiant, as though I had wielded the blade.

To think that, the last time I had seen him, his skin had burned with passion and his gaze with love, and his entire being had leapt with life. *In one brief hour, Fortune shows her darling lifted high in bliss, then headlong plunged in misery's abyss.* Love, on the other hand, burned as constant in my breast as the sacred fire of Vesta, extinguishable by no human hand.

I returned to Etienne's house that night with barely enough breath to sigh. As promised, my uncle had surrendered to the bishop of Paris on the condition that I confess to him all that Abelard and I had done: our love affair, conducted under his own roof—his first debasement, he said; our child, left to Bretons to raise—the second affront to his honor; our marriage, made in secret for Abelard's sake, and my denial, made falsely while accusing him among his own brethren of delirium; and my letter, which he produced for the bishop's perusal.

The bishop had said little as my uncle enumerated my sins, only lifted his eyebrows in surprise with each revelation. Suger, however, had plenty to say, especially against Etienne, who had been summoned to the bishop's palace to judge our case.

"What sort of archdeacon would conduct a marriage in secret? Why would he condone such a union, between a teacher and his student?"

"'He who is without sin among you, let him first cast the stone,'" Etienne said mildly.

"Ah! So you admit that you conducted the ceremony."

"Am *I* on trial?"

"Canon Fulbert says he was forced to keep his niece's honorable and legal marriage a secret so that her husband might defy the rules of the Church," Suger said. "Did you wed them?"

"I did not know that we would judge Master Petrus today—and in his absence."

Suger gritted his teeth. "Did you wed them, or did you not?"

"Ask *her*," my uncle said, pointing to me as if I were not the only woman in the bishop's chamber. "She agreed to confess everything."

I said nothing.

"Speak, Niece," Uncle Fulbert commanded. I lowered my eyes to look at my wringing hands, and at my uncle's tapping foot. "Tell them, by God's head! Tell them what he has done to you."

Why would I do so? Would they want to hear how Abelard had sharpened my wits and my tongue with the whetstone of his rigorous teaching? Did they desire to know how he had transformed me with his love from a shy, nervous mouse into a lioness shining with power? Would they rejoice at the one thousand blisses I had enjoyed in his arms?

"Master Petrus has taught me well," I said.

With no confession from me, and from Etienne only a steadfast refusal to try Abelard until he might defend himself, Suger could only gnash his teeth and curse us both under his breath.

Bishop Guibert, on the other hand, took my uncle into his care, offering him lodging in his own palace. "It is the only place suitable for a man of your birth to live while you await your trial." The bishop poured a cup of wine for my uncle from the flagon on the table. Of poor Jean, nursing his bleeding hands in the cold stone prison, no one said a word.

"Petrus is improved this evening," Etienne said as he escorted me to his house, but worry furrowed his face. Some of Abelard's students had entered Etienne's hall that day, he said, wanting to tell Abelard of the rumors spreading like fire through the city—all of them cruel, and all untrue. "I forbade them to see him, for he needs to rest. But he will hear the slander against him somehow. God only knows how he will react."

Abelard's future and mine, as well as Etienne's, I presumed, depended on the mercy of the Church fathers. "What rumors have you heard?"

What he said made me flinch: Abelard had fornicated with prostitutes and contracted a disease that he had given to me. He had fornicated with my uncle and me together, in the same bed. I had used my learning to conjure spells that drew him to me constantly and deprived him of his ability to resist . . .

To hear that scholars had slipped into Etienne's house made me grind my teeth. What if someone less friendly had reached him? I longed to dismount from that horse and hasten to him. But the nearer we drew to Etienne's house, the slower we moved, impeded by horses and riders, carts, and people walking in the street. Soon enough we saw the reason for our delay. Another crowd had gathered outside the house, not, this time, to call Abelard's name and cry for justice, but to listen to him speak. From the open windows he proclaimed himself innocent of any wrongdoing and a victim of conspiracy and debased my uncle with the foulest of insults.

12

I would not want to give you cause for finding me disobedient in anything, so I have set the bridle of your injunction on the words which issue from my unbounded grief.

—HELOISE TO ABELARD

With a cry, I slid off the horse and began to run, heedless of the mockery and laughter pelting me like flung stones.

"Abelard! Tell them to let me in," I cried. He did so and I, followed by Etienne, entered the gate and bounded up the stairs.

"Behold Heloise of my heart, whom I have made famous with my songs," he called out as I joined him before the windows. "Does she appear diseased? Have I abused her in any way? Tell them, Heloise, that I am innocent. Why would I marry you, my scholar? Philosophy is my life, and, indeed, my wife."

"Abelard," I said quietly, "you must come away. This is not the time. You need rest."

"How can I rest when all of Paris roils with lies and slithers with scandal?" he cried. "Are we married? Answer me, *sic* or *non.*"

I shook my head.

"*Voilà!* As I said, Canon Fulbert is a liar. He begged me to help him gain a promotion, and when he did not get it, he vowed to destroy me. But he has not destroyed Petrus Abaelardus—he has done the opposite. I am stronger than ever before!"

A great roar arose from the crowd as, with Etienne's help, I pulled him away and closed the window.

"I have not finished."

"Yes, you have," I said, as we led him toward the bed. Once he had settled, Etienne went to call for a fire and our supper.

"Heloise, you would not believe what people are saying—about me, about you!" Abelard clutched my hand as though I could save him. "The truth is not enough for their filthy minds. We are accused of every sort of perversion, disgusting acts—"

"Yes, including many things we never thought to try. And I had thought us quite imaginative."

"How can you jest?" He scowled. "Your uncle has destroyed my reputation, and yours."

"I care nothing for the opinions of others, as long as you think well of me, and I think well of you."

"Do you yet think well of me?"

"The best, sweetest. I love you beyond measure."

He sighed and sank back into his pillow. "You still love me, even after . . . everything."

"Of course I do. But you must not deliver any more lectures, not until we know what the bishop will do."

"Etienne is the judge. He will favor me—"

"Bishop Guibert has excused him from your case, at Suger's insistence."

"Suger." Abelard winced. "He hates me. Ever since that day in the court, when I laughed at his remark about 'young girls.'" A moan fell from his lips. "God, Heloise, it hurts. I felt nothing while it happened, but now I am all on fire. And yet, there is nothing to feel. How can that be?"

I took the bottle of serum the healer had left behind and administered a dose to him. Relief spread over his face, and his grip on my hand relaxed.

"Amica," he murmured, drowsy. Not *amor.* No longer "lover," but, now, "friend." Yet, what dearer name could I ask from him, the best friend I had ever known? Emotion crested like a wave and broke upon me. I could have sworn I was crying, but when I touched a finger to my eyes, they were dry.

Abelard slept. I sat near him, keeping watch lest he awaken in pain—needing more of the physician's "elixir of oblivion," as Abelard called it. For several days I remained by his side, desiring to relieve any discomfort, since I could do nothing to calm the storms of delirium that wracked him as he slept: his *Non!* like a clap of thunder, startling me, followed by unintelligible murmurs; his cries of *Stop!*; the toss of his head on the pillow, his perspiring brow; and then, the lightning crack: *Heloise! Mon Dieu!* My name screeched in my ears, a cataclysmic howl.

O Abelard! How patiently I waited those days and nights for his return to me, for his eyes glinting like starlight from under their insolent lids, for those soft, sweet lips curled like a question that I could not answer. When he did awaken, he only moaned for water, or for more of the serum. I offered him bread, soft cheese, meat, apples. He took only broth and a little milk. *Look at me,* I willed as I handed the bowl to him, and, as he returned it to me, *Look into my eyes. Look!* But, alas, he did not.

Even when he lay on his pillow and I sat on the bed beside him, holding his hand and waiting for the serum to take effect, he would not gaze at me as he once had done. If only I could see into those eyes again, feel their caress, dance in their light. Many years later, clinging to him as his life slipped away, I would remember those days and nights after his mutilation and shudder at my selfishness.

How could I have spared even one thought for myself while my Abelard suffered, robbed of his manhood and also of the glory that he so richly deserved? Already, Etienne told me, Bishop Guibert had appointed Abelard's replacement at the school, at Suger's urging. Abelard would be forbidden to teach, some whispered. His books would never be read.

The whole world, it seemed, hastened to condemn him, whom it never understood or even knew. Abelard loved me. No knife—nor instrument of any sort devised by man—could alter what we shared. We were husband and wife, bound to each other for life by our vows and by our son. When, now, would we go to Brittany for Atralabe? Yet I dared not ask. Just to think of mounting a horse would cause him distress.

When, after two weeks, Abelard had begun to move about again—even going to Etienne's window to wave to the scholars who still gathered outside, waiting for news—Bishop Guibert and Suger came to see him. I tried to forestall them, saying he needed rest. The bishop hesitated, but Suger insisted they be admitted.

"Canon Fulbert has been expelled from the cloister and his manservant castrated," he said. "It is time Petrus Abaelardus faced the consequences for *his* sins." He lifted his upper lip as though the word itself gave off a rank odor.

"Being butchered in one's bed does not suffice?" I forced him to meet my steady gaze.

"For another man, perhaps." He narrowed his little eyes. "But Petrus has a unique facility for turning even the worst humiliation into triumph. We have heard of the speech he gave denying his guilt. He has not grasped the gravity of his situation, it seems. A master does not seduce his own scholar without repercussions."

"He did not seduce me."

Bishop Guibert folded his hands and lowered his eyes. "We wish only to ask Petrus Abaelardus some questions essential to our investigation." Reassured by his quiet manner, I relented and went to prepare Abelard for visitors.

Although I found him sitting up in bed, surrounded by parchments and scribbling in a tablet, he slid down under the covers when I told him who had come. "Tell them I am unwell. I wish to see no one."

"They know of your appearances in the front window, and the speech you gave yesterday," I said. Hearing rumors that he would be replaced at the school, Abelard had accused Guibert of weakness, called Suger the "devil's mouthpiece," and encouraged his scholars to withdraw from classes in protest. The rousing cheers that had ensued surely resounded all the way to the bishop's palace.

"Besides, I cannot refuse the bishop of Paris."

"I have had a relapse." His groan sounded insincere. "I want more of that serum."

"Abelard, they are coming in. You may allow me to help you dress and greet them with dignity, or not."

"I will remain as I am. Let them see for themselves how I suffer."

With a sigh, I went to the kitchen to discuss the morning meal. I had hoped that Abelard might join Etienne and me at the table today, but he seemed determined to prolong his convalescence for as long as possible. My head ached at the thought of enduring his complaints and constant calls for even one more day. Astralabe in his infancy had not demanded so much care.

As I ordered a restorative soup for him and some greens from the garden, a servant entered the kitchen with a wax tablet in hand. "A letter has arrived from Master Abelard's brother in

Brittany. Shall I deliver it now or wait until His Grace and the monk have gone?"

I took it from him and went to the courtyard to sit and read what Dagobert had to say of our child, and when he might return to me. Two more weeks without him had passed, and the crack in my heart surely had widened.

Astralabe. My arms ached to hold him; I longed for the press of his soft cheek, the smell of his baby's skin. Had Dagobert and Denise told him that his mother was coming for him? *I will not be much longer, little one.*

I broke the seal and opened the tablet to read the letter, which was disappointingly short. *Denise will marry soon, and her husband does not wish the boy to accompany her to his household. Are you coming for him, as you said? My wife is with child again and cannot care for him. If he remains with us when Denise has departed, we must declare the boy abandoned and send him to a monastery.*

I pressed a hand to my thumping chest and willed my legs to be still, for they would have run up the stairs to Abelard before his visitors had gone. Coveting le Pallet for their own sons, Dagobert and his pinch-faced wife would stop at nothing to ensure their inheritance—including making an oblate of their own little nephew. Even Denise, who supposedly loved him, would forsake our boy. None, it seemed, had room in their lives or their hearts for Astralabe.

Yet, was I any different? I had abandoned him first of all, his own mother who had given him life and ought to give him a home. I closed my eyes, remembering how I had cried for my mother at Argenteuil. Thinking that I had not been good enough for her, I made myself obedient in hopes that she would return. I became a shining star of goodness, placating the Reverend Mother Basilia, submitting to my uncle's will, and, lately, considering Abelard's happiness over my own. Now, however, my child needed me. In my never-ending desire to please others— and to protect Abelard—I had failed my son as my mother had failed me. I was her child through and through, as my uncle had said.

But I was also the child of Robert of Arbrissel. He had endured slander and speculation far worse than anything being said about Abelard and me, never straying from the path to which God had called him. He had sinned, yes, but had then atoned for that sin by building Fontevraud Abbey and placing my mother at its head—elevating her in the esteem of the world and, more important, in the eyes of God. Had he known about me, would he have helped me, as well? His sickbed plea, his stricken eyes, told me that he would have done so. Now it was time for me to find my father's strength within myself and demand that our son come home to Paris. Astralabe needed me.

The servant came to say that Suger and the bishop had gone. I headed upstairs with the tablet in my hand, taking deep breaths in attempt to calm my jumping pulse. The brevity of the interview told me that the men had, indeed, presented only a few questions. Now I had more than a few of my own to ask.

Abelard lay in the same position in which I had left him, in bed, facing the empty fireplace, his back turned to the room. What had the bishop said? I asked. He merely grunted, expecting me, no doubt, to press him for details. But I had more interest in speaking than in listening.

"A letter arrived from your brother this morning."

Abelard remained quiet for a long moment before turning onto his back, pushing himself to sitting, and asking to see the letter. He frowned when I handed it to him, remarking on its broken seal.

"I wanted news of our son," I said, feeling myself flush and berating myself for it. Wasn't I his wife? I had been within my rights.

He opened the tablet and read his brother's note, then snapped it shut and closed his eyes. The servant entered the room. Dagobert's messenger wished to know if he should wait for Abelard's reply.

"No reply."

I cried out, stopping the man as he turned to depart. "You must write something to him, Abelard. He will send Astralabe to a monastery."

"He would never do so."

"But he says that Astralabe is a burden. Our son, Abelard!"

The servant lifted his brows in surprise. I sent him away for the time being, telling him to offer the messenger something to eat while he awaited our response.

"Dagobert says we must come for him now."

Abelard closed his eyes. "But of course, we cannot do so."

I snatched away the tablet. "You think only of what *you* want." I called for a blade and stylus.

"What are you doing?"

"If you will not reply, then I shall." Blade in hand, I began to scrape Dagobert's words from the wax. "I shall tell your brother to expect us within the month."

"That is quite impossible."

"Why?" I fumbled with the tablet; it slipped with a crash to the stone floor. With shaking hands I tried to put the pieces back together.

"Do you see? We are not meant to respond."

"Do not be ridiculous," I snapped. "Why can't we go and retrieve our son? If you cannot make the journey, then send me with a servant as you did before."

"That will not be. I am sorry, Heloise, but Astralabe must remain with my brother and his wife. We have no choice."

"What are you saying?" I let the tablet fall at my feet. "I want my son. I insist that you write to Dagobert now and tell him so." I called for another tablet.

"Have you forgotten?" Abelard gestured with his hands over his lap. "I, too, am broken, Heloise. Nothing is as it was before."

"Do you think our son cares about that? Do you think that I care?" I sat beside him and took his limp hand between both of mine, then pressed it to my breast. "Abelard, look at me. Please, dearest. Look at your Heloise."

At last he lifted his gaze to meet mine fully, gracing me with the beauty of his blue eyes—eyes that, I noted, held neither their former tenderness nor the mocking humor I had both hated and loved. I saw no expression of any kind in their depths. Had Jean's knife severed Abelard's soul, as well?

The man came in with the tablet, which I took and thrust at Abelard. "Write to your brother," I pleaded. "Tell him we are coming. Tell him that I am coming alone, and that he may give the child to me."

Abelard shook his head.

"If you will not write to him, then I shall do so." I took the stylus in hand.

"Give it to me." Abelard snatched the tablet and stylus from me, then began to write, scratching into the wax, reciting his words as he did so. "'Circumstances prevent my doing as you wish. We are unable to retrieve our son from your home, now or in the future.'" I cried out, but he continued to write. "'We pray that you will keep Astralabe in your care and give him the love he needs. He is, after all, your nephew.'"

"What are you saying?" I tried to wrest the tablet from his

hands, but enough of his strength had returned so that he easily pushed me away. "*Non*, Abelard," I begged.

"I tell you, I have no choice in the matter. The bishop of Paris has commanded me to enter the abbey at Saint-Denis."

"So he has not banished you from teaching?"

"Not as a teacher, Heloise. As a monk."

"My God," I whispered. "Abelard, no." How often had we derided the monks we saw in the cloister, laughing at their glumly pious faces, their bellies made fat from too much poverty? Abelard, one of them? I could not imagine it, or his living out his days in silence at Saint-Denis, shut off from the world. The cloistered life had been all but unbearable for me, but it would kill Abelard.

"As my wife," he continued, "Heloise will naturally do as I command. I have arranged for her to become a bride of Christ."

I laughed, thinking that he must surely be jesting. "Have you asked our Lord for his assent? Surely he knows that I am already married to you."

"In only a few weeks, Heloise will be my wife no more. The bishop of Paris has agreed: she is to take the veil as a consecrated nun and will remain for the rest of her life at the Argenteuil Royal Abbey."

The cry that sprang from my lips sounded far away. I would have snatched the tablet from Abelard, but clung to the bed, instead. Darkness spilled like ink across the room; Abelard's voice receded. *I am dying,* I thought as I fell, and thanked God.

13

Since my mind is turning with many concerns, it fails me, pierced by the sharp hook of love. . . .
—HELOISE TO ABELARD

*I*n Etienne's chapel, the very one where Abelard and I had wed, I prayed on my knees, oblivious of the time of day or anything else except the tomb in which my husband wished to bury me, and the fate of our son. How keenly did my breast yearn for Astralabe now, when I thought I might never hold him again.

Dear Lord, please. Take this bitter cup from me. Restore my son to me, Father, I beg you. Dear God, have mercy on my poor little babe. Do not punish him for my sins. He is innocent, as you know. Would you deprive him of his mother's love? Mother Mary, I know you would not. I beg you, return him to me.

Abelard! Have you ceased to love me altogether? You know I would rather die than go back to that cold place. Why didn't you fight for me? Dear God, have mercy. Do not let them send me back to Argenteuil.

What else could I do besides pray? I had no other recourse—a fact that made me want to laugh and also to cry. Had I thought to determine the course of my life? Even the wisdom and knowledge of the poets and philosophers through the ages could not assist me. Why, reading them, had I never realized that men reserve power for themselves alone? The huntress Atalanta had not wanted to marry. Hippomenes, desiring her, drew her eye with golden apples and claimed her for his own. How happily she might have lived, solitary and free, had he left her to herself! Instead, he took her in the temple as Abelard had taken me in the Argenteuil refectory, incurring the wrath of the Mother of the Gods. Now he and I would be chained as they had been—to the Church, our love denied for each other and for our son.

At the thought, I felt an ache spread through my chest like blood from a wound. Love was all I had ever wanted.

"Heloise." A hand on my shoulder interrupted my prayers: Agnes, standing over me like the angel of that mercy for which I had pleaded. "Papa and I came as soon as we heard. Oh, you poor dear."

I stood to welcome her soft embrace, felt her arms twine around me. How long had it been since anyone had comforted me? Concerned for Abelard and his loss, the world, it seemed, had forgotten about me, a woman without tears and so, it was assumed, without a heart.

"My son," I whispered. "He wants to take my son from me."

"Pierre is altered, Heloise. You cannot believe anything he says, not now."

"Can I believe the bishop, then?" I parted from her. "He confirms everything Abelard has told me. They have decided my fate. They tell me I must take the veil and forswear my son."

"You *must* do nothing, my dear. No abbey would accept a woman against her will."

My laugh was bitter. "If the bishop of Paris commands it, so will it be. Why did I ever believe him, Agnes? Abelard promised to return Astralabe to me, but his promises were false."

"*Non*, he did not lie. I know Pierre, have you forgotten? He would have brought Astralabe to Paris if he could. You should have seen his tears over the child! His own son, and he could do nothing for him. Your own anguish made him suffer even more, being its cause. He loved you so, Heloise."

I noticed that she spoke in the past tense, as if Abelard were dead or had ceased to love me.

"As you know, Pierre is accustomed to taking whatever he desires. But in this case, the world—and his fears—prevented him from claiming the child."

Suger, she said, had become increasingly powerful in the king's court. A brilliant architect, he had convinced King Louis to spend a fortune on a grand new cathedral at Saint-Denis. When the Garlande brothers opposed the expenditure, pointing to the needs of the growing city, Suger increased his attacks on them.

"He has turned King Louis against my father and Uncle Etienne for supporting King Philip's marriage to Queen Bertrade. Suger called the union an abomination, when everyone knows that she and King Philip loved each other deeply. Bertrade treated Louis kindly, but Suger says she tried to poison him so that her own son would become king."

I exclaimed. Queen Bertrade, a murderess? I could not imagine it of the woman who, on her deathbed, had sent for me so that I might know my mother had loved me.

"What proof does Suger offer?" I asked.

"None at all, but King Louis believes him." Agnes narrowed her eyes. "Amaury says Suger wanted to put Bertrade on trial. An abbess, on trial! Only her death prevented that humiliation."

Failing in this attempt, Suger focused his efforts on discrediting Agnes's father and disparaging Etienne for his patronage of Abelard.

"Pierre's songs have been banished from the court, did you know? Suger said they are too sensual, arousing sinful passions." The monk also accused Etienne, in the king's presence, of encouraging adulterers and fornicators.

"Uncle Etienne swore that you and Pierre were innocent of any sin. Suger produced no evidence of anything, of course, aside from Pierre's songs. But if it became known that you had a child . . ."

I shook my head. "Who is Suger? A mere monk, of unknown parentage. King's chaplain or not, he cannot harm me."

Agnes lifted one eyebrow. "Do not underestimate what any man might do for power."

I sighed. "Then you think I should take the veil?" The dark halls; the damp chill; the silence like a hand squeezing my throat.

"At your tender age? I should hope not." Agnes linked arms with me and led me indoors. "Being young and beautiful, you may easily marry again."

"Nothing could appeal to me less."

"Of course you feel that way today, while love for Pierre yet commands your heart. In time, though, you will forget. And with Pierre in the monastery, you will be free to do as you wish."

"The idea of sharing another man's bed fills me with revulsion."

Agnes laughed. "You will change your mind soon enough. Otherwise, how will you live? You may live here with me until I marry Amaury. But how would you care for yourself after that?"

"My mother had other brothers. I have a brother, as well." I had wanted to go to him, but Uncle had forbidden it. *Would he want to know what his mother had done? Would you reveal her secrets to benefit yourself?*

"Your relatives would quickly find a husband for you and increase their fortune. In our world, dear, the only doors open to women are those of the bridal chamber and the convent.

Otherwise, what would you do? Wash other people's clothes and raise your son with the beggars and rats?"

I thought of the neighborhoods through which Pauline and I had ridden in our search for Jean-Paul, and my spirits sank. Life in a monastery would be far better for Astralabe than that miserable, hungry existence. Pauline had endured it for a short time to be with her child, but she had hopes of working as a cook and marrying. I possessed no skills except reading and writing—useless talents for a woman except in the abbey.

"I could marry, I suppose, if doing so would return my son to me."

"*Non*, my dear friend. That child is lost to you now. Pierre is right about this: unless you would destroy the man you love, you must give up your son. Let him remain in Brittany, far from anyone's sight. Forget about him. But—don't look so gloomy about it, Heloise! You will give birth again."

After our dispute over Astralabe, Abelard returned to his studies and refused to answer any more of my questions. My eyes' accusations, he said, rebuked his tongue to silence. Only when Agnes and her father entered his room with Etienne did Abelard finally speak.

"They have forbidden me to teach, a more cruel punishment than any blade could inflict," he said, pacing the room, his pain overcome by outrage. At these words, I forgot my own travails for a moment. In their haste to rub the salt of their judgment into Abelard's wounds, would the men of the Church extinguish the light of his brilliance? They might as well blot out the sun for fear of being burned.

"Suger would destroy kingdoms if it would increase his status," Agnes's father said.

"By God's head, what does he gain by my diminishment? I possess nothing that he desires."

"Except Heloise," Agnes said. "Do you recall that day in the Saint-Etienne Cathedral when Bernard spoke? Suger glared at her throughout the sermon—with his hands crossed before his crotch. I wonder what he was hiding?"

"Having lived at Saint-Denis since he was a child, Suger knows nothing of women except what the Church has taught," Etienne said. "His own lustful thoughts terrify him. Forced to deny his natural desires, he blames women as the cause of his sin."

"Daughter of Eve," Agnes teased, seeing the color rise to my face.

"If so, then why wouldn't he blame me instead of Abelard for our sins?"

"I'm certain that he does blame you," Agnes's father said. "But to attack Pierre is to attack the brothers of Garlande. By diminishing us in King Louis's eyes, Suger aims to elevate himself."

"And now he would lock me away at Saint-Denis, where he can watch my every movement," Abelard said.

"As the abbot's secretary, he will do more than watch," Etienne said. "He will work to discredit you in every way, so as to harm my brother and me."

"That is all the more reason why Heloise ought to take the veil," Abelard said. "Then Suger could not threaten her, or any of us by accusing her."

Heat rose to my face. "Why should I sacrifice myself on the altar of that man's secret shame? Let him say what he desires. Our spotless lives shall speak for us."

As eagerly as I had longed to hear Abelard's laughter again, the sound now brought me no joy. "Spotless, did you say? With what soap have you cleansed *your* past?"

"I believe it is called marriage," I said tersely.

"God does not agree, or so it appears," he said.

When they had gone, Abelard slumped upon his bed. "I am finished."

"Why do you say so? Can the breath of any mortal blow out such a flame?" I went over to sit beside him and placed my hand on his, but he drew himself away.

"Of what benefit is a flame that burns where none can see its brightness or feel its heat?"

"Then—remain with me, Abelard. I shall be as a mirror reflecting your light for all to see. Pass on your wisdom and knowledge to our son. In time, the world will forget your shame and will welcome your music and your arguments again."

"The world will never forget. Or, if it did, the Church would not. No, Heloise, I must do as the bishop commands if I would continue my work. Guibert promised to disseminate my *Sic et Non* if I comply."

"Do as you must, then." I stood and brushed my palms together. "I shall do the same."

"You are my wife. You do as I command."

"Before husbandly rights come husbandly duties, none of which you desire to fulfill."

"As if desiring could make me a man again."

"Manhood comes not from the body, but from the willingness to do what is right."

"I know what is right for you."

"As you have demonstrated so competently in the months since our marriage? My son wrested from me, myself shut away in the very manner which you now dread, yourself attacked and now planning to abandon me—"

"I have made better arrangements for you than you ought to have hoped. Argenteuil would not admit you again, not after what we did there, without my help." Someone, it seemed, had spied us in the refectory—Sister Adela, I felt certain—and reported our transgression to the Reverend Mother. My face burned.

"You have done all for naught. I will not return to Argenteuil."

"You will. The bishop of Paris has declared it so."

"The bishop does not rule my life, as he seems to rule yours. I will retrieve our son and care for him myself."

"You mean to say that you will remarry." The spark of life returned to Abelard's eyes. "That I would never allow."

"Marry, and place myself under another man's control? I would sooner enter the convent."

"With what, then, do you intend to feed our child?"

"With the love that he is not getting now."

"And do you think love will sustain him? Come now, Heloise. If you will not take the veil, then you must marry. I will not be able to provide for you while I am cloistered."

"I shall write to my brother and my other uncles. They would not allow harm to befall me or our son."

"Why would your family aid you now, covered as you are with the dung others have heaped upon us? We reek, Heloise. No one can come near us without gagging from the stink of our sin."

I stared at him, uncomprehending. What had happened to my Abelard? Whence had gone the boaster, the swaggerer, the arrogant who had so confidently proclaimed that our love, far from being sinful, was God's most precious gift?

"We have atoned for our sins, if we ever sinned at all," I said, but my voice lacked conviction. "I always considered the pleasures we shared to be the most innocent of delights, given to each other with the highest intention, that is, love."

"And now we are ruined!" Tears filled Abelard's eyes as he stepped toward me. I stood as if in a dream, unable to believe that he was opening his arms to me at last.

"I have nothing to offer you, Heloise, except the little influence I still wield." Warmth filled me as I anticipated his embrace, but he only placed his hands on my shoulders. His eyes gazed into mine. I sought tenderness there but saw only pity—for himself.

"Your love is what I need," I said.

"Your obedience is what *I* need."

"I cannot do as you ask." I would have turned away but I dared not, for fear of losing Abelard completely again.

"You must, or your death will be on my head."

I smiled. "I have no plans to die anytime soon. I have a school to begin."

I told him of my plan, the seed of which had been planted long ago, when, denied my request to attend his class because of my sex, I began to think of opening a school for girls. Yes, I knew the arguments against such a school, but I also knew there was nothing else for me to do. Hadn't he taught me that I might accomplish anything to which I aspired?

"I can teach your dialectic to them," I said quickly, not daring to let him speak. "Your name and your teachings will live on then, even should the pope himself cast your books into the fire."

"Poor Heloise." He shook his head with a smile so condescending that, unable to bear it, I closed my eyes. "The Church would never allow what you want. Men would never allow it. Women are for bearing children and bringing them up—the matters of the home. The matters of the world are best left to men."

"*You* seemed to enjoy having a thinking wife."

"I am not like other men. And you are not like other women."

"Plenty of women would enjoy using their minds for more than needlework and nursery rhymes."

Yet my words rang feebly in my own ears. I thought of Agnes, who had been given the best tutors and yet possessed only a rudi-mentary grasp of Latin and none of literature. *What would be the use of filling my head with such nonsense?* she had said with a shrug—until Amaury came along. Now, however, she read not for her own edification, but to impress him. I thought of the ladies at King Louis's court, who, upon hearing Abelard's new, more sophisticated songs, had pronounced without shame that they preferred the simpler verses of his earlier works.

"*Oui*, and a place exists for women who crave the scholar's life," Abelard said. "There they may read and discuss to their heart's delight, without threatening the balance of the world that men have made for themselves. It is called the abbey, Heloise. If you aim to teach, as do I, then the abbey is the only place for us."

14

**When I was powerless to oppose you in anything, I found
strength at your command to destroy myself.**
—HELOISE TO ABELARD

I went at his command, that is to say, willingly, although
with ponderous steps, as though dragging my legs through
water. Was this how my mother had felt in the ceremony at Fontevraud? But she had joined the man she loved there, rather than
putting herself away from him. She had not given up her life for
my father's sake, but at my uncle's insistence.

Now, stepping with Abelard into the very life I dreaded, I understood at last. Mother might have kept me with her, but at
what price? My uncle, with his brothers' assent, had forced her
into abbey life sooner than she desired—for she would have gone
to Robert eventually, I imagine—but he had not taken me from
her. She had relinquished me willingly for the sake of her beloved, had left me fatherless for *his* sake, abandoning not only me
but also herself for the sake of love.

What is the meaning of love? Abelard and I had argued this question many times, but now, walking beside him with my hand in the
crook of his arm, I remembered something he had written to me.

*In this way will our love be immortal: if each of us strives to
outdo the other in a friendly and loving contest and if neither of us*

agrees to be outdone by the other. Wasn't this what Christ meant when he said, "Love your neighbor as I have loved you"? In giving his life for us, he created a debt that we can only repay by loving one another in turn. And so, only one type of love exists, as I had argued. Its authentic expression comes not in the uttering of words or in sweet gazes or even a fullness felt in the heart. To truly love, we must be willing to give of ourselves, even our very lives.

On that day in the Argenteuil chapel, in the gown I had worn for our wedding, I married Abelard as I had not done before, that is, with all my being and all my soul. Now, he must repay the debt. Elation soared in me at the thought. We, whose spirits had merged, whose bodies had dissolved and melded together, whose hearts had beat as one with the great and generous pulse of the world, had not finished, but had only begun.

He walked with me toward the chapel wearing the *bliaut* that I most admired, of brilliant blue silk embroidered with gold fleurs-de-lis, and a silver cross at his throat. For myself: that gown of deep red, the color of blood, soon to be shed for my beloved's sake. The abbey loomed before us like a great hulking predator. I clutched Abelard's arm, clinging to him for what was surely the last time.

"Steady, Heloise," he said when I stumbled. Not *sweetest* or *shining star* nor any of the other endearments that had sweetened his tongue in a past that was, for me, achingly present. *Hold still, you little beast,* my uncle had grunted as he'd carried me to the door that was, now, swinging open. The smoke of incense stung my nostrils. Women's voices sang of sacrifice and sorrow, and the mysteries of love. A man in robes stood in the entry, beckoning me into a darkness from which I would never return.

"I feel as though I were preparing a virgin for sacrifice," Agnes had said that morning, combing out my hair so that it fell in waves nearly to my waist. In the mirror I beheld my flushed cheeks, my red and trembling mouth, and my eyes glowing with a fire that burned unnaturally hot, as cinders do before they sputter to an end.

"My dear, you look divine. No—do not avert your eyes. Behold the beauty that God has given to you." She placed her hands on either side of my face and compelled me to face the mirror. "Surely it would be a sin to hide your shining light in that cellar."

Her words, a final attempt at dissuasion, had the opposite effect. Face and form meant nothing to me now, having ceased to please Abelard. Where once he had written songs in praise of my milk-white skin and eyes like dark stars, now he regarded my gifts with anguish, not able to bear the thought of another man's enjoying that which he, now, could not. Regarding outer beauty as I did, as the petals of a flower that would someday wither and drop, I could only smile at Agnes's words. Bereft of Abelard, what else was I to do except his bidding? My uncle's blade, in cutting him, had cut him off from me, and me from our son—an act for which I bore as much responsibility as Uncle Fulbert and for which I now would pay the price.

Oh, why hadn't I died that day by Abelard's bed when he had announced my fate? I had fainted to the floor, instead, "from exhaustion," the physician had said, but I knew that the shock had felled me. For me to die would have been kinder to Astralabe, who now must struggle to comprehend a mother's abandonment, as I had done. Perhaps he would learn the truth about me someday, if anyone dared to reveal it. But *non*—I had not died. I would tell him myself.

Bereft of my son, losing my beloved, I possessed nothing except my work. Removed from the cares of the world, I would devote myself to my studies and also to teaching, which I longed to do. So why did my throat constrict so tightly that, walking into the chilly Chapelle Saint-Jean-Baptiste, I could hardly breathe? The dim-flickering candles and grim-faced monks and canons and priests, the *De profundis* rising like a wail from the choir, the priest with the gleaming knife standing nearby: all filled me with dread as though death, not marriage, awaited me.

No one had to tell me what to do. I had already seen many novices walk this candlelit aisle, stepping in slow time, bedecked like brides with their father or a brother or an uncle—but never with a husband—by their side. No one had to tell me when to kneel, or when to bend my head to the knife that skimmed along my scalp, shearing my hair, which fell around me like a dark pool. I stood and turned to Abelard, triumphant in my submission, expecting to see his shock at the sight of me shorn, as fragile in appearance as though I were starving, which, in a way, I was. But his face remained as impassive as if he were blind, which, in a way, he was.

O Abelard! Had only a month passed since he'd embraced me so tenderly on these very grounds? *I will always love you, my only restoration, my only food, my one peace,* and his eyes had opened like windows through which I beheld my own soul. In them I saw restless wings beating, fanning my desire.

Standing in the chapel, shorn and cold, I knew I resembled nothing more than a frightened child, as did all novices. Would Abelard awaken to me at last, and to my sacrifices made for his sake? Every argument, every entreaty, every plea that I had uttered these past weeks had fallen on ears that had seemed, to me, deaf to anyone's interests but his own.

Cry, I urged myself. *Please, dear God, give me tears so that he will know the depth of my sorrow, and of my love.*

The sisters ceased their singing. The bishop performed a ceremony more elaborate than my wedding had been: waving the burning censer, filling my mouth and nose with the sickly-sweet smell; intoning the vows, to which I numbly gave my "I do"; placing a ring upon my finger; fitting my head with the veil. I turned to face the crowd that had gathered and saw the curious eyes of Abelard's scholars; the tear-swollen eyes of Agnes; the kind and solemn eyes of Etienne; the satisfied, glinting eyes of Suger; and a hundred other pairs, all watching, waiting, some shifting in anticipation of the ceremony's imminent end. But all was not finished, not yet.

I must try one final time to make Abelard see me.

"O noble husband," I cried out as best as I could from a throat choked with grief—not for the fate to which I submitted myself, but for the loss of Abelard's love, which, I believed, was complete and final. A hush fell over the chapel, save for the slamming of my heart against my breast.

"'O noble husband, too great for me to wed.'" What better poem than Lucan's *Pharsalia* to shake him from his trance?

"'Was it my fate to bend that lofty head?'"

"'Why did I marry you and bring about your fall?'" Oh, why? Countless times have I asked this question of myself, yet the answer is ever the same: because Abelard, my only love, commanded it.

I turned and looked directly at him, hoping yet to behold on his face the recognition of what I had done, the enormity of my sacrifice.

"'Now I accept the penalty,'" I said, faltering, for he had already begun to glance toward the open door, "'and see me gladly pay.'"

The sisters sang again. Their voices rose to the ceiling and out the door, carrying with them all my hopes. Finding no sympathy in Abelard, I looked to Agnes, but could not see her. I lifted my hand to rub my eyes and found my face wet with tears.

"Abelard!" I cried to his retreating back. "Abelard, look at me!" But he did not hear or, hearing, did not obey. Through the blur of tears that, now unstoppered, flowed like a melancholy river over my face and hands, I saw him step through that door, into the beaming, freewheeling sunlight. Then the door fell shut, and all was dark.

15

※

When her dead body was carried to the opened tomb, her
husband, who had died long before her, raised his arms to
receive her, and so clasped her closely in his embrace.
—ANONYMOUS ON HELOISE'S BURIAL

THE ORATORY OF THE PARACLETE
1164

What, against the span of eternity, are twenty-seven
years? They pass as quickly as a heartbeat, or a sigh,
or a single note in a love song performed in the place de Grève
market from under curling eyelashes. Yet, in the years between
the day that door closed on his retreating back and the night of
his death, Abelard and I might have known a lifetime of joy.

In twenty-seven years, we might have lived and loved together
and raised our son and bounced his children on our knees. Instead,
our Astralabe spent his childhood in Brittany with an aunt and uncle
who did not want him. He never knew his *maman* or *papa* and went
to the abbey as soon as he became of age. I saw him only once as a
youth, when, at Abelard's request, Dagobert brought him to me.
How like his father he appeared, with those heartbreaking blue eyes
and soft curls. I opened my arms to him but he shied away, averting
his gaze. On his second visit, as a young man nearing departure for
the Hauterive Abbey in Savoy—so distant, I knew I would never see

him again—he stammered when he spoke, and his hands shook, and he stared at me without ceasing, his eyes full of questions. I told him everything I knew. Before he departed, I gave him the collection of our songs that Abelard had entrusted to me. My son thanked me while holding the parchment to his chest, as though fearing I might wrest it away again—but then he embraced me with eyes full of moisture and kissed my cheeks and hands. "Mother," he called me, filling me with music as Abelard had done on the day we met.

If only we had remained true to our own song, and to our love, our lives might have held more joy than sorrow, and laughter rather than tears. Why did we part? Had we defied Guibert and Suger and clung to each other, what punishments might the men of the Church have meted out that they did not inflict upon Abelard, anyway? They tried excommunication, banishment, burning his books, harassment, even assassination, but Abelard would not be silenced. How gladly would I have endured these trials and more for his sake, and for that of our son.

During those twenty-seven years—nearly half of Abelard's too-brief life—I was forced into, then out of, Argenteuil, banished by Suger with my sisters and our Reverend Mother for crimes we did not commit. Abelard, taking pity on me, gave to me his only possession: his parcel of wild ground on the Ardusson River, on which to build an abbey of my own. My daughters and I endured starvation and robbers to tame that wilderness. With God's help we built an edifice that became renowned both near and far as the only abbey in the world governed for, and by, women alone, and guided by the first Rule for women, which I wrote. In time, the Oratory of the Paraclete grew to become one of the largest abbeys in the realm, with five daughter houses.

We were not completely without male influence, however. As the oratory's spiritual adviser, Abelard visited us many times, endearing himself to the sisters but keeping himself apart from me.

How I yearned for even one hour with him, to talk as intimately as we had done in the past! But he would not see me alone. Perhaps he dreaded provoking any more scandal. Perhaps he wanted to avoid any reminders of our former sins—sins for which he had repented, he said in his letters, admonishing me to do the same. But how could I do so? Now, as my own death nears, I dread God's punishment—will our Lord keep us apart in Paradise as men did on Earth?—but I hold in my heart an ember of hope that loving Abelard was, in fact, no sin at all.

During our years apart, Abelard wrote many works of true greatness, earning the glory denied to him. He threw his book on the Holy Trinity into the fire, as the Church commanded, then wrote it again even more brilliantly. For his efforts, the pope excommunicated him not once, but twice, and banished him to silence, forbidding him to teach or to publish any new writings. Yet I found him in the hours before his death sitting up in bed, surrounded by books, one hand gripping a stylus and the other holding a wax tablet onto which he scribbled as though each word might be his last.

In all the years between us, I never told my love the truth about the desperate letter I had written to my uncle that led to Abelard's mutilation. Now, riding my horse as fast as it would go, racing death, I anguished over this failure. Why hadn't I confessed? I could have written of it and, in fact, did so many times, but scraped the wax clean without sending anything. A written account, falling into the wrong hands, would damage us both, or so I told myself. But I also feared that, hearing the truth, Abelard might turn his back against me forever, shutting the door of his friendship, which was, now, all that remained.

Riding with as much haste as the pocked and scarred road would allow, I rehearsed my speech. *I thought you had left me in the Royal Abbey to die, either from laboring in the vineyards or from a spirit broken by your absence. I wrote to my uncle, then, out of desperation. Had I known what he would do to you, I would have cut off my hands rather than write even one word to him.*

How many nights had I shivered, contemplating the coldness in Abelard's eyes where once the fires of passion had raged? In all the time he spent at our Oratory of the Paraclete, he held himself apart from me, embracing my daughters but declining even to clasp my hand. With the sisters he engaged in long discussions, made merry, and performed new compositions written especially for our convent. With me, however, he spoke only of receipts, of repairs to the abbey, or of books we might acquire—and he addressed me never in private, but only in the presence of others. Thusly did he neglect his Heloise.

While those who had given him nothing feasted on the delights of his companionship, I who had given him everything pecked at the crumbs he let fall. For Abelard's sake, I'd sacrificed my son and all my hopes for life. Now, it seemed, he would never repay the debt. All I had wanted from him was, simply, himself—his acknowledgment of the extent of my losses, and his love. But to give of himself completely had always been an impossible task.

How would he react to my confession? With bitterness? With tears? Contemplating the possibilities, I felt calm. Abelard's anger would be preferable to his indifference. Once the storm of his outrage had passed he might forgive me, and I might live without him not joyously, but in peace.

I rode for four days, guarded by monks. At last I understood what the Scriptures mean when they admonish us to pray without ceasing. *Do not take him yet, dear God.* When the Saint-Marcel monastery came into view, we dismounted our horses and waited behind some trees, out of sight of the road, for nightfall. We must not tarry, the monks urged; Abelard's end lay near. But I would not risk being seen. The Church had denied Abelard's request to spend his final hours with me at the Paraclete. Loving us both, our friend Pierre the Venerable, the abbot at Cluny where Abelard had taken refuge, sent my beloved to this distant monastery so that we might be together during his final days. Alas, the journey had nearly killed him. *Let him live a little longer,* I prayed.

Darkness dropped its cloak but God brushed the clouds aside, and the waning moon illumined our path to the chapel door. There Pierre the Venerable greeted me with a kiss before leading me to the infirmary.

We entered the tiny hall, filled with flickering candles warding off the darkness like myriad stars. I had to smile at the sight of Abelard propped up with pillows, his brow creased in concentration, his fist clutching the stylus that he dropped when we entered. He lifted his eyes to me, and I began to cry, overcome by the pure and tender love shining, at last, in that blue gaze.

"Thanks be to God you have come," he said. "Heloise of my heart, here at last. Thanks be to God."

I wanted to fall to my knees and beg our Lord to prolong Abelard's life. Must I lose him now that he loved me again? Failing that, I would have asked him to take me, too. How could I live in a world without Abelard?

His gaze held mine, and all the years since he had first sung to me in the place de Grève market seemed to disappear. His sparse, stiff hair of pure white; his face etched by time and worry; his cracked lips; his rounded belly—all faded from my sight, and he became the Abelard of old, arrogant and proud, irreverent and more handsome than any other man I had ever beheld. I fancy that the changes time had wrought in me—silver strands in my hair, my thickened waist—might have vanished to restore me in his eyes to the youthful woman he had first loved.

"Please, Heloise, come and hold me," he said, sweeping tablet, books, stylus, and blade to the floor.

The monks in the room frowned, forbidding, but our friend Pierre nodded assent. I removed my mantle and handed it to him. He departed and the others followed, leaving us to ourselves. I gathered the heavy folds of my habit, lifted the bedcovers, and slid into bed beside Abelard. He pressed his face against my breast and wept, soaking my clothing with tears and shaking with a chill that, he said, emanated from his marrow. All the physician's potions and pastes had not warmed him; no fire could burn hotly enough. Yet, in my embrace, his bones ceased to rattle. He drew a deep, restful breath, then paused for so long that I thought his soul had departed. I whimpered—but then he spoke.

"Forgive me, Heloise. I wronged you and Astralabe most grievously." I dissuaded him from saying more, admonishing him to rest, but he persisted. "Thinking only of myself, I deprived you of our son and denied him his mother. I failed you both."

"No, my love," I said, reveling in the love in his eyes, swimming in it. "You did the only thing you could do, given the world in which we live." As I spoke the words, I realized their truth. Abelard and I had thought ourselves immune to the authority of men we considered our inferiors. Indeed, in our arrogance we had dared to defy God himself. Is it any wonder that the Lord struck us down? Were every man to live according to his desires alone, the world would descend into chaos.

Now, I knew, was the time for me to confess my sin, namely, the letter that had incited my uncle's attack. But how could I do so when Abelard had begun, again, to weep? Asking his forgiveness now might alleviate my agony, but it would only increase his own.

So I held my tongue and, stroking Abelard's damp hair and kissing his brow, listened to his confession.

He had seduced me, he said. For this, I readily forgave him, adding that I had desired him in equal measure.

He had deceived my uncle, he said. Again, I offered absolution, for hadn't I done the same and worse? Uncle Fulbert had provided for me and trusted me, yet I had given little thought to his feelings, if any at all.

He had forced me into the convent for selfish reasons, out of jealousy, loathing the thought of me with another man. I forgave him even of this, for hadn't I taken my vows of my own free will? As much as I dreaded the life he had chosen for me, I had submitted with an equally selfish motive, that is, the hope of reigniting his love.

"And I have neglected you for all these years," he said.

I made no reply at first, as the weight of every day without Abelard's care pressed against my chest and tongue and the backs of my eyes. How many days do twenty-seven years contain? I suffered through every one of them, deprived first of any word from him and then of any comfort when, attempting to talk with him of the love we had shared, I received his letter admonishing me to restrain my tongue. Desperate for contact with him, I obeyed and kept our correspondence as impersonal as our conversations had become, ignoring the promptings of my heart and stifling the cries of my soul for its other, better half.

"I thought you had ceased to love me," I said, "or that you had never loved me at all."

"You are the only one I have ever loved," he said, beginning to tremble again. I tightened my embrace, but, this time, his shivers did not abate for a long while. A sob formed in my throat but I swallowed it, not wanting to hinder his soul's unburdening in his final hours. My reward came soon enough, as, once his body had calmed, he told me through laboring breaths all that I had wanted to know.

Abelard had never blamed me for my uncle's cruel act, he said. Again, the urge to confess seized me, but again I forbore, not only because I feared extinguishing the light of love from his eyes but also because I would have him rest, now, in peace. If he had treated me coldly, he did so out of shame, he said, and also out of confusion. Even after his body's wounds had healed and the pain diminished, the desire that once had burned for me stirred him no more.

"When I beheld you—forgive me!—I felt nothing." Shame increased by his body's failure to feel what a man ought to feel, he wanted only to be rid of me, the reminder of all he once had been.

"And now I must confess. Heloise, the bishop of Paris did not decree that you must take the veil; nor did Suger suggest it. The idea was mine, and mine alone."

He began to weep anew, but I begged him to dry his tears. I'd given up my life for no one's sake but his, I said. Only Abelard could have prompted me to make that sacrifice.

"I hoped that you would repay your debt to me with your love," I said.

"How could I do so when I abhorred myself?"

His shivering commenced; I cradled his clattering bones awkwardly, as though clutching a bundle of twigs.

"I have never ceased to love you, my precious jewel; my unique one; my *amica, amor, dilectio,* and *caritas,*" he said.

I smiled through my tears. At last, he knew: love is love. I had won our debate.

Yet, I realized, Abelard's love had differed from mine. As I had argued so passionately all those years ago, each of us feels love differently. My experience of love—selfless, sacrificial, all-consuming—differed from his, which considered his own interests first and foremost. He loved himself first, but he did not love me less.

Out of love, he'd given me the most exquisite pleasures rather than simply taking his from me; out of love, he'd sent me to Brittany with all the money he could gather to ensure my safety and well-being. Out of love had he married me, imperiling all that he'd worked so long to build; out of love had Abelard moved me to Argenteuil to flee my uncle's abuse, knowing that Uncle might turn his hand against him, instead.

Out of love had Abelard given me his only possession in the world, his land for the Paraclete. Out of love had he made an abbess of me, knowing that I would be cared for no matter what might befall him, and also that, as the Paraclete's adviser, he would be able to visit me from time to time.

"I did not wish to harm you further," he gasped. "God is my witness, Heloise: all I have done since we parted has been for your sake. And yet mine is a selfish love, yes. I want you with me in heaven."

His eyes brimmed and overflowed, blue pools into which I yearned to dive, immersing myself in what had been denied to me for so long. Abelard loved me as much as I loved him, only differently. Why had I ever thought otherwise? Abandoned by my mother, never knowing my father, abused by my uncle, I had expected Abelard to hurt me, as well. Indeed, I thought many times that he had done so. I could not have erred more grievously. He had remained true to me since the day we met. He had not betrayed me, but, in allowing doubt to govern my mind, I had betrayed myself, and him.

I knew nothing else that night, cradling Abelard, my heart of hearts, but I knew this: he had never ceased to love me, and he never would. And, on that night, he repaid his debt to me.

His eyes pleaded. I opened my mouth to answer, *oui*, that I loved him, and always had loved him, and always would love him. But he foundered like a drowning man, grasping at my clothes as if to keep from slipping away.

"Pray for me, Heloise. Swear it. Take my body to the Paraclete. Pray over me every day. Ask for God's mercy and forgiveness. I should not have led you into sin. Please—beg him to forgive me."

"Shh. Do not speak of these things." Had he forgotten that I had never repented of our indulgences? Nor have I done so now, two decades after Abelard's death. Instead, I relive every hour we spent together and indulge, again, in every delightful transgression. Why would God listen to me, a sinner yet twisting with desire for my former lover and utterly unrepentant? I doubted that my prayers would provide any benefit—but I did not say so. Instead, I made the promise as he drifted away, his eyes' light diminishing, lanterns set on a vessel that, now, drifted out to sea.

"Abelard," I said, crying now, "don't leave me."

"Heloise," he said, gasping. "I shall never leave you. I will await you in heaven, my only one. We shall be together again someday, God willing."

"But what if God does not will it?" I began to sob. "I have never repented of sinning with you. I cannot, not in my heart. You say you have done so? Tell me how, I beg you."

His eyes' expression told me all. Elation swept through me. His admonishments; the calls for repentance in his letters; his claims that lust, not love, had ruled him—all were false.

"Or have you repented?" I whispered. "Are you forgiven?"

"I don't know."

He pressed his mouth to mine, as for a kiss. I felt my fears subside as, with a long sigh, he released his spirit, giving himself to me at last, the greatest gift of all, taking up residence in my soul, becoming a part of me as never before. Warmth rushed through my blood like the fresh breath of springtime, filling me with hope where, for so long, the cold winds of desolation had blown.

Every year without Abelard in my life has seemed, to me, a lifetime. But what are Earthly years? With his dying breath, he became mine for eternity.

And I, as ever, am his.

Love urges me to enlist in its service, to respect its laws,
And what I had not learnt, love forces me to learn.
No man but stone is he whom your beauty does not move.
I believe that I am moved, nor can I be stone.
Poets have tried hard to portray the body of Venus,
. . . .
But did they ever produce anyone equal to you? Certainly I
think not.
For your beauty surpasses even the goddesses themselves.
Should I go on or be silent? By your grace, I will speak.
I will speak, for a traitor is devoid of words . . .
You have conquered me, whom no woman could conquer.
Thus I burn more strongly, this being my first love;
For never before has that flame penetrated my marrow.
If ever there was love before, I was only lukewarm.
You alone make me eloquent; such glory has happened to
No one, that she be worthy of my song.
You are like no one else, you in whom nature has placed
Whatever excellence the world can have:
Beauty, noble birth, character—through which honor is
begotten—
All make you outstanding in our city.
So is it then surprising that I am lured by their brilliance,
If I succumb to you, conquered by your love?

—Abelard to Heloise

AUTHOR'S NOTE

⚜

*L*ove in all its passion, glory, pathos, and pain: That's what first drew me to the story of Heloise and Abelard, that "ill-starred" couple whose shocking tale has intrigued so many over the centuries. But where others have seen tragedy, I've found inspiration, especially in the life of Heloise d'Argenteuil. Her unconditional, self-sacrificial devotion to Abelard never wavered in spite of tremendous obstacles, including Abelard's own flawed humanity; nor did it prevent her becoming one of the most influential women of her day and one of the greatest writers of all time.

As soon as I encountered their story—while researching medieval philosophy for my thirteenth-century historical novel, *Four Sisters, All Queens*—I knew Heloise and Abelard would be the focus of my next book. Why did they appeal to me so? The tale's shock value grabbed my attention, of course, but so did the paradox of Heloise, a rare woman scholar who matched wits with the greatest of minds yet gave up everything that mattered for his sake.

When I began *The Sharp Hook of Love*, I was newly in love with an artistic man of true genius whose need for ample time and space alone clashed with my desire for companionship and connection. As we fought and parted, then reunited with passion and joy, our love deepened and grew—and I wrote and read and revised, searching for the true meaning of love, confronting my own deepest fears, anxieties, and desires.

My quest began with the couple's letters. Years after being forced to part, Heloise and Abelard continued to correspond. Eight of their letters survive, written when he was an abbot and she an abbess, starting with Abelard's autobiography, *Historia Calamitatum (The Story of My Misfortunes)*, in which he tells the tale of his affair with Heloise. She responded, correcting him in some of his accounts and embellishing others, and emphasizing that, in the fifteen years having passed since their parting, she had never stopped loving him.

Apparently, the same is true for Abelard. Before he died, Abelard asked permission to live his final days at the Oratory of the Paraclete, where Heloise was now abbess. The Church refused, so he requested that, after his death, his body go to the Paraclete so that Heloise might pray over him until she died—which she did for twenty years.

As for Heloise, her deathbed wish was to be buried with her beloved. "When her dead body was carried to the opened tomb, her husband, who had died long before her, raised his arms to receive her, and so clasped her closely in his embrace," an anonymous chronicler wrote, lending an air of legend to the lovers' already famous story.

When, one hundred years later, the great poet Jean de Meun translated their letters from Latin into French and excerpted them in his continuation of the popular tale *Roman de la Rose*, the pair became famous again, taking their place alongside Tristan and Iseult and Aucassin and Nicolette as embodying the spirit of enduring love against all odds—*Romeo and Juliet* before their time. Unlike these couples, however, Abelard and Heloise were not fictional characters. They truly lived, and loved.

Imagine my excitement to hear these lovers' tale for the first time. I *had* to retell it. As I began my research, my admiration for Heloise grew. Here was a woman of intellect, heart, and indomitable spirit who gave up her child, her freedom, her very life, for the sake of the man she loved. In doing so, she benefited not only Abelard but all posterity.

In 1129, twelve years or so after Heloise took the veil, Suger, now abbot at Saint-Denis, took possession of the Argenteuil Royal Abbey after accusing the nuns of "disgraceful and filthy relations." Suger expelled the sisters and their abbess, most of whom headed to the Saint-Marie-of-Malnoué convent in Brie. Heloise, however, followed a different path.

Abelard, hearing of her situation, had offered her his only possession, a tract of wild ground on the Ardusson River near Troyes, on which to build an abbey. She and her followers made the long journey to Abelard's oratory, which comprised a few mud-and-thatch huts and a small stone chapel. At first the women had to forage, hunt, and fish to stay alive, but in a few years the Oratory of the Paraclete had become one of the largest religious institutions in the French realm with five daughter houses, rivaling the Fontevraud Abbey.

As abbess, Heloise instituted a legacy benefiting future generations at the Paraclete: new rules governing convent life, the first ever written for women. She also left behind songs and poems, likely among those in the famous *Carmina Burana*, which scholars believe began as Abelard's personal collection.

And then, the letters. Even with only the aforementioned eight, the couple's story has captured imaginations for nearly nine hundred years. A glimpse at their Wikipedia entry reveals a long list of poems, music, novels, films, artworks, and more referring to the couple.

But in 1999, an extraordinary thing happened: a scholar in Australia, Professor Constant J. Mews, published excerpts from

113 more letters that he asserted the couple wrote to each other during their courtship. These "Lost Love Letters," exquisite in their poetry and extraordinary in their passion, provide a much different portrait of the love affair between Heloise and Abelard than we find in the *Historia Calamitatum*. Abelard, writing his autobiography to emphasize his own sinfulness and salvation, had positioned himself as a callous seducer of his innocent student. The "Lost Love Letters," however, show a Heloise fully engaged in the affair, an equal in love as well as intellect.

The Sharp Hook of Love is, to my knowledge, the first novel about the couple to incorporate these letters, not only their extraordinary language but also their themes, including the nature of true love. In this book, as in their letters, they debate whether different types of love exist, such as the love of a parent or child versus the love for a husband or wife versus the love for God, or whether love is, simply, love. They agree that, in considering the rightness or wrongness of an act, intention matters more than the deed itself. And they discuss the "perpetual debt" in which lovers ideally find themselves.

"You know, my heart's love, that the services of true love are properly fulfilled only when they are continually owed," Heloise writes. Abelard echoes this notion: "In this way will our love be immortal: if each of us strives to outdo the other in a friendly and loving contest and if neither of us agreed to be outdone by the other." To this day, debate rages over which of the two loved, and lost, more.

Incorporating the beautiful language from the couples' own letters was one of the great pleasures, for me, of writing *The Sharp Hook of Love*. Striving for authenticity of voice, I also wove in quotes from philosophers and poets they would have read— Boethius, Seneca, Cicero, Ovid—as well as from the Vulgate Scriptures. Knowing that Heloise and Abelard would have written and possibly spoken in Latin, I even tried to use only words of Latin origin. The result, I hope, is a book like no other in its blending of intellect and passion, of poetry and philosophy, of Heloise and Abelard.

If *The Sharp Hook of Love* and its poetry, themes, and story delight you as much as they do me, please spread the word about this book. Tell your friends and family members, your book group, your bookseller, your librarian, your social media friends and followers. Post your reviews wherever you hang out online.

And please do come to my website, http://authorsherryjones .com, for a plethora of resources to increase your understanding and appreciation of these remarkable lovers and the times in which they lived. While you're there, connect with me on the social media links posted there, and write to me as well. I would love to hear from you, and I always write back.

ACKNOWLEDGMENTS

My most heartfelt thanks go to Dr. Constant J. Mews, professor at Monash University in Australia and one of the world's preeminent authorities on Abelard and Heloise. Not only did he read an early version of this novel with an eye for historical accuracy as well as generously and promptly answer all my emails but he also, with his publisher, Palgrave, gave me permission to freely excerpt from his excellent 1999 book, *The Lost Love Letters of Heloise and Abelard*. I highly recommend this book to all who are interested in learning more about this fascinating couple.

I'm also deeply indebted to my literary agent, Natasha Kern, for her friendship, advice, and dedication to helping me further my career as an author; to my editor, Kate Dresser, for her brilliant editing suggestions and enthusiasm for this book; to Steven Boldt for first-rate copyediting; to friends who read early drafts and made comments so helpful: Richard Myers, AnneMarie Lewis, Todd Mowbray, Serena Belsby, and Mitchell James Kaplan; to my entire team at Gallery Books, including Louise Burke, Jen Bergstrom, Jean Anne Rose, and Liz Psaltis; to Kathy Sagan; and to the many friends, fans, librarians, and booksellers who continue to offer their support and love.

The Sharp Hook of Love

SHERRY JONES

INTRODUCTION

The Sharp Hook of Love retells the story of Heloise and Abelard, twelfth-century Parisian lovers. Beautifully incorporating language from the real couple's letters to each other, the novel traces the story of their romance as it blossoms from a meeting of the minds into a forbidden love affair. United by love even when pulled apart by families, friends, and society, Heloise and Abelard learn what it means to truly sacrifice one's life for a beloved. As intimate as it is erotic, as devastating as it is beautiful, *The Sharp Hook of Love* teaches readers that true love can never be thwarted.

QUESTIONS AND TOPICS FOR DISCUSSION

1. "For nothing is under less control than the heart—having no power to command it, we are forced to obey," writes the historical Heloise in a letter to Abelard. This quote is used by the author as an epigraph for the novel, and as such, it frames the story that ensues as one about control—or lack thereof. Who or what is in control in *The Sharp Hook of Love*? Who or what is out of control? Do any of the characters successfully disobey their heart?

2. Heloise, the narrator, begins her story by claiming, "I was born in silence" (ix). How does this statement act as an omen for what will occur in the novel? In addition to living a cloistered life, how else is Heloise silenced, literally and/or figuratively?

3. The idea of going home or of making a home is a central motif in the novel. For Heloise, the notion of *home* is not one of comfort but of fear and loneliness. That is, until she meets Abelard. What does the idea of *home* mean for each of the characters in the story? Do you think that Heloise and Abelard ever get home? Why or why not?

4. Discuss the role of women in *The Sharp Hook of Love*. How do women's roles in twelfth-century Paris differ from today? How are they similar? How did Heloise break stereotypes for women in her day?

5. Does Heloise's uncle Fulbert have any redeeming qualities, or is he pure evil? Do you think his intentions for Heloise were pure of heart, or motivated by self-interest? Is it possible that his intentions could be both?

6. Revisit the scene beginning on page 44 when Heloise nearly drowns in the Seine. Do you think this moment acts as a hinge for their relationship, swinging it in the direction of a full-blown affair? Why do you think this particular moment allows Heloise to trust in Abelard? Without this experience, do you think that Heloise would have given in to her feelings? Why or why not?

7. Do you agree that the inescapability of destiny is a possible theme of *The Sharp Hook of Love*? Do all the characters fulfill their destiny? Consider Heloise, Abelard, Uncle Fulbert, Jean, and Agnes in your response.

8. On page 113, Heloise and Abelard consummate their love for one another when Abelard takes Heloise when she is asleep, "imbuing [her] with his breath." How does this act, described as giving breath to Heloise, prefigure Abelard's kiss to Heloise on his deathbed? What symbolism can you glean from this action of filling another with your breath? Explore this scene in relation to the idioms *kiss of death* and *breath of life*.

9. In what ways are the characters in the novel motivated by self-interest? Do you think it's fair to classify all of the characters as

selfish, to some extent? Who might be the most selfish character, and why? Who might be the least?

10. "I pray that, someday, you will understand" (ix). These last words spoken to Heloise by her mother echo throughout the novel, haunting Heloise. Does Heloise come to understand, as her mother had hoped she would? What does Heloise mean when she says she has been "pierced by the sharp hook of love" (334)?

11. Is Heloise to blame for leaving her child to be raised by her in-laws? Do you think she makes the best possible decision, given the circumstances? Why or why not?

12. To varying degrees, Heloise and her mother both have trouble admitting the truth to their respective beloveds, Abelard and Robert. Why do you think they choose to keep their secrets to themselves? In the case of Heloise, would honesty have been the best policy with regard to the letter she wrote to her uncle that led to his attack on Abelard? Would Heloise have benefited from her mother's honesty about her father and the reason for her abandonment?

13. Do you agree with the definition of love presented by Heloise on page 345: "To truly love, we must be willing to give of ourselves, even our very lives." What does Heloise give up for her lover? What does Abelard give up? Do you think their sacrifices are equal? Why or why not?

14. "I lifted my hand to rub my eyes, and found my face wet with tears" (348), says Heloise near the end of the novel. What is the significance of this moment in the story? How does the inability to cry throughout most of the novel isolate Heloise or impact her relationships with others? What does it imply about her character—and the power of love—that she is finally able to cry as she watches Abelard leave the abbey?

ENHANCE YOUR BOOK CLUB

1. Heloise and Abelard's love grows out of a shared love for classical literature, philosophy, and rhetoric. Without Heloise's talent and interest in learning, the two might never have met. Explore some of the lover's favorite texts, including Ovid's *Heroides* (the text can be accessed here: http://www.theoi.com/Text/OvidHeroides1.html). Take turns reading part of this classic poem out loud to your book club. What similarities can you find between the lovers in Ovid's poem and the main characters in *The Sharp Hook of Love*? Why do you think Heloise and Abelard were drawn to this poem? Do stories of star-crossed lovers ever feel out of date? Discuss contemporary examples of ill-fated lovers. What does the proliferation of this type of story say about the human condition?

2. On page 26, Heloise describes the game of elocution she plays with Abelard through their letter writing, a game that turns into a series of confessions about the depth of feeling the two share. There is something deeply intimate about the act of letter writing, and so often people are able to put into words what they cannot say face-to-face. Have each member of your book club write a letter to a real or imagined beloved. Over dinner, share with your group the experience of writing a letter. Have you written to someone you love before? How does putting something in to a letter differ from saying it out loud?

3. Have a movie night with your book club, watching a couple of versions of *Romeo & Juliet* (1997, 1968). Draw parallels between these films and *The Sharp Hook of Love*. How are Heloise and Abelard similar to Romeo and Juliet? How do they differ? In your opinion, which couple suffers more?

4. Read another Sherry Jones book with your book club, such as *Four Sisters, All Queens*, or *The Jewel of Medina*. What do her characters all have in common? How would you characterize Jones's writing style? Pick your favorite scene in each book and share them with your book club.